Books by Howard Fast

THE PLEDGE*

THE DINNER PARTY*

CITIZEN TOM PAINE
(A Play)

THE IMMIGRANT'S
DAUGHTER*

THE OUTSIDER*

MAX*

TIME AND THE RIDDLE:
THIRTY-ONE ZEN
STORIES

THE LEGACY*

THE ESTABLISHMENT*

THE MAGIC DOOR

SECOND GENERATION*

THE IMMIGRANTS*

THE ART OF ZEN
MEDITATION

A TOUCH OF INFINITY

THE HESSIAN

THE CROSSING

THE GENERAL ZAPPED
AN ANGEL

THE JEWS: STORY OF A
PEOPLE*

THE HUNTER AND THE
TRAP

TORQUEMADA

THE HILL

AGRIPPA'S DAUGHTER

POWER

THE EDGE OF TOMORROW

APRIL MORNING

THE GOLDEN RIVER

THE WINSTON AFFAIR

MOSES, PRINCE OF EGYPT

THE LAST SUPPER

SILAS TIMBERMAN

THE PASSION OF SACCO
AND VANZETTI

SPARTACUS*

THE PROUD AND THE
FREE

DEPARTURE

MY GLORIOUS BROTHERS

CLARKTON

THE AMERICAN

FREEDOM ROAD

CITIZEN TOM PAINE

THE UNVANQUISHED

THE LAST FRONTIER

CONCEIVED IN LIBERTY

PLACE IN THE CITY

THE CHILDREN

STRANGE YESTERDAY

TWO VALLEYS

* In Dell Editions

QUANTITY SALES

Most Dell books are available at special quantity discounts when purchased in bulk by corporations, organizations, and special-interest groups. Custom imprinting or excerpting can also be done to fit special needs. For details write: Dell Publishing, 666 Fifth Avenue, New York, NY 10103. Attn.: Special Sales Department.

INDIVIDUAL SALES

Are there any Dell books you want but cannot find in your local stores? If so, you can order them directly from us. You can get any Dell book in print. Simply include the book's title, author, and ISBN number if you have it, along with a check or money order (no cash can be accepted) for the full retail price plus $2.00 to cover shipping and handling. Mail to: Dell Readers Service, P.O. Box 5057, Des Plaines, IL 60017.

"RIVETING, TIGHTLY PLOTTED. . . . Moves like greased lightning and will surely grip you from start to finish."
—*New York Newsday*

In the 1950s Howard Fast appeared before the Congressional Committee on Un-American Activities, which destroyed the reputations, careers, and lives of so many writers, artists, and entertainers. When he attempted to make a statement about his constitutional rights, Senator Joseph McCarthy stopped him, saying, "Write a book!" Howard Fast made a pledge: "I shall and I will!" This is that book —a stirring portrait of a time a nation must remember with anguish . . . and of an American we can honor with pride.

The Pledge
Howard Fast

"A REAL TRIUMPH: a deeply moving, heartfelt autobiographical story. . . . From the enticing opening scene in Calcutta to the gut-wrenching ending, this is a powerful book."
—*Modern Maturity*

"ADDRESSES THE POLITICAL AND MORAL UPHEAVAL OF THE McCARTHY ERA . . . [Fast] has a seasoned feeling for narrative flow and enjoys drawing savage portraits of J. Edgar Hoover and the young Richard Nixon."
—*The New York Times*

HOWARD FAST

The Pledge

A DELL BOOK

Published by
Dell Publishing
a division of
Bantam Doubleday Dell Publishing Group, Inc.
666 Fifth Avenue
New York, New York 10103

Copyright © 1988 by Howard Fast

All rights reserved. No part of this book may be reproduced or
transmitted in any form or by any means, electronic or mechanical,
including photocopying, recording, or by any information storage and
retrieval system, without the written permission of the Publisher, except
where permitted by law. For information address Houghton Mifflin
Company, Boston, Massachusetts.

The trademark Dell ® is registered in the U.S. Patent and Trademark
Office.

ISBN: 0-440-20470-4

Reprinted by arrangement with Houghton Mifflin Company

Printed in the United States of America
Published simultaneously in Canada

December 1989

10 9 8 7 6 5 4 3 2 1
OPM

For Daniel Fast, born December 11, 1987.
Welcome and blessings.

. . . WITH LIBERTY AND JUSTICE FOR ALL.

Calcutta

The many turns, twists, and circumstances that led Bruce Bacon down the curious path his life took probably threaded back through all his years on earth. No one is constructed instantly—in terms of mind and outlook—any more than one is changed instantly. The making and the changing are part of a process. But there is no question that in Bacon's case, the process climaxed in Calcutta in 1945. Bacon had been in Europe since the Normandy landing, writing for the *New York Tribune*, with the understanding that he could do magazine pieces for other publications, namely, *The New Yorker* and *The Saturday Evening Post*. His newspaper pieces were personalized and intimate, very much like the stuff that Ernie Pyle had been writing, and he had made a good name for himself, considering that he had just turned thirty.

By the time Berlin fell to the Allied armies, Bruce Bacon felt that he had seen enough of war and a war-shattered Europe. He had heard vaguely, from an officer who had been transferred from India to France, that the British, fearing a Japanese penetration of Assam and India, where they might be welcomed as liberators, had cornered the rice supply and contrived a famine, which broke the will of the people in Assam and in part of Bengal. The rumor held that hundreds of thousands had already died of starvation, and that thousands more were now in the process of dying. Bruce decided that it was an interesting and important story, something very different from the war stories he had been sending home, and well worth investigating.

Bruce returned to Paris with orders for Air Transport, and a few days later, after a stopover at New Delhi, a lumbering C-37 put him down outside Calcutta. He was quartered in a one-time rajah's palace that had been assigned to the press corps, where a tiny room, the size of a jail cell, became his home. There was a small, hard bed, on which he spent an uneasy night under mosquito netting, half choking in the heat.

Ignoring the advice of his colleagues, the old hands in Calcutta, he ventured out on his own. It didn't surprise him that they were uninterested in the source of the famine. It was everywhere around them; they hated it; they hated Calcutta, where there was no war; and nobody ever made a name as a war correspondent without a war. They hated the heat, the filth, the poverty, the stench, the gentle and so often abject people, whom they called "wogs" without discrimination, and they found solace drinking with their British counterparts and rewriting the dull handouts of the local army press office.

Bruce had the advantage of being new to it, and he was utterly entranced as well as horrified by the huge, throbbing, aching mass of humanity that was Calcutta. He walked miles through the streets; he rode the crowded streetcars for hours. He was enchanted by the big, ancient Buick touring cars that were the local taxicabs, each driven by two large, turbaned, bearded Sikhs, the clanging streetcars that were everywhere, the pools of water where the Bengalis washed and washed, endlessly observing their rite of cleanliness in very dirty water, the cows that wandered everywhere, worshipped and untouched by starving people, the thousands of peasant families living on the street, the focal point of their homes tiny charcoal fires, the dead mingled with the living. He saw the sleeping streets, set aside for the homeless to sleep on the pavement, and he saw them by night, when the broad streets were carpeted by living human beings, and he also saw them in the early hours of the morning, when the human skeletons that were alive had departed, leaving, scattered on the street, the human skeletons that had died during the night.

Bruce Bacon was a healthy, large-boned man, six feet in height, well dressed, well fed. The people he saw were short, skinny, many of them in rags, yet he never found anger or hostile words directed against him. Himself a product of middle-class America, he had not suffered in the Depression, the time of his childhood years. His father was a New York physician. His growing-up had been managed and sheltered, as an only child, by two loving and intelligent people, and until he saw the aftermath of an air raid on London, he had never actually seen a dead person. Like millions of other American young men, he was fed innocent into a world of death and horror, and in the course of three years of witnessing and writing about the largest mass slaughter in the history of the human race, he had come to the conclusion that nothing man did to man could shock him. Calcutta shocked him.

At the same time, it fascinated him. Essentially—like most men—he was a gentle person, fighting always for the macho that men were supposed to have and which women were blessedly exempt from. The things he saw in Calcutta ripped away the thin veneer of indifference that war had forced onto him, and he made the story he had come to write a sort of obsession. But no matter how many people he spoke to, no one could make the British connection for him. There was rice, millions of pounds of it, airplane hangars filled with bags of rice, warehouses of rice; but this, he was told, was the doing of the rich Muslim rice dealers, functioning within the doctrine that profits were not sinful, and that he who owned goods had the inalienable right to raise the price of those goods. But when he questioned why the British, who ruled the land, did not break the price, the answer was always that this was neither their right nor their function.

Then a U.S. Army sergeant, one Hal Legerman, found Bruce in the correspondents' palace, hunched over his typewriter in the smoking room, and said to him, "My name is Legerman, and if you'll stand for a dry martini, I'll put you on the track."

Looking at his watch, Bruce remarked that it was only four o'clock in the afternoon.

"I haven't had a martini in six months, so what the hell is the difference? I'm not allowed into this holy place; I bulled my way, and the Limeys don't know what a martini is anyway and they don't have vermouth, so just ask for straight gin."

"How come," Bruce asked suspiciously, "if you're that fond of gin, you waited six months?"

"I been up in the hills with the Tenth Air Force."

"And just what track are you going to put me on?"

"Jesus God, Bacon—you are Bacon, aren't you? At least that's what the guy at the bar said."

"I'm Bacon."

"OK. So you're trying to put the famine and the Limeys together, right?"

"How do you know that?"

"How do I know it? Shit, man, everyone in Calcutta knows it by now. I don't mean the people. I mean the assholes who run the place."

"Let's have that dry martini without vermouth," Bruce said.

It turned out that Hal Legerman had spent more than two years in the China-Burma-India Theater, otherwise known as the CBI. He was a supply sergeant, with tours of duty that included Burma and over the Hump into China, and there was not much in Bengal that he didn't know about. He was a conduit and a magnet for news, and when news came to him, he passed it on to the proper destination, as he saw it. He had friends at the local *Yank* office and at the two major Bengali newspapers, and he knew people in Karachi and Delhi and Bombay as well as in Calcutta. At home in New York, he had been a flack in a small public relations firm, but war does strange things to people, and now, sipping at his second gin on ice in the palace bar, he said to Bruce, "You're looking for a connection between this famine and the Limeys, something you can print, but even if you get it, nobody back home is going to print it."

"Why?"

"They'll tell you the war. That's the reason for everything, right? They knew the Jews were being murdered by the millions and they didn't do one damn thing. They wouldn't even bomb the camps. The war. More important targets."

"I saw the camps," Bruce said.

"All right. You're no fucken innocent. Do you know how many people have died already in this stinking famine?"

"Thousands."

"Millions. They do a body count that's as secret as a general's brain, and the latest figure is over five million. It'll be six million before it's over."

Bruce stared at him in disbelief. "You're kidding."

"Hell, no! I'm telling you the truth."

"That matches Hitler—damn near."

"You bet it does. And I'll tell you something, Bacon; you can hang in here for the next six months and you won't get anyone to verify that figure. Try to get your handle on any of this. Last week there was an argument between our local command and the Limeys that was pretty damn wild, considering that we're supposed to be allies. You've seen the sleeping streets?"

"I saw them. You can't be in Calcutta and not see them."

"Well, the Limeys were picking up over a thousand bodies each morning—just the urban crop—and they didn't have the trucks to handle it. So they demanded that we organize burial detail and use our trucks to help them out. Our CO told them to fuck off and pick up their own dead, not their troops, you understand, but the peasants who had poured into town when their food ran out, and it got ugly as hell."

"What happened?"

"It went up to the High Command and in the end we used our trucks—shit, Bacon, it's diseased, totally diseased. A human life around here is not worth two cents."

"You were going to put me on the track," Bruce said. "All you gave me so far are dead ends and closed doors."

"I'm not cadging a lousy shot of gin," Legerman said with annoyance. "I figured you for a good guy."

"Why? You don't know me from Adam."

"I don't know. You wear glasses. You look good. How the hell do I know? Maybe because you're on this story. Nobody else is."

"And putting me on the track?"

"OK. There's a Professor Chandra Chatterjee, teaches at the university here. I'll arrange for you to spend an evening with him. It should be profitable."

"He speaks English?"

"Come on, Bacon. This is India. Practically every educated Bengali talks English, most of them better than I do."

Professor Chatterjee's house, as Bruce saw it two days later, was a small stucco cottage, part of a cluster of such cottages near the university. It was pleasantly shaded by a large live oak and located at the opposite side of Calcutta, thus demanding a long twisting ride through an endless maze of streets and avenues. Fortunately, Bruce had the use of one of the three jeeps and a chauffeur, one of several that the army had assigned to the correspondents. When he reached the professor's house, he was introduced to two small children, nine and eleven, both boys, and to Professor Chatterjee's wife.

Mrs. Chatterjee, a small, dark-eyed, pretty woman, returned to the living room after she had taken the children to another part of the house. Aside from Chatterjee, a grayhaired wisp of a man with an eager yet unassuming manner, gold-rimmed glasses, and a gentle smile of greeting, there were two other people present: one was Sergeant Harold Legerman, and the other a thin, tall man with a lined, serious face, an Indian dressed in dhoti and sandals, as was Professor Chatterjee. Bruce knew of the Indian habit of dining very late in the evening and he had been told that they felt Westerners disapproved of their style of eating in part with their fingers, and thereby invited only close friends to dinner. Since it was now only six o'clock in the evening, Bruce knew that they would leave before dinner, and he looked to Legerman to make the appropriate decisions, whether to go and when to go.

Mrs. Chatterjee brought bottled water, glasses, and a tray of small fried cakes. Then she seated herself a bit apart from the four men. Legerman introduced Bruce to the professor and to the other man, whose name was Ashoka Majumdar. Majumdar shook hands heartily, smiling, an action that drove the gloom from his face and made it utterly enticing. It was Bruce's first time in an Indian home, and he found it both strange and familiar. Aside from a few pieces of polished teak, it might have been a room in a small apartment in New York. There was a pleasant drugget on the floor, and on the wall two reproductions of Indian paintings, which reminded Bruce of pictures he had seen in the Metropolitan Museum of Art at home. Yet for all this, the room possessed a quality of nakedness, bareness, indeed, poverty.

Noticing Bruce's appraisal of the room, Professor Chatterjee said, "You may be thinking of the contrast between our place and the palace, where the correspondents are quartered. But ours is a land of contrasts, Mr. Bacon, the poorest people in the world cheek by jowl with the richest. That is India under the Raj."

"And before the Raj?" Bruce asked.

"Not too different, and when the time of the Raj is over, it will take many years to change it."

"And that time—is it near?"

Majumdar answered, "Oh, near, dear sir. Very near."

Bruce was sensitive to language, sensitive to sound and accent, and the strange musical accent of Indian speech and its unembarrassed formality charmed him. He was trying to place these people in the complex Indian social scheme, but it was not easy.

"It is almost expectoration day," Majumdar answered, and Mrs. Chatterjee made a small sound of protest.

"A term my wife does not approve of," Professor Chatterjee said, "but nevertheless a very colorful expression. You see, Mr. Bacon, for years we have been telling our people that if they would only learn to spit once together, there would be a wave of water that would wash the British into the sea."

"And now they have learned?" Bruce asked.

"We think so. Yes, we think so. Very close. The time of the British Raj is over. But let us talk about you." Mrs. Chatterjee poured a glass of water, interrupting her husband apologetically to assure Bruce that the water was safe. "We boil it at least five minutes." She pressed one of the fried cakes on him, smiling tentatively. Her smile said that she would never have interrupted her husband under other circumstances. But he was a Westerner.

"I mean," Professor Chatterjee said, "that it is a shame that you had to be here so close to the terrible famine we have been through. Oh, Calcutta is not the most attractive place in the world, even without a famine, but there are qualities of life here—"

"I know," Bruce agreed. "Even under these conditions, I find it one of the most extraordinary cities I have ever seen."

"And horrible?" Majumdar wondered.

"I've lived with the horrible for so long that it no longer horrifies me."

"But different, different," Chatterjee said.

"Yes, different."

Majumdar watched him thoughtfully. He'll not be inappropriate, Bruce thought, and Majumdar said slowly, "In Europe you have been killing each other. Not you, of course, Mr. Bacon, but it has been the greatest killing since the beginning of time, over forty million I am told?"

Bruce nodded. "That's the latest estimate. Of course we don't have very good figures out of Russia. They have lost better than twenty million."

"And here Mother India weeps over her own dead, as she has always wept, and who will remember?"

"That's something we're trying to break through," Legerman put in, more comfortable with practical talk.

"Yes, in a moment. But tell me, Mr. Bacon, should we call you 'Captain'? You wear the uniform."

"No, I'm not army. All the correspondents wear the uniform. They brevet us captain, but I write for the *New York Tribune* and for myself. Not for the army."

The Indians appeared to be relieved. Mrs. Chatterjee smiled and offered her small cakes again. Bruce's was still untouched. Hal Legerman took a second one and said to Chatterjee, "They got Mr. Bacon here on a merry-go-round and he's been chasing his tail for days. He's seen the rice stores that the dealers put away, but he can't make a British connection, and the word's out, and nobody will talk to him or give him the time of the day."

"Of course, you can say that the British could impound the rice and give it out," Chatterjee said, smiling slightly. "And if you put that to them, they will say that the rice is not theirs to impound."

"And most of it came here only two weeks ago," Majumdar added.

"There was enough here six months ago," Legerman said. "Enough to break the famine. Punjee's warehouses were full of rice packs."

"My need is to find out whether it's a conspiracy, and if it is, to get some proof."

"It is, it is, no doubt," Majumdar said. "We know that, because the crop was good in so many places, and back when the Japanese had some push left and everyone thought they would overrun the plantations in the hills, the British decided they would break the people. You know, they were beginning to organize resistance in the hills, and with the Japanese to support them, well—"

"I can hardly think of the Japanese as liberators," Bruce said.

"Point of view," Legerman said.

"Ah, well," said Chatterjee, "you know, the British are very clever. A thing like this is done with whispered words, and the Muslims here are bitter against us. They would listen to the British. Ah, yes, certainly. But the British are very careful. The president of the university has excellent rapport with them, and they don't like student demonstrations. He begged the British to seize the rice. But this war—any and all horrors are met with sighs of what must be done. It is the war, you know. You will get no proof, Mr. Bacon, nothing like a document summing up the intentions of the British."

"And why couldn't you organize to seize the rice—I mean with all this death?"

They were smiling at him, and Bruce felt like a fool. Majumdar said, kindly, "You are a sensitive man, but this is India. There is a British army here, as there has been for over two hundred years, and there are two million American troops. We are not a free land. As to why we need two million American soldiers here—perhaps the British are afraid. I mean of the Japanese. I understand that it is very difficult for you to think of the Japanese as liberators, but a man in a cage does not question the morality of the man who opens the door."

Bruce nodded. Here was a world of upside-down, or was it the world he had come from that stood on its head? He could argue about the Japanese—indeed, he could argue about everything they had said—but they would be arguments without faith or real belief in whatever position he took. Somewhere, long, long ago, there was a world where people were not preoccupied with the business of killing each other, where his father practiced medicine. In that hazy other-reality, they lived in a huge old apartment on Riverside Drive in New York City, where they had family dinners together, and where people laughed and joked and embraced. But he was here, and the realities of that other place, if they were realities, were quite meaningless here.

Mrs. Chatterjee, who had been sitting quietly, now wondered why Bruce had not tasted his cake. "They are quite good, you know. Almost like besan barfi."

"Yes, I'll try it," Bruce said, "thank you," wondering what besan barfi were. Some marvelous treat that they had been saving for a guest like himself. Of course. The trouble was that, in the face of the famine, he was eating very little. Food mixed itself with guilt, which made no sense, as he admitted to himself, but still his appetite had shrunk away almost to nothing. He blamed it on the wet, oppressive heat; he was without hunger, but now he bit into the small confection, sweet, delicious.

"Very good."

The conversation had paused, and they were watching him. "Chickpeas and sugar and spices," Mrs. Chatterjee explained. What would have been impolite and embarrassing at home was quite different here. Bruce had been watching Professor Chatterjee. Bruce was yet to encounter air conditioning anywhere in this sweltering city, but overhead fans pervaded the place. There was one here, turning slowly, and at times it would drive an insect down on Chatterjee's dhoti, not a mosquito but a smaller bug, and when that occurred, Chatterjee would gently lift the bug and drop it to the floor.

Bruce forced himself to take another minimal bite of the confection.

Chatterjee was not insensitive. "I know how hard our sad
city is for you, Mr. Bacon. When I was a young man, I
made a trip to America with a grant I had won from a
foundation set up by your Mr. Rockefeller. It was not much
money, but it paid for my passage and for two weeks in
America, so I have memories of that wonderful place where
there is no famine ever. It put some reality into my dream of
democracy and freedom." He paused suddenly and closed
his eyes. Seconds ticked past, and then suddenly, without
preamble, "Three months ago, this famine was at its height.
My wife and I were sitting at that small table, there by the
window, having our dinner, a bowl of rice and a pickled
cucumber, and outside our window there was a family of
eight people. We could see them in the moonlight and we
heard their moans. They looked like the pictures in our
press of the Jews you liberated from the German concentration camps. In the morning, three were dead. A British
truck came and took away the three dead bodies. Those
living clung to the truck and with their last bit of strength
ran after it and then they fell in the roadway. The British
stopped the truck and the soldiers came back to the bodies
that lay in the roadway. Three of them were young children.
They were alive, and the British soldiers lifted them out of
the roadway and laid them on the grass. At least they would
not be run over by the traffic in the roadway. The other two
were either dead or close to it, out of the effort of running
after the truck. The British put their bodies in the truck.
The point I am making, Mr. Bacon, is that we did not do
what you certainly would have done."

After a long moment of silence, Bruce asked, "And what
is that, Professor Chatterjee?"

"Would you have given your dinner to those starving people?"

Bruce was tempted to say "Yes, of course," but swallowed
the words. The people in the room were silent. Finally,

Bruce said, "I have never been hungry—I mean, not hungry the way starving people are hungry."

"You are very honest. No, we did not give them our food. We had barely enough. If we had given them ten times as much, it would not have saved their lives. We ate our food. We must survive. Only if we survive will there be people who can force the British out and heal our poor broken land."

Silence again. Bruce felt it was incumbent upon him to say something, and he observed that their hatred for the British must be beyond measure. "I was at this British Officers' Club at the parade grounds. A correspondent for the *Times* invited me to join him for dinner there, and they have these steam baths and we took them before dinner. Then there were these attendants with towels—bearers, they call them. Well, we dried ourselves, but the British officers were being dried by these bearers, and they were drying their . . . well"—glancing uneasily at Mrs. Chatterjee—"their parts, and the officers appeared completely unaware of it, as if these were not men, not human—"

"Yet we don't hate them," Professor Chatterjee said.

"Ah, you see, you must understand the British," Majumdar said. "When I was working in Old Delhi two years ago, I would conduct an evening class in simple, beginning literacy. I must have had fifty or sixty students, bearers, tonga drivers, laborers, water carriers, rickshaw drivers. It was the most primitive thing, hardly better than *abc*, but there was such hope, such will, and all we had for a classroom was a small, flickering streetlight, a lamppost, where we all squatted together on the pavement. So I wrote a letter to the High Commissioner, who was a few miles away in New Delhi, and I explained that my students could barely see the scraps of paper on which they wrote their letters. Do you know what the British did?"

"I hope they provided a classroom."

"Ah, no. You must understand what they did, because it

will explain why we do not hate them, but they must go. They had a larger light bulb put into the streetlamp. You see, they were responsive—but to people they regarded as only a little better than animals. Like the bearers in the steam bath. They are so polite and sometimes considerate insofar as they understand. But the one thing they do not understand is that we are human beings, as human as they are."

Standing in front of Professor Chatterjee's little cottage later that evening, waiting for the jeep to pick them up, Legerman asked Bruce how he had enjoyed the evening.

"Enjoy is not the word."

"Interesting?"

"Damn interesting. But I don't have the story."

"I'm no writer, but it seems to me you got yourself a story."

"Maybe. Maybe it's another story." He didn't want to discuss the evening with Legerman. He didn't want to discuss it with anyone. He wanted to go back to his quarters, drink a glass of the warm British beer, and brood about food and hunger and life and death and people like Chatterjee and Majumdar.

"Who are they?" he asked Legerman.

"How do you mean that, Mr. Bacon?"

"Time you called me Bruce. Same as you, Sergeant. Who the hell are you and who is Chatterjee and who is Majumdar?"

"Well, me. You know who I am. Chatterjee teaches math and physics. Majumdar—well, he works on a local newspaper."

"What newspaper?"

"*Prasarah*, which I'm sure you never heard of. It's a communist newspaper, and *prasarah* is the old Sanskrit word for freedom or something of that sort. I guess it gives it a sort of universality, with India full of different languages."

"So Majumdar is a communist."

"That's right. Chatterjee, Majumdar, and me too. If you feel you were put on, I'm sorry."

"I don't know what I feel," Bruce said.

"You can sit around the palace like the rest of them and read the handouts and rewrite them, and it's no skin off my back. I thought you were looking for something."

"What are you getting so pissed off about?" Bruce demanded. "Did I say anything? Who the hell do you think I am, Howard Rushmore? I don't work for the *Journal.* I work for the *Tribune.*"

"OK, OK. You came here for a story that no one else wants. I think Chatterjee and Majumdar are two of the most connected people I know."

"I didn't see it tonight."

"Give it time. Give it time. Are you hungry?"

"I had to force myself to eat that damn cookie or whatever. Now I'm starving."

"Good. I'll take you to the Jewish restaurant."

Bruce didn't know what to expect, and he thought of the various possibilities that would place a Jewish restaurant in blacked-out, famine-stricken Calcutta. Now, in Calcutta nothing surprised him, and he watched, intrigued, as Legerman conducted the jeep driver through a seemingly endless maze of streets, the more so as the jeep rode without lights, with only the moon to light the way.

"What do you do when there's no moon?" he asked Legerman.

"Not a hell of a lot."

For Bruce, the city had become another world, a strange, ghostly place, painted over with silver. Families huddled together, asleep on the sidewalks; lean, half-starved cows were everywhere; and people awake moved slowly. An occasional streetcar thundered by, shattering the silver silence, and sometimes a taxi with the two fierce Sikhs sitting side by side, and sometimes an army vehicle, British or American, racing through the streets.

"When they hit someone, they don't stop," Legerman said, and the driver of the jeep, a Pfc from the motor pool, said, "I had officers in here told me to hit a wog. I told the fucken shitheads that a jeep can't do it. I told them to get an army truck, they wanted to hunt wogs."

"You're kidding," Bruce said.

"He ain't kidding," Legerman said.

It was ten o'clock when they reached the Jewish restaurant, a handsome building with a white stone front. Legerman told the driver to pick them up at midnight. The driver was dating a nurse at the general hospital, and he was pleased with the break. "This gives me an hour with Maddie. An hour is a challenge." Bruce, recalling the Sixth Avenue Delicatessen and mountainous sandwiches of hot pastrami and corned beef, was unprepared for the elegant dining room, the fourteen-foot-high ceilings with their gently revolving fans, the tables with their spotless white cloths and the well-dressed Hindus and Bengalis as well as British and American officers, dining with Red Cross women and nurses.

"Not the Sixth Avenue Deli," Bruce said.

The proprietor came to meet them and shook hands eagerly with Legerman and Bruce and ushered them to a table in a quiet corner, sitting with them for a few minutes and inquiring from Legerman what might be the progress of the war. His name was Abel Shar, a slender man with small, elegant features, a skin almost black, and silky black hair. When he left them, Bruce said, "I suppose he's Jewish?"

"That's right. They came here two thousand, three hundred years ago. He put on a big Passover dinner for Jewish GI's, and he serves cold beer. What more can you ask for, twelve thousand miles from home? We manage to find potatoes for him, a sack here and there that the army loses. He'll bring us Indian food if you want it, but mostly we have beer and potato pancakes when we're here. His potato pancakes are better than my mother's."

Bruce agreed that they were extraordinary potato pancakes, small, hot, and crisp, fried in deep fat; and he was also coming to the conclusion that Hal Legerman was an extraordinary man. His desire to be alone, to brood and weep over the immeasurable human suffering that was Calcutta disappeared. More GI's drifted into the restaurant, until a dozen young men were pressed around the table, eating potato pancakes and drinking ice cold beer, and arguing hotly about the past, the future, Adolf Hitler, Burma, Assam, the Japanese, the British, the Americans, hopes, dreams, indignities, horrors, and Atabrine. They all took Atabrine, a yellow medicine that gave their skin a golden glow and served as a more or less reliable preventive against malaria; and this kid, New York from his speech, Italian from the look of him and the cross he wore around his neck, was talking about a Southern GI who wouldn't take Atabrine. "He couldn't stand the color. The dumb bastard claimed it made him colored."

"What happened?"

"Malaria happened."

Hal Legerman said, "We are without question the worst bunch of racist bastards that ever infested this planet."

"Colonel Hallway says it's toilets, all toilets."

"Hallway is a total cretin."

"Who's Hallway?" Bruce asked Legerman.

"He's famous here. He's chief of orientation in this area and he gave a lecture about toilets. He says the world is divided into two groups, those who sit on toilets and those who whack it off the back and piss on the grass. That's the colored part of the world. No toilets, which means they haven't made what Hallway calls the final step into the human family."

"The fucken moron sent a mimeo of it to the *New York Times*," someone said. "Then he'd be in the PX every day to see if they printed it. He ordered that a paper be saved for him every day, and it got around and we'd manage to steal his paper. He tried to have the PX sarge court-martialed. Imagine, the PX sarge, the most important man in this shithead army."

Bruce listened to them. It was a forum of sorts. Men came and went, all enlisted men, no officers, an astonishing cross section, college men, men barely literate, men who sat and listened and never said a word and others who held the floor, egocentrics, easygoing, angry, every shade of mood, with a crazy assortment of ideas that ranged from the depopulation of Japan and Germany to mutiny in the enormous CBI Army, which for the most part did nothing but occupy the Indian subcontinent. When midnight came, Bruce rose reluctantly, fascinated by the conversation at this round corner table of what was called the Jewish restaurant.

"We can't keep the driver waiting," Legerman told him. "That guy has a short fuse."

"You talking about Johnson?" someone asked. "Johnson's jeep?"

There were three applicants for rides on the jeep. Legerman, meanwhile, had changed a dollar into pice, the bottom end of the local coinage, loading his pockets with the tiny coins. "I always keep a pocketful. With ten beggars per block, you bankrupt yourself or deal in pice."

"Fuck it," a voice said. "You can't deal with a million beggars."

"You can try," Legerman said. "It helps work off the guilt."

The city was asleep now, the moon lower, the streets darker. Johnson drove through dark passages, where Bruce saw very little. "He got antennas," someone said.

"The army runs a kind of bus service, trucks with boards for seats. They close up at midnight."

A figure stood in the road, waving his arms. Johnson jammed on his brakes, and another GI climbed into the jeep.

"Last one," Johnson said. "This is no half-track, and I don't stop for no fucken general."

"Can you believe it?" the rescued GI said. "Koorum Street. I told the fucken driver Koorum Street. I know a nurse quartered there. So he drops me at Goochum Street. Do you believe that. Where the hell is Goochum Street?"

"Where I picked you up," Johnson said.

"It happened to me once," Legerman said. "Lost in Calcutta at night. That has to be the scariest kind of thing you ever go up against."

"What did you do?"

"Walked all night."

Walked all night, Bruce thought, in this warren of six, eight, nine million people. Who knew? They lay on almost every street the jeep drove through, single men, single women, children, clusters of families, some awake, some asleep. How could they be counted? If more than five million had already perished, then there were at least a million or two or three more who had come into the city, hoping for a few grains of rice to sustain their lives another day, another hour, and in the middle of this, wealth, palaces, tropical gardens, and dozens of elegant restaurants where people dipped into platters of steaming food, as they had this evening in what was called the Jewish restaurant. And that night, as Bruce crawled under his mosquito netting, he decided that, including all the days he had spent in North Africa and in England and on the Continent with the invasion, this was by all means one of the strangest. But not the strangest. That happened a few days later.

Bruce never slept well during his time in Calcutta. Between the sickening wet heat and the things he had seen, even a few hours of sleep in his sweat-soaked bed was a blessing. Waking by night, he yearned for morning and release from the mosquito netting, which he felt covered him like a shroud, and as a result, when dawn broke he was out of bed and in the shower. By six o'clock, he would be dressed and breathing the somewhat cooler morning air, either in the garden behind the palace or on the front steps, where he could stretch out in the shade of the cool stone building. It was there, in front of the old palace, that Ashoka Majumdar found him.

"Greetings, Mr. Bacon. So early. I was prepared to wait. Do you ride a bicycle?" Majumdar was steadying two ancient bicycles, each with one hand.

By now, Bruce was accustomed to the apparent non sequiturs that were an integral part of Bengali thinking. Actually, they were not non sequiturs at all, but the result of a slightly different use of logic. Since Majumdar had appeared with two bicycles, it must be apparent to Bruce that they would take off on said bicycles, and regardless of his agreement or disagreement, the first question to be answered was whether or not he could ride a bicycle. He nodded and examined the bikes, old single-speed Raleighs that had been patched and wired and taken apart and put together so many times that it was doubtful whether they still deserved their original name.

"Yes," he replied, "I ride a bicycle—at least I did once." He shook his head. "But these?"

"Perfectly serviceable. But perhaps I presume. We are so happy you are interested in our sad picture here that we felt I should round it out. You know that I work for our newspaper, *Prasarah*. I also read for it. That is how I earn my keep."

"I don't understand."

"Ah. I explain poorly." Majumdar opened a small bag attached to his bicycle and took out of it a rolled-up sheet of paper. He unrolled it. It was half the size of the *Tribune*'s front page, and it was covered with tight print. The other side was bare. "Of course it is in Bengali," Majumdar said, "but I will sum up the stories for you as we go—if, of course, you will come with me. I can promise you that it will be enlightening."

"Where? Where are we going? And why? You know something, Majumdar? I can't help feeling that I am being hustled."

"What is 'hustled'?"

"Forget it, forget it."

"We should have some bottles of spring water from the bar. I drink ordinary water anywhere, but it could make you ill, since you have not made your peace with all the small, angry bacteria that live in Bengali water."

"That makes sense." The bar was closed, but in the kitchen a dollar bought him three bottles of water, which claimed to be as pure as a virgin, drawn from a sparkling spring high in the mountains of Kashmir.

"You must forgive our hyperbole," Majumdar said as he read the label. "This is very good water." He stowed the bottles in his canvas bag, placing the Bengali newspaper in the folds of his dhoti. "We are both newspapermen," he explained. "I write for our paper—I also distribute it and broadcast it, as you might say."

"That's the communist paper?"

"You say it as if it certainly must explode. No, sahib. It is a harmless sheet of paper with some facts the people need."

"Don't ever give me that 'sahib' shit again," Bruce said angrily. "You want to know what hustled means—me. I'm being hustled, but I know it. Just show me. I don't intend to apologize for one damned thing, because my world is just as weird as yours." He was relieved that it was so early in the morning, and that he wouldn't have to explain to any of his colleagues why he was taking off with a skinny, sad-looking Indian on a strange machine that pretended to be a bicycle.

"Will it hold together?"

"Oh, so many years it has held together. Why should the fates be against us now?"

The bicycle actually worked, and riding side by side, they took off along a maze of streets, dirt roads, and paths that led them out of the city into the countryside. Once out of the central part of the city, they saw fewer of the families crouched around their little fires of cow chips, fewer people sprawled on the street, fewer hands outstretched and pleading for alms. Unlike cities in the West, this city turned to country abruptly. They rode through heavy tropical growth and then into a countryside of rice paddies and vegetable fields, but all of it brown and dry before the monsoon.

Talking while they rode, Majumdar summed up the contents of his newspaper. "Our lead story, Mr. Bacon—"

"Hold on. Right there. If we're going to spend this day together, I'm Bruce and you're—"

"Jumdar. That's what they call me. Jumdar."

"OK. Jumdar. Bruce. None of this sahib shit and no Mr. Bacon. It's the fucken subservience here—"

"Which is the mark of oppression!" Majumdar said sharply. "Don't you understand one damned thing?"

Silence for fifty yards or so, and then Bruce said, "Thank you for getting angry. No, I don't know much or understand very much. War makes you used to death. It doesn't make you smart."

Majumdar nodded and was silent for a long moment. Then returned to the paper. "Our lead story is, of course, the famine. I interviewed Mohamout Arfet. He is one of the Congress leaders in our struggle for independence, and he feels, as I do, that somehow the blame for the famine must not rest only on the shoulders of the rice dealers. Most of them are Muslims, and God knows there is enough bitter feeling between the Hindus and the Muslims here in Bengal. The Congress people understand that we are very close to the peasants. The deep, original force behind the famine is the British, and the people must understand that. Then we have a story about a large landholder who has ground down his tenants so hard that sixty percent of them are dead of malaria and malnutrition."

"You blame the landlord for the malaria?"

"When you are weakened, starving, when your resistance

is very low, malaria can be fatal. I live with malaria. A starving man dies with it. Another story—you would call it a sidebar—points to the British lack of concern for the mosquitoes breeding in the swamplands. Then, of course, we have the Party program, a list of the things we propose. Right now, we have a united front with the Congress. The British must leave India. The time has come, and we will wait no longer. The day of the Empire is over. Programmatically, that is number one."

"And where do you fit in?" Bruce demanded. "Where does the Party fit in—the Communist Party, I mean? The British say you are tools of the Soviets, just waiting for the day the British leave and you can hand the country over to them."

Majumdar burst into laughter. "Don't, don't. I can't laugh and ride a bicycle at the same time. Bruce, do you really see me handing this subcontinent, with its four hundred million people, over to the Russians? I have never spoken to a Russian. They have enough to do for a hundred years, just putting together what Hitler has destroyed. Later we talk about this."

They had come to a tiny hamlet, about three or four miles from what Bruce considered the city line. Majumdar dismounted, as did Bruce, and they walked their bikes into the center of the hamlet, where there was a well, a watering trough, twenty-three people by count, babies, women, and children included, and a cluster of poor wattle shacks. The men and women and children, like most men and women and children in the vicinity of Calcutta, were thin, their clothes patched and worn, some of them in rags. They welcomed Majumdar warmly, and then looked down shyly when they were introduced to Bruce.

Apparently, they had been waiting for Majumdar, for they settled down in front of the well, sitting cross-legged in the dust, while Majumdar unrolled his newspaper and began to read. Bruce listened intently, although he could not un-

derstand a word of the Bengali, but watching the faces of
the illiterate village folk, he found responses that illumi-
nated the brief summary that Majumdar had given him.
When the reading was over, which took twelve minutes by
Bruce's watch, there were a few questions which Majumdar
answered. Then he opened his pouch, holding his bike
steady, while each one of the villagers, excepting the small
children, dropped a single grain of rice into it. Then
Majumdar closed the pouch, said a few words more to the
group, led Bruce across the road, and mounted his bike.

"Next village," Majumdar said. "About a mile from here.
Much larger. We'll have at least fifty people."

"Aren't any of them literate?"

"Would they stay there if they were?"

"And the rice—what did that mean? Is it a symbolic gesture?"

"Symbolic? I should say not. The rice is my pay. I try to
cover at least twenty villages—sometimes less, sometimes
only eight or ten if we have hot discussion. At the end of the
day, I have a small bag of rice. For a few pice, a vegetable to
cook in the rice. I remain well fed and healthy, more than
most in this hellish famine."

"This heat is impossible. I'm thirsty."

"It will be worse as the day wears on," Majumdar warned
him. "Try not to drink until ten. You know, you can still go
back. It's mostly straight road."

"And leave you to face the tigers alone? By the way,
where do you keep them?"

"Not around here, no tigers, no maharajahs on elephants,
nothing but very poor people and heat and sorrow."

Majumdar had underestimated the size of the crowd at
the next village, a place somewhat larger than the first one, a
trifle more prosperous, some women weaving, and cows being milked. Three of the men engaged Majumdar in rapid
conversation while the others pressed around to listen. It
appeared, as he explained to Bruce later, that there were

four families of Assamese here, who had come down from
the hills, where they were starving, and the village could no
longer take care of them and wished them to go off and find
a way to live in the streets of Calcutta. But the people from
Assam knew that no one lived on the streets of Calcutta; it
was a place to die, not to live.

Bruce seated himself under a huge baobab tree, which the
village was fortunate enough to possess, selling its leaves to
the pharmacists in Calcutta—although only to the old-fashioned ones—yet sufficient leaves remained to give him a degree of shade, and there he rested, listening to the frantic
discussion in a language of which he understood not a single
word. The small children of the village gathered around
him, and he was reminded of Hal Legerman's story of filling
his pockets with pice. He had only a handful of coins in his
pocket, and he distributed these among the children, who
first stared at the coins with awe and disbelief and then tried
to give them back. When Bruce refused to take them, the
children chattered rapidly and then raced away. Now half of
the men and women in the group were shouting at each
other, with Majumdar trying to quiet them and impose
some order. It took almost a half hour before Majumdar
could unroll his newspaper and read the news, and after
that, there was more discussion. When they rolled out of
there on their bicycles, Majumdar explained the problem to
Bruce.

"What decision did they come to? Or was the decision up
to you? They seemed to trust you."

"I hope so. The decision was theirs, but I pushed them a
little. I said that if the survival of the village depended on
sending the families into Calcutta, then it might be considered just and proper. On the other hand, they could not
send the children of these hill people to death without great
agony and terrible karma, terrible karma. Maybe it was the
thought of the karma. Possibly, the thought of separating

the children from their parents. They will allow the hill folk to remain."

"And the karma? Do you believe in karma—you, a communist?"

Majumdar smiled. "Does communism change the universe? Shall I not be accountable for my actions? Shall I be released from my karma?"

"No one gave you rice there," Bruce said.

"Quite true. They sacrificed. I must sacrifice."

Bruce wrestled with this as Majumdar went through his rite of reading the news at the next village. As before, the children gathered around him. He went through his pockets, but he had no more change and he felt uneasy about giving them paper money. His guilt—which he decided was totally unreasonable but nevertheless present and provocative—set him to brooding over the matter of karma. As well as he could remember, karma was the name given to the sum of a person's actions during the successive phases of existence, and his storehouse of karma, measured in some strange way by compassion, determined a person's destiny. Since Bruce, as a proper twentieth-century man, rejected any notion so preposterous as successive phases of existence, the problem of Majumdar, a man of obviously keen intelligence, believing in it, puzzled him—but no more than everything else in this strange land. The fact that he, Bruce Bacon, raised in the most proper middle-class circumstances in New York City, graduate of Williams College and postgraduate at the Columbia School of Journalism, was sitting in the shade of a wickerwork fence, a bony cow lying beside him chewing her cud and indifferent to his presence, his uniform soaked with sweat, listening to a communist organizer reading a newspaper in a language he did not understand, underlined that.

At the next village, Bruce finished the first of the three water bottles. Majumdar drank the village water wherever they were, so thirst was not his problem. "As far as food is concerned," Bruce told him, "I can't eat any of their food."

"You will not be offered food," Majumdar assured him. "We'll feel better in this heat if we don't eat until this evening."

"When you will be my guest for dinner."

Majumdar demurred, but Bruce insisted. "Ah, I shall have to find a clean dhoti." Majumdar sighed.

"I didn't mean I wouldn't eat their food," Bruce added hastily. "I mean, I'm not afraid to eat it. I mean the guilt—oh, hell, how can you eat in this heat?"

"Of course," Majumdar said.

Where their path crossed a larger road, they paused and stood with their bikes to watch a troop of British soldiers marching by. The soldiers wore chalk-white sun helmets over brown faces.

"They're Gurkhas," Majumdar whispered in contempt. "Stupid savages who kill for hire. Always one against the others with the British—Hindus against Muslims, Ghurkas against Bengalis—always one against another."

"I don't know that it makes a hell of a lot of difference," Bruce said tiredly. "For two years I've watched men slaughter each other. Killing is what we do best."

Majumdar nodded. The Ghurkas marched past.

Back at the palace, Majumdar took Bruce's bicycle, and they agreed to meet at nine o'clock at the same restaurant that Legerman had taken Bruce to. Bruce was utterly exhausted, soaked with sweat, his thighs and calves aching from the first bike ride he had taken in years. He had drunk and finished the three bottles of water they carried with them, and now his mind brimmed hopefully over a vision of a tall glass of beer, British or otherwise. It was after four, so the bar was open, and as he shuffled in, wiping his glasses and trying to adjust to the cool darkness, a man by the name of Peterson, accredited to the area through a Missouri newspaper, said to Bruce, "I see you been touristing with that tall nigger of yours. What are you on to?"

"Fuck off, you shithead!" Bruce shouted, drawing the attention of everyone at the bar.

"Easy," Peterson said, spreading his hands. "Easy. Maybe I said something out of place—"

"Oh, go to hell," Bruce muttered, walking to the end of the bar, past the curious and none too friendly glances of the other correspondents. He downed his beer quickly, reflecting that it was his fault. He had fallen into the trap of looking down at correspondents who had seen no action but sat out their assignments rewriting the army handouts, and he had gone out of his way to make no friends at the palace where he was quartered. He was suffering the painful response of a calm and reflective man who discovers that he is as capable of losing control as any hotheaded bully. His sudden disgust with himself displaced his vague notion of what his actions and discoveries of the past few weeks might lead to. He had done his part in this war; he had seen enough hell and horror and had committed enough of it to paper to establish a proper track record, and now why did he persist in remaining in this steaming charnel house called Calcutta? Why not take his typewriter and Valpack and find the quickest way home.

In his room, he stripped off his sweat-soaked uniform, and, naked, fell onto his cot. In a few minutes, he was asleep, and when he awakened it was dark outside. He switched on the light. Had he slept through his appointment with Majumdar? It was not yet eight o'clock. After a cold shower and with clean clothes, he felt human again. Downstairs, Johnson was waiting for him with a jeep, and a few minutes after nine, he was dropped off at the Jewish restaurant.

This time, at a small table for two, Majumdar ordered a dinner of Indian food. "You enjoy fish?" Majumdar asked him. "We will have some fish and vegetables and good bread. The waiter tells me they make fine tali machi here. Bits of fish coated with a chickpea batter and fried, and with it beans kari. Yes? That would please you?"

"Do you remember," Bruce said, "that after those Ghurkas had marched past us, we walked the bikes through that incredible field of golden mustard plants? And then, back at my quarters just now, I dropped down on my bed and slept for over three hours and I had this dream of the golden field covering the naked bodies of the starving children—oh, Christ, I'm making no sense, and then you talk about this food. What in hell are we doing here?"

"Eating, talking," Majumdar said gently. "For me, it is a great treat, because without feeling like a beggar—I despise begging—I am going to eat fine food that I have not tasted for many years. We return to the original proposition, my friend. Shall I deny myself? Another will eat the food, and who will it help? You are full of Christianity, as the British are. I am a Buddhist."

"And a communist. I thought you were a Hindu?"

"Ah, we are endlessly confusing you. I was born in Kashmir, a Hindu family, but in college I became a Buddhist, and then out of that I became a communist. I am still a Buddhist and a Hindu, but something in my karma, some awful presence there took me from Kashmir, which is heaven on earth, to this place called Calcutta, which before the monsoon is close to what you Christians call hell."

"Karma again. What is it? Fate? Kismet?"

"Oh, no. Nothing is fixed. If we wish to talk philosophically, everything is changing, everything is flux. Karma is in the nature of that flux. Your friend Hal Legerman fills his pockets with pice each day and he gives charity where he can. He comes from a place in your country called Brooklyn, where a display of emotion is not popular, so he covers his action with indifference. You wear your emotion more openly, so in a fit of guilt you gave rupees to the children in that poor village."

Thinking, What in hell gives him the right to lecture me? Bruce said coldly, "That's my damn karma."

"And now you are angry with me."

"Oh, no, no—but this place gets to me, palaces—like this restaurant, which is a damn palace, and palaces all over the city, sitting in an open sewer of human misery."

"True. I wouldn't have put it just that way, but it's true. That's the colonial system."

But for all his annoyance, Bruce ate with relish when the food appeared. The food was delicious, beautifully prepared and seasoned, and in the gentle coolness prompted by the slowly spinning ceiling fans, he was able to relax and put the local misery out of his mind. He realized that this was a unique privilege for him, to know Majumdar, to go out into the countryside with him, to be able to question him, a privilege that none of his colleagues enjoyed or sought. The end of the war, the suicide of Hitler, the taking of Berlin by the Russians, the washing out of the Japanese effort, had left small war news to write about here in India. Nor was he sending stories back about his attempt to get the truth about the famine—was it a natural or unnatural event, an act of God, or a crime against humanity?

"I think of today," he said to Majumdar, after they had finished eating and were sitting over small cups of sweet, thick Turkish coffee, "and what you did—day after day— why? What sense does being a communist make? You're such a poor, limited party. The Congress Party has millions of followers, and they don't even acknowledge you."

"That's true. There are millions of good people who will follow the Congress Party and the Mahatma. Gandhi is a saint and he has uplifted the whole nation. But still, day after day passes. Shall we sit back and wait? Someone must be the point, the reminder, the conscience, the gadfly. Someone most go to the poorest of the poor. Someone must be beyond betrayal, sellout, confusion. Are we that? I don't know. We try." Majumdar went on, telling Bruce how he had been sent to Calcutta to take part in an organizing drive in the jute mills, how he had been jailed, beaten, tortured, followed for months at a time by police spies, how it became a matter of life and death for him to go near the mills. That was when he took the job on the newspaper and began to work with the peasants. He was forty-seven years old and he had spent eleven of the forty-seven years in British jails.

When they parted that night, just before midnight, he took both of Bruce's hands in his and held them for a moment. "We have become very close," he told Bruce. "It must have occurred to you that I am using you. To some extent, that is true, but someday, perhaps, you will see it in another way. In my faith, all men are knit together. I want you to tell the truth about this famine."

"I'll try," Bruce said. Those were the last words he ever said to Ashoka Majumdar.

When Johnson dropped Bruce back at the palace, the bar had closed, and aside from Greenberg, an old, sour *Daily News* man, sitting in a corner and chewing on a dead cigar, the lounge was empty. Bruce's typewriter was upstairs in his room, but he felt that this, in any case, was something that should be handwritten and not punched out on a typewriter. He took a sheet of writing paper, with its fancy CBI inscription, and began to write:

"Calcutta, India

"Mrs. Bruce Bacon

"Dear Pru,

"I have been carrying around your letter."

He crossed that out. What in hell did it mean, carrying around your letter? He began again, "I have your letter. Since it is the first letter that has reached me in six weeks, I was relieved to hear that you were well." He was determined not to be sentimental. She had not been sentimental. "I must agree with you that romantic love, so slightly rooted, does not bear the test of absence very well, and I am ready to believe that your feelings about Captain Dennis are

more firmly rooted in reality." There, damn it, he had
rooted himself in reality twice in the same paragraph. Well,
the hell with it. Fuck her! The unspoken oath hit him like a
sledgehammer. Was that it? Was he so indifferent to a beautiful young woman who was his wife that he could sling
such curses at her? Why wasn't his heart broken? Three
years ago, the very creation of such a thought would have
been unthinkable. He tore up the paper and began again:

"Dear Pru,

"Congratulations. You have found someone to love. Even
if his goddamned destroyer had not been in 'grave jeopardy,'
as you put it, I would not have thought less of you. The
point is, love dies. You remember Swinburne, 'love grown
faint and fretful'? Well, the damned, bitter truth is that I
have been neck deep in something and I forgot about your
letter. By all means, have the marriage annulled. Tomorrow,
I'll find whatever the army equivalent of a notary public is,
and I'll swear under oath that the marriage was never con-
summated. I will certainly never contest the proceeding. I
don't want the ring back. I am not angry, not even greatly
disappointed. Whatever was between us, this lousy war destroyed. It destroyed many other things as well. I wish you
happiness."

Later, Bruce would regret the letter and realize the un-
necessary agony it might have caused a woman he had once
loved. But he never knew how she responded, and he felt
that it was at least a truthful letter. He had come to a point
where he neither missed her nor thought a great deal about
her.

The postal clerk usually kept stamps in the lower left-
hand drawer of the big center table. The drawer was empty
now. Greenberg took the cigar out of his mouth and asked
whether Bruce was looking for a stamp. "The native kids
steal from the drawer. I can spare you one."

"Thanks." Bruce accepted the stamp.

"How are you making out with the famine?" Greenberg asked him.

"You know about that?"

"It's around."

"Not good. Not anything I can send back to print."

"The trouble is," Greenberg said, yawning, "that there's too much killing around to score a beat that anyone gives a damn about. Yesterday, I heard the new estimate of the number of people put to death in Hitler's death camps. Nine million, and they figure that six million of them are Jews. One out of every two Jews on the face of the earth, and do you think anyone really gives a damn? You want them to weep over Indians?"

"I'm not in the weeping business," Bruce said. "I want to get at the truth and print it."

"Listen, kid," Greenberg said, not unkindly, "you know who made this famine and I know who made this famine, and every *shmuck* correspondent who's quartered in this stinking palace knows who made the famine, and nobody is ever going to print it except maybe that commie sheet they call *Prasas* or something of the sort." He laid his cigar down in the ashtray. "Never press out a cigar. You allow it to die, nobly." And with that bit of sage advice, he said his good night and lumbered upstairs to his quarters.

Alone in the lounge, Bruce remembered that there were other unwritten letters, letters to his father and mother, letters to friends. But not tonight. He was bone tired, and his bike muscles hurt like the very devil. He went to his room, took three aspirins, and crawled naked under the mosquito netting. But sleep came hard. He was back on the misbegotten British bike, his sore ass growing raw on the wire that poked through the leather seat, the coconut palms leaning over the dusty road, and on one side, stretching away forever, the waving fields of yellow mustard, a golden, glowing ornament to this hellish place. Why did sorrow and beauty go so well together?

Very early in the morning of the third day after this, a GI
brought a note from Public Relations at army headquarters.
The note requested him to report to Lieutenant Colonel
Frank Scott, Public Relations, if possible on this same day.
The GI who brought the note drove a jeep, and he said he
was told to wait if Captain Bacon would return with him.

"I'm no captain," Bruce said. "It's a warrant commission.
I'm a correspondent."

"It never hurts to be sure," the GI said, and Bruce said
that he was ready to go now, but since it was no great
distance, he could just as well walk.

"I was told to get you, sir, so I might just as well get
you."

"All right, you got me," Bruce agreed. He had been
thinking about Prudence Carter Bacon since the night before, when he had a long, absurd dream about her, in which
he seduced her mother. The Carters were an old Boston
family, with excellent small features, who aged well, although since Pru's mother was only in her late forties, one
could hardly speak of her as aged. She was very good-looking, as was her daughter, and Pru's father was president of
the First Eastern Bank of Massachusetts, which had been
organized in 1811, and all of it added up to a very fortunate
marriage—although Bruce never regarded it as such. His
parents did. The Carters were an old, cultured, and impec-
cably well-mannered family. Mr. Carter had gone to Harvard, and Mrs. Carter to Wellesley, as had Prudence.
Bruce's mother—Chicago-born, as was his father—had
helped put William Bacon through medical school by working nights as a waitress while she was getting her master's at
Hunter College. They had come a distance since then, and
since they were Congregational Church members at that
time and engaged in what the Carters regarded as suitable
professions, the Bacon son was approved as a match for
Prudence. Bruce had met her in the home department of the
Tribune, where she was gainfully employed creating recipes

for rationed foods. There was a whirlwind courtship, a proper marriage, and then Bruce was off overseas.

During the short ride to headquarters, Bruce tried to shake loose from both Carter women and decide whether to seek for at least a modest romance among the many nurses and Red Cross ladies who worked in the hospital across the road from the palace. His growing guilts impeded him, not guilt because of what he had done to Prudence—for he had done very little in that direction—but guilts concerning the character of a man like himself, who could let go of one so lovely and certainly decent as Prudence, without a tear. No solutions offered themselves by the time the jeep reached headquarters, and Bruce comforted himself with the thought that all his emotional responses had been shaken out of context here in Calcutta. Or replaced by other responses totally unfamiliar to him. Within sight of headquarters was one of the many pools that abounded in Calcutta, large square basins of filthy water that were a response to the Bengali lust for cleanliness where no cleanliness was possible; and these pools were crowded with kids swimming and adults washing and cleaning dhotis and shirts and dresses, and, seeing the pool this morning, Bruce was brought back to a book he had read as a child, *The Water Babies*, by Charles Kingsley, and the refrain that ran through the book, something like "he who would be clean could be clean," perhaps the strangest connection imaginable—or perhaps not so strange at all.

"Sir?" the jeep driver said.

Bruce left the jeep and entered the building. There was a long mirror just inside the entry, and the sight of himself was curiously unfamiliar, a tall man with brown hair, hazel eyes and glasses, nondescript features, all of it encased in a wrinkled uniform. His appearance won no points from Colonel Scott, very proper and military and not too long ago the head of a large New York advertising agency. Colonel Scott felt that war must be appreciated, and he had already made up his mind that Bacon was one of those whose appreciation of war was limited.

"I have just a few points to make with you, Bacon," Colonel Scott said. "Then Major Hillton would like to have a talk with you."

"Who is Hillton?"

"Army Intelligence."

"And what does Intelligence want of me? My own is strained to the breaking point."

"I presume that's a joke. I think you might take a more serious view of things."

"What things?" Bruce asked angrily, finding a convenient target for his stifled frustration and irritation. "I want to remind you, Colonel, that I am a civilian. I am a newspaper man, and I have been covering this godforsaken war where it was fought, in Africa and on the Continent. You dragged me over here without so much as a by your leave—"

"Oh, come on," Scott interrupted. "I sent a jeep for you. You weren't dragged anywhere."

"OK. You want to see me. Why?"

"Nothing very serious on my part. Major Hillton informed me that he desired to have a talk with you and would I send for you, and since you're here, I thought I might mention a thing or two, small matters."

"All right. Mention them."

"I don't understand your hostility," Colonel Scott said. "We have done everything conceivable to make matters easy and as pleasant as possible, considering that this is Calcutta, for correspondents stationed here." He paused, and when Bruce did not elucidate on his hostility, continued, "The shirt you are wearing. I noticed the same shirt or type of shirt on two occasions when I briefed the correspondents at the palace. Aside from the fact that it is khaki, it bears no resemblance whatsoever to government issue. It has no theater patch, no epaulets, and no other sign of military distinction."

Containing himself, Bruce said, "I came here directly from Europe, Colonel. The shirts I owned were heavy. My mother bought three shirts at Abercrombie's and sent them to me. Are you against motherhood, Colonel?"

"Just for the record, I'm not against motherhood, and I damn well don't know what that has to do with it."

"Oh, fuck the whole thing, Colonel. What are you going to do to me? God be praised, I'm a civilian."

Very stiffly, the colonel said, "I'd suggest you wear government issue, and a little politeness might not be amiss." He opened the door of the office and instructed the sergeant to escort Mr. Bacon to Major Hillton's office. Then he slammed his door emphatically, and the sergeant said, "Colonel's angry. Sorry. No business of mine. You want a Coke? There's a machine right down the hallway here."

"I'd love a Coke," Bruce agreed. His mother-purchased shirt was wet with sweat, even though a sort of air conditioning was struggling with the interior heat. "This is lousy," the sergeant said, commenting on the atmosphere. "Fans are better. I could hear Pinhead calling you out." He dropped two nickels into the machine. "The Cokes are on me. What paper are you with?"

"*New York Tribune.*"

"Great. I'm from Baltimore. I was a stringer for the *Sun.* Well, not exactly. I was a copy boy, and when I was called up, I became their stringer at the training camp. I sent them letters. They printed three of them. Do you know, I knew Mencken. I mean I shook hands with him. He used to call me Brutus. My name's Harvey, but he always called me Brutus. I don't know why."

They finished the Cokes and went on down the hallway. It opened up into polished railings, people in uniform sitting at typewriters, spinning mimeographs, files, fans, officers in a tight knot, discussing things in low key, all very official. A good-looking young woman in uniform, one who had mastered the art of not sweating, sat guard at Major Hillton's door. She was expecting Mr. Bacon.

"Good luck," the sergeant whispered.

Major Hillton was a small, tight-muscled man, burned brown as a berry, needle features, curling British-colonial mustache, and small, pale blue eyes. He shook hands without energy, and then he motioned for Bruce to be seated.

"You're here on a voluntary basis," the major said, clearing the legal ground first. "I suggested that you come here. You came."

"That's right."

"Any notion why?"

"Because you suggested it," Bruce said tiredly. "I'm not clever enough to know much about Intelligence, as you call it."

"You don't take things very seriously, do you, Mr. Bacon?"

"Serious things I take seriously."

"All right. Let's not beat around the bush. I know you work for the *New York Tribune,* and I know you have a damn good reputation. That's why I want to talk to you off the record."

"Thank you." Bruce nodded.

Hillton picked up a clip of three sheets of paper. "This is a verbatim report of your interview with General Felix Shorham, commander of the British Bengal Sector. I won't read all of it, but just what is to the point."

"You don't have to read it," Bruce said. "I remember the interview. I have my own notes."

"I prefer to read it, if you will spare me the time."

"I'm in no hurry," Bruce said.

"Very well. I'll skip the first part of the interview, although General Shorham says some very important things about the Anglo-American alliance being more than an alliance between two nations, but a blood brotherhood—"

"Please spare me that," Bruce interjected. "General Shorham's rhetoric gives me a pain in the ass."

Major Hillton regarded Bruce coldly and said he would overlook the remark. Bruce shrugged. Hillton stared at Bruce in silence for a moment or two; then, abruptly, he began to read:

"Bacon: 'I've spoken to two of the largest rice dealers, and their response is that this is not Russia, that the market makes the price, and since they pay so much and so much for the rice, they must either sell it at a profit or go bankrupt, and then there will be rice for no one. Not their exact words, but the substance.'

"Shorham: 'Understandable.'

"Bacon: 'Perhaps in ordinary circumstances. These are not ordinary circumstances.'

"Shorham: 'How long have you been in Calcutta, Mr. Bacon?'

"Bacon: 'About a month.'

"Shorham: 'I'm making the point that there have been famines here before and there will be again. We cannot control these matters.'

"Bacon: 'But there were and still are enormous supplies of rice here in Calcutta. You could have confiscated the rice, paid the dealer a reasonable sum, and either distributed or sold the rice to the people. I'm not saying you could have averted all that happened, but thousands of lives could have been saved.'

"Shorham: 'You forget. We have no authority to do anything of the kind. This is not Russia. We respect property.'

"Bacon: 'In March, when Indians raided one of the rice warehouses, you gave your troops orders to shoot to kill. Eleven people died.'

"Shorham: 'A mob action which we had to deal with. A mob is a mob. There's no bloody difference.'

"Bacon: 'General Shorham, I am pressing my questions because I have been told by a number of people, in Europe as well as here, that this famine was the result of a British decision, in the face of a then threatening Japanese advance into India, to break the will of the people in Assam as well as eastern Bengal so that they could not welcome the Japanese as liberators and join them against the British. I am not offering any evidence for this. I have no evidence in writing, but I do have the word of people who claim to have absolute knowledge of this.'

"Shorham: 'Who the hell do you think you are, Bacon? You dare to come here with some bloody slander worthy of Julius Streicher—to accuse His Majesty's Government here in India of a slaughter so great that it deserves to stand beside the worst that the Nazis have done? Are you out of your fucken mind? How dare you!'

"Bacon: 'I have only repeated what I have heard, and all I desire from you, General, is a denial.'

"Shorham: 'I will not dignify it with a denial.' "

Major Hillton finished reading from the interview and dropped the papers on his desk. He maintained his silence long enough, as he saw it, for Bruce to become thoroughly uncomfortable. From Bruce's point of view, it was not discomfort but irritation at being subjected to a lecture by a fool.

"You do know," Hillton went on, "that we and the British are allies, and that the alliance is signed with the blood of thousands of British and American young men."

"Major Hillton," Bruce said softly, "I am not some eighteen-year-old GI, standing in front of you with his eyes on the ground. I have been a part of this war for more than three years."

"And the war goes on. We still face the Japanese, Mr. Bacon, and in the face of that fact, you come here to a country that you don't know—not one damn thing, with problems you have never faced, which we must face—"

Enamored with the word *face*, Bruce thought.

"—and then you throw this goddamn crazy accusation at

the British High Command. Do you realize what you have done?"

"I've done my work. I'm a journalist."

"And the war? As an American are you beyond any responsibility for that?"

"Major, there are two million American troops in this country, and no Japanese have yet set foot on Indian soil nor is there the slightest likelihood that they ever will. If they're here for anything, they're here to stop the Indians from rising, and if that is what I believe, I am going to damn well write it."

"Mr. Bacon, you have created more difficulties between us and the British than you can possibly imagine. We have labored for months to make our alliance work. You've thrown a bomb into the heart of it."

"What the devil gives with you, Major? You're in a city where for months the streets have been littered with the bodies of men and women and children who have died of starvation, and you know damn well that Limey general was lying. This famine could have been broken, and it's one of the biggest stories out of this war, and I'm going to write it."

"Your orders will be cut tomorrow. You are not wanted in this theater. Don't think for a moment that your dealings with Ashoka Majumdar and Professor Chandra Chatterjee have gone unnoticed. Professor Chatterjee is a local subversive with a long record, and as for Majumdar, he is a communist organizer with a prison record. You have behaved and spoken witlessly, and now you're paying the price."

"Major," Bruce said softly, "have you ever stopped to reflect on the fact that on this great subcontinent, four hundred million people are being held in subjugation by the British, with nationality set against nationality and religion against religion?"

"On that point, Mr. Bacon, let me just note that they are niggers without any talent to govern themselves. They should thank God for the British."

"I have nothing else to say to you!" Bruce snapped, getting to his feet, turning on his heel, and leaving the room.

There was no jeep waiting to take him home, now that the sun was well up and beginning to bake the street. In this climate, it was quite proper to hold that "mad dogs and Englishmen go out in the midday sun." After ten steps, his shirt was moist and sticking to his body. He walked along the streetcar tracks, the shortest way to the palace, staring morosely at the lines of old, rotting buildings that lined the street, the stucco peeling off their stained fronts. Rickshaw drivers came trotting by, trying to entice his patronage, but he hated to ride in a rickshaw, finding the sensation both degrading and humiliating, a small, lean trotting man become an animal and pulling him in his little carriage, as a trotting horse would. Hal Legerman had argued with him on this point. "They have to live," Legerman insisted. "We pay them five times what the Limeys do—at least, that's how I tip them." Still, he could not be at ease riding in a rickshaw. Like Legerman, he kept a pocketful of pice. He had calculated that in Calcutta, there was a beggar or a street family every fifty feet—in what the British called "the glorious city of palaces." One night he had lain under his mosquito netting weeping; and told himself sourly, the following morning, that such empathy came out of the guilts conditioned by washing machines, Ford cars, and packaged cereals. Yet in all this filth, there was a frantic effort by the population to be clean, washing themselves endlessly in dirty, polluted water. Why did his thoughts always come back to this? The moment he set foot in America, this world would cease to exist, and, as he vaguely hoped, it would no longer trouble him. Why not? It didn't trouble his American colleagues; and his British colleagues, and the British officers who hung out at the press club for the cheap American drinks and who upheld the gentility of their clan by proving to Bruce that one could use the word *fuck* at least five times in the average sentence—well, they felt Calcutta to be one of the prime glories of the Empire, an absolutely *pukka* place to be stationed.

At the palace, Bruce showered and changed his shirt—for another nongovernment issue that his mother had provided —and then, hearing a voice shout his name, went downstairs to answer a telephone call. It was Legerman calling, and he said he wanted to talk to Bruce, very important, but he didn't want to come to the palace. Would Bruce meet him at the old Cricket Club in the Maidan, the park. Did Bruce know where it was?

"I think I know where the Cricket Club is."

"Outside, there are some benches, shaded. I'll meet you there in an hour."

The thing that had stayed with Bruce after a stroll in the Maidan was that the fine green lawns were cut and kept smooth as carpeting, not with machines of any sort, not even with hand-pushed lawn mowers, but by natives who, on hands and knees, cut the grass with clippers. Why not? If the cost of a lawn mower could pay the wages of a bearer for a full year, why bother to purchase the lawn mower? Like all other things in India, it made sense in a weird, senseless way.

When Bruce reached the Cricket Club, Legerman was sprawled on a bench, in the shade of a great live oak, straw in mouth, sipping a bottle of Coca-Cola.

"Got one for you," he told Bruce, reaching down next to the bench and coming up with another bottle of Coca-Cola, straw already inserted. When things were needed, Legerman produced them at the proper moment.

"Legerman," Bruce said, staring gratefully at the Coca-Cola, "don't you have anything that pins you down? You are a sergeant in an army run by the sergeants, so you must have duties, responsibilities?"

"I arrange time to do my own thing. You know, I was a p.r. man around Broadway, and you're a newspaperman, and one day, God willing, this lunacy will be over—and well, one hand washes the other. You're in trouble."

"How do you know? God damn it," Bruce went on, "how the hell do you know everything that goes on around here?"

"I keep my ears open. Also, I occasionally date that cute little Wac who guards shithead Hillton's door. Would you believe it, Major Hillton got his job in Intelligence out of being a clerk at police headquarters in Cleveland—not even a real cop, but a clerk. Officers are no bargain, but those cookies who got their jobs by appointment out of civilian life —they're the worst."

"OK," Bruce said, "I'm in trouble. Forgive me. I had a lousy morning."

"They cutting orders for your departure?"

"So they tell me."

"And of course you're not going. You're going to stand on your rights as a journalist accredited to this theater and remain right here in Calcutta, and get your newspaper into it and maybe make a real case out of it."

"I had something of that sort in mind," Bruce agreed.

"Sure. Why not?" Legerman nodded. "Your thinking is high class. That's because you're an American. Me too. We're both full of motherhood and apple pie, even after Hitler, even after the gas ovens, even after what we both seen in this lousy town, because we're pure. You know what happens, you fight this thing?"

"Tell me."

"Sure I'll tell you, and don't get your ass up and get sore at me, because I can see that's what you're doing. I had a girl friend back home, and you know what she used to call characters like you—*shiksa boys*. Good, educated parents who spoke real English right from the start, good private schools, good colleges, entry to anything. Bruce Bacon. You grow up with a name like that and with your looks and six feet from eating good food instead of garbage, and you don't even need brains. You're an American, Jack Armstrong.

You remember Jack Armstrong on the radio, raise the flag for Hudson High, boys, Jack Armstrong loves Wheaties and so should you."

"Oh, Christ, can it."

"I'm getting to you."

"I'm staying here," Bruce said. "They're not forcing me out. They haven't got a leg to stand on, and I can blow this famine thing sky high."

"Sure you can. Otherwise, what happens to apple pie and motherhood? Now let me suggest what will happen if you decide to stay here. One: they will remove your accreditation, and no wire service will be available to you. Two: they will stop your mail, and don't think they can't do it. Three: they will toss you out of your quarters at the palace. No hotel in town will book you. Where are you going to sleep? You go to someone like Chandra Chatterjee, and they'll arrest him. This goes with three. They arrested Majumdar last night—"

"When? Why?"

"Hold on," Legerman said. "We'll talk about that. We're only up to four. Four: they'll plant something on you. The Limeys are brilliant at that. Plans, papers, whatever. Espionage. All or any of the above, and finally, five. Five might even be *one* if you're too damn annoying. Five is making you dead, completely dead. Run over by a half-track. Beaten to death by bandits. The streets of Calcutta swarm with killers —or didn't you know? Now I'm not making up crazy movie plots, believe me. I like you. You're straight. You're decent and honest. I want you at home, where there are few enough like you."

"What happened to Majumdar?" Bruce asked, his voice hoarse.

"He was with the professor last night. They walked in and arrested him. British specials. That's it."

"Well, what happens now? What do they do with him?"

"You guess."

"Torture him, kill him? Is that what you're intimating?"

"Not intimating."

"My God, Hal, can't we do something? I work for a great newspaper. I write for *The Saturday Evening Post.* These are important and powerful entities. They can reach into Washington—into the White House itself. I know people who know President Roosevelt—"

"Forget it," Legerman said harshly. "It's done. We'll never see Majumdar again. He may be dead already. You don't know what workmanship is until you've watched these sweethearts. No, it's over for us. Get out of here. These fellers will take care of things themselves. They don't need you. Do you hear me?"

Bruce nodded.

"I want you out of here. Today."

"I can't leave today. It's out of the question."

"God damn you, will you listen? Why are we sitting here instead of at the palace? Because my guess is that they're there already. I have your orders right here in my pocket." He took out of his jacket a long brown envelope and handed it to Bruce. "Waiting for you. From now on, you'll be watched, day and night. Who knows whether these orders would have gotten to you? Jill cut them, and then she put them on the major's desk. He countersigned them and left the office. Jill passed them to me. She'll claim innocence. They disappeared. Done. I signed Soutine's name and wrote A-One priority. No one will question it. No one ever questions such things in the army. I want you out of here."

"You said Soutine?" Bruce asked weakly. "You mean General Soutine, the top theater commander?"

"That's right."

"You're crazy. This is the craziest damn thing I ever heard about. This is crazy. You'll end up in the stockade for life."

"Hell, no. I know what I'm doing." Legerman grinned. "You know, I got you into this—the worst of it anyway. I

owe you, and I like you. Don't worry about me, Bruce. I
know my way around, and it ain't that different from Brooklyn."

"I can't—my clothes, my notes, my typewriter—I just
can't."

"Listen," Legerman said gently. "I know the bearer who
works the door at the palace. I'll buy him a pint of hooch,
and being that he's a Muslim, he'll be so happy for a chance
to sin, he'll steal me the tiles in the lobby. He'll bring out
your notes, and I'll bring them back. You got my word on
that. Just give me your address." He took out his notebook
and a stub of pencil. Bruce gave him his parents' address on
Riverside Drive and One hundred and eighth Street in New
York, since Prudence was at the apartment and he had more
or less given her possession.

"I left it there," Legerman said, nodding at a jeep that
was parked about fifty feet away. He stood up. "Let's go."

Bruce stared at Legerman as if he had never seen him
before, as perhaps he never had, a heavyset man of twenty-
seven years, wide face, full lips, dark skin, heavy beard that
turned his skin purple, and under a pair of shaggy brows,
light blue eyes utterly at variance with everything else about
him.

"How did you get a jeep?"

"Borrowed it," Legerman said.

He walked to the jeep. Bruce followed, shaking his head,
astonished, bewildered by what he was about to do, staring
at Legerman, who was a genius, a lunatic, or a crook. If he
was the last, Bruce couldn't for the life of him figure out
what he was getting from this. On the other hand, he himself, Bruce Bacon, was engaged in something new in his life.
Until now, with all the danger and killing and horror he had
witnessed in Europe, it had always been inside the strong,
indomitable arms of the United States Army, cherishing
him, feeding him, protecting him, making sure that they
would not have another dead correspondent on their hands.

But this was something else entirely, with both the British High Command and the American High Command lined up against him because he had committed, or was attempting to commit, the unforgivable sin of breaking a story that no one wanted broken. He realized that neither the British nor the Americans knew how much evidence he had, nor was there any way he could prove to them that he had no evidence at all, and say to them, Look, fellers, let's drop the whole thing.

But what odds that they would drop the whole thing? Here was a nosy American correspondent who would not accept the fact that over five million—almost six million—people had died of a famine that was no more nor less than an act of God, aided and abetted by some hungry rice dealers, who were only doing what one was supposed to do in any business, which was to make a reasonable or even an unreasonable profit. It spelled trouble, and with a war still going on, even though Germany had been defeated, he who shook the boat was an enemy of the people, and in war, especially in this war, there was neither time nor mercy for such. The war effort was an enormous blanket that covered almost all of everything, even in India, where there was no war.

"You're crazy, I'm crazy," he said to Legerman as the jeep rolled toward the airport.

"We're pretty sane. It's the rest of the world that's smoking opium."

"You know they can pick me up stateside."

"For what? What have you done? Your orders are valid. You've committed no crime. Come on, Bruce, shape up. Look at those coconut palms. This is the finest avenue of palm trees in Bengal. Doesn't that make you want to stand up and cheer? The hell with them! Once you're out of here, the whole thing will be forgotten."

"But my luggage, my Valpack, my typewriter—a man

who runs out on his luggage is suspect. There's no way around that."

"Who says you're running out on your luggage. You had to catch this C-Forty-seven up to Delhi. It's the only Air Transport out of here today. Write a note when we reach the airport, and I'll have your stuff sent home via Ship Transport. It won't reach you for maybe a few months, but you got another typewriter. Right?"

"Right," Bruce said weakly, realizing that Legerman was simply flying by the seat of his pants. He was desperate to get Bruce out of the China-Burma-India Theater of operations. Whether the danger he proposed to Bruce was real or not was something Bruce couldn't know. He found himself trusting Legerman because Legerman had the attitude of a man to be trusted.

An hour later, Bruce was sitting in a C-47 that had taken off en route to Delhi. Legerman had bustled him onto the plane with such an air of urgency and importance that the night officer at control, a young captain engrossed in a conversation with a blond Red Cross lady, never even questioned the A-1 priority for a correspondent. At Delhi airport, Bruce had only an hour of waiting time, and then his priority put him on a C-54 to Egypt. The C-54 refueled in Egypt and then took off for the Azores, refueled again, and finally deposited him in Long Island, where, after fifteen minutes with customs, he was able to step into a big, comfortable Checker cab that drove him to his folks' apartment on Riverside Drive.

Three weeks later, an atom bomb was dropped on Hiroshima, and the war with Japan was over.

New York City
Uptown

He loved New York City. He loved the big, lumbering yellow streetcars. He loved the crowds, the endless parade of faces. He had read somewhere once that all the people, the bodies, the faces, were linked in a sort of network of vibrations that one felt without knowing that one felt it, and that buoyed up the spirit. Then would it have been the very opposite of it that he had sensed in Calcutta? But he was here now, dressed in civilian clothes, thin gray flannels, clean white shirt, and striped tie. The sun was shining. All was right with the world, and McGregor, who was his friend as well as the editor of a great national magazine, had invited him to lunch at "21," and the week before, he had met a love of a girl at, of all places, church.

By and large, neither church nor religion played much of a role in the Bacons' lives. But there were moments when Elizabeth Bacon, Bruce's mother, felt that she must offer either gratitude or prayers in a more spiritual place than their apartment. The return of her son, unharmed, marked such a moment, and although she had been born a Congregationalist, she felt a little more comfortable among the Unitarians. William Bacon, Bruce's father, was indifferent to the whole thing, but being a good-natured man, he trailed along without demur; and it was on this occasion, at the Church of All Souls on Lexington Avenue, that Bruce met Sally Pringle, twenty-three years old, unmarried, and a year out of Vassar.

It was like a scene out of time, or out of Shakespeare, and where else, as Bruce pointed out later, does one meet the woman one loves but in church? In this case, it was facilitated by the fact that Elizabeth Bacon, Bruce's mother, and Denny Pringle, Sally's mother, were old chums who had not seen each other for at least thirty years. They met. Bruce, no loner, no swinger, no one-nighter, was instantly enchanted. If someone had asked him what he was looking for, physically, he would have admitted to the tall, long-legged type, firm, solid, fine regular features, light brown hair, blue eyes —and if a mind came with it, so much the better. That it was also a fair description of Prudence, whose "Dear John" letter had taken her out of his life at a distance of twelve thousand miles, mattered not at all.

So it was that, with the good feeling of a life disrupted and finally coming together with just the right ingredients, Bruce faced Jack McGregor and hoisted a celebratory dry martini. As a rule, Bruce did not drink before dark, but this was worth breaking a rule. He had spoken to McGregor on the telephone, and this was their first postwar meeting. He had sent McGregor a major piece of fifteen thousand words. McGregor had read it, but would not comment over the telephone. Thus the luncheon meeting. Such a luncheon was almost ritually divided: before the main course and with the drink, one discussed social matters; during the meal, one spoke of the city, the nation, the weather, etc.; with the coffee, one got down to business, which in this case was an abrupt declaration by McGregor:

"Bruce, I have to put it to you flatly. There is absolutely no way in the world that we can publish your piece."

After a moment of silence, Bruce said, "Just like that."

"Ah, no. No. You're no neophyte. You're in there with the best, and this is one hell of an article. It's an earth-shaker."

"But you can't publish it. So you feel free to lay it on," Bruce said sourly.

"That's not called for."

"No? Tell me why. Maybe I should be grateful."

"Bruce, for Christ's sake, get off your indignation and come back to the world we live in. We've just wound up the biggest, goddamned awfulest war in the history of the human race. We killed the monster, and now we look at what he left behind. Have you read the reports about the killing camps, the abattoirs, the gas ovens? Do you know what the figures are that they're putting together—that Hitler cold-bloodedly murdered six million Jews? It's not something the mind can encompass, because there is no precedent. It almost makes you sick to be a member of the same race. And now, when we're stiffening up against a Soviet takeover of the whole Continent, you want me to print something that accuses the British, our number one ally, of an action almost as inhuman, as unbelievable."

"Jack, you're missing the point," Bruce argued. "Nowhere in what I've written do I accuse the British of engineering this famine, because I have no proof that they did. But I have plenty of proof that they never lifted a hand to stop it. I saw the rice, thousands of sacks of rice, and I interviewed the dealers. It's all in there. I write that the common belief around Calcutta was that the British had done it, but I specify that I have no proof that I could go into court with. But this is not simply an accusation thrown at the British—it's the whole world indifferent to the death of millions."

"The war was at its highest point. How could you expect the nations to drop—"

"Jack, don't give me that. It wouldn't have made a particle of difference in the war effort if those starving people were fed."

"You're not hearing me, Bruce."

"I hear you. I sent you a story that was a clear, clean beat. No newspaper, no magazine touched it. It's good, decent professional work, and now you tell me that you won't print it."

"What did the *Trib* say?"

"It's fifteen thousand words. It's not a newspaper piece, it's a magazine piece. You know that."

He walked uptown from that lunch meeting at "21." It was a fine fall day, a sweet day, not too cold and not too warm, one of those very special days that New York is blessed with occasionally. It was a sort of benediction on a world finally at peace, a world with all possible futures achievable, a world not yet actually aware of the atom bomb. Bruce couldn't remain depressed. Prudence had moved out of their one-bedroom apartment in a brownstone on East Seventy-sixth Street, leaving it for him, furnishings intact. Very decent of her, he thought, recalling a conversation with a psychiatrist about "Jewish guilt." He didn't think it measured up to white Protestant New England guilt. He could think of Prudence very objectively, and that bothered him. Had he ever loved her? Like everything else during this war, relationships had changed; but if the word *love* defined something else, he didn't know what that might be. Should he have doubts about Sally Pringle? But why? She pleased him, she excited him—or did she? Now, as he walked up Madison Avenue, he wondered why, when he started a train of thought, it would end up either confused or shattering some belief that he had accepted as the rock and foundation of his existence. Somewhere, all the rocks and foundations had become slithery. There was the matter of his friends. Before the war he had friends all over the place, people on the newspaper, leftovers from college, magazine people he dealt with, older people who were family friends. Of course, some of them were in the service, but they were starting to trickle back. The trouble was that after he had shared lunch with them, with one or another, and occasionally double-dated, he had no desire to see them again. What had happened to him?

He brought the matter up with his father. He had always been close to his father, and after three years of separation, he found they could talk together as grown men. His father, Dr. William Bacon, sixty-three, had aged noticeably during Bruce's absence. He was a tall, slender man with a rather forbidding face that melted under a smile. His smile made his patients adore him, and his unsmiling face, when the need arose, made them follow his orders.

"You've undergone what might be called," his father said to him, "the ultimate experience that anyone could endure on this earth. You would have to be either a fool or pathological not to be affected by it, and you are neither."

He recalled it this fine October day, walking uptown along Madison Avenue and wondering why Jack McGregor's rejection of the story he had worked on so carefully had not devastated him. Yet it had not, and perhaps the reason was that somewhere down deep he had expected precisely that kind of response. What do you do? he asked himself. He had entertained some thoughts of doing the Indian experience as a book, fleshed out perhaps by his prior experience in the European war. Of course, a slew of books about the war, fiction as well as nonfiction, would be pouring into the bookstores. Every correspondent had a story to tell, yet his own story would be different. Insofar as he knew, no one else would be telling it. On the other hand, if he sat down to write a full-length book, he would have to ask for a leave of absence from the *Tribune*, and then it was a question of money. He and Prudence had a joint account for the money gifts that had come with their wedding, but as far as the earnings of each was concerned, they kept separate accounts. The twelve thousand dollars they had received as gifts, Prudence had split evenly between them, and in his own account, almost thirty-six thousand dollars had accumulated during the years abroad. The way he lived, Bruce decided, forty-two thousand would see him through the next five years, and he was young enough not to worry about what would happen after that. The thing to do now was to get home, take a shower, change clothes, and meet Sally. Tomorrow was time enough to start talking to publishers.

Sally was a model, sport clothes. She worked for Hillsdale Fashions, a very large garment company on Seventh Avenue, and at nine thousand dollars a year, she was well paid indeed. This was information conveyed to Bruce at their first date after meeting her in church, and after having told him this, Sally observed that he appeared surprised if not shocked.

"You aren't shocked, really, are you?"

"No. Oh, no."

"Then why so surprised?"

"Well, you know—"

"I don't know," Sally said. "Tell me."

We're starting off on the wrong foot, Bruce decided, and what can I say that won't make it worse? The truth of the matter was that after the church meeting, Mrs. Pringle, a widow, and her daughter were asked to tea at the Bacons'. In one corner of the room, Bruce chatted away with Sally, and his impression was of a very bright, well-informed young lady. They talked about a number of things, but mostly it was directed toward Bruce, and while he was very impressed with her, he didn't learn that she was a model until he took her to dinner two nights later.

"Well, you know, one—"

"You said that before."

"Did I? I mean, well, you know. Yes. What I mean is that one develops certain stereotypes and one applies them to a model—"

She burst out laughing. "Oh, Bruce Bacon, you are precisely the kind of man one would meet in church."

"Hey, come on," Bruce said, "that was the first time I've been to church since I was in school."

"Oh, I'm not putting you down, believe me. I mean you

have such a delicious lack of sophistication—I mean you're the way guys should be but aren't. Oh, hell, I'm making you feel foolish."

He felt foolish, damn foolish. She reached across the table and took his hand. "Bruce, I model sport clothes. In college I majored in biology, and I thought I would do postgraduate work and become a marine biologist. That was the thing a few years ago. Very romantic. Then I met this designer— purely by accident—his name was Phil Sturtz, and he's a part owner of Hillsdale. I met him at a party, and he asked me to help him out because one of his girls was sick, and that's about it, and it's as prissy and proper a job as one could have, and Hillsdale is a very large corporation, and listed on the New York Stock Exchange, and they had a very good war—"

"What did you say?"

"I said they had a good war."

"Explain it, please," Bruce said. "What is a good war?"

"Bruce, you've been away too long, and I know exactly what you're thinking, but people have made scads of money out of the war, and they say this one or that one had a good war, and it's nothing I invented—"

They worked it out. Bruce was able to confront his indignation and put it in its place. Sally was quite right; it was nothing that she had invented. Sally was bright, practical, and pragmatic, and indeed she helped anchor Bruce in a world called "postwar U.S.A." It was a world apparently untouched by the incredible suffering the war had caused, and while there were those who wept for the dead, there were infinitely more untouched and unmoved who wanted to forget the extermination camps and Hiroshima and Nagasaki. The bleak, jobless days of the Depression were behind them forever, and there was a brisk, strutting little haberdasher who had come into the presidency. Nothing was the same, and Bruce might just as well come down to earth and realize that nothing was the same.

On his second date, he took Sally to bed. There had been a French girl whom he met in Páris, and who was sweet and willing, and whom he had taken to bed in a brief affair that lasted for the three days he was in the city at the time; but beyond that he had not been unfaithful to Prudence. Now his passion exploded, and when their lovemaking was over, Sally studied him with surprise and new interest. She had not dreamed of such passion.

"I want to marry you," Bruce said. Actually, he was not expressing a need or even a desire; he was reacting to the sudden erasure of his loneliness, to the warm, wonderful feeling that he was part of another human being. Sally, on the other hand, had no thoughts or intentions of marriage, and certainly not to a newspaperman who spoke of giving up his job to write a book. Yet she found in Bruce qualities lacking in so many of the men she met: he was warm, nonjudgmental, well educated, better in bed than she could have expected, reasonably tall and good-looking, and well mannered. Sally had grown up with a mother who had very urgent social pretensions. She hardly could have escaped being influenced by those social pretensions and sharing in them to a certain degree, and while Bruce's family were not a part of what went for society or celebrity—the two becoming interchangeable in New York City—they had enough breeding and elegance and money to satisfy her. But as for marriage, that was another thing entirely.

"Do you?" she said, kissing him and stroking his cheek. "It was very nice. Did that decide you?"

"Sex? Good sex?"

"It was very good. There should have been all sorts of awful problems, but there weren't," Sally said, laughing. "But one has to get out of bed occasionally."

"I hate to think so. Look, Sally, I don't mean tomorrow."

"You just wanted to stake out a claim?"

"I don't even know how you feel about me."

"I'm in bed with you, Bruce. That's how I feel about you."

Afterward, Bruce was relieved that Sally had not accepted his offer of marriage. He hardly knew her. What did she think about anything? What were her dreams? She certainly made good money, but her apartment on Central Park South was almost regal—at least in terms of his tiny place on Seventy-sixth Street—and out of this he came to have a sense of escape vying with his need for a permanent connection. He stopped by the desk of Joey Kemp, who did an "on the town" column for the newspaper, and asked him what he knew about Phil Sturtz.

"Sturtz? Why Sturtz?"

"Curiosity."

"A good newspaperman don't have curiosity, old buddy. You got something going, tell me about it."

"Just curiosity."

"Well," said Joey, "when the curiosity matures, buzz me. Meanwhile, Phil Sturtz is one of a new crop of fancy clothes designers that's come to life since the war. They're native, by which I mean they don't genuflect to Paris, and they've changed the *shmata* game to very big business—listed on the stock exchange and all that—and at the same time, they're the neon lights of the new top fast crowd in town. But that's off your beat, right?"

"You could say that. What does he look like?"

"Tall, dark, and handsome. What goes on, Bacon, is he competition?"

"I wonder."

There was too much running around in his mind, like a spinning cage full of hamsters, and nothing adding up to a direction or even a point of view. The paper put him on full salary for two months, making up for unclaimed vacation time, and then the managing editor called him in for a talk. "What about it, Bruce, what kind of assignment do you

want? The way we feel about you, you can pretty damn well
name it."

"Even after I raised such hell about your not printing the
famine story?" Bruce asked cautiously.

"You were entitled. We never turned down any dispatch
of yours, but we have an editorial board and only so many
pages. You know that things get turned down for a variety
of reasons."

"I know that," Bruce agreed. He had given up on arguments for the famine story.

"So you name it. The big story today is Berlin. Fitz is
there, but he wants to come home. Can you speak German?"

"I can get by with it, but I don't think I want to go to
Berlin."

"What else? Name it."

"I don't know," Bruce said slowly. He could feel his heart
tightening. This was a city where people would kill, lie, con-
nive, to work on a major newspaper. Right at this moment,
he was still a hotshot correspondent, a younger Ernie Pyle, a
man who had crawled into foxholes with the ordinary un-
striped dogfaces, who had been under fire and faced it and
written about what he saw and felt. But that was yesterday,
and he had come to understand full well that the American
public had a memory and a concentration span that could
wash out in twenty-four hours. Already, people he met who
had been in the service had put away their "ruptured
ducks," the tiny brass pins that marked them as ex-GI's.

The managing editor was watching him thoughtfully.

"I think," Bruce said, "I want to write a book."

"Come on!"

"Yes, sir. That's what I think."

"Jesus God, Bruce, every goddamn correspondent who
ever left this shore is writing a book. There are going to be
so many books about this war that a man would have to live
to be a hundred to read half of them."

"I guess you're right, but I still think I have to write a book, so what I really want is six months' leave. If you can do that, I'll be grateful."

It was not a problem. His editor assured him that it was not a problem. The job would be waiting for him. He walked out into the sunlight and shook himself, the way a dog shakes off water. Again, as with Sally, the feeling of liberation fought the feeling of being lost, of having taken the wrong step. It was not the wrong step, he told himself; it was being back here after so long that made him uncertain of so many things. Actually, what was there to worry about? He was single, he was far from broke, and he was free.

He walked on, block after block. He wanted to see the city, feel it, know it again. In a circle, he went down to Fourteenth Street, and then walked east across Fourteenth Street. There was Lüchow's. He had eaten there with his father and mother when he was fifteen, a festive, heavy meal of German food that made his mother cringe. She was one of the new nutritionists, whole wheat bread and salad vegetables. He looked through the glass windows at the old chandeliers and dark woodwork. How strange that after the mortal struggle against the Germans, and having seen the horrors of the death camps, he should have only the teenage memories. Nothing here connected with what he had seen in Europe. He walked uptown to Gramercy Park, pausing outside the Players' Club. He had an Uncle Bert who was a member and who had promised that when he came home, he would be put up for membership. But Uncle Bert, his mother's older brother, had died while Bruce was overseas, and right now, he had no desire to join any club. He walked up Lexington Avenue, recalling a wonderful Armenian restaurant in the upper Twenties, where they would go occasionally to feast on rice and lamb broiled on a spit. He remembered introducing the place to Prudence. He knew the city better than she did, and each part that he showed her was like a small gift. Odd that he could think about

Prudence so objectively, as if she were cut from cardboard, simply the picture of her and no existence beyond that. He turned left toward Fourth Avenue, and sure enough, there was the restaurant. Things don't dissolve in three years. He walked on north to where Fourth Avenue became Park Avenue, and then down the hill to Forty-second Street, past Grand Central Station and west on Forty-second Street. It was all there, different but still there, the color, the variety of people, the old, beautiful bulk of the Public Library, and then Times Square with its crowds, its bums, its hookers, its tangle of traffic, and the wonderful clanging, bell-ringing yellow streetcars soon to disappear forever.

It was late afternoon when he reached his place on Seventy-sixth Street. A man in a Panama hat stood outside the town house, and he looked at Bruce, and then said, "Bacon? Are you Mr. Bacon?"

"Most of the time," Bruce said.

The tall man in the Panama hat ignored the humor, took out his wallet, showed his credentials, and identified himself as Carl Jorgenson of the Federal Bureau of Investigation. "I'd like to talk to you if I might," Jorgenson said.

"If you wish," Bruce said. "If I could be helpful, why not?"

In his living room, Jorgenson complimented him on the appearance of the place.

"My wife decorated it. We're divorced now."

"Away too long?"

Bruce shrugged.

"That's the way the war did it," Jorgenson said sympathetically. "Nobody counts those casualties."

He was pleasant enough. He wore a ruptured duck to show that he had not been left out of things, and if that was a bit gauche at this date, he did work for the government, and who knew what their rules were? It was Bruce's first encounter with the FBI, and his feelings were absolutely neutral. If he felt anything about them, it was an underlying sense of them as a secret police, and a secret police was nothing he could applaud. He excused himself for a moment, went into his tiny kitchen, took ice cubes from the refrigerator, and came back into the living room with ice, glasses, and a bottle of gin.

"Can I pour you a drink? Just gin on the rocks. It's all I have."

"Thank you. Not on the job," Jorgenson said.

"And how do I fit into the job?" Bruce wanted to know.

Jorgenson's face was long and sad. A smile might have helped it, but he didn't smile. "If you could answer a few questions?" he said. "You don't have to. This is a very informal visit, but we would appreciate it if you could."

"I don't know what the hell you're doing here, and if you want me to answer questions, suppose you tell me what this is all about." He felt anger beginning, and he didn't know why he should be angry except that a finger was being pointed at him. What did they say—spinach was without empathy, chopped liver was funny, raisins were a medium laugh—and FBI? What was FBI? Why did it do something cold and constricting to his stomach?

"My questions will explain that."

His feelings crystallized. Throw the bastard out! Since when do you, Bruce Bacon, hold out your hand to secret police cops! But then his curiosity took hold.

"Go ahead," he said, dropping ice into a glass and pouring gin. "You don't mind if I have a drink?"

"Not at all."

"You don't mind if I smoke?"

"Oh, no. Go right ahead." Jorgenson watched him stuff a pipe, a new pipe. Bruce had smoked pipes years ago and then dropped it overseas. This was a pipe he had picked up a week before, but he found he had lost the habit. Why then was he smoking now?

Jorgenson had taken a notebook out of his pocket. He

glanced in it now and said suddenly, "Legerman. Harold Legerman. You know him?"

Bruce put the pipe aside, thinking, The hell with it! I don't know why I want the damn thing. The name didn't register for a long moment, and then he said, "Hal Legerman? What on earth do you want with Legerman?"

"I asked whether you know him?"

"Know him? Sure. I met him in the CBI."

"How well do you know him?"

Suddenly, Bruce backed off and became cautious. "Casually. I was a correspondent overseas. I knew GI's, a hundred of them, maybe a thousand."

"You don't recall a thousand names. You remember Legerman. Right?"

"I said you could ask me questions. I didn't say you could grill me. This is ridiculous."

"Perhaps to you. To us it's a very serious matter, Mr. Bacon. Is Legerman a communist?"

"Ask him."

"I'm asking you if you know or do not know whether Mr. Legerman is a communist?"

"Mr. Jorgenson, I don't even know whether you're a communist. Are you?"

"For the record, I am not."

"I was trying to be cute. I'm not good at it. I couldn't care less about who is or is not a communist. I have my own problems."

"Nevertheless, I am very serious. Do you know whether or not Mr. Legerman is a communist?"

"I don't know, and if I knew I wouldn't tell you."

"Why not? I am a representative of your government— trying to serve this country, which is your country."

"That's a hell of a locution. Does it come with the job? I mean, do you memorize it?"

"I am trying to be polite and straightforward, sir."

"Look," Bruce said impatiently, "don't feed me shit. You

are not a representative of my government, you are a god-damn member of a secret police. Why don't you ask me whether I'm a communist?"

"Are you?"

"No. Why don't you ask me whether I'm a Democrat or a Republican?"

"Because that's no business of mine," Jorgenson said patiently. "Those are legitimate American institutions. I have been both polite and patient, Mr. Bacon. I cannot for the life of me understand why you refuse to answer a few simple questions."

"Am I refusing? You asked me whether Legerman is a member of the Communist Party. I said I don't know."

"When you were in India, did you attend any Communist Party meetings with him?"

"No."

"Do you know a Professor Chandra Chatterjee?"

"Yes. I mean by that that I spent an evening at his home. I wouldn't say that constitutes knowing him."

"Did you know that Professor Chatterjee is a member of the Central Committee of the Communist Party of Bengal?"

"Now hold on, Jorgenson, just hold on. This is setting up like a bad spy novel. You want to know about me, ask me. I am nonpolitical. My father, who is a very nice man, is a registered Republican. That's all right with me. I went to college at Williams. Other colleges were very political. Williams was not, and what politicking went on there I had nothing to do with. I don't like you. I resent your being here in my apartment, and I think you'd better go before I get very nasty and say things to you that I may regret."

Jorgenson rose and put on his Panama hat. "It's a reaction I wouldn't expect from a man like you. I'm sorry you couldn't be more relaxed about it. I was only doing my job."

"I suppose you were," Bruce agreed. "I tend to get nasty when I'm pushed. It's a character flaw. Forgive me." But there was no note of apology or interest in Bruce's tone, and Jorgenson left without saying anything more.

Bruce had dinner with his parents the following week, and after dinner his father asked him into his study and consulting room, where he could smoke a cigar with his coffee—something Bruce's mother did not permit in any other room in the house. Cigars were his father's single large vice, at least according to his mother. He smoked only two a day, one in the morning and one after dinner, and endured his wife's unhappiness. Bruce loved his father's study. In one corner, there was a human skeleton, hanging from an iron support, wired together, a thing that even in his childhood delighted him instead of frightening him. It was *de rigueur* in the early part of the century, when his father had been a medical student. The desk was an old, beautiful partners' desk, where he loved to sit facing his father, and where he seated himself now. There were two big black leather chairs, a polished hardwood floor, and on the walls framed engravings of his father's respected colleagues, Louis Pasteur, Sigmund Freud, Albert Einstein, and Mark Twain. Neither his wife nor his son understood his selection, but Bruce had always felt that his father's love of Samuel Clemens had eased his own struggle out of medicine and into journalism. It was quite a break. His father was the third generation of physicians in the Bacon family.

"You never tried a cigar?" his father asked him, lighting a long Cuban panatela.

"I tried it. You asked me that before."

"Yes, I forgot. Before this wretched war. I hate cigarettes, unhealthy, coffin nails. But a cigar is something else. Tell me, how's it coming?"

"Not too bad. Getting used to things all over again."

"Yes, of course. That's a nice girl, that Sally Pringle."

"Yes, very nice," Bruce agreed.

Dr. Bacon studied his cigar, took a gentle puff, and then

watched the wisp of smoke circle up, after which he said, "I hear you've taken a leave of absence from the paper."

"Word gets around, doesn't it? How did you hear that?"

"Dr. Benedict knows your managing editor."

"Well, I'll be damned. You're telling me I'm important enough to be a subject of their conversation?"

"Bruce, you're more important than you imagine. Your stuff has been read all over this country for years."

"The war's over, finished, and the American public has the memory of a mosquito."

"We won't argue that. I'm sure you know exactly what you're doing."

"I'm going to write a book."

His father nodded. "I'll look forward to it. Have you started?"

"Trying to get it together in my head. That's the first step."

"How long do you imagine it will take?"

"I don't know." Bruce had left that open. "I've never written a book. Maybe a year, maybe two years."

"Well—you know, you'll have to live," Dr. Bacon said uneasily.

"Is that what it's leading up to?" Bruce said, grinning. "Thanks, Dad, but I'm well fixed financially."

"Good. However, if the occasion should arise—"

"I hope not." Then he went on to explain his financial condition. "I suppose the best break for me at this moment is that Pru left me the apartment. She had paid the rent right through this year's lease. I imagine she had guilts, but she was very decent about the whole thing."

"She's a fine woman. I wish this hadn't happened." It was the first time either his father or his mother had spoken about the divorce.

"It had to happen. It didn't hurt. We had become strangers to each other."

"That happens."

They went on talking. It was a good hour, and the first time in his life that Bruce had opened up entirely to his father. They talked about the war, and how it had been to see it happening and yet not be a part of it, the senselessness and cruelty and madness, the things that imprint and remain for a lifetime, the opening of a concentration camp and the release of its inmates, the time he was in a jeep, trying to catch up to the advance, and he saw by the road the body of a German soldier, the trunk and the legs, the upper body and head blown away, leaving the lower body intact from the waist down, the body of a child, headless, like a doll, with a woman staring at it, motionless, catatonic. He told his father about the comparatively brief aftermath in India.

"You know, it adds up to nothing," Bruce said. "Yes, we destroyed Hitler and Nazism, but I've been thinking lately that we created him, and when we found he was not to our exact specifications, we had to destroy him. I remember way back, in the late thirties or maybe the middle thirties, I read an article in *Collier's* magazine about Hitler and his Brown House, and they were not without admiration for what he was setting up, and somewhere in Germany, I was sitting next to a tough old regular army colonel, and I said some words of opinion concerning Adolf Hitler, and this colonel —he came from Mississippi—this guy says to me, Why do you hate him, because he's their son of a bitch? If he was our son of a bitch, you'd write eulogies about him. Would I, Dad? I don't know."

"You've seen something I never saw," Dr. Bacon said. "You'd have to make judgments very different from mine."

"Trouble is, I can't make judgments. My thinking is too screwed up. I don't know up from down or right from wrong. A few of us from the paper got together the other night—all of them correspondents who'd been in Africa or the Pacific or in Europe, and we had dinner and talked about things and got a little drunk, and none of them gave a good goddamn whether anything was right or wrong, and

then the question of Dresden came up, and you remember
when you and Mom took me to Europe—I was only thirteen—and we stayed overnight in Dresden, it was like a
fairyland city, and then the next time I went through Dresden it was with the army and the city was gone, nothing but
rubble and ruins. We had wiped it out of existence, perhaps
not as totally as we wiped Hiroshima and Nagasaki out of
existence, but for all practical purposes the same, and thousands and thousands of people died there in a fire bombing
that made the attacks on London seem like child's play, and
this argument came up with the men I was eating and drinking with, and their attitude was: So what? The bastards deserved it. They'll think twice before they start another war
with the United States. But who deserved it? The children
who died in Dresden? The children who died in the concentration camps? The Indians I told you about? Who deserved
to die? I remember one night when you came home from the
hospital, and you were white as a ghost and shaking and
told us that you had spent nine hours in the operating room
trying to put together a kid who had been run over by a
truck, and you couldn't keep back the tears when you told
Mom about it and how it didn't work and he died anyway, a
little Negro kid who nobody gave a damn about, and you
had your team of four doctors working with you and the
two best scrub nurses in the hospital. It was the only time I
ever saw you cry. And then nobody claimed the body, just a
homeless runaway kid. And we do that. We try to work
miracles to save one life, and then without blinking an eye-
lash, we put millions to death."

His father drew on the cigar and watched the smoke.
Then he rose, went to his medicine cabinet, and found two
brandy glasses and a bottle of cognac. "Helps the throat,"
he told Bruce. "Maybe it helps the soul a little, too." He
studied his son thoughtfully. "That's the way it is," he said.
"You can go round in circles and hammer your head against
the wall, but that's the way it is. At least we tried to save the

kid, and if there's a heaven or a god or anything of that sort, well, perhaps it counts for something."

When they had stepped into his father's study, Bruce intended to tell his father about the visit from Jorgenson, just as an interesting and curious incident; but then he realized that if he spoke about Jorgenson, he would also have to go into his acquaintance with Legerman and his peremptory flight from India and his time spent with Majumdar and Chatterjee, all of which he had erased from his account to his father of the time spent in India—an account sketchy at best. Later, he asked himself whether there was a measure of guilt involved—or was it something almost ominous in the air of this postwar America? Did he really know whether or not Legerman was a communist, even though Legerman had admitted it? And exactly what was a communist? He could not recall ever having met someone who said, "Bruce, I'm a card-carrying communist." Or were there cards? He tried to remember what Legerman had said to him on the subject, but his memory was fuzzy in that area. He knew that both Chatterjee and Majumdar were Communist Party members, but a Communist Party in another country, especially a country so distant and so poverty-stricken as India, seemed to have little if any relationship to the newspaper stories denouncing the Communist Party and accusing them of everything from the rash of strikes that were flaring up all over the country to the conveyance of the secrets of the atom bomb to the Soviet Union. He finally admitted to himself that he did not speak of Legerman for the same reason that he did not try to find Legerman and tell him that an FBI agent was asking about him, and he softened his self-critical sense with the excuse that he had no notion where Legerman might be. And where was his luggage and his typewriter and his notes that Legerman had promised so faithfully to send to him?

Exactly eleven months after Bruce had left India, his luggage arrived, care of the newspaper where he had worked.

New York City
Downtown

The months passed, and Bruce realized that whatever the writing of a book was to others, to him it was imprisonment combined with not a little torture. Other books appeared, were reviewed and read by whatever number of people purchased them, and then disappeared to somber graves in libraries. He wrote over a hundred pages on England before the Normandy invasion, and then destroyed what he had written. The least difficult was the intensity of the battle on the European mainland, but even there his memory of battle was not what he sought, but an inner truth that might describe the unwritten horror that used war as its camouflage. He remembered Tolstoy's dictum only too well, that every story of war and battle was a lie; but when he went to *War and Peace,* seeking Tolstoy's own circumvention of that trap, he could not find it. But *War and Peace* was fiction, and he, Bruce Bacon, was seeking the truth—or was fiction the only place that truth could be found? He would watch his typewriter turning into the enemy, and then recall sitting at the bottom of a shellhole, in slime and mud and dirty water, taking down the names of the four soldiers there in the mud with him, that he might credit them for the stories they were telling him, and writing their names and his notes with a stub of a pencil in a damp little notebook, and then finding that he had managed one or two fine, strong phrases; and remembering this now, he would take a pencil and a legal pad and go into Central Park, and sit there on a bench, scribbling away.

But this was a small and rather worthless remedy; all it created that was positive was a sojourn of a few hours in the fresh air and the sunshine. On the other hand, he had spent endless hours in the New York Public Library, going through the back issues of the wartime years to see how the other correspondents on the *Times* and the *Daily News* had handled their dispatches. But that was a mine that yielded no metal of any use to him; he would have to find his own way or give it up entirely.

His romance with Sally Pringle, if one could call it that, appeared to disintegrate as the intensity of his absorption with his book increased. One day she called him with a pair of tickets for a Broadway opening, and he pleaded that he had to work that evening.

"Bruce, what on earth do you mean, you have to work?"

"I'm trying to work out a problem."

"Which you give yourself. It's your own project."

She slammed down the telephone in disgust, but a week later, when he made his apologies and his pleas, she consented to see him again. But romance was corroding. An editor of a leading fashion magazine, a competitor of *Harper's Bazaar,* told her that he had offered Bruce an in-house job for twenty thousand a year, a princely sum at the time, and Bruce had turned it down out of hand. Bruce was tall, good-looking, and much admired in circles that Sally enjoyed; but to her he appeared to be going nowhere, bound to a book which she felt would never be finished.

Also, their dates were becoming argumentative. She could not comprehend his horror at the bombing of Hiroshima. When he recalled what he had seen in the concentration camps, she said, "No. No, I will not believe that the Germans put six million Jews to death. I know Germans. Mother and I were in Germany twice before that awful war." In bed, she was delicious, wildly emotional and enthusiastic. Bruce realized how well they were in tune with each other's sexual drives and needs. But they were not in love, either of them, and both of them realized that.

The months went by, and he wrote and rewrote, and tore up much of what he wrote, and at long last he had something over a hundred pages of manuscript that he was satisfied with. At least it was a beginning and proof that eventually he would do what he had set out to do. If not in celebration, at least in relief, Bruce went outside and began to walk. It was mid-November in 1946, a cool, windy day, the best kind of a day in New York City. He felt more relaxed and alive than he had felt in weeks. He wore an old sport jacket of Harris tweed over a sleeveless sweater, and old gray flannels and comfortable shoes. He walked south down Lexington Avenue, easily and swiftly. At Forty-second Street, he responded to thirst and hunger and took himself into an Automat, where he put coffee, fried eggs, and bacon on a tray and found a table for himself.

A few moments later, a voice said, "If you're not waiting for someone, I'll join you."

Bruce glanced up to see the broad, smiling, toadlike face of Milton Greenberg. It took a moment to make the connection with the press club in Calcutta, and then he rose and shook hands eagerly.

"I must say you look happier than the last time I saw you in Calcutta."

"I feel happier. Sit down."

Greenberg had a cup of coffee in his hand.

"Getting something to eat?"

"I've eaten," Greenberg said. "What are you doing on my turf?"

"Still with the *Daily News*?"

"I been there twenty years." He set the coffee on the table. "I hear they threw you out of the CBI?"

"Sort of."

"Boychik, it's a distinction to be thrown out of a whole

damn theater. It means you're on to something nobody else is."

"Only the famine. You saw it."

"I did. I certainly did. I also hear that you put the *Trib* on hold to write a book."

"You're going to tell me everyone else is writing a book. Anyway, how do you know?"

"Word gets around. And don't feed me that crap about everyone else writing a book. Lousy books. There hasn't been a good book out of this war yet."

"Mine can make the same garbage heap. You know, Greenberg, it's good to see you. You're something real. I came back by Air Transport, booked right through. It was like closing my eyes in Calcutta and waking up here. At the airport, customs cleared me without waiting, and there was one of those big green Checkers waiting, and an hour later I was in my apartment. Women on the streets walking their babies, clean, neat, beautiful. Summer dresses. High, beautiful tits. Clean streets. No mud, no blood, no guts . . ." His voice died away.

"I know what you mean," Greenberg said.

"You're real. You bear witness. That's what I'm trying to do with this book of mine."

"You got any of it finished?"

"About a hundred pages that I can read without feeling sick."

"Have you shown it to anyone?"

"No," Bruce said quickly. "I can't. I got this girl I hang out with, and she begs me to let her see it. I can't."

"Don't. Don't show it to anyone except your publisher. People don't know a damn thing about writing, and they'll just give you shit and louse you up. You got a publisher?"

"I thought I might look for an agent—a literary agent."

"You could, but I might save you that step and the piece they grab. I know the editor-in-chief at Scandia Press. His name is Mel Bronson, and Scandia is a rich and very respected house, and if you show him a hundred pages and he likes it and he feels you're on the track, he'll come across with a very nice advance."

"Like what?"

"Maybe twenty, thirty thousand."

"I could use that very nicely," Bruce said. "Would it be asking too much if—well, say you called him?"

"Sure. But Bruce, nobody has to open doors for you. With your track record during the war, any editor in town will be delighted to talk to you. I just think Bronson is a bright guy and Scandia is maybe a shade better than most houses."

The following day, when Bruce decided to call Bronson and give him what he had written, he reflected that it was decent of Greenberg to set it up. After all, he hardly knew Greenberg, aside from sharing quarters with him in Calcutta and passing the time of day, and as good as his word, he had spoken to Bronson.

"By all means," Bronson agreed, after Bruce had reached him by telephone. "Suppose we say three o'clock today. I followed your stuff during the war, and it was damn good and damn enlightening, and I'm just pleased as punch to look at your manuscript. First look, you said?"

Scandia's offices were on Fourth Avenue, between Twenty-ninth and Thirtieth Streets, and Bronson himself was a large, white-haired man of about sixty, pink-skinned and hearty in his manner and his welcome. He accepted Bruce's manuscript as if it were eggshell precious. "I shall read it with great expectations," he said. "You say it's different? Bless you. What the world needs is a book about this war that is different. I'll read this over the weekend and call you next week." He took the manuscript out of its brown envelope and laid it reverently on his desk. "You don't have an agent, do you?"

"I'm afraid not."

"Puts the onus on me. Ah, well, I can be honest if pressed. I shall certainly read it over the weekend."

It was a very long and difficult weekend for Bruce. He had a date with Sally Pringle for Saturday night, and it was difficult for him to focus. It nettled her. "Do you have a television?" she wanted to know, repeating the question a second time.

"You know I don't," Bruce said. "What on earth would I want with a television set?"

"You might want to connect with what's happening in the real world. Here's a great big change in my life, and you ask me what you would want with a television set. You might want to look at me."

"I love looking at you," Bruce said.

"I left my job."

"Why?" He was not displeased that she had parted company with Hillsdale Fashions and the handsome Phil Sturtz. Whatever had been happening to their relationship, she was still the woman he was dating and taking to bed, even if all talk of marriage had ceased and even if on occasion she went to bed with another. Since he had no hard evidence of this, he preferred not to linger over the notion. If there was only nominal passion, there was pleasant sex and they made a handsome couple.

"Because I've just signed a three-year contract with the DTB network as fashion consultant and women's editor. I'll be on the air each afternoon at four o'clock, and if you don't think television's the wave of the future, Bruce, you're simply not with it. They've agreed to double what I got at Hillsdale—and it's going somewhere. Have you seen any of the statistics on the proliferation of television sets?"

"I haven't noticed."

"You will. You certainly will."

Bruce made a mental note that on Monday he would buy a television set. Since his mother's arthritis was making it increasingly difficult for her to walk any distance, Dr. Bacon had purchased a television set. Bruce had watched it on occasion and had not found it terribly enlightening, but then he had not been much of a radio fan as a kid. He had preferred the movies or the printed word.

Sunday dragged on forever, and on Monday he decided not to leave his apartment until Bronson called him. But Bronson never called on Monday, and that night Bruce lay awake for most of the dark hours, convinced that a year of work had been a total failure, and wondering whether the fact that he had doubled his time of leave at the paper would militate against his getting his job back. Tuesday morning, at eleven o'clock, his telephone rang. It was Mel Bronson, and he said to Bruce, "Forgive me for not calling yesterday. I had about twenty pages still to read, and it was one of those days. Bruce—if I may call you Bruce—Bruce, you have the beginnings of one hell of a book there, and if you'll meet me at a place called the Balkans, on Twenty-ninth between Lexington and Fourth, we'll have lunch and talk about it. Say one o'clock? Can you make that?"

Wild horses couldn't keep him away. "I'll be there," Bruce said.

The Balkans was another Armenian restaurant that Bruce vaguely recalled from before the war, a place popular with the Fourth Avenue publishing houses. Bronson was waiting for him when he arrived, and over stuffed mussels and shish-kabob, he talked about Bruce's book, about his perspective on war, the development of his pacifist convictions, his lack of the hatred that pervaded so much war writing, his contempt for the so-called bravery of the German soldier, his analysis of courage in wartime and human conscience in wartime. "It is different," Bronson said. "It's different thinking and it's new thinking, and if the next few hundred pages are as good as this, we've certainly got something."

"Thank you," Bruce said. "I've been living in the dark. You're the first one to read this. I would have shown it to some others, friends, perhaps my father, but Greenberg was very insistent that I show it to no one but a professional editor."

"He was absolutely right. Interesting chap, Milt Greenberg. When he was a kid, he covered World War One for the old *New York World*. Got a special congressional citation. I've been begging him to write a book. He won't."

"I can understand that," Bruce said. "Once is enough for me."

"I hope not. Now look, Bruce, we have to come to some arrangement, and since you don't have an agent, I have to do some honorable bargaining. On the basis of this section— by the way, how many of these manuscript pages do you feel it will be?"

"About four hundred and fifty or so. At least, that's what the material adds up to, the way I have it now."

"Good enough. Now, on the basis of this section, what I have already read, I can make the following offer: a signed contract at this point, with an advance of ten thousand dollars—or an agreement on our part to pay an advance of fifty thousand dollars when you bring in the completed manuscript, based of course on our willingness to accept the manuscript for publication. On that score, I have no doubt about the quality of the completed book. Now think about it for a moment."

"And what happens if I accept the ten thousand, and then you decide not to publish?"

"If that should be the case, which I doubt, the ten thousand comes off whatever advance you get from another publisher. No publisher, you don't repay it."

"And the fifty you pay when I finish the book—that comes with an agreement to publish—right?"

"Absolutely."

"I'll finish the book and take the fifty," Bruce decided.

"You're sure you don't want to sleep on it? Ask the advice of a third party? Another opinion?"

"No. No thank you, Mr. Bronson. I have enough money

to finish the book. At this point, I think I'm secure enough to gamble. The main thing is that you like it, that you've given me an opinion I can trust."

"All right. I respect your decision."

But afterward, Bruce wondered whether he wouldn't have been better off had he accepted the ten thousand. Hearing that the first part was so good, he was weighed down by the need to perform to the standards set. For two days, he found himself tearing up page after page, but that did not last. By Friday, he was at work again and in control of what he wrote. It was on the same Friday that Greenberg telephoned him to find out how it had gone from his point of view. He explained that he had already spoken to Bronson, who was very excited about the project.

"It went well," Bruce said. "I have to thank you."

"Then I'll ask a favor from you," Greenberg said.

"Feel free. Anything I can do."

"Well, it's no big deal, and you can say no, if you wish. We have a group called the Broadway Forum, mostly news people and magazine people and a nice sprinkling of theater characters—you know, some actors, directors—and we get together once a month at the Murray Hill Hotel in their big room, anywhere from a hundred to a hundred and fifty people, and we listen to a speaker and then talk about it. Well, they heard me mention that I knew you, and they're asking you to come and speak Monday a week." Greenberg drew a long breath and waited while the silence lengthened.

Then Bruce said, "You know, I never made a public speech in all my life."

"You're kidding."

"No." Bruce shook his head and stared at the telephone.

"Bruce?"

"I've just been thinking about it. Thing is, the thought scares the hell out of me. I mean, why should anyone want to listen to me?"

"Because you been around the way few people have. You

were right in the middle of the worst trauma this planet ever experienced, and you're a damn good newspaperman."

"Oh, hell, I'm one in a hundred. You know that."

"OK. I'm the messenger boy, that's all. I told them you'd probably say no."

"Hold on," Bruce said. "I want to think about it. Can you call back in, say, half an hour?"

"Absolutely."

Bruce put down the telephone, dropped into a chair, and thought about it. Astonishing; here he was, embarking on the fourth decade of his life, and he had never delivered a talk in public. He reviewed his postteenage life: the four years at Williams College, the two years of postgraduate journalism at Columbia, the job of a cub reporter on the *Tribune,* and then the moment of good or bad fortune— depending on how one saw it—that took him to England as the war began. Where was his life, his experience, his need to belong to a human race that was not preoccupied in the art of killing? He had holed up in his little apartment like a hermit who had taken a vow of solitude. He had a strange relationship with a woman who fitted some remote Williams College definition of what a proper mate should be, and while he slept with her, there was no idea, thought, or conceivable future that they shared. And now, asked by Greenberg to talk to a group of his peers about the only experience that really defined his life, World War Two, he had begged off with the excuse of fear.

When Greenberg called back, Bruce said, "Sure. I'll do it. How long do you want me to speak?"

"As long as you wish, twenty minutes, half an hour. You can field some questions afterward if you wish, or not. Whatever you decide. No one expects you to do anything that might make you uncomfortable."

If the thought didn't frighten him, it still worried him. He brooded over it for the next week, and it messed up his writing schedule. He disliked talking about his war experience for two reasons: first, because the notion of war and battle that most people had was derived from newspaper stories, books about the war, and movies—even servicemen were inclined to accept this notion, since most of them by far had never seen action; and second, because it depressed him and caused him to suppress his real feelings, his decision that war was madness beyond justification in any case.

Whereby, when he came to the Murray Hill Hotel and stood in front of the crowded room, at least a hundred and fifty people, he said: "Tonight, in spite of the fact that most of you who read my dispatches associate me with the war in Europe, I decided not to speak about that, but rather about a much shorter experience in the Far East."

He then went on to tell them what had taken him to India, and rather briefly of his pursuit of the truth about the famine. "In the course of which," he said, "I came to know a man named Ashoka Majumdar." After that, Bruce told the story of the day he had spent with Majumdar. The audience was with him, intent upon what he was saying, and this gave him sufficient sense of security to put down his notes and talk from memory. When he finished, a man by the name of Jerry Gionni, a sort of chairman, asked Bruce whether he would field some questions.

"I can try."

"All right"—to the audience—"but make them short and to the point."

A woman asked, "This theory of yours that the British were responsible for the famine—do you still believe so?"

"I still do. Yes."

"Do you have any new evidence?" from an older man.

"No. Nothing more than I had before."

A man of about thirty: "Did it ever occur to you that you were being used by the local communists?"

"Well, yes and no. In one sense, every correspondent in a war zone is being used. I never met a senior officer who didn't want his name in the papers. Big competition there.

The war is their moment. Then the High Command uses us to give out what they want to give out, and the press officers use us to push whatever they're pushing, and I'm sure that the two men I told you about were using me to get the horror of the situation across to people on stateside. But this does not impugn their integrity. I know this country is going a little crazy on the question of communism, but don't forget that while it was only a couple of years ago, it was another world. I saw Russian and American soldiers embrace each other with tears in their eyes, and I also know, from my own eyewitness, that there was no way in the world that we could have defeated the Germans without the Red Army as our allies. So I saw no reason to make any judgments about the communists I met in Bengal."

"But you'll admit," another voice said, "that the Russians couldn't have survived the war without our Lend Lease."

"Perhaps. I have no strong opinions about that."

A tall redheaded woman stood up and said, "Mr. Bacon, what's your opinion about the wave of anticommunist hysteria and the loyalty oaths that go with it?"

The question brought him up sharp, and he had to ask himself whether to answer it honestly or accept the inner voice that told him this was a very hot potato indeed, and that the smart thing to do was to sidestep it. The audience was waiting.

"Well, I can say this. I have a squeaky, unhappy feeling that it resembles the first tactics of Adolf Hitler after he took power. He used the communists as an excuse for every rotten provision in his program. I can also say that, like millions of my fellow Americans, I take comfort in the fact that I know nothing very much about communism and have never associated with communists; but that's poor comfort when I recall the German who said, When they came for the communists, I was not afraid. I was not a communist. When they came for the socialists, I was not afraid. I was not a socialist. When they came for the Jews, I was not afraid. I wasn't a Jew. And when they came for me, I was alone. It was too late. Maybe that exaggerates the situation. I can't say. It's simply not the kind of thing I like to see happening in my country."

When the meeting was over, Bruce had to admit to himself that he had enjoyed it. After his self-enforced isolation, it was in the way of a relief to talk about ideas, to exchange points of view. The audience drifted out. Greenberg shook his hand and told him that he had done very well. Jerry Gionni shook his hand and then gave him a check for two hundred dollars.

"Hey, hold on," Bruce said.

"We don't pay a fortune, but we also don't expect you to come in and do this for nothing. We're taking advantage of you. If we reached you through an agency, it would have cost us three times as much."

Bruce took the check. He hadn't expected pay of any kind, but he knew he could use the money. Greenberg had left. As Bruce came into the lobby, the redheaded woman who had asked him the provocative question was there, waiting for him, and she smiled at him and said, "Can I lure you into the bar for a drink? I'd like to talk to you." It was not a pickup. It was absolutely straightforward and on the line. She was a tall woman, at least five foot nine or ten, well shaped, strong long-fingered hands, good-looking if not beautiful, eyes blue, and her flame-colored red hair tied in a knot behind her neck.

"You won't have to do much luring," Bruce said. "What's your name?"

"Molly Maguire, Mr. Bacon, and you can ask for a gin and bitters for me." They were at the bar. Bruce asked for two of the same, and then they took their drinks to a table in the corner.

"If we're going to talk," Bruce said, "I'm Bruce and you're Molly, if that's OK with you." He was trying to assess her age, and he decided that she was probably the same age as himself.

"Good enough, Bruce. I'm Molly, I'm thirty years old, because the first thing a man tries to guess seated next to a woman is how old she is, and I'm divorced to answer the second thing, and that's now out of the way. I know all about you because I've been reading your dispatches for many moons, and I read a piece Skeets Andrews wrote about you when you met him in Paris. Myself, I was born in Boston and grew up there, and right now I'm a reporter for the *New York Daily Worker.*"

"You're kidding."

"Why should I kid about something like that? Did you ever read the *Daily Worker*?"

"Yes, once," Bruce recalled. "Your friend Skeets Andrews gave me a copy to read. Yeah—that was the one time I met him. I forgot about that completely. Did he actually write a piece about me?"

"You never saw it?"

"No. Never knew about it. I met Andrews in Paris a few days after Liberation. Met him in a hotel bar, and we had a few drinks and talked—nice guy. I thought he was working for *The Nation*? Or was it *The New Republic*?"

"Actually, it was neither. But he did some stuff for the *Daily Worker* and *The Nation*. He started it in North Africa, and he would sign those pieces Africanus, a pen name he kept. His assignment was from the *Sun*. You know, he spoke highly of you. He thought you were an honorable man."

"That sounds old-fashioned," Bruce said.

"Do you remember what you thought of the *Worker* then?"

"The commie paper?"

"That doesn't sound too honorable," Molly Maguire said. "Call it red or communist, not commie."

"Fair enough."

"You said you read the issue Skeets gave you?"

She was hard to decipher. Was she goading him, teasing him, or seriously trying to get something from him? She was not beautiful. She had one of those strong Irish faces, a high, narrow nose, full lips, and a wide mouth. Or was she beautiful? The freckled face and the freckled arms gave her a strange girlish appearance. He kept seeing the image of a kid running barefoot in the field.

"You're staring at me, and you don't even know what I asked."

"My opinion of the *Worker*. That was years ago. Let me think."

She picked up their two empty glasses. "I'll refurbish while you think."

"Oh, no. Let me."

"You think," she said. She came back with two more gins. "I didn't pay for them," she said. "I make forty dollars a week. You got a wife, kids, girl friend?"

"No wife, no kids, and maybe no girl friend."

"What's she like?"

"That's the trouble. I don't really know," Bruce admitted.

"All right. We drink to two lonely strangers. Tell me your opinion of my paper."

"It's too long ago. All I really remember is that it smelled of poverty and that it was self-serving."

"And the *Trib* and the *Times* are not?"

"Of course they are. But they're not a whisper in the cheering squad. They're the cheerleaders."

"You make a point." She opened the big purse she carried and took out a thin newspaper. "Here's today's issue."

Bruce took it and scanned the front page. The headline read: TWELVE NAZI WAR LEADERS SENTENCED TO BE HANGED. "Same headline as the *Times*," Bruce said.

"We agree on some things. That was a hell of a story, over there in Nuremberg. Are you sorry you missed it?"

"No. I've had my share of the Old World. Tell me, why are we sitting here?"

"You do come right to the point. I wanted to talk to you," she said.

"Why? You don't have to come to a lecture to pick up men."

"I don't pick up men."

"You picked me up," Bruce said. "Thank God. I never would have had the nerve to stop you and talk to you."

"You're kidding."

"No. That's the truth."

"All right, Bacon—here's my truth. I was divorced six years ago, I hate living alone, and I haven't met anyone who wasn't married who grabbed me enough to interest me. Tonight, I said to myself, He could finish, walk right out of this place, and I'd never see him again. What do I do then? Do I get your phone number and call you and say, I was at the Murray Hill when you spoke and I want to see you? We don't do things that way, do we?"

"Good heavens, Maguire, we don't know the first thing about each other."

"We're not Bruce and Molly anymore. That's too formal, so we've made the first step. Well, I was married to a man for three years, and I never knew the first thing about him, so that's the way it goes."

"You're going to call me Bacon," he said hopelessly. "For the rest of my life, you're going to call me Bacon. I never liked the name. Bacon. God be praised."

"You know," she said, "no one talks like you anymore. 'Good heavens,' 'God be praised.' You're out of another time, Bacon. As the Bacon fried, she sighed and dreamed of far Cathay. Maguire, not Tennyson or some such. Do you think we're both a little drunk?"

"This is the strangest courtship I been—I have ever been, that's better—involved in. Your glass is empty. I will go to the bar."

At the bar, he was told that the room would close in

fifteen minutes. "We make a proper drink here," the bartender said. "I hope you're not driving."

"I'm not even walking," Bruce replied sagely. He paid the bill and went to their table and said, "We have to vacate this place in fifteen minutes, so drink up. Where do you live?"

"I think—Twenty-ninth Street. Just east of Fourth Avenue. We could make it on our hands and knees if we have to. I live in a brownstone. I have one studio room. You said this is a strange courtship. Why the hell don't you court me?"

"We'll talk about it," Bruce said. "Do you have anything to drink at home?"

"Three gins are enough. And how do you know you're coming home with me? It's twelve o'clock."

"Whatever you say, Maguire."

"Sure. Whatever I say."

He wasn't drunk, not even when they finished the third gin, but high and pleased with the world, and feeling unwound and more at ease with himself than he had been in years. Who was this wild, redheaded, vulgar woman who wrote for a communist paper? As he walked home with her, she sang softly a little ballad about a man called Kevin Barry, who fought the British Army all around a little bakery, and Bruce wondered how the devil the word *vulgar* had leaped into his mind. Vulgar? This was the most unusual, straight-on woman he had ever met.

"What the hell is wrong with me?" he asked her.

"How do you mean that? I don't know you well enough to even guess what's wrong with you. You use a word like *courtship*. Nobody's used that word in twenty-five, thirty years."

"You used it."

"A gift from you."

"Am I prissy?"

"You're innocent," Molly said. "You're as innocent as the first light of dawn, when the birds begin to sing."

"That's very poetic," Bruce said, "but how can I be innocent? You know where I've been, what I've seen."

"But you've never killed anyone, not even in your heart. The 'Dear John' letter either enrages men, or saddens them, or liberates them. And you—"

Molly Maguire's room, or apartment, was one half of the third floor in a fine old brownstone on East Twenty-ninth Street. It made for a room twenty by twenty-two feet, simply furnished with one double bed, two overstuffed chairs, a kitchen table painted and decorated, four chairs to the table, two cheap Indian carpets on the floor, some bright prints on the walls, and a long bookcase, the length of one wall, six feet high and stuffed with books. A bathroom and a tiny kitchen completed the apartment.

By the time they reached her apartment, their moods had changed and the gaiety had gone. Molly made coffee, and they sat in the overstuffed chairs and talked. They talked about themselves and they talked about each other, and he spelled out the difficulties he had understanding why anyone in this postwar world should be a communist.

"I could see it in the thirties. Not that I ever felt the Depression. My father was and still is a successful surgeon, and we had enough money. I went to private school and then to Williams up in Williamstown, Massachusetts. Have you ever been there?"

Molly shook her head. She was untying her hair, and it fell out in a mass around her shoulders.

"Well, you have middle class and upper middle class at Harvard and Yale, but Williams is something else. It's a beautiful, elegant school, perched up in the Berkshires in the shadow of Mount Greylock. The world doesn't touch it. Oh, I knew there was a depression and I knew that the country was in a crisis, but it wasn't very real. Do you know that when you untie your hair with a lamp behind you like that, you're framed in a kind of golden—"

"Back to Williams, Bacon," she said. "I want to know

who I picked up. Not something I do every day of the week."

"We had a tiny left-wing group on the campus. I remember the fuss they made about the slaughter at Republic Steel —but that's about the only thing of its kind that stayed with me."

"The slaughter at Republic Steel," Molly said slowly. "I was there. I was just a kid. It was my first big assignment. Go on."

"No—you were there. What was it like?"

"You know, Bruce, you're very strange. For three years, you watched the greatest slaughter in the history of man, and now you want to know what Republic Steel was like. It was very small. Republic was on strike. Tom Girdler, who ran the place, hired an army of armed guards. The strikers organized a march across the flat prairie where the plant was, and the guards stopped them and began clubbing— especially on the women—and I was watching it and then the shooting began. I remember that, because it didn't sound the way I thought shooting should sound."

"No, it doesn't."

"Just *pop, pop, pop,* like toy fireworks, and seven strikers were dead and more than a hundred wounded, and then the Communist Party workers laid out the dead bodies and people talked and more than two hundred of the strikers signed Communist Party cards right then and there—because we were with them and we were willing to die for them, and you say you can't understand why anyone should be a communist now, because a couple of years have gone by and nobody remembers that the Red Army destroyed the Wermacht."

"I remember," Bruce said, "but for heaven's sake, it is a different world, isn't it?"

"It's always a different world. I'm not pushing you or trying to convince you of anything, Bruce. Something is finished. It is different, damn different."

"The truth is," Bruce confessed, "that I've only known two communists in my life, I mean aside from those I met in India, and you are one and the other is a fellow by the name of Legerman."

"Hal Legerman? So that's who you were talking about in your lecture. Why didn't you name his name?"

"I don't know. In this current lunacy and anticommunist hysteria—I don't know. I suppose I wanted to protect him. Then you know him?"

"A little. Before the war, he was a flack around Broadway. Now he's out on the Coast. I hear he got a job as a screenwriter. Something like that. He used to feed me bits and pieces. I suppose he felt it was something to have your name in print—even in the *Daily Worker.* Funny thing about the *Worker,* we never run much more than fifty thousand copies, and for a metropolitan daily, that's nothing, but it gets around. I got to interview Leland Harringwell—you know, he has more money than God and a bit of power to go with it—and he said to me that there are only two papers in the United States that he trusts, the *Wall Street Journal* and the *Daily Worker,* and he reads both."

"He has the advantage of me. The only copy I ever saw is the one Skeets Andrews gave me."

"And the one I gave you? Do you know, Bruce, for a smart guy, you're a dumbbell."

"Thank you. I haven't read your copy yet."

"I have a byline, so read it. You know, if I were your mother, I would have called you Candide."

"Thank God you're not my mother. What about your mother? Father?"

"You want to put me up there with Sally Pringle? My God, you're a man, flesh and blood, maybe a hundred and eighty pounds of you—you have a heart, compassion, understanding, and you witness three years of hell, and you marry a girl whose name is Prudence—Prudence, God help me—and now you're shacked up with a Sally Pringle?"

"Well—that's sort of intimate, isn't it? I mean, this is—"

"Oh, shit, no! It is not intimate. It is you, and you are what interests me. You want to know about Molly Maguire? Here's line and word. She's the daughter of Sean Maguire, whom I know only from his picture, but I could see a sweet lad who never had enough to eat in all his blessed life, and came here at the turn of the century as a kid from county Mayo in the old country. He was exalted. He worked his way up from being a construction laborer to being a fireman on a locomotive and breathed enough coal dust to give him tuberculosis. He died two months before I was born, and there was my mother, left with three daughters to raise and not one damned Prudence or Patience or Sally to stretch out a hand to help her, but sweet Jesus be praised, there was Frank O'Malley, the crooked ward heeler whom they hustled off to jail eventually, but he kept us in potatoes and cabbage until he got my blessed mother a job scrubbing floors in the old Hancock Building." She paused, her wide blue eyes half closed, a hint of a smile on her lips. "Ah, poor decent Bacon, I am jumping on you with both feet, am I not?"

Bruce shook his head. He didn't want her to stop, he didn't want her to tell him that it was very late, that he should go along home. He was filled with desire for this long-limbed Irish woman with her pale skin and her flaming hair, but he also sensed very deeply that this was not the time and that she was not someone who opens her arms and says, Come jump into them.

"And still I haven't answered your question, dear Bruce, me who would be a little lost Mick, a guttersnipe, were it not for the blessings of the Boston Public Library, and what is it that made me a communist? There was my mother, working on the floors with her scrub brush and pail, and along comes Mr. Lowell Wordsworth, a very big banker who was working late, and he sees, sticking out of the basket in which my mother carries her lunch and whatever, a copy of the *Daily Worker*—I've had a subscription for her as long as I've been on the paper—and he sees it sticking out, and he says to her, 'Mrs. Maguire, I am shocked. You, a good Catholic, reading that communist rag.' A good Catholic! Imagine! Catherine O'Brian Maguire, my mother, has her name written on the golden gates as the number one Catholic in the Boston diocese. There was no room in our apartment without at least two crucifixes, and my mother has sore knees more from prayer than from scrubbing floors, and this godless white Protestant banker dares to scold her with taunts like, You, a good Catholic. Well, Mom just looked at him and said, 'Mr. Wordsworth, I have three beautiful daughters. One I have given to God for his blessed goodness to me, and she's a nun; and one I have given to the poor abused women in this life, that they might take some comfort, and she is a hairdresser; and my youngest daughter I have given to the working people, to God's poor children, and she writes for a communist paper. So I'll not have you looking down on me.' There's my history and if you can't figure out from that why I am a communist, then you have beans for brains, which is also not uncommon."

"I don't know what to say," Bruce complained. "My mother and father put me in the way of being a white Protestant. One of my mother's tragedies is that she was not born in Boston. I'd say that's one for you, except that you're from the wrong side of the tracks. But I like your mother."

"There's points for you." She rose to refill his coffee cup, but it didn't help. She was shaking him gently and the room was full of the morning light. "Wake up, Bruce. It's half past seven."

"Here in this chair all night?"

"I'm afraid so," she said.

She made eggs and sausage, and they had breakfast together, and then he walked with her to the *Worker* building on Twelfth Street, kissed her on the cheek, and then left her.

The Subpoena

It would have been less of a dilemma for someone else, but for Bruce the fact that he had twice asked Sally Pringle to marry him prevented him from calling Molly Maguire and telling her that he must see her again, that he could not just wipe her out of his consciousness and pretend that she did not exist, and that he could not go on staring at his typewriter and thinking of her, of that flaming red hair and snow-white skin, and asking himself silly questions, like did she ever sit in the sunshine, or did she wear a wide, wide hat, or did she have some current lover whom she had simply failed to mention? Nevertheless, he could not escape that he had been to bed with Sally Pringle dozens of times and had made passionate love to her, which she returned. Molly Maguire might hoot and laugh, being Boston-born and Irish, but Sally was a most passionate and loving woman— or was she? The two times Bruce had asked her to marry him, she laughed and assured him that such flattery would get him anything and everything; but she never said yes— the same laugh that replied to his declaration that he loved her.

And if he loved her, why had six weeks gone by since he had last spoken to her? And why had she not called him? And, damn it all, why should he, a grown man who had seen something of life and death, be influenced by his mother, who felt and stated that Sally Pringle was an absolute dear and precisely the sort of wife that Bruce wanted?

In any case, it was six weeks, and he went to the telephone and called her at the television network where she now worked.

When Sally answered, and Bruce said, "Sally, this is Bruce," her reply was hushed. "I can't hear you," Bruce said.

She said, "Hold on, please. I must transfer this call." And then, after perhaps a minute, she was on the phone again and said to him, "I'll call you back, Bruce. In ten or fifteen minutes. Are you at home?"

"Nowhere else." He put down the telephone and walked to the window and stared out at the street below. Why? Someone, obviously, was in her office. Whoever it was, she couldn't talk in front of him or her. It meant nothing, absolutely nothing—unless, of course, she had a new lover. He had not called her for six weeks; why had it never entered his head that she had not called him during that time? It was not as if she had never called him. At the beginning of their relationship, she had called him at least a dozen times. What then? Was it over? He brooded until the telephone rang.

"Bruce," Sally said, "it's all right now. I'm in a booth in the entry downstairs."

"Sally, what's all right?"

"I didn't dare to talk from my office. My secretary could overhear me. Who knows who else? Bruce—Bruce, dear, you must not call me here ever again."

"Why not? What the devil's gotten into you?"

"I thought you knew, and that's why you'd stopped calling me."

"Knew what? Talk some sense."

"I'm talking very good sense. Bruce, they have put together a list of writers and actors whom the network will not employ because they are communists. Bruce, you're on that list. Bruce, I love my job, but if they find out that we have a relationship, I'm finished. I can't have that. I won't. I can't."

Her voice rose. She was on the point of hysteria when Bruce told her to stop it. "Right now!" he insisted. "No more of that! Listen to me. I am not a communist. I have never been a communist. I don't give a damn about the Communist Party, and if my name's on that list, it's a setup and a damn lie!"

"Yes," softly. She was at the point of tears.

"Do you believe me?"

"It makes no difference whether or not I believe you. If the network discovers that I see you, if they find out that we've been—oh, God, you know what I mean."

"They won't find out that we slept together. No one knows that."

"I can't see you again and you mustn't call me again."

"Sally, do you know what you're saying?"

"Yes."

"Don't you want to sit down with me and talk about this?"

"No, no, no, please!"

"All right. Don't get upset again. I promise never to call you again. And I won't see you. If that's what you want, all right. Whatever makes you happy."

"It doesn't make me happy. It doesn't make me happy at all." She was calm now. She had the situation in hand.

"I just hate to see it end this way," Bruce said, and though he was shaken by her report on the blacklist, he was not at all certain, even while talking to her, that he hated to see it end this way or any other way.

"I mean, I don't want you to think me utterly heartless."

"I wouldn't think that."

"Of course you would," she insisted. "But what am I to do, Bruce? That beastly list."

It had gone on too long. "Sally," he said firmly, "I understand. We had better not talk anymore."

"Oh, Bruce" was the last thing she said.

He put down the phone and slumped into a chair and tried to sort out his thoughts, telling himself first that he was an utterly despicable and heartless cad not to shed a tear over Sally's departure and to be relieved in the bargain. Of course, Molly Maguire would pluck out the word *cad* and say something to the effect of nobody using that word since F. Scott Fitzgerald, and why the devil was he thinking of Molly Maguire when he should be brooding over his presence on a blacklist? And there was a ridiculous mystery. He had never written anything for television, and he had never written anything for radio. He was essentially, and above all, a newspaperman, so what was he doing on a network blacklist? Like everyone else, he had read about the blacklists, that strange new phenomenon that was being stitched into the fabric of what they had begun to call, in this postwar world, "the American way of life." Somehow, before Pearl Harbor, no one referred to the American way of life. If you had a job, you were lucky; a lot of people did not have one, but no one talked up an American way of life.

But blacklists were for communists.

He asked himself, What in hell was he thinking? Sally wasn't lying to him. She was hardly so consummate an actress that she could manufacture that note of sheer terror. And as for Sally—well, she was as far from being a communist as one could get. And wasn't he? How did he land on the blacklist, and, more important, how did blacklists come into being? Where did a television network get either the impetus or the right to create a blacklist? The airwaves belonged to the people, and a television network operated by virtue of a franchise granted to it by the Federal government. Then either it was violating some very basic laws of the United States, or the names in the blacklist were fed to it, at least in part, by the very government that had granted its franchise. As for himself, what could he have said to the FBI agent, Carl Jorgenson, that would pin the communist label on him? Or were they so thorough in the United States Army Intelligence that the communist thing had been passed on to the FBI from Calcutta? That was not his experience of the army. Thorough—they could lose a division just from their slipshod and inefficient paperwork—but he couldn't imagine this as a lead to a blacklist. Or might it be his connection with Legerman? Or with Molly Maguire? But who knew about that? Or with Greenberg? Was Greenberg a communist? Or was he, Bruce Bacon, losing his mind? Why was he thinking of Greenberg? Because Greenberg was Jewish? Jews equal communists; was that it?

"This is crazy," he said aloud, slowly. "This is totally insane, and it can't be happening to me."

He was a reporter, wasn't he? A damn good reporter, and the thing to do now was to get himself down to the network and see the top man there, and say, "What the hell is this about a blacklist? About your network running a blacklist? Do you have a blacklist with the names of writers and actors—" Or was it actors as well as writers? Had Sally said actors, or was he thinking about Hollywood and the stories coming out of there about actors as well as writers being named as communists? All right, he'll put it to them as a writer: "I am a writer, and therefore I'm putting it to you flatly. My name is Bruce Bacon. If you were reading the *Tribune* two years ago, you saw my byline."

"You are dreaming," he said aloud.

He knew how it would go. Like this:

Blacklist? Mr. Bacon, we have no blacklist.

And what paper do you represent? The Tribune? *Oh, you no longer work for the* Tribune.

And how did you come by this information, Mr. Bacon? You say from an employee of the network? And what is the name of this employee?

You do understand, Mr. Bacon, that if you should print this, we will not hesitate to take action, and this is very actionable.

It just wouldn't play, no matter how he innovated. In the first place, it would wash out Sally's job. He had picked her up at her office, spoken to people who worked with her, and they would make the connection. Whatever he felt about Sally, he could not destroy her career. That was impossible, particularly since he was pleased that she had ended their affair, relieving him of the guilts he would have lived with. And even if he were to write the story, why should he think that the *Tribune* would print it? They were an honest, decent newspaper, one of the best in the country, but he had seen no story in the *Tribune* about the blacklist.

In effect, that was the way it was, and there wasn't one damn thing he could do about it. Or was there? He could begin to avoid anyone he suspected of being very left wing— or a communist, or a liberal? he asked himself. Where did it stop? He experienced a wave of self-disgust that the idea had even shaped itself in his mind.

Forget it, he told himself. It's over. It's done. You're on the goddamn list, and you'll just have to earn your daily bread without the networks, since if one of them has that list, you can be damn sure that they all have it.

Bruce put the incident away as something he had to live with, telling himself that at least he was not a communist and therefore had less to worry about than the more obvious victims of the witch hunt. But as the witch hunt became more apparent on the American landscape, his certainty was shaken. He had refrained from mentioning the incident with Sally to Molly—indeed, refrained now from mentioning Sally at all when he was with Molly; but having dinner with Molly, one evening a few weeks after the Sally debacle, he raised the question of her own security. "Aren't you afraid, or at least worried, the way this lunacy is spreading?"

Her answer seemed inappropriate: "Have you never wondered about my name, Bruce?"

"Your name? Why, and what has that got to do with it?"

"You're as poorly educated as the rest of your lot, Harvard and Yale and Williams notwithstanding. If you had a bit of knowledge of your own land, you'd know that after the Civil War there was a big movement of Irish immigrant lads into the hard-coal fields around Scranton, and the mine operators were squeezing the blood and life out of them, the men dying of the black lung and kids in the mines at age ten and twelve, never with a chance to be a kid or eat a decent bowl of food. So the Irish miners got together and organized a secret union, which they called the Molly Maguires, and they went on strike for a living wage. Well, the strike was broken, and twenty of the lads were hanged, which was the price of putting together a trade union in those days, but my father remembered them and took great pride in them, and he said to my mother, If the third should be a girl, call her Molly after the heroic miners. Well, Bruce, with that in my mother's milk, I'll be damned if I let the likes of John Rankin or Dickie Nixon scare me. What can they do to me? Ask me if I'm a communist?"

It was then that Bruce told her about the blacklist and about his final parting with Sally.

"Ah, Bruce," she said, "you make such lousy choices. I love you. I hope I'm not a lousy choice."

"You love me? I mean—in what way?"

She burst out laughing and stretched across the table and took his hand in hers. "How many ways are there? We'll talk about that later. I want to know about this list. You know, we all took it for granted that the networks and film companies had blacklists, but hard evidence—did she say there actually was a printed or a typewritten list that she saw with her own eyes?"

"She indicated as much. Oh, yes, I would have to conclude that. I mean not that she actually saw the list. Someone else could have seen and said to her, You know, Sally, that guy with the glasses who was with you the other day, you said he was Bacon, the correspondent, well his name is on a blacklist—or something of the sort."

"Or something of the sort. But I'm inclined," Molly said, "to believe that she actually saw the list, probably in her boss's office."

"Probably. So what do I do? I'm new at the whipping boy act. I plead for life to be rational."

"After what you saw in Europe?"

"Still I plead for life to be rational. Tell me why this is happening. What are they after? What are they thinking? What do they suspect me of? If this whole damn Federal Bureau of Investigation doesn't have enough common sense to know that Dr. William Bacon's boy never even pulled a traffic ticket, then a lot of taxpayers' money is going right down the drain."

"Eat your spaghetti," Molly said. "Why do you always order spaghetti?"

"Because my mother never served it, or something of the sort. Don't try to evade my question. I rely on you. You're my only link to that foul conspiracy you call communism. Why don't you ever talk about it? Why don't you try to charm me into it? I read the *Communist Manifesto* by Mr. Marx. It's as pertinent to what is happening in America today as that idiot Tennyson's 'Charge of the Light Brigade,' and don't think they don't have something in common."

"I'd hardly compare Karl Marx to Alfred Tennyson."

"They're both Victorian antiques. I tried *Das Kapital* and got fifty pages into it—bored to tears. Did you ever read it?"

"No."

"Then why the hell are you a communist?"

"I tried to explain, but you're too dumb to get it. Let's stop worrying about me being a communist and get on to your case. Go ahead, eat."

"You're the only woman I ever took to dinner who worried about how much I ate."

"I went to bed with you," Molly said. "Do you think I'd go to bed with you if I didn't love you? That's why I worry about how much you eat. It's the shanty Irish way of demonstrating love. Food and whiskey. You know, there's one thing you'll never really understand, Mr. Bacon, and that's how it is to be poor."

"I've seen that in India."

"That doesn't mean you understand it. Now let's get down to what's happening to you. If you want to understand lunacy, you have to think like a lunatic. There are three connections you have: first with Harold Legerman, second with Ashoka Majumdar—that was his name?"

"Yes."

"And third with the famine in Bengal. Or maybe that should go together with Majumdar. Now let's examine it carefully. What happened to Majumdar?"

"I don't know. When I was leaving, Legerman indicated that the British had tortured him and had then beaten him to death, a not uncommon practice among our British cousins in India. They certainly don't like the Congress people, and they have a maniacal hatred for the communists."

"OK. Let's go from there."

"Do you want dessert and coffee?" he asked her.

"You don't take it seriously, do you?" Molly said. "You just can't believe that this could happen to the all-American boy? In Jack Armstrong's world, there is apple pie, mother, and absolute justice."

"Why the hell are you always sticking a knife into me and twisting it? One moment you tell me you love me—"

"Good! Get angry! And listen to me, damn you. You're in the middle of something, and you can't believe it's happening to you. If they tortured Majumdar and killed him— why? It's not illegal to be a communist in Calcutta, is it?"

"I'm not sure."

"Jesus be praised, you sure as hell don't know very much. You never walked the dark side of the street. Well, that's the way you are, and someday you'll grow up."

"If we're going to talk, talk," Bruce said angrily. "Don't

lecture me on what a horse's ass I am, and I'm damned tired of being told I don't have minimal street smarts. I don't! Period."

She lifted his hand to her lips and whispered, "I'm sorry. I'm so sorry."

"You're forgiven."

"It's too easy. I love you, Bacon. Now please listen to me. They knew that you were after the famine story. They knew that you associated with Majumdar. Put it together. They knew that Majumdar had something on the famine and who made it."

"Majumdar had nothing. If he had anything, he would have given it to me. I think he trusted me. He knew I was after the story, and he knew how big the story was."

"It doesn't matter," Molly insisted. "Try to think the way they think. They pick up Majumdar. They tell him, very nicely, You have something we want. Oh, no, says Majumdar. I have nothing. Then they beat him. Then they beat him some more. But from what you say, this Majumdar is a stubborn critter and they keep beating him and finally he turns up dead. Tell me something, did you try writing to Majumdar?"

A chill went through Bruce's body, a chill of cold, primitive fear. Until now, he could explain away everything unusual that had happened to him. He was living in a strange, new world, a place that the United States of America had never been before. It was a place of fear and suspicion and cheap betrayal, and the key word, the word that was bringing people to their knees, was *communism*. But he had been apart from all this; he had no record of being involved with the Communist Party. When others were accused and he read about it in the newspapers, he half agreed with the accusations. He had no way of knowing. He had even whispered to himself at times, This is not Russia and this is not India. This is the U.S.A., and if they're not tools of the Russians, why are they what they are? Why not Democrats, if they were liberals? It was still the party of Roosevelt—or was it? And here was himself, Bruce Bacon, sitting opposite a red as red as red could be, a tall, strapping, handsome Irishwoman, who was exactly that thing and made no effort to conceal it.

"Bruce, did you hear me?" she asked. "Did you write to Majumdar?"

"Yes," very weakly.

"Bruce, it's not the end of the world. Let's talk about it."

"I wrote to him twice," Bruce admitted. "Both times at the offices of his paper, *Prasarah*. That means truth or freedom or such, in Sanskrit. Molly, what the devil has happened to me? When I was there in India, I felt that communists were good and even noble people, and now I'm back here—"

"And you're wondering why you ever got mixed up with me. But you're going too quickly, Bruce. It's not the end of the world. The Limeys may be playing footsie with our new set of nuts, who call themselves the Central Intelligence Agency, or it may be that it's your connection with Hal Legerman or maybe with me."

"Not you. No, I won't accept that. Anyway, no one knows. It's always just the two of us."

"I know," Molly said, "but that's no good either. I can assure you that the FBI knows. The Party is lousy with them. Sometimes I feel that the whole damned Bureau has joined the Party. We have nothing to hide, and I have to step into your world and you have to step into mine. Or else—we end this."

"No, we don't end it," Bruce said. "Not now, not ever."

That night, he clutched her in his arms as if she were the only reality in a world of senseless flux.

Then he had a spell of frustration and destruction, which he told himself had nothing to do with his name on that ridiculous network list. For three weeks, he was satisfied with nothing he wrote. He filled his wastepaper basket with

torn, crumpled manuscript paper. When he opened the
weekly book sections of the *New York Times* and the *New
York Tribune,* he burned with envy of and resentment
against this world of people who wrote books so easily and
who understood war and peace and despair and hope and
murder and innocence as if it was all simply an extended *abc*
of an adult-extended childhood. For himself, he understood
less and less. Williams College had given him no leads into
the world that was and is. Molly had not pushed beyond the
single question: Had he written to Majumdar? She didn't
have to call his attention to the fact that he lived in a demented world where the act of writing to the gentle and
compassionate Majumdar might cause his own death; his
learning on that score was instantaneous.

It was not that communism lured him; it exhibited a kind
of total immersion that was no more pleasant or enticing to
him than the total immersion of the born-again Southern
Baptist, yet recalling the four communists he had met in his
lifetime—Chatterjee, Majumdar, Legerman, and Molly
Maguire—he had to admit that if one looked upon the
world as a place of good and bad people—as most human
beings did look upon it—he would have to place those four
among the good. He could not accept their ideology. He
could not believe in a communist brotherhood of man any
more than he could accept the notion of a Christian brotherhood of man. Someone who looks into an open burial pit in
a Nazi death camp and sees a thousand bodies of men,
women, and children piled like cordwood, stiff in death, is
not too likely to preach brotherhood or believe in it—or is
he? Or is Bruce Bacon? And what in God's name does
Bruce Bacon believe in? And why did he have to know?
Why couldn't he go ahead and write the damn book as any
writer writes a book?

He put a page in his typewriter and typed, slowly, a totally new beginning for his book: "There is no good war,
there is no just war, there is no righteous war. We, the hu-

man race, have been flimflammed, and what follows is the
story of one man's witness to the flimflam."

He called Molly at her office at the paper. She had warned
him that, in all probability, the telephones at the *Daily
Worker* were tapped, but Bruce's position was that if he gave
in to this mindless fear of FBI-tapped telephones, a fear that
was beginning to permeate New York, he would give up and
move to Tasmania or some such place. Anyway, he didn't
give a damn, convinced that nothing he might say had much
value to anyone anywhere. "I must see you tonight," he told
her. "Have dinner with me, please."

"I'm working too late for dinner. How about my apartment, say nine o'clock?"

"Will you have eaten?"

"I'll grab a sandwich."

"I'll bring Chinese," Bruce said. He loved Chinese food,
the assortment of wonderful dishes that were the forbidden
fruit of his childhood. They were still wonderful. Molly
laughed at his delight in such things. "You're like a kid,"
she told him. "Everything new is wonderful."

"Or terrible."

Tonight, he arrived at her place about fifteen minutes before she did. They had exchanged keys as an alternative to
living together. They never spoke of marriage, and when in
his fantasy he asked her to move in and live with him, he
always thought better of it. Simply on the basis of not deliberately putting his foot in a bear trap. You couldn't be free
and aloof from the Communist Party if you lived with someone who was blatantly a member of the Party. He added to
this the fact that his relationship with Molly Maguire was
totally different from any of his previous affairs or en-
counters. There was no flirtation, no maybe or perhaps, no
playing of mating games; they simply accepted each other.
"You're what I want," she had explained once. "A little
askew here and there, but basically right." He felt the same
way, and tonight as he emptied the containers into dishes,

putting them in the oven set at Warm, he thought of how different it had been with Sally and Prudence.

They finished the food before he told Molly what had brought him to call her and insist on their being together tonight. "Of course," he began, with the intent to say something about going on this way without living together; but then he choked the rest of it. "Of course, it's damned selfish of me," he said instead. "I demand and you do it."

"If I want to." She was clearing the table. "Good food. You bring food, the door's open. Tell me about the crisis."

"I suppose it is a crisis."

She sat opposite him now, grinned, and poured tea. She had large, strong hands. He was constantly engaged by her competence; she did things well.

"You see," he said, "I'm trying to place myself. Am I insane or do I live in an insane world? Then why me? Why should I be any more sane than the next guy? I never faced up to any of this. All the months I lived in a butcher shop, I accepted the butchery. Hitler had brought it on himself and his people. I saw a little girl of perhaps nine or ten years who had been cut in half. The whole lower part of her body had been blown away, and yet the head and neck and arms had survived without damage. She had blue eyes and flaxen hair, and that touched the part of me that is still racist, and I dream about her at night and she speaks to me. When a child is dying of starvation, the flesh disappears, and the oversized, hollow-eyed head sits on a skeleton. That's India. The blue-eyed child was German. I saw a nineteen-year-old infantryman go crazy, and he put the muzzle of his rifle under his chin and he pulled the trigger, and his head exploded in a burst of brains and bone. An officer watching it remarked that he had never seen a hard-nosed bullet act that way. His only comment. Six million Jews die, and no one gives a damn. Six million Indians die, and no one gives a damn. Mr. Truman blows two Japanese cities off the map, and no one gives a damn."

She didn't interrupt him. When he finished, Molly said, "That's true—more or less. Some hyperbole, but that's only to be expected. But you knew this."

"I suppose. But I never faced it."

"Some of us faced it. It doesn't change much."

"What happened with me," Bruce explained, "is that I face a wall, a dead end. I sit in front of that damn type-writer, and I have no place to go. Molly, I'm no amateur. I've written my stories under the worst conditions, and I got them through. I told what I saw. It's not enough."

"If you see clearly, why not?"

Taking a folded sheet of paper out of his pocket, un-folding it on the table, and pushing it toward Molly, Bruce said, "I've written over two hundred pages, and then the wall. For two weeks, I've been tearing up everything I put down. I fill a wastebasket and my brain is empty."

He paused, and Molly read, "There is no good war, there is no just war, there is no righteous war. We, the human race, have been flimflammed—" She looked up from the paper. "What else is new?"

"Is that all you have to say?"

"I don't know what else to say," she confessed, almost sadly. "Please don't be angry, Bruce. We are both of us very simple people. I think that's why we get along with each other. But there are things I've known since I was a little kid, and when you discover some of these things, it blows your mind."

"Which is another way of saying I'm both innocent and stupid."

"No!" she exclaimed. "God damn it, no! You are not stupid. I never said you were stupid. But innocent—oh, yes. What is innocence? To be upright and artless, which you are, thank God. If you were sitting here with one of those half-ass intellectuals who are now leading the new crusade against the left, they'd spend the rest of the night convincing you that there is good war and bad war and good murder and bad murder, because that's the function of society. Well, yes, it's my hyperbole—I exaggerate. You made a discovery —it's not the last. The only advantage I have over you is that I never went to college. I cribbed my education as a packing clerk in Filene's basement, so I made the choices. By the time I was fourteen, I had read Shaw's *Intelligent Woman's Guide to Socialism and Capitalism,* Bellamy's *Looking Backward,* Veblin's *Leisure Class,* Jack London's *Iron Heel,* John Reed's *Ten Days That Shook the World*—to mention only a few. We sang a song where the refrain was 'No Irish need apply,' and we had a teacher called poverty that cut to the core of things, and when I was eighteen, I met a wonderful Irish lady, name of Elizabeth Gurley Flynn, who talked me into joining this subversive organization—oh, damn it, I run off at the mouth like some silly schoolteacher, but I have to make the point, Bruce, and I'm the stone in the pudding. You made the most important discovery of your life, and I say, So what? But that's it—so what? Nothing changes except your mind."

"And that's not important?" Bruce asked softly.

"Damned important."

"So why are you putting me down?"

"Because if I know you, you're ready to tear up your book and go into a passionate denunciation of war. Don't. Please. Write what you saw, and believe me, it will come out right. I don't want you to be a preacher. I don't want you to join the Communist Party. The Party would shrink your soul and destroy you. I want you to be what you are—a decent, upright man who knows the difference between right and wrong—and when you write what you see, the reader will know it too."

"Let's not have tea," Bruce said. "Let's have some gin or whatever's handy. You get points for confusion, and I might as well be drunk. You're a first-rate news lady, and yet you work for forty bucks a week on a communist paper, and you tell me that the same Party would shrink my soul and destroy me, and I'm supposed to make sense of all this?"

"No more than anyone else does, and if we start to drink, you won't go home. Well, why not? And about the Party, it's like everything else. There are people in it who are damned near saints and there are others I don't want to know or talk about, and God only knows how many have sold out to the FBI and how many were FBI from the beginning, and if there were something better around, I'd join it in a minute. But there isn't anything else that isn't totally corrupt, and as for the Democrats and the Republicans, well, you name them and that's enough said. As for the C.P., it's being attacked from every side, the government is determined to destroy it, its leaders are narrow and not bright, we lose membership, we're afraid to stand up and attack what's wrong in the Soviet Union, and a hell of a lot is wrong"—she spread her arms—"so it crumbles."

"And yet you stay with it."

"Much as I may hate a lot of what goes on in the Party, I have even more contempt and hatred for those who leave the Party and go over to the other side and make a cheap bundle out of becoming anti-Party hacks. No matter how wrong we are, no matter how much we choke creative people and isolate ourselves from the rest of the country— which is one reason I don't want you in it—we still have never betrayed the workers or peace or the Negro people or the women's movement. Show me another party in this country that will face death for its beliefs—"

"Come off it," Bruce said. "I ask you questions, and you don't really try to answer them, and as for facing death, millions of us faced death, and I don't find virtue in it, not on your side, not on the other side—"

"Stop," she said. "We're building up to an awful fight. Let's go to bed and make love. It's better."

"It's better," Bruce agreed.

Yet during the ensuing days, Bruce followed Molly's ad-

vice. He went on writing plainly and straightforwardly
about what he had seen, nor did he destroy what he had
already written. Yet as his inner self matured and changed,
so did his reflection on his own experience. During this time,
he often thought of breaking his connection with Molly
Maguire. He sometimes asked himself whether his view of
communism was so different from the general public's view,
as reflected in the media. It was something mysterious and
unreal and menacing. And Molly, if not menacing, was so
different from any other person he had ever known, including Legerman and Majumdar, that she might have dropped
out of another planet. All of her premises were different, at
least from what his had been. She shattered every icon he
had lived by. When he asked her how she, a member of an
atheist organization, could consider herself a good Catholic,
she replied that one had nothing to do with the other, and
when he objected that atheism and Catholicism were not
compatible, she replied that no one was really an atheist,
and when he asked when she had last been in a church, she
replied that a church was the last place in the world where
one should look for God. She loved America and considered
its economy and its government to be a disaster for the
world, and at the same time inscribed it as the best place on
earth. She had taken a job in a shipyard to support the war,
taking a leave from the paper, yet she condemned the war as
a stupid and bloody result of twenty years of British and
American stupidity. She displayed a mind that was a cross
between a steel trap and the dreams and fancies of a poor
Irish kid in the streets of Boston. She had apparently read
every book he had ever heard of, and one evening in her
apartment, after dinner with Ronnie Gilbert and Pete Seeger, she sang along with them in an endless flow of song that
went on for hours. She canvassed for the Party in the Puerto
Rican section of East Harlem, and he went with her one
day, amazed by her Spanish and by the ease and compassion
with which she dealt with the people.

"Where did you learn Spanish?"

"A year in high school. I picked up the rest."

He was troubled by his affair with her; he was also in awe of her, enchanted by her, and madly in love with her. His fantasy terror was that one day she would decide, This Bacon character is hopeless, and why am I wasting time with him?

But his writing went better and easier, and the end of his book was in sight.

Each time he had a chapter finished, he brought it to her to read. She was a good critic, clever enough to get him to see for himself where he had gone off the track. "You must understand," she said to him, "that there are things here that I wouldn't write the way you write them. That's OK. You're not me and you're not a communist, and I don't ever want you to become one. You have a clear, pure vision, and no one must ever tell you how to write or what to write." She often spoke of "parlor pinks," well-to-do, comfortable liberals who echoed the Party line and never walked a picket line. "You have to be in this neck deep," she said to him, "to realize how isolated we are, the mistakes we've made, the writers we've squeezed dry until they fled from us. It's lovely to talk about the things we believe in and sit safe and comfortable. Don't do it, Bruce."

One evening, Bruce went with her to the home of Professor Ernest Goland, who had worked on the Manhattan Project, and who was subsequently thrown off it and out of his job at Cornell University because it was discovered that as a young man in Germany of the thirties, he had been a member of the Communist Party. His wife, Nell Goland, was an important and gifted gynecologist and, like her husband, a one-time fugitive from the Nazis. They lived in a big old apartment on West End Avenue, and when they opened the door for Bruce and Molly, they embraced and welcomed Molly with the enthusiasm of a father and mother greeting a long-away daughter.

"This is Bruce Bacon," Molly said. "He's the best thing that has happened to me in a long time."

"Bruce Bacon," Professor Goland said thoughtfully. "The same one? Africa? Europe and then India?"

Bruce nodded.

"Then indeed I'm honored. You're an honest writer—and also very good."

The apartment reminded Bruce of his father's place, the high beamed ceilings, the dining room and living room separated by big sliding doors, the massive dining room table, the overstuffed pieces in the living room, the maps and steel engravings and etchings on the walls, the clutter by people interested in practically everything; but different from his youthful home in its feeling of another culture and a rather forlorn attempt to reproduce it.

Alone with Molly for a moment as another guest arrived, Bruce whispered, "The parlor pinks you spoke of?"

"Not the professor. He puts his life on the line. Others? There'll be some. Find them yourself."

Most of the guests were familiar to Molly. A handsome woman in her forties was introduced to Bruce as Betty Anderson. He would keep asking himself, Is she a communist? Is he? This was a new kind of place for him. Abe Kinholt, a fat, imposing man in his fifties—next to be met and greeted. Bruce was still focused on Betty Anderson. He had seen her in at least a dozen films when he was a kid. Of course, she had been blacklisted. "The *Liberal Day*," Kinholt said. "One should be properly identified in this den of reds. I'm the editor of the best of what Westbrook Pegler called the 'butcher paper' magazines." Frank Collins was in his late twenties, slight and blond. His wife, slighter, blonder, looked like a small twin sister. Kinholt overwhelmed them. They stood in the background, modestly, almost sheepishly, while Kinholt's voice filled the room. Bruce realized he was staring at Collins, and Molly nudged him.

"What is it?" she whispered.

He pushed past Kinholt to where Collins stood with his look-alike wife, and said to him softly, "Frank Collins? Captain Collins?"

Collins said, "Do I know you, sir?" Apologetically, as if he, Collins, had no right to ask the question. His wife smiled, also diffidently. Professor Goland joined them and said, "This is Josie and Frank Collins. Good teachers. Good honest teachers."

Kinholt stopped talking to Molly. They all turned toward the Collinses.

"We teach at Stuyvesant High School. We met there. It's such an honor—I mean to be back there and teaching there. It's such a very good school."

"I'm Bruce Bacon," Bruce said to Collins. "I interviewed you in Domfront, August of 'forty-four."

"Yes—yes, of course, we were both covered with mud. You must forgive me for not recognizing you."

Collins obviously did not care to talk about it, although he was pressed with questions, particularly by Kinholt. "There's a story there," Kinholt said, and the professor replied that there was a story everywhere, and it was time for everyone to sit down to dinner. In the European manner, he served no drinks before dinner, but there was wine and beer on the big table. Bruce managed to whisper to Molly, "I'll tell you later. He was a lieutenant in the infantry. He won a field commission for distinguished bravery. Not too common."

The food was German food, pot-roasted brisket of beef, roast potatoes, a dumpling loaf, and, almost apologetically, spinach. The food was delicious, heavy and old-fashioned, and Bruce loved it, washing it down with sweet dark beer. Bruce learned that Frank Collins, who taught trigonometry at Stuyvesant High, attended a small evening group at Professor Goland's apartment, where Goland lectured on nuclear mechanics. Thus their connection. Betty Anderson was an old friend and one-time patient of Nell Goland's,

and Kinholt was an old friend of the family. Bruce knew his
magazine, but not too well, having never done more than
glance at an issue, and he was enough of a movie fan to be in
awe of Betty Anderson, who was talking about the situation
in Hollywood.

"The sad thing is," she was saying, "that people are so
terrified."

"With reason," Kinholt said.

"Oh, no, no," Betty Anderson protested. "Everyone
keeps comparing the situation to Nazi Germany before the
war. But I can't make sense of such a comparison. Do you
think it's valid, Professor?" she asked Goland.

A plump, short man, his head surrounded by a halo of
fluffy white hair, his blue eyes eager and alert behind gold-
rimmed spectacles, Professor Goland responded to a question by pursing his lips for a long moment and nodding,
whether his answer was in the affirmative or the negative.
This time he agreed with Betty Anderson. "No—not a valid
comparison at all. Mr. Truman does not want a fascist country. But he does want an absolute and deep break with the
Soviet Union. They're not afraid of communism here, where
the Party is so small and fragile, but he is very afraid indeed
of the communist parties of France and of Italy. Because the
communists led the resistance, they have become great mass
parties, and Mr. Truman's nightmare is that these parties
could take over the European Continent. They cannot, of
course, and they will not, but can you tell that to Truman?"

"But the terror is real," Miss Anderson insisted. "I went
into a restaurant in Beverly Hills last week, and there were
two people I've known over twenty years, and they looked
the other way the moment they saw me, and then pretended
not to have seen me or noticed that I was there. And this
isn't the first time."

"And you don't think it began this way in Germany?"
Kinholt said.

"No way. No. The conditions are too different."

"Then what becomes of the Communist Party here?"

When no one leaped at that, Molly said, "They'll destroy us. Ten years ago, we were rooted in the trade unions. Not today. We made too many mistakes, and that wretched little bastard J. Edgar Hoover has become too smart. Our membership is down to thirty thousand at the most, and maybe a thousand of them are FBI agents."

"That bad?" Betty Anderson asked. "I saw the May Day parade here in nineteen forty-six. We had thirteen thousand men in uniform marching under the Party's banners. And just in New York."

"It changes quickly," the professor said.

"We never joined the Party here," his wife said. "Of course, we suffered all the torment of being communists without joining the Party, and now who knows whether I'll be able to cling to my operating privileges. But we were in the Party in Germany, and we thought we had support. But the support became quiet with fear, and in one night, Hitler put a hundred thousand communists to death. Nobody remembers that or wants to remember it."

"We're all being so bleak," Frank Collins said softly. "I search everywhere for dark beer and never find it. Yet when I come here, there is always dark beer."

"That is positive," Molly said.

"And we won't have fascism here," Collins continued. "Even if they wipe out the Party. We're not Germans. With all the fear that's going around, it's still only a handful—and when it gets large enough, the people will fight back, believe me. It may take time, but we won't have fascism."

"No, they're not putting us in jail, not yet," Betty Anderson said. "But they take away our jobs, our careers. I know at least twenty people who can't work in film. They are blacklisted."

"The same in the schools. We're holding our breath."

"You're taking it lying down," Kinholt said.

"You want barricades?"

"Abe is a literary leftist," the professor said.

"Molly's the lucky one. They can't fire her."

"Just don't you believe that. Communism's like Christianity—as Mark Twain put it, Christianity's a fine religion that's never been tried. So be it with communism. I used to think that Russia would give it a shot, but like the Pope, Stalin doesn't understand the religion he preaches and doesn't dare to give it a chance to work. Lenin said you build socialism with the bricks of capitalism. Paraphrase," Molly said, smiling wanly, "you try to build it with the pricks of capitalism. So don't think they can't fire me. They bring me up on charges every couple of weeks for what I write."

"Too bitter, Molly," the professor said. "You're the best thing they have on that paper. They won't expel you from the Party. No, couldn't be."

Kinholt said to Bruce, "We haven't heard a word from you, Bacon. You're the odd man out, since I never remember you standing left of center, and here you are in this den of reds. I remember reading your stuff and thinking what a joy it would be to have you write for me. I know what brings you here. I'd join the Republican Party for one of the looks your redheaded friend casts on you. But is it beauty alone?"

"Oh, don't be such an oaf, Kinholt," Betty Anderson said.

Bruce did not like the man, but he smiled and said, "If you're asking whether I'm a communist—the answer is no. And I don't expect to be one in the future."

"You know, Abe," the professor said, "you do put your foot in your mouth, if that's the expression. When I testified on the bomb, a senator asked me whether I was Jewish. I said yes, even though I was born Jewish. He asked me why I said that? I told him because, although from your name and looks you were apparently born a Christian, nothing you have said lends any credence to it." And, turning to Bruce, "Forgive him. He's a good man." His manner was so gentle that Kinholt couldn't take offense, and Collins leaped into the gap.

"Mr. Bacon is no stranger to me. I don't think he'd be a stranger anywhere good people come together. I met him in Europe after a nasty battle, and we both sat in the mud while he interviewed me with a pencil stub and a tiny notebook that was damp."

"The notebook's a sort of badge or something," Bruce said. "I have a good memory. I remember that one particularly, because when you were done—well, do you remember what you said to me?"

"I remember very well. I said to you, 'I'm finished. I'll never fire a gun again.' Yes, that's more or less what I said."

"And did you?"

They were all listening now. The silence lengthened, and then Collins said, "Did I fire my gun again? No. Never. I had killed twelve men, God help me. I became a pacifist at that moment, although it doesn't heal anything. If there's a God, He can't forgive me, and if there isn't one, I can never forgive myself. I didn't have enough guts to refuse the field commission they gave me. I like to feel I was still in shock, but it was the guts I lacked."

"I don't understand," Bruce said. "You can't be a communist."

"I can't be anything else. Who else is fighting for peace?"

"And the force and violence?"

"That's the press's whipping boy. The only force and violence I know about have been directed toward me."

Walking slowly with Molly toward the subway station, asked how he felt about the evening, Bruce replied, "Confused—and I ate too much."

"You ate like a poor, hungry child."

"I know. The food and the beer were marvelous."

"What confused you?"

"You're supposed to be atheists?"

"Well, they don't expel us for believing in God."

"Do you? I never asked you that before."

"Only if She's a woman," Molly said.

"I'm serious."

"So am I. What else confused you?"

"You know," Bruce said, "we never have a real argument. I know, I do get pissed off when you start throwing your brains and information around, but I mean a real argument. I expected one tonight. I said to myself, Here she's bringing me into—well, into—"

"Den of reds."

"Right. And I was going to face the lot of you and fight you on your own grounds, and then, damn it, there was nothing to fight about."

"We can try again. I'll change the crowd."

"Go soak your head."

"You call that nice?" Molly asked. "That's hoodlum talk. The fact that I'm a little smarter than you doesn't make me want to be treated like less than a lady. Six months ago, you wouldn't have dared. I was so pleased to find an actual, living, breathing gentleman, just like in the books of Richard Harding Davis."

"Good God, you read Richard Harding Davis?"

"I read everything, sonny, and don't you ever forget that."

Then they went into the subway and rode downtown to her place and drank Alka-Seltzer and went to bed.

A week later, Bruce received a telephone call from an old associate at the *Tribune*. They had been copy boys together, and today this man, Jerome Rogers, was a highly paid staff writer on *Life*. Bruce had not seen him since before the war. He had found Bruce's number in the phone book, and now he asked Bruce to meet him at the St. Regis bar on a matter of great importance. He was waiting for Bruce in front of the big Maxfield Parrish King Cole panel, and after they shook hands, he sounded off on what a great piece of folk painting the King Cole panel was. Bruce thought otherwise, but was in no mood to argue aesthetics. He resented being summoned like this and then greeted as if they were no different from the two kids of seven years ago. He had never been very fond of Rogers, and he had no great admiration for the costume of sneakers, flannels, and leather-patched jacket that Rogers wore.

After initial praise—"Hey, great stuff, great writing—you *were* in that war. I was in England, but you *were* in it right up to the neck"—he ordered drinks. It was four-thirty in the afternoon. Bruce had a beer, Rogers a martini.

"I felt I could do you a favor," Rogers said. "I owe it."

"You don't owe me."

"I owe myself. I watch this crazy anticommunist crusade, and I keep saying to myself, Nazi Germany all over again." He dropped his voice. "I was in Henry Luce's office yesterday, and J. Edgar Hoover came in. J. Edgar himself. Luce doesn't ask me to go, so I just sit there. Hoover is there only a few minutes. He hands a fat brown paper envelope to Luce, and then he says, 'I still haven't found out whether Simpson works for them. He's got to be a commie, but we can't get a trace on it.' And then Luce says, 'I have my own man on their National Committee. Just hold on.' Then Luce dials a number direct, and he says, 'Hello?' He listens. Then he says, 'About Buckingham Simpson, is he in the Party?' Then he listens. Then he puts down the telephone, turns to Hoover, and says to him, 'No. He's not a member.' 'Can you trust this man?' Hoover wants to know, and Luce says, 'He's on their National Committee and he's been on my payroll for years.' "

Bruce listened quietly until Rogers had finished, and then he said, "Why are you telling me this?"

"Call it an act of conscience. I don't agree with you guys about anything, but this is no way to do it."

"Who are *you guys*?"

"Come on, Bruce, you know what I mean."

"Please tell me."

"What are you sore at? What in hell did I do to make you sore at me? You're the only communist I know. I bring you this to save you some grief."

"So I'm a communist? Where did that come from?"

"It's around. If I knew anyone else in the Party, I wouldn't have come to you."

"I'm sorry," Bruce said. "I guess I'm on a short fuse these days. I'm trying to finish a book, and anything that takes me away from it provokes me. I'm not a communist, Jerry, never have been one."

"I'm sorry as hell, my turn now," Rogers said. "I feel like a horse's ass of the first water."

"Forget it."

"Do you know anyone? Can you pass it on?"

"Maybe. Why don't you forget about it. I don't think it means a damned thing anyway."

But thinking about it, Bruce decided that possibly it did mean something of importance in Molly's world, and he told her the gist of it that same night.

"I don't know why he decided I was a communist," Bruce said.

"Well, you date me, and that gets around, and then there's the blacklist at the networks. If one has it, they all have it. But do you think this Rogers guy was telling the truth?"

"If he could invent that story of J. Edgar Hoover in Henry Luce's office, my hat goes off to him. About the National Committee—what is the National Committee?"

"That's the top leadership of the C.P. It's supposed to go up and down, starting with neighborhood or factory units, then the county, then the state, and then the top, the National Committee. But mostly it just goes down from the top, and that's most of what's wrong with us. You're sure he said this guy Luce is paying off is in the National Committee?"

"As he told it."

"And no name? He couldn't come up with a name?"

"Apparently not. The way he said he heard it, there was a private line and the man on the other end recognized Luce's voice."

"Oh, Jesus be praised," Molly said hopelessly, "that's no way to sleep better at night. Their own man in the Central Committee—sounds like a cheap spy novel. The Trotskyites say that Stalin was a czarist police spy. I'm getting too old for this, love."

"Are you going to pass this up to them, to the Central Committee or National Committee? Both the same?"

"Same thing. No. There's enough junk floating around in the movement, and it won't help any if they don't know who he is, and how are they going to find out who he is? They'll want to know where I got it, and then if I name you, it will get thicker and thicker—oh, the hell with it, Bruce. I'm beginning to be frightened—a little. I was never frightened before."

For the first time since he had met her, he said, "Molly, get out of it—please."

She stared at him unhappily.

"I know I never raised this before. You never asked me to get into it. I never asked you to get out of it—until now."

Her reply was unexpected. "Sure, Bruce, and what do I dream about then? Do I go back to the church? But, you know, this is a church, too. It's the only dream of the brotherhood of man. They call us atheists—which is nonsense. Why do you think we have so many Catholics and Jews? Because we're believers. And if I stop believing—"

"There are other things to believe in." He was begging now.

"I wonder." She put her arms around him and held him tight. "Ah, baby, we're not onto solving these strange mysteries. You know, as the poem says, It's Mary, the Mother of God, who brings the gentle sleep from heaven. That's enough. We'll go to bed."

"But you'll think about it."

He stayed the night with her and went back to his own apartment at ten in the morning of the following day. A man was waiting in front of his house, a dour, scruffy sort of man, brown hat, brown suit, tie full of food stains, and he said to Bruce, "You live here?"

"Yes. What's it to you?"

"Your name Bacon? Bruce Bacon?"

"Yes."

"This is for you," he said, offering Bruce an envelope.

Bruce stared at him.

"Damn it, it's for you. There's your name on it."

His name was on it. Bruce reached out and took it. "What is it?" he asked.

"It's a subpoena. You accepted service." The man turned on his heel and walked away.

A
Wall Street
Lawyer

Bruce went upstairs to his apartment, took off his jacket and tie, washed his face in cold water, and then looked at the subpoena, which summoned him to Washington, to the House Office Building, to appear in three weeks' time before the House Committee on Un-American Activities, the same infamous HUAC that was driving a nation toward fear and silence. He dropped into a chair and closed his eyes and tried to think. Then he turned on his radio. He always thought better in the presence of music. Someone was singing the "Ballad for Americans," popular since it had been chosen as the theme song for the Republican National Convention. Hadn't Molly mentioned that both the writers were communists? And "This Land Is My Land" and "The House I Live In" and the "Ballad of John Brown"—and how many more? The books, the plays, the songs, and the poems—all written by communists. The list was endless, and now, the clear soprano was singing, "Nobody who was anybody believed it, everybody who was anybody, they doubted it—and they are doubting still—" Doubting America; he switched off the radio and closed his eyes, and tried to recall what had happened to those who had already appeared before the House Committee. It was painful. He couldn't bear to think about it right now, and certainly not clearly, because it always returned to his own indifference. Why hadn't he rung bells from the church towers? Why hadn't his father, his friends, his newspaper associates, rung bells? Suddenly, he was totally alone, and he understood about others who received such subpoenas.

Well, what now? What's the next step? His immediate impulse was to call Molly; but he realized that this impulse had become all too frequent and he resisted it, allowing himself to think that a hell of a lot of it was her fault. No, that was crazy. Some of it, at least. How did Jerome Rogers get the notion that he was a communist? No. He would have to keep telling himself and remembering that it had started in India, before he ever met Molly. All right, then try to think. The lines of the "Ballad" kept jumping into his mind, and that did not help. He was a lost kid; he had no one in the world to turn to; he was filled with self-pity. If he went to his father, he would be scrutinized dubiously. Where there's smoke, there's fire. His mother, an otherwise sweet and reasonably gentle person, had a muted fear of "foreigners" who were debasing the country. A quiet fear, since her son's feelings were so very different, and by foreigners she meant anyone who was not white, who was not Protestant, and who was not what she referred to as "our kind." Did he tell his father and his mother? But how could he tell them?

Finally, he used up his immediate response and returned to the more or less normal Bruce Bacon who had occupied his clothes before the subpoena arrived, and having returned there, he was deeply ashamed of his initial reaction. Nothing had happened, and he had nothing to hide, and if the bastards thought he did, they'd know better. This was the deliberate dissemination of terror, a reversal of the basis of the whole legal system of the country, a proposition that instead of being innocent until proven guilty, a man was now guilty until he could establish his innocence. And guilty of what? Of belonging to a perfectly legal party that ran candidates in every election. But now it came home to him that they really did not give a tinker's damn who was a communist or who was not. The weapon worked against anyone they chose to subpoena.

Silently, he apologized to Molly, with the addendum, You, Bacon, are a spineless shit. Then he called her.

"I'll be home early," she replied. "About seven o'clock."

"I'll be there."

"I'll cook spaghetti. We'll eat at home."

He bought twenty-five dollars' worth of white roses, and when she opened the door, he embraced her and kissed her passionately.

"What are you apologizing for?" Molly demanded.

"Some things I thought."

"That I got you into all this? That's a legitimate thought. I don't think I did. I think you got you into it because you're Bruce Bacon, and let's eat before we talk about your subpoena."

She piled his plate with spaghetti and butter and garlic and grated cheese, and he ate ravenously. "I forgot about lunch," he explained.

"It's a plus and a minus from living alone. It keeps your weight down, but too much of it is dangerous. You know, Bacon, things are pretty much coming apart at the seams. Frédéric Joliot-Curie, Irène Curie's husband, is in New York, and I interviewed him today, and I asked him whether Russia has the atom bomb. It was an exclusive interview and he didn't hesitate to talk. He said that the Soviets have five atom bombs, and their present production rate is two a month. He said that will increase, and in six months they'll be making two hundred a month. I asked him whether it was a secret and whether he was talking to me off the record. He said absolutely not. We're printing in tomorrow's *Daily Worker*. Of course, the CIA is too damned stupid to believe us, but it gives me a queasy feeling. At the same time, it's leaking through that they're going to indict the Communist Party leadership, on the grounds of their attempting to overthrow the government by force and violence."

"Come on, from what you've been telling me, you couldn't overthrow a baby carriage by force and violence."

"That's the way it looks."

"What happens to you?" he demanded anxiously.

"I'm OK. I'm not a communist leader, only a reporter on the *Daily Worker,* and they're going to think twice before they touch anyone on the paper. When you're working out the first step of a police state, you don't close down the press. That's First Amendment stuff."

"And the stuff about the bomb. Do you believe it?"

"I think so," Molly said. "I don't know just what it means, but I think it puts off war with Russia, which is what they're playing for. If they have the bomb and we have the bomb, it has to slow things down."

He dried the dishes while she washed them. "We still haven't talked about the subpoena."

"All in good time. I'm thinking about it."

When the dishes were finished, she steered him to a chair and brought out a bottle of Irish Cream, poured for both of them, handed him the liqueur. "I didn't spring for it, love. It's a present from my sister Bernadette. She's the nun, and don't ask me how nuns handle finances. But drink it slowly. Did you say that on occasion you like a cigar? Well, here's a Romeo and Juliet, pure Cuban. They assured me it's the very best cigar in the world. I want you to smoke the cigar and sip that sweet Irish junk and we'll relax and talk about those sons of bitches in Washington and that lousy subpoena. But give it to me and let me read it first."

"In my jacket on the chair. If you're going to spoil me rotten like this, I'm going to accept with glee. By the way, just to add to the increment, I got back my piece on the famine in Bengal. I have sent it to fourteen magazines to date. Not one of them will touch it."

She was reading the subpoena. Still reading, she pulled up a chair and sat facing him.

Bruce bit the end of his cigar, lit it, and watched Molly

through the curl of smoke. There was nothing set or fixed about her face. It was no beautiful lifeless icon that could make the cover of a magazine, but a living thing, plain one moment, beautiful the next, dour when she concentrated and then wonderful when she smiled. He found himself wishing that either of them had a fireplace, that he might look at her face and mass of red hair in the flickering light a fire cast. The set of her face changed now as she glanced up with a slight smile.

"Very worried?"

"Sort of." He grinned sheepishly. "Not only have I never been in trouble with the law, but I'm the righteous type."

"You had me fooled."

"I get the feeling you're always sort of laughing at me," Bruce said.

"Let's talk about this subpoena. I only laugh with love, but let's be cold and practical. This calls you to testify before a committee of the House of Representatives. Supposedly, congressional committees hear witnesses to aid in the framing of legislation, but this committee has turned itself into an instrument of terror. They call witnesses for two reasons, to terrify the witness and liberals in general and to gain publicity for themselves."

"What can they do to me—I mean when all the chips are down?"

"Cite you for contempt. Indict you in a Federal court, try you, and give you a year in prison—"

"All for not being able to prove that you're not a communist?"

"Oh, no. No, they don't give a damn whether you're a communist or not. I told you that. Terror and fame. Think of the peculiar bastards on that committee: Dick Nixon— Tricky Dick they call him, congressman from California— John Rankin, wrapped in a Confederate flag, Parnell Thomas, stupid fat pig of a man. These are the dregs of Congress, the dregs of the nation, too. No, it's not communists they're looking for. If they want to know whether Bruce Bacon's a communist, all they have to do is telephone J. Edgar Hoover and ask him."

Bruce puffed the cigar gently and tasted the Irish Cream again. "Do you know, Molly," he said, "before one of Joe Louis's fights, a feller from the other fighter's camp came into Joe's dressing room and spelled out all the dreadful things that he was going to do to Joe. Joe listened calmly, and then Joe said to him, What will I be doing while he's doing all that to me? That's my position. What will I be doing and what can I do?"

"First thing, get a lawyer. You can't go into this armed only with integrity. Anyway, the word's been dropped from the language."

"What kind of a lawyer? You must know lawyers who know their way down these dark alleys."

"Oh, sure, Bruce. I know a few damned good left-wing lawyers. But I don't think you want one of them. I'd like to see you walk in there with a Wall Street lawyer, a good, solid, conservative house that has been in business for at least a century—south of Wall Street. You know what I mean?"

"I know exactly what you mean. You mean Frank Britain of Lennox, Britain, Delloway, and Jones. Dad's lawyer. They don't touch criminal law."

"How about white collar crime?"

"They don't call it crime. But that's a thought. Are you really serious?"

"Of course I am. If you come into court with a left-wing lawyer, you're testifying against yourself. Now according to this subpoena, you testify in executive session. That means your lawyer does not go into the room where you'll testify. He'll be sitting outside, and you can come out to consult him, but mostly you're on your own."

Bruce nodded. "American History One. What the textbooks called the Star Chamber system. It's a tired notion, but doesn't the Constitution sort of forbid that kind of thing?"

"In a courtroom, sure. This is not a court and you're not on trial."

"Beautiful."

She smiled. "Well, maybe not beautiful. Nice. Poor, dear Bruce. Don't you think you could learn to dissemble—just a bit? I do love you so."

Bruce's father responded differently from what Bruce had expected. Bruce was there the following night for dinner, and after the meal he maneuvered his father into his consulting room. His mother readily accepted such exclusion. She disliked the discussion of anything political. Hers was a fragile world that had begun to disintegrate in the first decade of the twentieth century.

Once in Dr. Bacon's office, the door closed behind him, Bruce took out the subpoena and passed it over to his father. Dr. Bacon read it carefully, occasionally glancing up at his son as if to refresh his memory. When he finished, he said, "You'd better tell me about this, Bruce."

It was a long story. He began with Bengal, and then added all the various steps since then. His father listened intently, without interrupting, and then took a cigar from the humidor on his desk. He looked inquiringly at his son.

"I had one last night at Molly's place. That does it for a while."

"This Molly—you intend to marry her?"

"I don't know. We don't talk about marriage."

"Let's go back to the subpoena. I read the papers, so I'm not overly surprised, but they can't be so stupid that they think you're a communist."

"No—or maybe they're just that stupid."

Dr. Bacon studied his cigar for a long moment. "You know, Bruce, a lot of strange things are going on these days. Old friend of mine, Claud Fergeson by name, came down from Cornell for a small operation, resetting a poorly set finger that he broke last year. He teaches physics at the college, and he has a national reputation in the nuclear field. Well, he tells me that they called him down to Washington about a month ago, and he appeared before the Joint Chiefs of Staff, and the question they asked him was what would be the result of one hundred atom bombs exploded simultaneously in a restricted area. Would the explosion ignite the atmosphere and end life on earth? Would it make Europe, for example, uninhabitable? Would the wind carry the fallout to us? Obviously, they were talking about an atomic raid on Russia. He said it made his skin crawl, these automatons in uniform, rigid, mindless faces discussing the pros and cons of ending life on earth. I've been a Republican all my life, and I regard this wretched little man in the White House as one of the less pleasant accidents of history, but Fergy is a Democrat, way-out liberal left, and he's shaking in his boots."

"What did he tell them?"

"He said no one knew, no one could even anticipate what might happen. Then Fergy learned that at least a dozen physicists he knew had been called down to the Joint Chiefs and asked the same question. Strange times. Now let's get back to this subpoena. I'll talk to Frank Britain tomorrow. By all means, he must represent you, and he will. I've operated on him and on his wife, so I have a pound of flesh to obligate him. He'll take care of things. On the other hand— your mother. I'll have to tell her."

"After I leave—please, Dad."

"As you wish. I can sympathize with that. She'll be very distraught. And on that, you never answered my question. Do you intend to marry Molly Maguire?"

"I told you, Dad, it hasn't come up."

"Stop the nonsense, Bruce," he said sharply. "You see one woman month after month, you sleep with her, you cling to her—you have damn well thought about whether or not you want to marry her."

"I've thought about it."

"Well?"

"I'm afraid to ask her."

"You'll get over that. Meanwhile, make a date with your mother to bring her here to dinner."

"What! Oh, no, Dad."

"You're not being very practical, Bruce."

"Dad, she's a communist, a Catholic, shanty Irish background, her mother's a scrubwoman in an office building in Boston, one sister's a hairdresser and the other one is a nun, and both her father and her mother came over here from county Mayo in Ireland, and you want me to bring her here and introduce her to Mom?"

"Are you going to marry her?"

"I hope so, someday."

"Then sooner or later we have to meet her. Don't worry about your mother. She's survived worse. And how come she's a Catholic? I thought communists were atheists."

"I don't know exactly what she is that way. It's complicated. You really want me to bring her here?"

"I do."

Bruce sighed and said, "OK, if that's what you want."

Molly reacted warily to the invitation. "It's the wrong time," she said. "It's walking into a spider web in the best of times, but with the subpoena hanging over you, it's the worst of times."

This was two days later. They were having lunch at Tony Marino's place on Eighth Street, and Bruce was on his way to his appointment with Frank Britain at three o'clock.

"Then we'll put it off," Bruce agreed.

"Why do they want to meet me?"

"I guess they think I intend to marry you."

"Oh? Don't you have to ask me first?"

"Well," Bruce said uneasily, "I mean, that was my father's notion. I told him I haven't asked you."

"Why haven't you? It's over a year since we met."

"Why haven't I?" Bruce considered it. "I figured you'd say no. That would make things very uncomfortable."

"Ask me."

"Just like that?"

"Any way you like."

"All right. Would you?"

"Sure. Now let's talk about this lawyer—"

"Wait a minute! Hold on!" Bruce shouted. Heads turned from all over the restaurant. Molly put her finger to her lips, and Bruce said in a hoarse whisper, "I asked you to marry me."

"I said sure."

He shook his head bewilderedly.

"I said I'd marry you, dear Bruce. You asked me. I said yes, sure. Whenever you want. Now let's talk about Frank Britain. The name is dubious, but since he's a classy lawyer, we won't fault his name. Now these guys charge a bundle. Who's paying the bills?"

Staring at her, studying her as if he had never seen her before, his mouth slightly open, he offered a picture of oafishness. He was trying to think.

"Bruce?"

"Yes," he said. "I'm just trying to put it together. You said you'd marry me whenever I wanted to. Do I have that right?"

"More or less."

"What do you mean, more or less? You're not reneging?"

"I mean not today. You have to see your lawyer today."

"Yes, of course. You asked me something about him."

"I asked you who's paying him? Also, what is he charging you?"

"I don't want to talk about that. I want to talk about marriage."

"Bruce, will you get your head back on? Who's paying for this?"

"I am."

"All right. But before you say a word or he does, ask what it's going to cost you. That's the trouble with you rich kids. You never ask what anything costs."

"Right. We ought to decide which apartment we want to give up."

"Pay your check," Molly said. "I'll see you tonight."

Bruce paid the check, kissed her passionately once they were outside the restaurant, and then strode downtown, barely conscious of where he was going, far more conscious of the fact that Molly Maguire intended to marry him. Well, at least no one could say he had stumbled into this one. They had been together for over a year; they knew each other if not entirely, at least with some depth and understanding, and if there were problems, they would be worked out. That there were problems he could not deny. She was a communist; he was at best a fairly committed liberal who believed strongly in the type of government that existed in the land of his birth; but she was not a fanatical communist. She disagreed with too much that the party was doing to be bound and chained to the movement. She wanted some peace in her life, and from the glowing manner she spoke about her hairdresser sister's children, he felt that she wanted children of her own. She was almost as old as Bruce, and she had mentioned her fear of losing her childbearing years, of allowing them to slip away. She was so much of a woman, full-breasted, wide-hipped, shaped to bear children easily; and just as easily, as Bruce saw her in her parents' land, to do the work of a woman bound to the soil. It would work out. He called to mind the night Pete Seeger sat in her apartment with his banjo, singing, and there was a song about John Brown freeing the slaves at Harpers Ferry, and the refrain said, "America's working folks are all remembering of the day," and after Pete and Ronnie left, he and Molly had talked about the songs, and he said to Molly, "The trouble with your songs is that you lie to yourselves, and then you believe the lies. Your whole program is threaded with those lies—"

Molly was enraged and demanded to know what lies, and he had said to her, "Well, that line about America's working folks remembering the day John Brown was hanged. It's a lie. They don't even know who John Brown was, and they don't give two damns that he was hanged, and all that talk about the working class, and the workers don't give a damn for your Party and they're not lifting a finger to stop what's happening to it, and in Germany the workers supported Hitler, and where are they today, with the red hunters running loose like madmen, and McCarthy sounding off like a demented Mussolini? Has one trade union lifted their voice against the committee or in support of your party? You lie to yourselves as much as the government lies to the people."

He had expected an explosion after that, but nothing of the kind took place. Instead, she remained silent, staring at him, her wonderful pale eyes misting, and then finally said, "It's true, isn't it?"

Well, she would do what she had to do, and she wouldn't demand any meaningless sacrifice on his part. Meanwhile, as these thoughts were going through his head, he had been walking downtown with long, energetic strides. It was a cool, sunny day, the weather of the best of days in New York, and his heart beat in measure to the sounds of the street and the sweetness of the air—a sweetness that blows in on the wind from the bay. He walked down Broadway to where the high building that housed Lennox, Britain, Delloway, and Jones stood within sight of the Battery. It was a high-rise, but distinguished, not like the new glass towers going up uptown, but a big, solid pile of limestone, granite, and white brick. The bronze plate outside that announced the firm's presence contained not only the names of the founders and their children, the present senior partners, but thirty-two associated members of the firm; and inside, they occupied three full floors of offices.

Bruce dwindled as he entered here. He had been around, but this was new to him, a rarefied region paved with gold. A beautiful young woman, seated behind not a desk but a delicate and venerable Adam table, her hair dyed a quiet ash blond, took his name and asked him to be seated in the outer waiting room, and from there another beautiful young woman escorted him to an inner waiting room, where the décor was Queen Anne rather than Adam. Presently, Frank Britain appeared and escorted him to his office, furnished in rather heavy Chippendale and boasting a splendid view of the harbor. Britain himself was a tall, cadaverous man in his sixties, at least six feet and three inches in height, taller than Bruce, who topped six feet, with a long, narrow head and a fine, well-modulated voice. He greeted Bruce with a warm handshake and put him in a mahogany signer's chair that might have come from Convention Hall in Philadelphia. They faced each other across his desk, and Britain smiled pleasantly, a smile that removed him from American Gothic and made him quite human.

"So you're Bill Bacon's boy, and I hear you put your foot in one of Washington's new bear traps."

"I didn't step into it. It reached up and grabbed me."

"Let me see the subpoena," Britain said.

Bruce handed it to him. He studied it thoughtfully for a minute or two, and then he gave it back to Bruce. "I don't think it's anything to worry about. It's part of the lunacy that's been going around since the war. Now, your dad told me something of your predicament, but I'd like to ask you a few questions, if you don't mind."

"Go ahead," Bruce said.

"I'll start with the first question they'll throw at you: Are you or have you ever been a member of the Communist Party?"

"No to both."

"Good. That clears the air. Now, Bruce, you know what they mean when they speak of a communist front? An organization of mostly noncommunists organized or directed by communists or so accused. Belong to any such thing?"

"I'm a card-carrying member of only one organization, the Newspaper Guild. That's it. I carry a library card and a Social Security card."

"Fine," Britain said. "Just fine. Your dad tells me that you have honorable intentions toward a young lady who writes for the *Daily Worker.*"

"We'll be married one day soon."

"And I presume she'll give up her job on the *Worker*?"

"I hope so," Bruce said. "I sure hope so."

"And how do you feel about communists?"

"Not a great deal. I've known some. I think they're good people in pursuit of an impossible and unworkable dream. I'm not a red baiter, I couldn't be."

"All right. Now let me explain something about contempt of Congress in the legal sense. You must forget about the judgmental sense; if that were part of it, I would be in jail tomorrow, since I have the utmost contempt for this committee of Congress. In the legal sense, contempt is basically the refusal of cooperation. Refusal to answer a question most often, and of course perjury. Now, there is a legal shield against the coercion by a committee, and that is to rest upon the Fifth Amendment to the Constitution, which holds that no person can be forced to give evidence against himself. But it carries an implication of guilt, and as far as I can see, it's a tactic you don't need. You have no guilt in any measure, and it would seem to me that in your straightforward position, you are well armed. Answer fully and straightforwardly and you will not be in harm's way. I would guess that this subpoena stems from your public association with Miss Maguire and with your job at the *Tribune.* They dislike both the *Times* and the *Tribune,* and they'd be as pleased as punch to uncover a communist plot at the *Tribune.* But the whole notion is ridiculous. I am a loyal reader of the *Tribune,* and I read every column you wrote during the war years, avidly, since I had two sons in the service, and to my mind, it was fine reporting, perhaps the best of its kind.

"Now, this subpoena of yours calls for an appearance before the committee in executive session, which means closed session. In other words, I cannot be in the room with you. I could be outside in the waiting room, and you could come out to consult me after each question, but I don't regard that as very profitable. It won't surprise you if I tell you that we are a very expensive firm, and if I were to accompany you to Washington, I would have to charge you what would sound like a most unreasonable figure. As far as this present consultation is concerned, there will be no charge at all. You're the son of an old friend."

"I'm not asking for favors," Bruce said. "I'm ready to pay."

"I'm sure you are. But we'll stand on our right not to charge. I won't go with you to Washington because it will not help you. As senior partners, we do accompany corporate clients to Washington, but you are not in a comparable situation. I don't feel that you are being abandoned. I think you will handle it very nicely. We have a little pamphlet which we give to any client facing a congressional committee, and I'll let you have a copy to study. However, if you have apprehension——"

Bruce cut him off. "I don't."

"You feel you can handle it? I want you to be absolutely forthright with me."

"I can handle it. Yes, sir."

"Fine. Your hearing is on the twenty-second of the month. Suppose you stop by here at the same time on the twenty-fourth."

"Yes, sir. Certainly."

"And remember—you have nothing to hide."

"Yes, sir."

"And I'll see you on the twenty-fourth."

He left Britain's office in a totally ambivalent state, unable to decide whether to go along as Britain had suggested or to find another lawyer. But he had no stomach to go shopping for lawyers, and it might very well be that Britain had given him the best advice he could expect. In the street, walking down to Battery Park, breathing the pungent sea air, it was hard to be depressed. After all, his book was just about finished, a bit of rewriting here and there, a little more editing, and there it was. He was going to marry a most beautiful and remarkable woman, he was only a couple of years past thirty, and he was in good health. After the House committee business had been put to bed, he would go back to the *Tribune,* provided they gave him a stateside assignment. Mel Bronson had spoken of an advance of fifty thousand dollars, and together with his wartime nest egg, it would solve his and Molly's problems for another year, even if neither of them could find jobs.

A headline in a newspaper caught his eyes: A YEAR OF FREEDOM. He bought the paper and sat down in Battery Park to read it. It had come at long last, and now it was a year since freedom came to hundreds of millions of people in India who had been a virtual possession of a tiry ruling class of a tiny island thousands of miles away. True, India had been split, and there was a Muslim Pakistan and a Hindu India, but it was freedom, and if there was still hunger, there were no more contrived famines to break the bodies and the souls of the people.

His mind filled with thoughts of Professor Chatterjee and Ashoka Majumdar, Bruce walked uptown in the fading afternoon light. He had a sense of his Bengal experience being an eternity ago. The war had finished. The Nuremberg trials had finished, and a dozen Nazis had been sentenced to death, among them Ribbentrop and Goering, and India was free. He felt a sense of sadness. People live and die for a cause—fifty million had died in this recent war, and for what? For peace? To destroy Hitler? We make vile gods and kill millions to destroy the gods we make. Was Majumdar alive? Had *Prasarah,* that strange single-sheet newspaper, survived? And what would *Prasarah* be in the future?

He stopped at a telephone booth and called Molly. "I want to celebrate," he told her. "I want to celebrate life."

"I can understand that," she agreed. "Where?"

"I'll meet you at the King Cole Bar of the Saint Regis at seven. We'll go on from there."

They went on and on from there, and at midnight or so, they ended up in bed at her apartment, where he whispered to her, "That was true about marrying me?"

"Body and soul. Drop your arms so that I can cross myself."

"You still cross yourself?"

"Only at very important moments of truth—like this."

"Amen, my dear love."

After that day with Britain, Bruce's life quickened its pace. He felt that he had been in a sort of torpor. He was more alive now than he had ever been, as if the subpoena had acted as adrenaline, at least when matched with the fact that Molly would marry him. By the end of the first of the three weeks between receiving the subpoena and his impending date in Washington, he sat up into the small hours of the morning and finished his book, six hundred and twenty manuscript pages, with two maps, which he drew himself and which he hoped would tell the truth about two battles that were being mythologized. He packed it into a cardboard box and bore it in triumph to Mel Bronson at Scandia Press.

"Here it is," Bruce said, putting the heavy package down on Bronson's desk. "Almost three years out of my life."

Bronson touched it tenderly. "In my life, this is sacred. It sounds as pretentious as hell, Bruce, but we are not only money-grubbing businessmen, we are the keepers of a flame that since the beginning of history has sanctified civilization. Nothing else has. How wise those old words 'In the beginning was the Word, and the Word was with God and God was the Word.' "

"That's too much for me to deal with right now, but very nice." He felt much too pleased with himself to tell Bronson that his bit of fantasy was rubbish. They were family now. This man was his publisher, and soon would be sending him a check for fifty thousand dollars.

"Of course, it's not something you read overnight," Bronson said. "Give me a few weeks on this, Bruce."

"Sure. I'm flattered. If you told me you intended to read it overnight, I'd be worried."

"Not only myself," Bronson said. "Anything that our readers report on positively gets three readings, myself and two of the editors. Not that the readers will ever touch this, but still three readings take time."

"Of course."

He told Molly of the delivery and then added, "I use *delivery* advisedly. A whole new experience for me. You know, they say that a woman, after the delivery of a baby, feels empty, depressed. Well, I don't feel depressed, but empty, yes."

"Advice?" Molly asked him.

"Well, yes, absolutely."

"Then hike down and see your old boss tomorrow. Tell him you want your job back. Tell him the book is finished and you'll soon be famous, but you'll do him the honor of coming back on the paper before you get too famous."

"That'll be the day." Bruce laughed.

"All right, tell it your way. Tell him you want your job or you'll break his back. It is waiting for you, isn't it?" she asked, a new note of concern in her voice.

"Maybe. I hope so. But you remember, I was overseas. When I first came back, they offered me everything but the moon, so long as I got out of the country. Maybe they figured that a foreign correspondent can't handle City Hall. Who knows? Maybe now they'll decide I'm a red. The old where-there's-smoke-there's-fire routine. I'm beginning to feel damn smoky."

Nevertheless, he realized that it was good advice, and the next day he went down to the paper and made himself known, as he thought of it. "The book is done," he said.

"Cheers!" The editor took a bottle of Old Overholt out of his desk drawer and poured two shot glasses full. "Cheers," he said again.

"Well," Bruce said, "here I am—for better or worse."

"Leave out the worse. You're a damn sight better than most."

"I need a job," Bruce said.

"If you just finished the book, could be you need a breather."

"What's that supposed to mean?"

"Nothing very serious, Bruce. Just a little time to loosen up."

"Loosening up won't do a damn thing for me. I have to eat and I have to pay my rent and I've been known to need a new pair of shoes. I need a job."

"Bruce, I'm not conning you. It's just not that easy. We're running with a full staff and we're losing money. I can't just say, Here's your job. It doesn't depend on me. I have to take it upstairs."

"In other words," Bruce said, "you're thinking about the subpoena."

"Come on, that's a hell of a note. Don't accuse us of playing ball with that lousy committee. I'm hurt that it should even come up in our conversation. You read the paper. You know what we think of the dirty little men who run it."

"Tell me about it!" Bruce said angrily. "I gave you three years of damn good stuff, and I didn't get it by taking a streetcar down to City Hall. Then I asked for a leave, and you said fine. Now I'm told that the paper's losing money."

"Just take it easy, Bruce. Take it easy."

But he was in no mood to take it easy, and he went from the paper to the Newspaper Guild offices, where he sat down with Mike Levenson, who took care of such things; and Mike said to him: "Just how did you part company, Bruce? Did you get some kind of a letter of agreement that your leave would be so many weeks or months, and that at the end of that period your job would be waiting for you?"

"Who'd think of it? You come back from three years of writing blood and horror, and you've survived—well, you tell yourself that you've paid your dues."

"Bruce, what in hell do we have a union for? You never pay your dues. It's their club, not ours. Do you have anything in writing?"

"No, nothing."

"Oh, beautiful. Just beautiful. Do you know what you did, Bruce? You walked out. You quit your job. Sure they said, Take a leave Bruce. Don't worry about a thing, Bruce. Whenever you want it, the job will be waiting. But what they said doesn't mean a thing. You remember Samuel Goldwyn's line, 'A verbal agreement is not worth the paper it's written on.' That's what it amounts to."

"So you think I'm through at the *Trib?*"

"Maybe, maybe not. All I'm saying is that they have no obligation to give you back the job. Maybe they will. You have a damned good name. The war's not so long ago that it's forgotten. There's the *Times,* the *News,* the *World-Telegram,* the *Sun.*"

"And there's my subpoena."

"The hell with those creeps. You're no communist, and anyone who says so is out of his mind."

Grateful for encouragement if not aid, Bruce sat at his desk in his apartment making a list of newspapers and periodicals where he might find work when he learned that the gates at the *Tribune* were finally closed. He was unwilling to believe what he had thrown at his former boss, that the subpoena was enough for them to bar him. Other places, possibly, but not at the *New York Tribune.* His brooding was interrupted by a call from his father, who said that after he had told Bruce's mother—under severe pressure—that a wife was in the picture, she would have nothing but that Bruce should bring her to dinner.

The silence that followed that announcement provoked him to ask "Did you hear me, Bruce?"

"I heard you. I love my mother, so don't hold anything I say against me."

"What on earth are you talking about?"

"Does she know about the subpoena?" Bruce asked.

"No. She doesn't read the papers, and I see no reason to tell her. Frank Britain assures me that you have nothing to worry about."

"Come on, Dad. Some dear friend will call her and inform her, and she'll want to destroy Molly before she ever lays eyes on her."

"Why do you say that?"

"Because she'll blame Molly. Does she know that Molly works for the *Daily Worker?*"

"Let's cross that bridge when we come to it."

Molly, on the other hand, was equally doubtful. "You know, Bruce, a few years ago I would have said, The hell with your mother and father. They'll take me the way I am, or shove it. I suppose I've changed. I love you, and I don't want it to be all crapped up. Did you hear what I just said? That's the way I talk."

"You're a big girl. You'll talk the way you want to talk."

"And what do I tell your mother? Who was your father? Where is your mother? What schools did you go to?"

"Tell her the truth. Either she lives with it, or she refuses to believe it and tells herself it's not so."

"That's pretty damned cavalier."

"What are the alternatives? Do I marry a woman never to be seen by my mother and father? Or do we dress you up in a suit of lies? I hate lies. This world stinks of lies. Not only do I love you, but you're beautiful and one hell of a remarkable woman."

"All right, damn you. Dress me. What do I wear?"

"Flats, to begin. They're not tall, and I don't want you to tower over them. I think my father's five-ten or so. Mother is five-six, if I remember."

"OK. Hair?"

"Tight in back. Do it in a bun. No lipstick."

"How many times have you seen me with lipstick? Or didn't you notice? Oh, the hell with all this! I have a decent gray flannel skirt and a white silk blouse."

"You brought it up," Bruce said. "I never would have presumed to tell you what to wear."

"Oh, shit!" she exploded. "Sometimes I wonder how I ever got into this. I'm a Mick kid. I have no graces, and I'm not going to learn any to please a couple of American Gothic characters who don't know which side is up."

"You're spoiling for a fight that isn't going to take place. You have more graces than anyone I ever knew, and you just happen to be the most well-read and the most erudite lady I ever encountered. So don't give me any crap about being an ignorant Mick kid. You cling to those memories of yours the way one of those cheap royal clowns we bumped in the war clings to his memories of being a king."

She burst into laughter. "What a hodgepodge of mixed metaphors. No, we won't fight, baby. Anyone who raised you can't be wrong. Tell me, were you ever an Eagle Scout?"

"That's a hell of a thing to throw at me. Half the time around you, I don't know whether I'm being insulted, put down, or praised. OK. I was an Eagle Scout. Make something out of it."

She threw her arms around him and said, "Darling, I love you so much, and I would have been disappointed if you hadn't been an Eagle Scout, and I only laugh at you because you're so delicious and because I never knew anyone like you."

And when Bruce came to pick her up to take her to his parents' home, he might have well said that he had never known anyone like her. She had bought herself a new skirt that fell halfway down her calf in the courtly sweep of the New Look, a bold kelly green that was perfect with her red hair. The hair in the bun was no less startling in color, and her broad hips and straight shoulders gave her a queenly presence.

"Beautiful," Bruce said. "You are something."

"We're also pretty stodgy," Molly admitted. "Back in the early thirties, Party members never bothered about such niceties as marriage or parents. I feel an awful cloak of respectability settling upon me. Also, I think they're going to fire me down at the *Worker*. I have too many fights with them. Today I wrote a story about a young Negro girl. I was told that there were no Negro girls because that was a term of oppression, and I argued that I had been a girl and was still an aging girl, and nobody was oppressing me except this stupid editor at the city desk, and I refused to make the change, and I told him that if he made it, I'd buy a bow and arrow and shoot one into his private parts—"

"No kidding."

"God's truth. I told him he had the mind of a pettifogging Jesuit. I'm not long for that place."

"None of that at Mother's," Bruce said sternly. "She never heard of the *Worker*, and we'll keep it that way."

"What floor are you on?" Molly asked, as they entered the old stone apartment house on Riverside Drive.

"Ninth floor—wonderful view of the river. It's a sort of Columbia University place, at least a dozen professors and a few of the truly rich. It used to be posh, but now the neighborhood's changing."

"It's plenty posh for me."

She was wary as a cat. Standing in front of the apartment door, she whispered that she shouldn't have worn a kelly green skirt. That was crazy. Why had he ever allowed it? He squeezed her hand. A young woman with a Scandinavian accent opened the door for them into the wide entryway, and Bruce's father appeared to greet them. He smiled with pleasure at Molly. Men did that. The maid wore a black dress with a starched white apron. She took their coats and disappeared, and Bruce said, "This is my father, Dr. Bacon. And this is Molly."

She held out her hand to him and he took it in a warm grasp, and said, "I'm glad you could come."

His mother was waiting for them in the living room. She sometimes did that, but more often she came to the door to greet a guest. This was for Molly, and he wondered whether Molly knew. Of course she knew. She had antennae all over her. She missed nothing, finding every detail of the place without any appearance of awe or blatant curiosity, the beamed ceilings, the polished walnut woodwork, the oil paintings, each with its own little light to illuminate it, the somber etchings, the Persian rugs on the floors, the big overstuffed chairs and the antique wood pieces, and, of course, Mrs. Bacon. She was in her sixties, slender, delicate, dressed for the evening in muted, rose-colored crêpe de Chine, as if she had anticipated the kelly green skirt and the flame-red hair.

She held out her hand for Molly, but there was no enthusiasm in the grasp. When Bruce said, "This is Molly Maguire, Mother," she merely nodded and attempted a smile. The wide folds of the green skirt became a flagrant assault of color in an otherwise colorless room. Nothing about Molly Maguire blended with the place. After ten minutes or so of trying to be demure, she returned to herself. Dr. Bacon had mixed martinis. "I'm not one for cocktails," he said, "but occasionally a celebratory drink is called for." Mrs. Bacon refused. Bruce and Molly accepted with pleasure. A limited time was allowed for such nerve-soothing measures, during which time Mrs. Bacon directed at least a dozen covert glances at the kelly green skirt. Once seated at the dinner table, Mrs. Bacon could not resist mentioning the color. She supposed that Molly's background found security in green.

"Well, not security, Mrs. Bacon. I think it goes with my hair. At least, people tell me so. I don't have enough clothes to make real problems, and I saw this skirt in a window in the Village, and I decided that as long as I tempered it with a white blouse, it might be very nice. Don't you think so?"

Oh, wonderful, wonderful, Bruce told himself.

"Of course," Mrs. Bacon said.

When it came to her father, Molly simply said that he had died long ago. And were all the daughters married?

"Oh, I should hope not," Molly said. "My sister Bernadette is a nun. It wouldn't do for her to be married, would it?"

"No, indeed," Mrs. Bacon admitted.

Dr. Bacon tried to move the conversation by mentioning a very curious operation, the restoration of a severed thumb, but Mrs. Bacon cut that off with a reminder that there is no medical talk at the table when guests are present.

"I don't think of Molly as simply a guest."

Worser and worser, Bruce decided, his head beginning to ache with visions of the tea party in *Alice in Wonderland.* Molly sat serenely, having dealt summarily with a thick slice of roast beef, potatoes, and spinach.

"I was so hungry," she said to Mrs. Bacon, "and this food is so delicious."

"Thank you, dear," Mrs. Bacon said graciously. "You mentioned another sister."

"My sister Mary. Oh, yes, she is married. She married Joe Carlino, and they live in Brookline and they have four kids. Still, she goes on with her work."

"Professionally?"

"Yes, of course. She's a hairdresser."

"And your mother is still alive, Miss Maguire?"

Bruce leaped into the breach with "Dad, do you remem-

ber the baseball games we used to go to when I was a kid—
the time we saw Babe Ruth hit two of them over the fence in
the same game? Well, Molly's never been to Yankee Sta-
dium, and I'm taking her there Sunday morning, and we're
due for a double-header and I have no idea whether I could
sit through two games today or whether I'd want to, because it has to be at least fifteen years since I saw a baseball
game—"

"Mrs. Bacon," Molly said sweetly, "my mother is alive
and well in Boston, and of course someday you must meet
her."

"Bless you," Bruce said, once they were outside, "and all
things considered, I do believe it came off better than I had
expected."

"Come on, Bruce, you know what I did. The damn skirt
was a provocation, and then I felt so ashamed of myself,
because they're both such sweet people. I ought to grow up.
It's time, isn't it?"

"You could say that."

"Do you still love me?"

"More or less."

"What the hell does that mean?"

"It means," Bruce said, "that it's mostly more and once
in a while less."

"All right. I can live with that. Now listen, that classy
lawyer may not think you need him down there in Washington, but you need someone. You are not going in there like a
lamb to slaughter. That's a dark, lousy world down there,
and you're not walking into it alone."

"Molly, for God's sake, I'm a big boy. I can deal with it."

"Maybe you can. But I want to be with you."

"They may not let you in."

"I've seen these things. I'll be in the waiting room. But I'll
be there."

"Yes, and if I get hung up, I tell them that Molly

Maguire's outside and I have to question her about something."

"No good, even as a joke. I'm not a lawyer. You can step out only to consult a lawyer."

"Will the paper give you the time?"

"Either that or I'll take it."

The
Star Chamber

The train from New York to Washington marked the first trip they had ever taken together, and in spite of the fact that his destination was nothing to glow about, Bruce felt excited and pleased. Most of the time in the train they spent in the dining car. They split a bottle of excellent wine, and the food was not half bad.

"Can we call it a honeymoon—premarriage?" Bruce wondered.

"Why not?"

"Oh, I thought of something esoteric, maybe India. I'd like to see what a free India is like. Different. Take you up to the hill country, Kashmir, or to see the Taj. There are so damn many things we have to do together."

"All in good time."

"Kids?"

"Oh, you bet your sweet life," Molly said. "At least three before my birth clock runs out."

"And speaking of first things first, we have to get up to Boston and meet your mother and sisters Mary and Bernadette."

"True, not to mention getting married."

"My mother's not entirely into that yet. We'll work it slowly."

He greeted Washington dubiously, hesitantly, yet with enormous curiosity. "Do you know," he said to Molly, "this is my first time as an adult?"

"No. It's just a hoot and a holler from New York."

"A war comes. Four years of college, two years of graduate school, and then more than three years of war. It changes the normal progression of a life. Last time I was here was with my father, age fourteen. I don't remember too much, just an endless parade of white buildings, sort of like a great cemetery."

They put up at the Mayflower Hotel. He had registered as Mr. and Mrs. Bacon. He had suddenly become very conscious of violating the law, but neither he nor Molly could think of anything that covered this. "Anyway," she said, sprawled on the bed and watching him unpack his wardrobe of clean shirt, tie, and underwear and socks, "in the eyes of God, we've been married a good long time."

"You do work God," he said.

"Why not? I'm a Catholic. My sister's a nun. I'm as properly set with God as anyone."

"You're also a communist and you belong to what purports to be an atheist organization. And didn't Marx say that religion is the opiate of the people?"

"Maybe so. I don't push it too hard."

"Every time I think I understand you," Bruce said, "I come to a new angle that makes no sense whatsoever."

"That's as it should be."

"Anyway, first time in a hotel. Can you believe it, I never thought going to bed with you was anything but an act of worship—"

"What? Are you nutty?"

"Absolutely. Tonight, it's pure sin."

They had both worked themselves into a state of light pretense that did away with any thought of the committee, putting it neatly aside and downgrading it to the condition of a nasty nuisance and no more than that. On the way to the House Office Building, where the hearing was to take place, the pretense that this was a vacation or a picnic disappeared. Molly began to go over procedure again, reminding him that the trap was always in the question. He must not refuse to answer anything. He had all the time in the world, and they must not be permitted to hurry him or rattle him.

"I don't get rattled too easily."

"All right. You're brave and decent, which means nothing in this den of thieves. You were telling me about a minefield you once walked through?"

"Yes."

"And the procedure?"

"Yes."

"Same thing here."

The anteroom to the hearing room was a rather dismal place, two rows of chairs lined up against facing walls, with the door to the hearing room on the right as one entered. There were Venetian blinds on the windows at one end of the room, but no drapes, and the walls were painted what Bruce always thought of as government green, a dismal olive color. The chairs were the heavy oak institutional furniture that existed wherever the government paid the rent. A guard showed them into the waiting room, informing them that the quorum was already present. They were to wait.

There was no one else in the room. "Evidently, today is ours," Bruce said. "Unless it's like a doctor's waiting room and fills up gradually."

"Offer nothing," Molly said. "Remember. Just answer questions. No hostility. You're an A-One American gentleman, which is why I love you."

"Bullshit," he whispered. The door to the hearing room was opening, and a tall, skinny, dour man came into the waiting room and introduced himself: "Gerald Crown. I'm counsel for the committee. You're Bruce Bacon?"

Bruce stood up and nodded.

"And this lady is your attorney," pointing to Molly.

"No, just a friend."

"You have no attorney? Or is he to show? Is he late?"

"No attorney. I understand that even with an attorney, he's barred from the room?"

"You can always step outside to consult. I'm afraid not with this lady. Was there difficulty in obtaining counsel?"

"No. I have nothing to hide from the committee. Why would I need a lawyer?"

Crown shrugged, turned to the door of the committee room, and bowed slightly. "We can start now, Mr. Bacon. If you would?"

Bruce entered the hearing room with much the same feeling with which Scrooge, in *The Christmas Carol,* had greeted the ghost of Christmas Past, as the result of something indigestible that he had eaten the day before. It was there and it existed and it was totally unreal, the oval table, the men seated around it, the American flag drooping in one corner, as if to apologize for its presence in such company, the large photo-portrait of Franklin Delano Roosevelt on one wall, the even larger photo-portrait of Abraham Lincoln on the other wall, and the quiet, hunched-over stenotypist in the corner, his face impassively humble.

Five men sat around the oval table. Bruce recognized the faces of four of them. There was John S. Wood, co-chairman with Rankin, pudgy, comfortable middle America, taken from drugstore or haberdashery to confront strange creatures, and then Rankin, a face like an old hound dog, drooping folds of flesh, yellowed teeth, and a look of suspicious dislike. Richard Nixon, as improbable in appearance as Rankin, was a sort of balance. He was young, a terrier ready to leap and snap, his ski-jump nose and very dark shaven beard giving him the appearance of a cartoon character, made even more unreal by his cheeks, which puffed out as if each contained a Ping-Pong ball. He had accusatory beady little eyes, and Bruce could picture him standing before a mirror, trying to look stern and eliminate the youthful jack rabbit visage. There was another member Bruce could not place, and, finally, J. Parnell Thomas, a fat piggish face, tiny eyes encased in fat, thick neck, and fat body. Only he greeted Bruce with a silly grin, as if to play good cop to the others' bad cop.

Crown offered Bruce a seat at the head of the table, and asked him whether he had any objections to taking the oath.

"None." He put his hand on the Bible and took the oath.

Crown walked away from him, took a small sheaf of notes from the table, and then faced Bruce, still standing, leaning against the wall and about halfway across the room, and said, "Would you state your full name and your address?"

"Bruce Bacon, and I live at One twenty-six East Seventy-sixth Street, in New York."

"Is that your name?" Parnell Thomas asked sharply. "You are under oath, sir. I don't think that's your name."

Nonplussed, Bruce groped for air. "Yes, sir. I don't know what you can be thinking. My name is Bruce Bacon."

"I think Mr. Thomas is asking for your full name."

"Oh, I see. I have a middle name. My name is actually Bruce Nathaniel Bacon. I haven't used my middle name for years. You all know who Nathaniel Bacon was, of course, and we have pretensions toward the same family. Of course, it's so hard to tell, since he did his thing three hundred years ago." He knew that they didn't have the slightest notion who Nathaniel Bacon was and that they would be ashamed to ask.

Gerald Crown was playing a neutral role. That point had been made in the pamphlet Britain had given him. If, among the legislators, there were pros and cons, the counsel strove for a balance. But there were no pros here, only cons.

Crown said, "Thank you, sir. Now I will ask you: Are you now or have you ever been a member of the Communist Party of the United States?"

"Not ever and not now."

"Very well. Have you ever been a member of a communist front organization?"

"You'll have to be more specific," Bruce said. "I'm really

not certain of what a communist front organization is. This is not a refusal to answer your question. I simply wish to be enlightened as to its breadth."

"Very well," Crown said, still wearing his amiable mask. "I'll give you an example. You spoke to a group called the Broadway Forum, at the Murray Hill Hotel. The Broadway Forum is on the Attorney General's list of communist front organizations."

"I see." Bruce nodded, unwilling to probe deeper into what was or was not a communist front organization. "I don't belong to the Broadway Forum, if indeed it has a membership. I was invited to speak to a group of journalists, and I did."

"You haven't answered my question. Do you belong to or have you supported any other communist front organizations?"

"I think not," Bruce replied. "Unless the Newspaper Guild is on the Attorney General's list. I am a member of the Guild."

"Are you indicating that the Newspaper Guild is a communist front organization?"

"Oh, absolutely not."

"Then you know it is not a communist front organization?"

"Well, yes—" Bruce paused, hesitated. Where was he headed? He was just beginning to recognize the pattern Crown was following in his questioning. It was not a simple case of answering or refusing to answer. He had not read the Attorney General's list. Suppose the Attorney General had listed the Newspaper Guild as a communist front organization. Now if he denied that it was a front organization, he was on a hook.

"As far as I know," Bruce said.

"Oh?"

"I mean, as far as I know, the Newspaper Guild is simply

a trade union. I belong to it as a member of a trade union. That's as far as my knowledge goes."

"I see. And you are associated with no other communist front organization?"

"No."

"Very well. We'll return to that." He turned to John Rankin. "Sir?"

"I was told, sir," Rankin said, "that when the Newspaper Guild was organized, certain communists played a major role in that process of organization. Can you tell us anything about that, son?" Rankin was from Mississippi, and his Southern accent was thick, his words slow. Bruce had the feeling that the accent was part of the persona Rankin assumed at hearings such as this.

"No, sir. If that was the case, I know nothing about it."

"We had testimony here to that effect. How come you know nothing about it?"

"I was overseas during the war years, and as far as the Guild is concerned, I appreciate its role as a trade union, but I don't take part in any of its internal affairs. I should as a decent union man. I just haven't."

Crown took up the questioning here: "Mr. Bacon, I am going to read a list of names. I want you to tell me which of these names you recognize." He took a sheet of paper from the table. "I will ask for a comment with each name. We begin with Gautam Sharma. Do you know this man?"

"No."

"Did you—well, allow me to put it this way. Were you ever at a meeting or a party where he was present?"

"Not so far as I know," Bruce replied. "I presume these names relate to Bengal?"

"India," Chairman Wood corrected. "India, sir."

"Yes, sir," Crown said. "Bengal is part of India."

"Then let's stick to the whole, not the part."

"Yes, sir," Crown agreed. "Now, Mr. Bacon, I ask you about Chandra Chatterjee. Do you recognize the name?"

"Yes, if you mean the same Chatterjee who is a professor at the University of Calcutta. Chatterjee is a common name in Bengal."

"I presume it's the same man. I've given you both his first and last name. Is he a member of the Communist Party of India?"

Bruce hesitated, telling himself at the same time that even hesitation is an answer of sorts. But how sure was he about Chatterjee? "I don't know," he said.

Staring at a loose-leaf book, one such being in front of each of the five men around the table, and without looking up, Nixon snapped, "You spent an evening with him and you don't know whether he was a communist?"

"But Mr. Nixon," Bruce said gently, "if you were a secret communist, I might spend an evening or even a weekend with you and never know it."

"We'll have that stricken from the record," Nixon said angrily, and, pointing a finger at Bruce, "That kind of smart-ass response will only get your ass in a sling!" And then to the stenotypist, "We'll keep that off the record as well."

Crown smoothed the waters. He had not yet made a reliable assessment of Bruce Bacon; and the big, shambling writer, taller than anyone else in the room, but slightly stooped now as he stared at the men in the committee, squinting a bit behind his heavy horn-rimmed glasses, defied proper analysis. He could be an innocent, a boob, a smart red, or someone with his own game to play. The latter designation appealed to Crown. He continued, "Romila Thapar." He spelled it out for the stenotypist. "Do you know this man?"

"No, sir."

"You have never met him? You have never been in company where he was present?"

"No, sir. Not as far as I know."

"Krishna Sinha?"

"No, sir. I don't know him, I never met him. I have never been in company where he was present."

"You don't have to anticipate my questions, Mr. Bacon."

"I'm sorry. I thought we might get on with it."

"We will get on with it, Mr. Bacon."

Bruce spread his hands and smiled slightly.

"Ashoka Majumdar," Crown said. "Is that name familiar to you?"

"Yes."

"Did you meet this man in Calcutta in nineteen forty-five?"

"Yes."

"Is he a communist?"

"Is he?" Bruce asked. "You use the present tense. Does that mean that he's still alive?"

"Do you have reason to think otherwise? Do you maintain connections with Calcutta?"

Here, he had done it again, given Crown a lead down a path that didn't exist. "No, I have no connection with Calcutta."

"Or with the Communist Party of India?"

"No. Absolutely not."

Parnell Thomas's fat round face broke into a smile as he looked up from his loose-leaf notebook and said, "I been under the impression that all you Communist Parties are linked together. So how come you profess no knowledge at all about what goes on there in India?"

"I'm not a communist, Mr. Thomas."

"Check." He was still grinning pleasantly.

"Let's return to Ashoka Majumdar. What was your interest in him?"

"I was after information about a story I was working on."

"I ask you again: Was Ashoka Majumdar a communist?"

"I suppose so. He made no secret of it, and he worked for a communist newspaper."

"What was the name of that newspaper?"

"Prasarah—if I remember correctly."

"Would you spell it, please?" the stenotypist said.

Bruce spelled it.

Rankin said, "Does this here communist paper have some connection with the *New York Daily Worker*?"

"I can't imagine that it does, but there's no way in the world for me to know for sure."

Crown said, "I take it from your answer that you also don't know that it doesn't."

Bruce thought about that and nodded, telling himself, Careful, Bruce, careful. You have taken them for a bunch of malignant idiots, but when it comes to what they do they are damned sneaky and cunning.

"Mr. Bacon," Crown said, "have you ever given an interview to the newspaper called *Prasarah*? Do I pronounce it correctly?"

"Yes, I'm sure you do. In answer to your question, no, I never gave them an interview. Overseas, I was a working correspondent. I looked for interviews, but why on earth would anyone try to interview me?"

"Why indeed? Here is a translation, provided to us by British Intelligence, of an early June nineteen forty-five edition of *Prasarah*. Let me quote from it: 'The question I put to Mr. Bruce Bacon, a renowned American correspondent, is this: Do you believe that the famine was contrived in a conspiracy between the British and the rice dealers? His answer was that he suspects this to be the case, and hopes that he will find evidence to support his conjecture.' Wouldn't you call that an interview, Mr. Bacon?"

"I could have said that. Yes. But simply as an answer to a question, not as any part of an interview."

"Son," Rankin put in, "am I hearing that in the midst of a struggle to preserve the world from such as Adolf Hitler and Joseph Stalin, you were ready to accuse our allies, the British, of aiding and abetting in the deaths of millions of people? Is that what I am hearing, son?"

"The war with Germany was over," Bruce said angrily, "and so far as I know, we were not at war with Russia. They were our allies."

"We are always at war with Russia," Rankin said.

"The war with Japan was still on," Nixon put in. "The British were our allies."

Bruce was silent, thinking that, once again, he had taken their bait. But how to avoid it? He had spent hours with Majumdar. They had spoken of many things, and it was no breach of faith on Majumdar's part to quote him so long as he quoted him correctly. And he had. Nevertheless, Bruce felt himself being entangled in a spider's web of intrigue. Why would a committee of the House of Representatives have information from British Intelligence? So far, he had published nothing on the situation in Calcutta. What was happening, and where did he stand?

Crown was studying his notes. "Milton Greenberg," he said. "Does that name mean anything to you?"

"Yes, I know Mr. Greenberg. He works for the *New York Daily News.*"

"No longer, you'll be pleased to know. He refused to sign a loyalty oath and he was discharged. How do you know Mr. Greenberg?"

"I met him in India and subsequently in New York."

"Did he ask you to appear before the Broadway Forum?"

"Yes."

"Is he a member of the Communist Party?"

"I have no idea," Bruce said.

"I'd like you to confine your answer to a simple yes or no."

"That makes no sense," Bruce said. "How can I say yes or no when I don't know?"

"Then you refuse to either affirm it or deny it?"

"What the hell are you up to?" Bruce exploded. "You know damned well that I can't give you a yes or a no answer!"

"Very well. We'll continue. Harold Legerman. When you spent time with him in Calcutta, he was a sergeant in the United States Army. Is that so?"

"Yes."

"Is Harold Legerman a member of the Communist Party?"

"I don't know."

"Once again," Crown said very deliberately, "I am seeking a yes or no answer."

The anger had gone. You can't be sensible if you're angry, Bruce told himself. Quietly, quietly. "You know, Mr. Crown, that a yes or no answer is impossible and that I will not give you a yes or no answer."

"Speak up," Congressman Wood said. "I don't hear you. Please speak up. Did you say that this here Legerman is a communist?" His accent was even broader than Rankin's.

"No, sir."

"Then you're saying he is not a communist?"

"No, sir. I told Mr. Crown here that I did not know whether Mr. Legerman was or was not a communist."

"Well, don't think you have us there, sonny. Just don't think so at all."

"Molly Maguire," Crown said.

Finally, at long last, Molly Maguire. Did they know that she was sitting outside in the waiting room? Probably not, and without a subpoena they could not even ask her the time of day. What had she said? They were afraid to subpoena any member of the press, whether from the *Daily Worker* or the *New York Times*. It made sense.

"Do you know her?"

"Yes, I do."

"Do you know that she is an employee of the *Daily Worker*?"

A long moment went by, while Bruce worked desperately to put his thoughts, his life, and his principles together. The moment stretched out. He went back to when he was a kid in the best of all possible worlds. He was a funny kind of kid, without anger or hostility. He was sent to camp, and he won the award for all-around camper. He never had to work very hard at being a good athlete. The body had been given to him, and he took care of it, even though, apart from summer camp, he had no particular interest in athletics. He read everything he could lay hands on. He became the editor of his college paper, and the forces railed at him because he refused to be judgmental. He could see both sides of a question all too easily. He believed in motherhood, God, true love, and country, and when they played "America the Beautiful," he felt prickles on his scalp. Even when an old reporter on the *Tribune* said to him, "Bacon, you are the epitome of what Mencken calls *Boobus Americanus,* but how you combine it with a degree of intelligence, I don't know," it did not shake him. It took a war to strip him of almost every illusion, but somehow he maintained his view of his country, even though it was tarnished somewhat. Coming home from the horrors of a Europe destroyed by war and an Asia ridden with poverty and misery, he had embraced the cleanliness, the orderliness, the beauty and comfort of America.

"Mr. Bacon!" Crown said sharply.

"Yes—I'm sorry. I was thinking."

"Concerning one Molly Maguire, I asked you whether you know that she's an employee of the *Daily Worker*?"

"You know that as well as I do, and your question is pointless. Now I have something to say to you. Since I am here as a witness before a congressional committee, I will answer any—"

Nixon cut him off. "Will you please answer the question!"

"I will answer any question about myself. I will not answer any question about Molly Maguire. I have broken no law. Neither has she, and under the law and usage of this land, I am not required indeed to answer any of your questions. If I do, I degrade myself."

"Is Molly Maguire a member of the Communist Party?" Crown asked.

"I have watched and written about a world conflict to rid this earth of Adolf Hitler and Nazism. I find your tactics no different from his—"

They were all shouting at him at once now.

"Damn you filthy bastards!" he shouted at the top of his lungs. "Listen to me! You disgrace the Congress of the United States!"

"Call the marshal! Call the marshal!" Nixon was yelling. "Call the marshal!"

"You foul this nation! You sicken me!"

Someone must have pressed a button, for the marshal entered now and took Bruce, who was on his feet, looming over the table, by the arm and said, firmly, "Come along, young feller. If you resist, it spells a lot of trouble."

The energy and anger collapsed, and Bruce allowed himself to be led out of the hearing room, meek as a lamb now. In the waiting room, the guard said to Molly, "He's yours?"

Molly nodded.

"Then take him along and buy him a cup of coffee." He waited until they had left the waiting room and then watched them as they went down the corridor to the elevator. Molly said nothing. Bruce said nothing. They reached the street, and then Bruce said, "All right, I'll—"

She touched his lips. "No. We need a couple of double martinis, and we'll find that in the hotel bar. Until then, well, the door was by no means soundproof. When you shouted, 'Damn you filthy bastards,' they heard you all over the building."

"You heard it?"

"And much more."

"Oh, Lord. Why don't you dump me and run?"

"Oh, no." She gave him a peck on the cheek. "You're lovely. It's not your fault that God gave you a pincushion instead of a brain."

It was one o'clock, and the bar at the hotel had just opened. Bruce wondered whether they shouldn't have lunch first.

"Oh, no. Gin now, lunch later," Molly said. "My world is very shaky."

"If you say so," he agreed meekly.

"Come on, love," Molly said. "I can't have you groveling every time you do what any decent red-blooded white Protestant American boy would do." The drinks came. "Mud in your eye," Molly said. "Now tell me all about it. The shouting I heard. What came before it?"

"You don't want me to tell you first how I flubbed it?"

"We'll save that. Start at the beginning."

"Yes. Well, that's the strange part of it. First, you know, the stuff you hear all over the place, which is a sort of a cliché at this point. Were you ever and are you now a member? Then, out of left field, we're back in India, and they begin to throw Indian names at me."

"Names you knew?"

"Two of them, yes. You remember I told you about Professor Chatterjee and Ashoka Majumdar? Those were two of the names. I said yes, I knew them. The other names were strange to me. Then, again out of left field, they bring in British Intelligence."

"Hold on. What do you mean, they bring in British Intelligence? How do they bring in British Intelligence?"

"I'll explain."

"You mean they had someone in there from British Intelligence? If they did, it invalidates everything." This with great excitement.

"Will you slow down? I'll explain. Do you remember my telling you about the communist newspaper Majumdar worked for?"

"Of course I do. It filled me with guilt. I would fall asleep at night asking myself what I was doing here where nobody really needed me when I should be out there doing what your Majumdar does."

"Well, evidently Majumdar printed a few sentences from our discussions in the paper. Something to the effect of did I believe that the British helped organize the famine? I said that I suspected it was so but that I had no evidence. Now this character, Crown, he's counsel for the committee, has the translation and reads it to me, and then Rankin and Nixon get into the act, scolding me for thinking bad thoughts about our British cousins, and then they drop it."

"Just like that?"

"Just like that."

"And up until now," Molly said, "you've been a proper, upstanding young man. How did you manage to louse it all up and start calling them names?"

"It just turned into shit, if you'll forgive the expression. You know, Molly, just living your life normally, if there is such a thing, you dissemble constantly. You're polite to people you detest, you lie a hundred times a day—no, I'm not tired, when you can't keep your eyes open; he's great, when he's really a louse; very interesting, when the thing is pure garbage—and you live with it so easily you forget you're doing it. So there I am, going along with this idiot committee, trying not to think how utterly ridiculous and profane this whole procedure is, and your name comes up. So I told them to forget it. I said I'll answer any questions about myself, but I will not become an informer on Molly Maguire."

"Beautiful," Molly said softly. "You beautiful dumb bastard. I want to cry. I think I'm going to cry. Give me a handkerchief or something."

He gave her his handkerchief. He had never seen her cry before.

Through her tears, she mumbled, "And you're not even Irish. You have to be Irish to do anything as stupid as that.

You're very noble and you're going to jail. What in hell did you think you were accomplishing?"

"I wasn't trying to accomplish anything. For God's sake, Molly, give me a break."

She dried her eyes and pushed her drink away.

"You're really mad."

"Mad? No, I'm not mad. I'm just trying to figure out how I got mixed up with a Boy Scout. Why in hell couldn't you do what we planned? They know all there is to know about both of us. They know I'm a communist."

"Since when does knowledge take the curse off an informer? Must I be an informer to exist in this cockeyed, lunatic world?"

"Ah, Jesus," Molly said, "it's almost two, and checkout time is three. Let's go upstairs and make love and forget that those bastards and their lousy committee even exist."

"I'm with you."

"When I was a kid," Molly said, "I read *Pilgrim's Progress.*"

"I know," Bruce said.

"Pay the check, and then let's get upstairs and make one good thing happen to us in this stinking city."

As
Such Things Go

About ten days after Bruce returned from Washington, Dave Buttonfield, the managing editor of the *Tribune,* telephoned and asked him to stop by at his office. Six months earlier, Bruce would have presumed that Buttonfield had decided to rehire him, but by now, Bruce realized that the world he lived in at the moment did not function that way, and in this, he was right. Buttonfield handed Bruce a sheet of paper and informed him that it had just come over the AP wire. The AP dispatch said that the House of Representatives had just voted to cite Bruce Nathaniel Bacon for contempt. It went on to say that the House Committee on Un-American Activities had reason to believe that Mr. Bacon was linked to the international communist conspiracy, and that during the war he had cooperated with the Communist Party of Bengal.

"We thought," Buttonfield said, "that before we printed this, we ought to hear your side of the story and give you a chance to state your own case. Is there any truth in it?"

"Are you asking me that with a straight face?"

"Yes."

"Then the answer is no. No truth in it. I'm not a communist. If there's an international communist conspiracy, I don't know one damned thing about it, and during the war, I was a correspondent of this paper. That's it."

"Do you want to give us a sidebar? We'll print it."

"Thanks. That's very decent of you."

"Bruce," Buttonfield said, "we've had your application for reinstatement under consideration—I might say favorable consideration. This sets us back."

"I was sure it would."

"I can understand your bitterness. These are strange times."

"You can say that again."

Buttonfield led Bruce to the city room, where a young reporter named Calahan interviewed him for the sidebar. In his mind's eye, he read the proposed piece with embarrassment: Mr. Bacon denies that he has ever been a member of the Communist Party, and so forth and so on. Guilt was underlined by the denial. He finished the interview and left the building, resisted an impulse to have a drink with the injunction to himself that he was not going to lay whatever had happened or was going to happen on a bar for solace. To hell with that. He was not a singular, misunderstood martyr; he was a part of something dark and ugly that was happening in America, and a great many other people were also a part of it.

The telephone was ringing when he entered his apartment, and when he picked it up, Molly's voice asked where he had been and did he know? Her voice was so full of concern that he could almost feel her reaching out to comfort him.

"I'm all right. Yes, I heard."

"I wrote the story for the paper. At least one place will print the truth about what happened."

"I'll see you at dinner," Bruce said.

"Do you know," he said to Molly when he saw her later, "this afternoon, I just sat in my apartment and looked at the wall and did absolutely nothing. I didn't read. I didn't turn on the TV. I just looked at the wall. Jesus God, Molly, they're reducing me."

"No—those bastards can't reduce you. They're not fit to wipe your shoes."

"Unfortunately, they're not in that line of work. But look at it. No newspaper will hire me. What do I do? I've written a book, a very large book, and that's the hardest thing I ever did in my life, and I gave it to Bronson over three weeks ago, and I haven't heard word one, and I haven't got the guts to call him."

"Bruce, don't worry. That's a massive tome you wrote, and it takes time. No publisher accepts a book on one reading. But you've written a wonderful book, a beautiful book —I think the best book on this war that I've read. But let's talk about what has happened."

There was a great deal to talk about in terms of what had happened. What would be the next step? Would they indict him and put him on trial? And what was the punishment if he went on trial and was found guilty?

"The contempt of Congress is only a misdemeanor, and they can't give you more than a year in prison for that. On the other hand, if they decide to go after you for perjury— no, we shouldn't be talking about that. You have to have a lawyer."

"Trouble is, I can't afford a lawyer."

"Of course you can. What you can't afford is Frank Britain."

The next day, Frank Britain called and told Bruce that a serious talk was required and as soon as possible. His father had already conveyed word that his mother was deeply worried. Thus he had both his parents and Frank Britain on the same day. Britain was the easier of the two.

"I have the transcript of your hearing," he told Bruce, handing him a printed leaflet, "an extra one for you. I wish I had gone with you."

"I don't think it would have made much difference," Bruce said. "I wouldn't have stepped out of the room until they threw me out."

"Perhaps. Now, Bruce, as you know, I am a Republican and a conservative. I don't understand what's going on today, and I don't think I approve of it. You have given me your word that these allegations are untrue, and I accept it. But it would appear to me that the manner in which these members of the committee are proceeding indicates that they intend to indict you. I think you have very good grounds for defense—primarily in the field of the lawful work of a congressional committee. Such committees are constituted to gather information that will help in the writing of new legislation. They have broad powers, but for a defined purpose. However, these are strange times. You realize that?"

"I do indeed."

"And you must realize that we are corporate attorneys. We don't deal with criminal law, and I'm afraid we lack the facilities to do so."

Bruce smiled. "And yet you had enough congressional committee business to print a pamphlet?"

"These are hearings, Bruce, not trials. As a favor to your father, I have given you legal advice, for which the firm is not charging you."

"For which I am grateful."

"And you must understand that our services are very expensive. There are very few if any legal firms in this city who charge more for their services than we do."

"I have been told," Bruce said deliberately, "that if I have distinguished counsel, I am a foot ahead in this thing. Your firm is probably the only opportunity I have to enlist distinguished counsel. You indicated during our previous conversation that you would be willing to take on the case—or so I understood."

"I think you understand incorrectly," Britain said, offering his own smile this time.

"If it's a question of money, I can borrow the money from my father."

"It's not simply a question of money, Bruce."

"Then why don't you come out and say that, having read

this transcript and knowing what I am accused of, you no longer can see your way toward representing me, that there's dirt in the water now and you don't want to put your hands in it?"

"If you are trying to say that we will not represent a person accused of communism, I must reject your statement. On the other hand, Bruce, we have only your witness that these assertions have no truth to them."

Bruce rose and said, "I don't want to press this point. You have been very kind. Thank you." With which he turned and walked out.

The evening with his mother and father was more painful, since he arrived at his parents' apartment while his father was still in surgery at the hospital. He had been asked to come at seven for dinner at eight, but when he got to the door of the apartment, he found that it had been left open a crack so that he would not have to ring, and inside he was greeted by the maid, who told him in a whisper, "Mrs. Bacon is lying down with a sick headache. She said to call her when you come, but since Dr. Bacon is held up at the hospital, I thought I might let her rest a while longer."

"Very good thinking," Bruce said. "Suppose we let her rest another half hour or so."

In the living room, Bruce found the *Tribune* with the story of his citation for contempt. He blessed makeup for putting it on page six, with a straightforward headline that did not name him: TRIBUNE REPORTER CITED FOR CONTEMPT. His sidebar was almost as large. But if his mother had not seen this, why was she in her room with a sick headache?

He learned later that Calahan, the young man who had interviewed him for the sidebar, had called and spoken to his mother; but for the moment the important thing was that she knew and Bruce had to face her. He rose as she came into the living room a few minutes after he had arrived, and she took him to her bosom. "My poor, poor darling."

"Mother, sit down, please," leading her to the couch.

"No, I can't sit on the couch," she said forlornly. "At my age, Bruce dear, one wants a hard chair."

He took that as a good sign. True grief would not be so selective where chairs were concerned. She was worried, but not too worried, and she must have discussed it at some length with his father. The maid came in with a folded napkin, which Elizabeth Bacon pressed to her forehead for a moment or two and then put on an ashtray.

"What will happen, Bruce? What awful thing will happen now?"

"Nothing terribly awful, Mother."

"You treat everything that way. You wrote all those cute little letters during the war, as if I didn't know what dreadful things went on over there in Europe. Can't you take anything seriously?"

"It's not that serious, Mother."

"Bruce, don't you understand?" The tone reached back twenty years. "They're saying you're a communist. That's such a dreadful thing to say about anyone, and they're saying it about you."

"Mother, I'm no more a communist than you are. You know that. And all the worrying you did during the war was to no end, and here you are worrying again. It's not good for you. You know that."

"You keep saying I know this and that. I don't, Bruce. Will they send you to prison?"

"I don't see why. I haven't done anything criminal."

"Bruce," she said, turning her glance away from him, "I know this will upset you, but I must ask you. That girl you brought here, the one with the red hair that you're so fond of—"

"You mean Molly Maguire, Mother."

"Yes, the Irish girl. I never asked you what she did, I was

so sure you'd get over that infatuation. But I have a feeling she's involved in this?"

"No, Mother."

"Are you still seeing her?"

"Yes. She's a fine person. When you know her a little, you'll realize that."

"Doesn't she work for a radical newspaper of some kind?"

"Yes." He smiled and went to his mother and kissed her. Prejudices that in another person might have made him furious were meaningless where his mother was concerned, even when she said dolefully that they had never had a Catholic in the family before. "And I know you want to marry her," she added. "You do want to, don't you?"

"At times, Mother."

"I knew it."

Dr. Bacon came in at that point, and all through dinner he and Bruce steered the conversation away from his session with the Un-American Committee. But after dinner, in his father's consulting room, lighting the cigar he smoked when offered to him, he agreed that there was a possible jail sentence in sight.

"What are your chances?"

"I don't know," Bruce said. "It's very strange, a sort of Alice in Wonderland thing. They seem to be spreading their net for anything they can catch."

"And Britain, that bastard—he threw you out."

"How do you know?"

"I hear things," the doctor said, watching the smoke of his cigar. "Fifty million people died in the worst war in history, and our own inheritance is prosperity, intolerance, and corruption. I operated with Dr. Goldstein today, and when we were washing up, he offered me this sad little joke. Nineteen fifty, and Cohen meets Levy in Berlin. What happened to Stein? Cohen asks Levy, and Levy says, He never got out of America. Horrible little joke, but it says something."

"I'm afraid it does," Bruce agreed.

"As for Britain, well, there are other lawyers. We're not rich, Bruce, but we're not poor, and the money is there when you need it."

"I know. But I think this business of distinguished counsel is out. I don't want it. I'll find a competent lawyer who fits into my budget."

"Just remember that I'm here. I spoke to Berman, the hospital manager. He's a lawyer and smart, and he says he can't see how they can convict you. To him, it's an open-and-shut case."

But it was nothing of the kind to the lawyer Molly brought him to. Sylvia Kline had graduated from law school with honors two years before, and since then had been a public defender in New York. A month earlier, she had opened her own office at Eighteenth Street and Sixth Avenue and became licensed to practice in Washington, as well. Molly had gotten to know her during her time as a public defender. "She's smart and decent and on the side of the angels," Molly told Bruce. "She's not a communist, which is all to the good, and from what you tell me of your Comrade Britain, she's got it over him in spades."

Sylvia Kline's place was small, a tiny waiting room, a receptionist-stenographer-secretary behind a desk, a room with books and a table, and a very small office. She was a thin, birdlike woman with a delicious smile, a tousled head of brown hair, bright blue eyes, and apparently bursting with energy.

"I am so proud to be able to help you—if you want me to," she said to Bruce. "I lived through the war with you— with you and Ernie Pyle; but you did more. You made me hate it more. Now, we'll talk about price first, before we talk about your case. Price is put away in a drawer by high-class lawyers, but I am not a high-class lawyer. Now, even if they

don't move for an indictment—and I pray they don't—we'll
need some hours of discussion and consultation, because we
must be prepared, and for this my charge will be three hundred dollars. If we go to trial, the trial will be held in Washington, since that's the Federal district where the misdemeanor took place, and I must stress that we will, if
possible, refer to this as a misdemeanor and not as a crime.
It is being used viciously and with malice, but it still remains
on the level of a speeding ticket or smoking in the subway.
However, the punishment can amount to a year in prison,
and that is not to be dismissed lightly. Now, as to the trial—
if we go to trial—my charge will be five hundred dollars a
day during the trial term, plus expenses. Since I can hardly
anticipate circumstances where the trial will last more than
five days, your overall charge should be no more than
twenty-five hundred dollars and in all probability less. Can
you afford that?"

"No problem there."

"Very good. Suppose we have our first session next week.
There's no hurry. Even if they should move immediately for
indictment, the calendar down there is tight, and they probably would not set a trial date sooner than two or three
months, and I can have it postponed at least a month or two
more. I feel that the country can't get much crazier, and
maybe a few months from now, we'll begin to come to our
senses. Don't you think so, Molly?"

"I'm afraid not. We're going downhill fast. But I agree
that we should postpone as long as possible. They haven't
indicted yet."

He had his first real fight with Molly the day after this.
He had picked her up at the *Worker* offices on East Twelfth
Street, and since it was a pleasant evening, they decided to
walk downtown and find some place near Foley Square.
Molly was silent and moody, and when he pressed her about
her mood, she told him that twelve leaders of the Commu-

nist Party had been arrested and indicted under the Smith Act.

"What's the Smith Act?" he asked.

"Oh, Jesus God, you're a journalist and supposedly alive and you're asking me what the Smith Act is!"

"That's right. I know how to tie my shoelaces and I'm able to read. And what the devil makes you so damned hostile?"

"I grew that way. It's a part of my nature."

"Bullshit."

"I wonder if you'd say that to some of those titless beauties you courted."

"Oh, come off it."

"And I suppose that if Sylvia Kline was a male with a desiccated nose and desiccated balls, you would have crawled on your knees to her. But I'll tell you this—she wouldn't have sent you down into that nest of thieves without a lawyer."

"Then why the devil didn't you introduce me to her before I went down to Washington?"

"Because you couldn't see anything but that Wall Street *gonif* your father sicked you onto."

"Anything that isn't poverty, pure, unvarnished, and unwashed, is corrupt to you. Didn't it ever occur to you, my dear Molly, that you are a little crazy on this subject? Did it ever occur to you that your proletarian virtue might be as phony as that lousy committee?"

"Oh, beautiful. That's all I need today!"

"We're shouting at each other."

"Otherwise, you don't hear me!" Molly yelled. "You don't hear anything!" She turned on her heel and strode off; passing people stopped to listen and look. A truck driver shouted, "I'm with you, baby!" Bruce started after her, taking long strides, and she turned on her heel and snapped, "Don't follow me. I have nothing to say to you. Nothing!"

"All right!" he shouted after her. "When you come to your senses, call me."

But almost a week passed, and she did not call him. The newspapers were filled with the indictment of the twelve communist leaders. He had fallen into the habit of buying the *Daily Worker* when Molly didn't give him a copy so that he could read whatever she was writing, and between that and the *Tribune,* he discovered that the Smith Act had been passed in 1940, revised a month before the indictment, and that it proposed that anyone who conspired to teach the overthrow of the government by force and violence could be sentenced to five years' imprisonment.

During that time, Bruce called Mel Bronson three times. The first two calls were not returned. The third call was answered by Bronson's secretary, who made an appointment for Bruce three days in advance. But before then, Sylvia Kline called him, and they had their first session.

For Bruce, there was nothing very new in the first hour and a half he spent with Sylvia Kline. They went through the printed version of his hearing line by line, and then she questioned him carefully about his being visited by an FBI agent the year before. Finally, she said, "I can't go on with this, Bruce, if you're going to perform like a man at the point of death. What's happened between the last time I saw you and today? Did someone close to you die?"

"I can't talk about it."

She studied him shrewdly for a long moment, and then said, "Molly?"

He shrugged.

"I'm your lawyer. Talk to me."

"We had a ghastly, stupid fight."

"So what? Everybody fights."

"I suppose so," he agreed. "Are you a communist?"

"Glory oh! What's gotten into you? You don't go around asking people whether they're communists. Not today."

"I'm sorry," he said, so miserably that she rose from be-

hind her desk, came around to face him, bent, and gave him
a peck on the cheek. "Cheers!"

It was very funny. He began to laugh.

"That's better. That's much better."

"Do you kiss all your clients?"

"When they look the way you looked a few moments ago,
yes, absolutely. Molly's a dear old friend. You're going to be
married."

"Huh!"

"What did you fight about? Come on—you can tell a
lawyer anything." She perched on the edge of her desk,
studying him.

"The Smith Act. I asked her what it was. To me, it was a
perfectly normal question. She blew her top, and awful led
to worse. Marry me? I don't think she'll ever talk to me
again."

"Oh, she'll talk to you again, and if I didn't think so, I'd
never let you out of this office. Now listen to me. You're
older than me and maybe you're older than Molly, but we
grew up different. We're the children of immigrants. We're
street kids, and we have something called street smarts, for
want of a better word. You may come to understand this,
but you'll never feel it. We clawed our way up. We're educated differently, when we are educated. The tables I waited,
the dishes I washed, the discovery that you can survive on
four hours' sleep each night. You know what Molly's life
was. My father was a tailor. He didn't own a shop or anything classy like that. He sat in a corner and repaired men's
clothes, and I had to fight this miserable world on scholar-
ship. I'm not complaining, I'm explaining Molly. We're
close. We've talked this out for hours. You asked her what
the Smith Act is. You're a writer. You exist as something
more than a paid voice by virtue of the First Amendment to
the Constitution. Do you know what the Smith Act does? It
wipes out the First Amendment. Suppose a professor at Yale
teaches Marxism. Suppose he discusses his teaching with

another professor. Technically, they have both violated the
Smith Act and they are each subject to five years' imprisonment. It used to be twenty years' imprisonment; last month
they revised it down. Suppose someone had collaborated
with you on your book and in your book you wrote about
communism and Marxism. You're both in technical violation and subject to trial and imprisonment. This is the most
vicious, fascist law that has ever been put on the books in all
the history of this country, and it's not just you asking
Molly what it meant—but the same lack of knowledge right
across the country. Here's a law that can put her away for
five years of her life, and you don't know about it. There's
different kinds of education—and a big gap between you.
You reached out and she reached out—it's a big gap."

Outside, on the street, it was almost ninety degrees. Even
his seersucker jacket was unbearable, and he removed his
tie, stuffed it into the pocket of his jacket, and then slung the
jacket over his shoulder, holding it by the loop. He had to
think, and that meant he had to walk. He had to retrace his
steps and see what brought him to where he was now. He
had to resurrect that long hot day he had spent on a bicycle
with Ashoka Majumdar. What exactly had happened to
him? Suppose he had remained in Europe? What strange
need led him to flee Europe after hanging in right through to
the final victory? His colleagues had a ball wallowing in the
immensity of Germany's defeat, the slaying of the Nazi
dragon, the total horror of the concentration camps. He had
seen a concentration camp liberated. Had he fled from that?
Or had he sought a balance of justice in a world where there
was no justice? What had happened in his mind when he
heard the first rumor that the British had engineered a famine that took the lives of six million people? Six million
Indians, six million Jews, twenty million Russians.

He turned his thoughts to Legerman. Suppose he had
never met Harold Legerman? If he had been trapped, where
was the trap set? But there was no trap. The more he

thought about it, the more he realized that it was his mind that had steered him to his destiny, not Legerman, not Molly, not Greenberg. He thought about communism and the Communist Party. He had no belief in communism, no real knowledge of what it meant. He had a healthy distaste for Stalin, but on the other hand he had witnessed the war. He saw the core of the Russian army wiped out or taken prisoner by the Nazis, and then he saw them produce another army and wipe the Nazis from the face of the earth.

But it was India that had brought about the deepest change. Suddenly, he ceased to see the war as a struggle between right and wrong—it had lost that semiromantic shape and had become of a piece, a great killing, the greatest killing since civilization began, fifty million men and women and children eliminated, wiped from the face of the earth. He recalled his father mentioning that when he, his father, had been in grade school, the population of the United States had only been slightly more than fifty million, so Bruce could make an image of every man, woman, and child in his own country put to death. He was slow to hate, and mostly his hate had been reserved for the Nazis. All other evil withered before this. Still—

Molly never argued the case of communism. She had made the situation plain to him from the beginning: "I am what I am," she told him, "and I have certain loyalties. This isn't my way anymore. It got derailed a long time ago, and the whispers I hear about Stalin make me ill. But this is something you don't have to share with me. You're not a communist, and I don't want you to be one."

Not that there was much chance that he ever would be one, but what was he? He was someone who had never heard of the Smith Act, yet by what he had heard today, it was a monstrous inversion of the whole principle of free speech. Before he left Sylvia Kline's office, he had asked her if she thought the twelve communist leaders would be convicted.

"Of course they will. Do you think that any jury in this country could be put together that would acquit them?"

And then he had asked her, "Could any jury be put together that would acquit me?"

"I don't know," she had answered slowly.

It was too hot to walk. His shirt was soaked with sweat. His own apartment boasted only an antique shower, hand-held. In his parents' house, there was a splendid shower, a large, comfortable stall shower. His mother and father had left a few days ago for their summer place on Indian Lake in the Adirondacks after futilely urging him to accompany them, and he decided to take advantage of the stall shower. It was odd at this moment to make that decision and to excuse it on the basis of heat. He suspended all thought while he sat in the cab that took him uptown, but later, prowling through the big apartment in which he had spent his growing and formative years, the shades drawn, the place so dark and cool, he was able to face the fact that he was looking at his childhood. Here was where he had been shaped by two loving and strict people, but always shaped, protected, sent as a small boy to the Allen Stevenson School, then to Choate, and then to Williams, and shaped as a Boy Scout in between. As he had once expounded to Molly, "A scout is trustworthy, loyal, helpful, friendly, courteous, kind, obedient, cheerful, thrifty, brave, clean, and reverent." They had both burst into laughter. "Can you believe it?" he had asked her.

The truth was that he believed it, and remembering his troop of Boy Scouts and what a foul bunch a good part of them had turned out to be, he still believed it; and nowhere, not even in the most secret apologetic places of the heart, could Molly believe it or not wonder how many of the men on the Un-American Committee and in and about the White House and various and sundry city halls had been Boy Scouts.

I don't ask her to change, he said to himself. I don't ask

her to be like me; I only ask her to try to comprehend me as I am trying to comprehend her.

He took his shower. It was fine to stand under the cleansing gush of water, and scrub himself with soap and then wash himself so clean. What had Kingsley said? Something like "Who will be clean will be clean." He had discussed Kingsley with Molly once, presuming that she knew nothing of him, but she exploded, "That disgusting, brainless upperclass fool!" "Oh, not that much; too much," he had protested. He found a loophole once with Proust. She had never read Proust. "That witless titmouse. I have only so much time on earth. I don't have time to read Proust." "But you've never read him. How can you stand in judgment?" "Exactly," she had replied, at her most provoking; and then she burst into laughter. How do you travel from him to her, from her to him?

He dried himself and dressed, dropping his wet shirt into the laundry basket and borrowing one of his father's. His father wore fifteen and a half; Bruce wore sixteen and a half, but as long as the collar was not buttoned, it would be snug but wearable. Not since his college days, when he still spent his holidays at home, had Bruce worn one of his father's shirts. He came out of it with a shock. What in hell am I doing? he asked himself. Am I frightened and trying to crawl back into my childhood?

He scribbled a note to his father and placed it on the desk in the study. It was twilight when he left the apartment and walked downtown along Riverside Drive. It was certainly the most beautiful avenue in New York, but slowly sinking into decay as the town houses in the side streets became rooming houses and were let to drug pushers and prostitutes. Then the sun sank behind the Jersey shore, and Bruce walked over to Broadway, where he found a cab to take him home.

When he entered his apartment, the lights were on, and

for a moment he drew back in surprise and fear; but then he saw that it was Molly. She was sprawled in a chair.

She stood up and went into his arms, and they stood, locking their embrace tighter and tighter.

"Oh, God, I love you so much," she said.

"Yes. I know."

"Do you love me? Do you want me at all?"

"I can't go on living without you. Don't you know that? Don't you?"

"I whisper it to myself—sometimes."

"Why don't you shout it?"

"Ah, dear Bruce, I have such guilts over you. You found yourself a redheaded Irish girl and you walked into a bear trap, and all I can give you is some love."

"I want to marry you."

"Oh, yes, yes, bless your sweet heart. For the moment, let's go to bed and find each other again, and then tomorrow, if you want to, I'll get the day off and we'll go up to Boston and you can meet my mother and my sisters, which is something you want to do before you plant yourself in any family."

"Not tomorrow," Bruce said. "Tomorrow is the day before I get to hear the fate of my book, and it makes no sense to try to come and go in one day."

"And what about the book?"

"Ah, well may you ask. Bronson has put me off for weeks, and it's damn near taken him and his editors as long to read the book as it took me to write it."

"Bruce, it's not a novel. It's a large, important work, and it says something about the war that no one else has had the guts to say."

"I'll keep my fingers crossed, but I'm not happy about it."

Neither was Bronson as he sat behind his desk facing Bruce, the manuscript of Bruce's book resting in a large box in full view. He tugged on his lower lip, his eyes going from the manuscript to Bruce and then back to the manuscript.

"I should have called you earlier," he said to Bruce. "I hate
to put writers off, but I had to think this one out. You've
written an extraordinary book, Bruce, but I can't publish it.
It's not for our house."

"And you waited all these weeks to tell me that? That was
not your opinion when you read the first piece of it. You
were ready to put your money on the line."

"The first piece was not the whole book," Bronson said
unhappily.

"You're talking rubbish," Bruce said, his anger increasing. "You damn well know that. The book is of a piece. The
first hundred pages defined it and specified it, and now you
tell me you couldn't publish because the theme changed.
You sit with the book for weeks. First you tell me editors are
reading it, and then you don't return my phone calls."
Bruce picked up the manuscript, started for the door, and
then turned to Bronson and spat out, "Do you know what I
think, sir? I think you're a damn liar and a damn coward!"

Bronson leaped to his feet, a big, fleshy man, his face
reddening, came around his desk to face Bruce and tell him
that no one had ever spoken to him like that before. "Damn
you," he said to Bruce, "by what right?" His voice turned
into a shout, and his secretary opened the door to his office.

"Are you all right?"

"Get out of here!" Bronson snapped.

She fled, closing the door behind her, and now the two
men stood facing each other.

"You had no right," Bronson said. "You damn well owe
me an apology."

"Then you damn well owe me the truth," Bruce retorted.
"I'm no novice. I know what I've written."

Bronson took a deep breath, and then he seemed to de-
flate, to collapse in upon himself. He took a few paces across
his office and back, and then he said to Bruce, "Sit down,
please." When Bruce remained standing, Bronson went

around his desk and dropped into his chair. "Please, Bruce, sit down," he said again. "We'll talk."

Bruce dropped into a chair, facing him.

"You called me a coward," Bronson said. "Do you know anyone who isn't?"

"A few."

"Introduce me to them. It hurts worse to call me a liar. If you had told me a year ago that I would sit here and say what I am going to say, I would have replied that you are out of your mind and dreaming nightmares. About three weeks ago, an FBI man came here to my office and informed me that the Director—J. Edgar Hoover, they call him the Director—anyway, the Director did not wish the book that Bruce Bacon had written to appear in print."

"Come on—you're kidding."

"No, no. Now you're getting the truth, naked, unvarnished. As naked as I feel right at this minute."

"And you agreed to that? You let yourself be threatened by some horse's ass in the FBI? You dismantled the Bill of Rights and concurred in a filthy suppression that has no precedent in American history? You're telling me that you succumbed to this kind of pressure?"

"Take it easy, Bacon. Don't be so goddamned holy! And for your information, I did not toss your book out of the window at that point. I'm not defending myself, but for God's sake, don't brush me off like some damned right-wing bastard!"

No, Bruce thought to himself, like some liberal son of a bitch.

"That wasn't the end of it," Bronson went on, pleading now. "I went down to Washington to the Federal Bureau of Investigation, and I saw Mr. Hoover—yes, J. Edgar himself, the esteemed head of the Federal Bureau. You know, during the worst of the Depression, I joined one of those left-wing organizations for a short time. Maybe two, three hundred members. Hoover had it all there in a folder on his desk. He told me I had been given an anti-American book, and if I published it, I should be ready for the consequences. They knew what women I had been to bed with. Once, during the war, we paid off a printer to get paper a little better than our quota provided for. He had that. He knew how many times I pissed. He had a précis of your manuscript, obviously given to him by some little shit in our company. He told me that the précis had been shown to the British and they had taken the matter to the White House. I don't know how much I believed of his threats, but he convinced me that if we published your book we would be out of business in very short order." He paused, took a deep breath, and said, "All right. That's it. I don't function alone in this company. I have stockholders, I have a board of directors."

"I'm sure," Bruce said, rising and taking his manuscript. "I suppose I can be grateful that he didn't order you to burn the book. I'm sure you would have." And then he turned and walked out of the room.

It was still early in the day, and with the manuscript under his arm, Bruce found a telephone booth in a drugstore, found the number he wanted in the phone book, and then called another publisher with a reputation as good as Scandia. He gave the young woman who answered his name and asked to speak to one of the editors.

"Will you hold on, please?"

The minutes ticked by while he searched his pockets for another nickel, found one, and dropped it into the slot. The woman was back on the line, informing him that Mr. Williams would speak to him.

"Is this the same Bruce Bacon who covered the war for the *Tribune*?"

"The same Bruce Bacon."

"Oh, how very nice—how very nice indeed. I was a great fan of yours. What can we do for you?"

"I have a manuscript I would like you to read."

"Book length?"

"Over six hundred manuscript pages."

"And do you want to submit it to us? I mean, it's rather strange. Most of our submissions come from literary agents. Do you have an agent?"

"I'm afraid not," Bruce admitted.

"Well, no reason why you should if you feel you don't need one."

"I would like to come by your office right now, if you don't mind, and leave the manuscript at your reception desk. There is no need for me to speak to anyone. My name, address, and telephone number are all on the manuscript box. Would that be all right?"

"Well, very unusual, Mr. Bacon, but quite all right. With your name, well, it won't go through our readers. One of our editors will read it himself."

It was within walking distance, and that way, Bruce left his manuscript at the reception desk at the publishing house of Harley-Cummings. Telling the story of his experience that day, Bruce experienced a curious feeling of unreality, as if the day's happenings had unrolled slowly and turgidly in a surrealist painting.

When he finished, Molly was silent.

"What do you think?"

"I have cold shivers running up and down my spine, and you want me to think."

"It seems to me," Bruce said, "that somewhere down there in Washington, they have made the decision to wipe out the Communist Party, root and branch, and anyone associated with it. God knows why. There was a time when you people organized the trade unions and you sang with the voice of the people. I admit it. You made our songs and you gave this country a sense of itself it never had before. I've read all that and heard all that. You fought for the Negroes and for women's rights, and maybe it was a fight worth dying for, regardless of what went on in Russia. But what have you done since the war?"

"Fought for our existence, and that way we become more and more rigid and more and more impotent. We don't think anymore, and I'm not the only one who feels the life is being choked out of him. Our leadership, if you can call it that, has been arrested and will go on trial, and some of us estimate that there are maybe a thousand, twelve hundred FBI agents in the Party, which has a total membership today of about thirty thousand."

"Then why are they so desperate to destroy you?"

"I can make a good guess. They're planning war with the Soviet Union, and we don't fit into their plans. They have already built three enormous concentration camps. For the *day,* when it arrives."

"No—I go a long way with you, Molly, but not down that street. I simply don't believe it."

"And if I told you yesterday that the FBI would blackmail a publisher out of publishing your book, you wouldn't have believed that either."

"Not concentration camps. Who's in them?"

"No one at this point. They're built and ready, that's all."

"Then why hasn't it broken as a story in any paper?"

"It sort of did in the *Times.* Slantwise with innuendo that makes it acey-deucy. Oh, Mother of God, I don't know. I've had enough, and I can't walk away from it. Not now. Not when the whole ship is sinking."

A week passed, and Bruce heard nothing from Harley-Cummings. He began another book, planned as a much shorter work, a story of the Normandy landing and his own personal experience during that time. Molly, meanwhile, had arranged for both of them to visit Boston and meet her family. The party would be at her sister Mary's house, since her mother's tiny one-room apartment would scarcely be suitable for a family dinner. Mary had a pleasant house in Brookline. She and her husband, Joe Carlino, had their own hairdressing shop and they did very well with it. "But they're nice, decent, simple people," Molly explained. "They have four kids, which makes me jealous, and they don't know a hell of a lot about anything except being honest and raising their kids as nice kids, and that's a lot, believe me."

Bruce rented a two-door Ford, and they drove up to Boston on a cool August day. The sky was blue and full of cotton-ball clouds, and it was a rare and important outing for them. They talked and sang songs and talked again and enjoyed what modest scenery presented itself along the Merritt Parkway and Route 15. Bruce explained about the book, "It's pretty crazy, isn't it? I mean, here's my first book, two years of damned hard work, and it seems not to have the chance of a snowball in hell to be published, and I'm beginning a second one. I suppose it's a condition by now. If I don't write, I begin to wonder what I'm doing in this foolish world. I suppose some of the material will duplicate what I've written, but with another point of view. I went ashore there. I want to try to put down what I felt—the quality of my own terror."

"It's a wonderful notion. You read so much of war and so little of the terror that goes with it."

It was an odd feeling to drive again, after not having driven for years. At the end of the summer before, he had spent a weekend with his folks in their summer place at Indian Lake. They kept an ancient Buick at the lake, which was jacked up on blocks each fall, greased, and wrapped away for the winter. It was a wonderful antique, but something had gone wrong with it, and he lost his opportunity of driving it that summer.

"Like riding a bicycle," he told Molly, "you don't forget."

He had lured her onto a bicycle in Central Park. She protested that she had not sat on a bicycle since her thirteenth birthday. "I never owned one," she confessed. "We were hand to mouth, and you don't buy bikes instead of food. But Nancy O'Hare had a bike, and she let me use it now and then, just up the block and down. She would have killed me had I gotten out of her sight." But on a rented bike in Central Park, she rode very decently, and it became a favorite thing for Sunday mornings. He loved the way people stared at her, her long, straight red hair flying in the wind, her head high, her legs strong and lovely.

"Do you drive a car?" he asked her now.

"I do indeed."

"Then we'll take turns."

"If you wish. I'll drive and you can tell me one of your wonderful stories."

When she took her turn at the wheel, Bruce said, "Did I ever tell you about Majumdar and the police spy?"

"No, I don't think so."

"He was working out of Old Delhi then. You know, there's an Old Delhi and a New Delhi, and they stand a few miles apart. New Delhi is a mass of great grand government buildings that the British put up as a place to run India. Old Delhi is an Indian city, crowded, full of twisting lanes, crumbling houses, and assorted dirt and disease. I was only there for a few days, so I can't be too specific about it."

"But this happened to Majumdar, not to you?"

"Oh, yes—yes, indeed. Years before I met him. In those days, every radical had a police spy attached to him—oh, not everyone, of course, but the important ones—and labor was very cheap, so why not? Well, Majumdar was doing much the same thing as in Calcutta, going from village to village with his newspapers, sometimes on foot, sometimes on a bike, and when he was on his bike, slow as he might ride, his police spy had to move at a run to keep up with him. Finally, the police spy pleaded with Majumdar that if he kept this up, he, the police spy, would surely die. He was forty years old, and he had a wife and four children, and if he dropped dead, the way the rickshaw runners dropped dead, who would feed his family? At first Majumdar was in no mood to help a police spy, but then he reasoned that the police spies were exploited by the British as much as anyone else, and thus he agreed to give the police spy a résumé each day of where he had been and what he had said."

"Oh, no!" Molly cried. "I don't believe you."

"I tell you only what Majumdar told me. Well, this police spy, and I can't remember his name—well, he asked Majumdar to talk to some friends of his who were also police spies, and the upshot of it was that Majumdar organized them into the police spy trade union."

"You invented the whole thing."

"No. And I don't think Majumdar did."

"And what happened to the police spy? Did Majumdar tell you that? Are you going to tell me that he became a powerful trade union leader in India?"

"Hardly. The British arrested him, according to Majumdar. They broke his legs and his arms. He can't walk or crawl. He pulls himself along on his belly."

"What a horrible end, poor devil. It doesn't sound like something that happened, Bruce. It sounds like a folk story of long, long ago."

"It is long, long ago, and India is free now, and who remembers, Molly? That's what I can't comprehend about this whole radical thing. Who knows, who remembers? You shout into the darkness. You die to make a labor union, to free a black man in the South. Who knows? Who cares? Who remembers? You walk on a picket line because some poor bastards are out on strike, and a cop fractures your skull with his club and kills you. Who cares? Would the *Times* offer you a free inch on the obit page? Who would remember that Molly Maguire gave her life to raise the wages of some worker ten cents an hour? Who would shed a tear?"

"You would, dear Bruce."

"Come on, Molly. Try to answer me. I love you. I want to know why you are what you are."

"And you think I know?" She put her fingers to her lips and then touched Bruce's hand. "Father Cogan—he's a

Paulist priest in Brookline—he says that some of us are God's laughter and some of us are God's tears."

"That's a smart apple, your Father Cogan, but the fact remains that if there is a God, He's bequeathed this beautiful earth of His to a pack of unmitigated scoundrels and murderous bastards, and that goes for every government on the planet, including ours and including your Soviet Union—"

"Not mine, Bruce!"

"—and if one of His commandments is *Thou shalt not kill,* it has to be the most abused instruction in history. And damn it, what kind of a Catholic are you?"

"You're beating up on me," Molly said primly, "and I'm not going to get angry. I'm a very good Catholic—that is, the part of me that believes in God. That's Molly Maguire at four o'clock in the morning. In daylight, I'm a much more independent thinker. You see, I had God with me when I was a little girl, and then one day, He went out to lunch or Mexico or some such place and never came back. Jesus is much more reliable, because you can hang Him up over your bed, and I can understand Him because I like Jews. The first thing Mom said when I told her I was bringing you home was, Is he Jewish? I asked her when she ever knew a Jew whose name was Bacon, and she said that she knew a rabbi in Ireland whose name was Moriarity, but she probably made that up. She's very sharp and she makes up things like that."

It was late afternoon when they drove up to the small white house in Brookline. The four Carlino children, Joe Jr., nine, Peter, seven, Lucy, five, and Agnes, a very small three, were lined up in front of the house, a sort of greeting committee, but silent, a presence without a voice. They all had more or less the same red hair. "The perseverance of a stout gene," Molly said. Then Molly's mother, sisters, and brother-in-law came out of the house, and there was a lot of hugging and kissing, and the silent children dissolved in laughter. Molly's mother, also Mary by name, six inches shorter than her daughters, a round, white-haired cheerful woman, did not wait for introductions but threw her arms around Bruce and went up on her toes to kiss him. "He's a fine man," she decided in immediate judgment. The others were introduced more formally: Mary, the middle sister, very much like Molly but older and work-tired and thinner; her husband, Joe Carlino, slender, good-looking, too good-looking, Bruce thought, for an aging, tired wife and four kids; and last, retiring, waiting, her smile gentle and tentative, Bernadette, in her gray nun's habit.

They were all kind and warm. Evidently, through the months since she met Bruce, Molly had kept them up to date on the man as well as the progress of the love affair. It was a kind of family gathering that Bruce had not experienced before, outgoing, sometimes everyone talking at the same time, a bottle of champagne opened almost on their arrival, toasts made seriously yet lovingly beyond anything Bruce had encountered. They were all on best behavior, and Bruce in turn fought with himself not to be embarrassed. Much of his wartime stuff had been syndicated in Boston, in the *Boston Herald,* and whether they had read the *Herald* or not, they all gave voice to remembering and liking what he had written. Except Bernadette, who hardly spoke at all. He noticed her greeting Molly, a long, clutching embrace, and later Molly whispered to him, "She prays for me constantly, poor dear." There was a large crucifix in the living room, a smaller one in the dining room, an apparent religiosity that at first struck him as morbid, and that he realized, as the evening went on, was so integral as to be a thing in passing. Coming from a family that relegated religion to Christmas dinner and Easter in church, he found it strange but hardly oppressive. Molly's mother knew about his appearance before the Un-American Committee, since she read the *Daily Worker* Molly sent her, and at the dinner table she argued the case against the uneasy opposition of Joe Carlino, who was a formal anti-communist, a matter-of-course thing; but also unwilling to offend their guest. His attitude was also modified by Mrs. Maguire, who was a staunch supporter of her daughter and a pillar of the church. Bernadette took no part in the discussion, sitting in silence, for the most part. When she spoke, it was to mention a project she was working on to establish a day care center for Negro children.

Carlino said to Bruce, "You see, to me that's communism."

"Ah, so my Bernadette's a communist too," Molly's mother said.

"I mean, that's what communism should be."

"He'll write a book about it," Mary said.

The table groaned with food, a twelve-pound turkey roasted to golden brown, a bowl of roast potatoes, salad, string beans, turnips, a Jell-O mold of fruit—"We didn't know if you'd like Italian food," Mary said, "so we made it strictly American."

Bruce forbore from informing her that he loved Italian food.

And at a point in the dinner, Bernadette said gently, "Some say Jesus was a communist, don't they?"

"Tim Murphy," Mrs. Maguire said, "worked in the mines in Pennsylvania until his lungs gave out, and then he came back here to Boston to die where his people were, and he told me that one day in the mines, he saw Jesus standing in front of him, plain as day, and he called to the Protestant lads who were working with him, and not a thing could they see—meaning no offense to you, of course, Bruce, but it was his faith that took hold of him, and as he told me, Jesus wore the work clothes of a miner and was no different even to the lamp on His head, except that it gave out light like a halo."

"And that I'll believe when pigs have wings," Carlino said, to which his wife responded, "You got to have a brain to believe."

Driving back to New York late that evening, Molly asked him what he thought of her family.

"I think your mother is a very remarkable woman," he said. "I begin to see you more clearly."

"Because of my mother?"

"How old is she?"

"Sixty."

"She's very wise."

"I think so," Molly agreed. "Sometimes, when I compare women like my mother and my sisters to the run of your sex, I get very discouraged."

"I can well imagine."

"You are in a cheerful mood," Molly said.

"I think I know you better than I knew you before, and that's important. I never knew a devil of a lot about the Irish. I read Farrell's Studs Lonigan books, and they put me off, making out the lot of you to be a race of barbarians—"

"Sure and we are," Molly said, "but not Farrell's barbarians. The worm that crawls through Farrell's books comes out of him, not our people, or maybe he knows a race of Irish I never met with. You know what my mother once said to me? She was fifty-one years old and long a widow, and never in her life had she bought a book or had the money to spend for one. But a year past fifty, she said to herself, I will not live my life without buying a book, and she went into a bookstore and bought a copy of *Destiny Bay* by Byrne, and read every word of it, even though it disappointed her by being about the north of Ireland and not the south. She had never even set foot in my own church of God, the Boston Public Library, but after that, Mary and I would find her books. Did you like the kids?"

"The kids are great."

"You like the way they look? You're not as dark as Joe, but our kids will probably look the same. I'm gonna have a lot of kids, you might as well know."

"I think I can live with it."

"I'm glad that's over with."

"Why?" Bruce wondered.

"I was a little afraid. You probably don't think of yourself and your folks as a part of the upper classes."

"I certainly don't."

"Well," said Molly, "it depends on where you're coming from and where you're going."

Then she fell asleep, curled up against him, while he drove the rest of the way into New York, well occupied in trying to work out where he was coming from and where he was going.

A week later, he received a call from Douglas Williams at the publishing house of Harley-Cummings. He had only spoken to Williams on the telephone; meeting him, Bruce found to his pleasure an open-faced young man of about his own age, a long, narrow head, sandy hair, and gold-rimmed glasses. Williams shook his hand eagerly. "What a hell of a wonderful book you've written! I couldn't put it down, and finally I stayed up half the night to finish it. The chapters about General Patton and General Clark are the most exciting and revealing stuff I've read in years—and I have such a deep sense of the truth. You are a brave and damned eloquent man, Mr. Bacon. You have put this war and all war in a new perspective, and if we have a volcano here, then heaven bless volcanoes. This is the kind of thing that happens to an editor once or twice in a lifetime, if he's lucky, and I'm enjoying it."

Bruce stood transfixed.

"Sit down, please. Has no one else told you that? It seems so lucky and unlikely, you coming in off the street, no literary agent—and you are a well-known writer, if I may say so. Surely someone else said what I'm saying."

"The woman I'm going to marry," Bruce said. "You can't believe anyone who loves you when it comes to literary criticism. Let me get my breath."

"Well, there it is. But mine is not the last word. The

chapter about India is shocking, to put it mildly, and God
only knows what will happen when your book sees the light.
But it's going to sell like crazy, and that is the bottom line,
isn't it?"

"What do you mean when you say yours is not the last
word?"

"It has to go to the board. That means three more readings, and perhaps a World War Two expert in the bargain.
But don't let that worry you. There isn't a book on our list
that I'm as certain about as this one."

He wondered, at that moment, whether he should reveal
to Williams the history of the manuscript at Scandia Press;
but since the question had not been asked of him directly, he
decided not to bring up the matter.

When he told Molly of his interview with Williams, she
decided it was the occasion for a proper celebration, and
that he would be her guest at Dinty Moore's. They both
dressed for the night, Bruce in his single operative gray flannel suit and Molly in her kelly green skirt, and they ordered
the famous Dinty Moore gefilte fish, followed by the famous
Dinty Moore corned beef and cabbage. They started with
martinis, drank two beers each through dinner, and then put
it to rest with doubles of Irish Cream. They were filled with
good food, comfortable, just a bit glazed, and in love with
each other. After dinner, they went to Roseland and danced.
It was Bruce's first time at Roseland.

"Let's get married tonight," he said to Molly.

"You've asked me that before. You can't do it in one
night. You got to have Wassermans and a license, and you
got to have someone to marry you. Bless you, Bacon, which
mother's heart do we break?"

"You're kidding," Bruce said, stopping in the middle of
the floor. "You mean she wants the real thing, a priest and
all that?"

"That's what she wants."

"She can't afford it."

"The church is pretty cheap. It's not a Jewish or Italian wedding. We don't have to feed anyone."

They were dancing again. "I know," he said. "You reserve that for the wake."

"Don't be Wasp-nasty."

"All right. I ignore the insult, but let's be practical. You're divorced, I'm divorced. So how on earth can we be married in a Catholic church?"

"Poor dear Bruce. The church is no monster, and my faith is that God understands. About my first husband— well, he was Jewish, and the church, in a fine piece of arrogance, will not recognize a marriage to a Jew. As for your marriage, we will never mention it, and what no one knows hurts no one."

"You'd do that?"

"Why not? My God understands such things. In fact, I turn to Mary, who is very wise in the devious things a woman must do to live in a world where men make the rules, and what have any of these rules got to do with the fact that we love each other? Now will you put the problem away? I will manage it, and I'll say no more in the way of needles under your skin."

"You can't get under my skin tonight. I have been told by at least one person that I've written a great book."

"Two persons. I am number one. Williams is number two."

It was a fine night, one that Bruce would remember for a good while to come, and his ecstasy survived for exactly eighteen days. During that time, he outlined the second book he intended to write.

On the eighteenth day after his talk with Douglas Williams, he received a call from Williams's secretary, asking him to come down to the offices of Harley-Cummings.

Williams's face and tone were full of despair as he looked at Bruce and told him that he couldn't bring himself to send the manuscript back with a letter. "No, I had to see you and talk to you. I have been witness to a despicable action, shameful, cowardly—"

"What are you trying to say to me? That you won't publish my book?"

"Two people on the board read it. Their opinion matched mine, although they were a little uneasy about certain parts. Then we got word of Mel Bronson's discussion with J. Edgar Hoover. The publishing business is a comparatively small and tight affair, and the story of the dictum laid down by J. Edgar to Bronson is all over the industry—"

"And you're telling me," Bruce said slowly, "that this dirty little man in Washington can tear up the Constitution and throw the fear of God into the whole publishing community?"

"I'm afraid so. I stormed, shouted, threatened to resign, but all of it to no end. If I thought it would make one iota of difference, I would resign."

"Then that's it. You won't publish the book?"

"I'm afraid so. It sickens me to have to tell you that, but I don't own this house. I work here, that's all."

Bruce had the book copied, retyped with carbons, and he thus circulated four copies. Over the following three months, he sent the book to eleven publishing houses. All of them rejected it. One house, one of the most distinguished publishers in New York and a house that specialized in beautifully designed and crafted books of quality, and that had a reputation for publishing the best of European literature, sent the manuscript back to him unopened, with an abusive letter from the publisher. The letter announced that the publisher, a loyal American, would not deign to look at the writing of a man like Bruce Bacon.

A Curious
Courtroom

Sitting facing him in her office, Sylvia Kline said to Bruce, "I wanted you to hear this from me, and I just got the news from Washington. You've been indicted."

"When did this happen?"

"Early today."

"It's a relief in a way," Bruce admitted. "I kept waiting for it to happen. Now it's happened. What do we do?"

"The first thing we do is to shake it all out and see where we stand. When you committed your contempt of Congress, you had committed a misdemeanor, and as I told you, a misdemeanor is punishable by one year in prison at most, specifically, one day less than a year, and that is not a statutory punishment but the limit. Many contempt cases are dealt with only with fines, and others with thirty or sixty days in the slammer. Your case is something else. It's a building block in this structure of fear that they're creating —and a very important building block, if I may say so."

"Why me? Why on God's earth do they want to put me in jail?"

"Think about it," Sylvia Kline said, "and see the pattern. They've arrested twelve leaders of the Communist Party, and now they're on trial. But they are communists—no question of whether they are or are not Party members. They're moving against a list of college and public school teachers—suspicion of being communists. The Hollywood people, writers, actors, a few stars, also very left and maybe some communists. But in your case, they take another very important step because you are not a communist and never have been one, and they know it. Prior to the war, nothing. You weren't a left-winger, you had no visible trade union sympathies, except the Newspaper Guild, and yet they got you—and if they can get Bacon, they can get anyone. That puts a whole new face on this business. It's not just lunatics on the Un-American Committee, but there's this totally besotted and very dangerous Senator McCarthy charging that the whole State Department is saturated with communists. So you become a step in that, Bruce, and we must see it clearly, the way it is."

"I'll have a trial?"

"No question about that."

"When?"

"They'll probably set a date in a few weeks. No reason to postpone."

"Well," Bruce said, "we'll have a trial and we'll win. No jury would convict me on the basis of that absurd hearing."

"Wrong," Sylvia said, "because the trial will take place in Washington, and if we find a jury there that won't convict you, it will be a miracle. Washington is the core of this lunacy, and it's a company town, and no government worker in today's climate would dare to vote to acquit in a case like this."

"If that's true, what hope is there?"

"Some hope. Maybe even a Washington jury can be moved, and then on appeal we don't have to deal with a jury. So we'll play all our best shots, and we'll try to work out a proper game plan. That is, if you still want me to represent you?"

"I think I do," Bruce said. "I wouldn't want to bring this to anyone else now. I think you understand my situation and you know how I stand with Molly. Let me try to clarify my own position since the war, which adds up to the main reason why I could not be a communist. You haven't read my book, but I'll get a copy to you before we go on trial. My book is a commentary upon war, and what threads through it is my deep personal belief that there is no just war. I begin my book with World War One and its fruits, but a reading of the book would make it plain to anyone that the author is a pacifist. I am a pacifist—totally, and this is the position from which I write of the demented slaughter of World War One, and how it led to the even more demented slaughter of World War Two. I've seen good, decent, and brave people who were communists, but whatever the cause or need, I cannot engage in acts of violence and I cannot justify them. I don't regard the accusation of communism as slanderous or degrading; it is simply not my way of thinking or life."

There was a stretch of silence after that, and then Sylvia nodded and said, "I'm glad you shared that with me, and now there are certain questions."

"Shoot."

"Did you ever know anyone in British Intelligence?"

"I don't think so, but I can't be sure. On and off, I met up with a good many British correspondents, but who could say? At the various press clubs overseas, you'd see a good many Limey officers who'd come in to cadge drinks and tell you how great they were, but I don't know that I could spot one as Intelligence. Do you think they have a finger in this pot?"

"Maybe. What about American Intelligence?"

"That would be Army Intelligence—harder to tell. They don't advertise either."

"Do you have scrapbooks of all your dispatches?"

"I have some. My father has all of them. I'm sure he'd let you see them whenever you like."

"I'll make a note of that. Give me his address and telephone number. His name—?"

"Dr. William Bacon."

"Good. Now, I would like to use Molly as my chief witness. Do you have any quarrel with that?"

"I wouldn't want to see her put to pain or embarrassment."

"She won't be. Is your father a Mason?"

"I'm afraid not."

"And you?"

"No."

"I wish one of you were. It helps. I want dates, prep school—you went to Choate and Williams. Right?"

"Right."

"Born April twenty-seventh, nineteen fifteen?"

"Right again."

"What about distinguished family or ancestors? Molly said something about Nathaniel Bacon?"

"You're kidding."

"Oh, no," she said. "Everything counts. You see, we're not dealing with a crime here. We're dealing with an attitude, and we have to approach it in a very special way."

"OK, I'll go along with you. We claim the relationship, but who knows? My folks were born in the Middle West—ah, the hell with it. They can't check any more than we can, so use it for whatever it's worth. You know, Sylvia, I get the feeling that we're doing a charade and that no matter what we do, I will end up in the slammer. That's predestined, isn't it?"

She thought about it for a moment or two, and then she said, "Bruce, you're a nice guy, and I could give you all kinds of hopes and say that we'll go in there and face those morons and beat the stuffing out of them, but that's not what the handwriting on the wall says. You'd go in there full of hope and righteousness, and you'd come out of it heartbroken and bitter. I don't want that. I want you to know the score in advance. If a miracle happens, we might win. If we lose, a fearless and incorruptible judge might demand a token fine or thirty days in jail, as he would if it were one of their own boys. But I've never met a fearless and incorruptible judge. Of course, I'm young. Who knows what lies down the road?"

Bruce was laughing. She was a delightful, incisive person, and he had the feeling that, in her own way, she would do a good job of it.

On his part, Bruce felt a little proper publicity might help his case, and with that in mind, he wrote the story of the progress of his manuscript since he first gave it to Mel Bronson. The piece was six typewritten pages, and he took it down to Jack Garland, who was one of the editors at the *Tribune* book section, a gentle, white-haired man who had developed a fondness for Bruce when Bruce was a cub reporter. He greeted Bruce with pleasure and commiserated with him about his problems. Would he read the piece? Of course he would, and he told Bruce to have the single chair in a little office piled with books and manuscripts while he sat behind his desk and read what Bruce had written. He finished, stuffed an old pipe with tobacco, and expressed anger and disgust.

"It's hard to believe how low we've sunk."

"Will you use it, Jack?"

"I can take it to the board," he said, "and of course I will, but there's not a chance they'll use it, either here or in the news section. My word, Bruce, you name names, too many names. Putting aside slander, the names you name advertise here. Of course they'll all deny it. They'll say your piece is worthless. You know the line—Bacon's a brilliant reporter, but when it comes to organizing his material for a full-length article, he just is not with it. We would have to call everyone you mention for confirmation, including that little bastard J. Edgar Hoover. You know that."

"I'm afraid I do."

"You might try a piece on the general beating they're giving you, without naming publishers and editors."

"It's old hat already. We have an impatient public, Jack, and these are things they're not happy to know about. Last week's news is a hundred years old, and the Hollywood cases are a lot more glamorous and interesting. But thanks for reading this and listening to me."

"It's a privilege."

That night, Molly said to him, "It's not that we don't have decent people, Bruce. This feller Garland sounds like a perfect darling, and there are thousands like him—as I suppose there were in Nazi Germany. What scares me is how easily they're intimidated, how quick they are to give up and say, Well, if this is the way it must be, then this is the way it must be."

The trial date was set for the following November, and in the interim Molly left the *Daily Worker.* She had become increasingly uncomfortable in her job, stubbornly resisting the clerical inhibitions that were a part of the paper. When she wrote with great sympathy of the creation of Israel, she was accused of succumbing to Zionist propaganda. When she refused to do away with the use of *boy* or *girl* in writing about blacks, she was accused of white chauvinism. When she wrote of the stupidity of Soviet propaganda, particularly in their attack on baseball, her story was scrapped, and when she did a special piece on Bruce, it came to a showdown.

The Party's position was that Bruce had invited his situation, that far from being a hapless victim of a grotesque turn his country had taken, he, as a totally nonpolitical creature, had invited his fate and, along with many thousands like him, would invite fascism to happen in America. Molly rejected this. She could not accept the inevitable victory of the collection of madmen who, with Senator McCarthy at the helm, were trying so desperately to remake the country according to their image. Bruce was not a political innocent or failure, and it was precisely because of his delving into the mystery of the Bengal famine that he had become a target for the committee. Rather than give in and rewrite her story, Molly tore it up and walked out.

"I can live with anything except the man who tells me what I must write or what I cannot write, because if I can't write what I have to write, my brain stops being mine. There's no damned sense living if you give your mind away," Molly told Bruce.

"Was it the story about me? Molly, I don't give a damn what they or the *Times* or the *Daily News* says about me. The press was once sacrosanct. There was a time when I would have defined it as a priesthood of freedom, which is merely my penchant for bullshit. Since this started, not one damned paper in this city has given me at least the poor crutch of an editorial. Nothing. Yes—except your paper. So score one for the *Daily Worker*."

"I'm not putting them down," Molly agreed. "They're good guys and they're dedicated, but that's not enough."

"But what does it mean?" Bruce asked her. "Does it mean you're out of it, through with the Party?" How many times he had said to himself, Please God or whatever there is, please get her out of it before someone jails her or kills her. He was saying it now, and in spite of his determination never to demand this of her, he could not keep the note of excitement and anticipation out of his voice.

Molly heard it. "Poor Bruce, you want so desperately for me to be out of it."

"But this means you're out of it."

"No, darling—not unless they expel me. Maybe they will. I doubt it. The movement's going down, and in a way that breaks my heart. We meant something to this country. We go back half a century to the Wobblies, the lumber workers in Washington state and Oregon state, and we never turned our backs on wrong and we never put our tail between our legs and ran. We taught this country something about truth and courage and we left our dead wherever the battle was, and then it went wrong. Somehow, it went wrong as hell, not those slimy little bastards like Rankin and Nixon and the rest of them, but inside us, and instead of opening our arms, we're nitpicking us into hell. Oh, Jesus, I don't know. When I sang with the Southie chorus, and we sang 'The Minstrel Boy,' I knew who I was and what my life had to be; you know, 'His father's sword he has girded on, and his wild harp slung behind him.' That was me; it had to be me and my wild harp, and now it's gone—ah, Mother of God, where do we go from here?"

He took her in his arms, and she clung to him, sobbing. He tried to tell her that if she wanted her job back, they would give it to her; she had years behind her; but she knew better and through her tears tried to explain that none of it could be reversed. She was right, of course, and he knew it well and deeply. That at least he had seen better than she, that beginning as something unique and wonderful, coming out of all the different and remote American movements toward peace and brotherhood, a socialist movement began and flowered and then, through a freakish turn of history, hooked itself onto the tail of a man called Stalin and the little circle around him. He didn't see it clearly or scientifically or as a historian, which he was not; but he felt it and he absorbed it through all that Molly had told him; and he knew as well as she did that she couldn't go back.

"What in hell am I crying about?" she demanded, pulling out of his arms. "We have work to do. We have to get you through this stupid trial, and I have to find myself a job—no sweat," she added as she saw the look on Bruce's face. "I can sling hash, I can type, I can use a sewing machine—no problem at all." The next day she was waiting tables at the Downtown Café at Eighth Avenue and Twenty-fourth Street, and on the same day, Bruce was informed that his trial date had been set for late November.

"We can postpone the trial," Sylvia Kline told him.

"To what end? Do we need more time than that?"

"No, we don't. Perhaps you do."

"No—unless it runs into Christmas. I'd look forward to

Christmas at home with my family. Can it stretch out more than three weeks?"

"Bless your heart, Bruce, not a chance. Three, four days —five at the most. You have been, by their lights, contemptacious. You haven't robbed a bank. They'll give us a day to pick the jury, and then they'll be on with it. We'll want your father down there as a character witness, and the editor of the *Tribune,* if you can talk him into it. Now, as I told you, I don't expect to win this shot, but I think I can do a good appeal. Contempts are rarely appealed, but this is something different."

Everything was different, and he, Bruce Bacon, was being remade. When Molly first informed him that she had taken a job as a waitress, he was ready to explode with objections —to the tune of: No, absolutely not. You don't have to do that kind of work, I have enough money for both of us. Yet he controlled himself and managed to nod calmly, convinced that she'd never know what that took.

"For a few weeks, darling," she said. "I can step out of it any time I want to. Look, I'm a big girl, and the way men put it, I'm built like a brick shithouse. I walk into a lunch place, and the job is mine if there's a job there to be had. I've done it before and I can do it again."

"At least come and live with me. We don't have to pay two rents."

"Sylvia says no."

"You mean you raised it with her?" He was astonished.

"Of course. But she said not until after the trial, and I have so much junk, enough papers and books to sink your place. All in good time, dear love."

Bruce was shaken and confused. She had used a phrase that stuck in his mind, "built like a brick shithouse," a phrase he had heard a thousand times during the war, just as he had heard every foul word in the language a thousand times, and not the phrase itself but her use of it, the ease with which she identified herself, the ease with which she had walked into a job at some cheap restaurant. If he, Bruce Bacon, was being remade, what in God's name was the direction and the result? He had just asked her to give up her apartment and live with him, and the understanding was that they'd be married; but who was he marrying, looking at this tall, self-confident woman, self-confident to the point of arrogance? Or was it arrogance that allowed her to burst into tears the other day? Who was she? How did she connect with him? She had led him into a world beyond his experience, and now he'd be going to prison without rhyme or reason. He was in love with her. The thought was without content, and at this moment in his life, he would not attest to being in love with anyone. If you have to try to find love within yourself, where is it and what is it?

Bruce left Molly with the feeling that he would like nothing better than to get in a car and drive day after day after day, without any destination, but away from everything happening here. A child dreams that way: fix it in your mind and it will happen, except that in this case it would not happen and he would do what had been planned. Tonight was dinner at his parents' place. They had not suggested that he come with Molly or without her; he said he would come alone, and that was quite conscious, an action he had taken and then removed from his own right of inquiry, telling himself, They'll be pleased to be with me, just the family. They do have problems with Molly.

But it was not just the family. His folks had invited two old friends of his father, Dr. Jules Steinmott and his wife, Ellen, and since Molly was not to be present, they had asked the Steinmotts to bring their daughter, Roberta, who was a resident at Dr. Bacon's hospital. It was a family thing, and Bruce had known Roberta since they were kids. She was four years younger than he, a bright, pretty young woman, round-cheeked, with large, wide-spaced brown eyes. Ellen Steinmott was a medical researcher, and where Steinmott was plump, pince-nez, and very bedside, his wife was thin and ebullient.

There had apparently been a prior decision by all but Bruce not to talk about his current trouble or the Un-American Committee, and to Bruce that was something of a relief. Roberta, who had not seen Bruce since before the war, was in awe of his romantic image, if not of him, and kept turning away his questions about the pros and cons of being a lady doctor in a world where there were so few; she would much rather hear his own stories. Was it true, for instance, that soldiers under fire never caught cold, regardless of the weather conditions? That they got trench foot, but not colds? She had read a paper on psychosomatic causes of the common cold. Bruce could offer no evidence either way. He was in a more difficult position with Mrs. Steinmott and India. Some years past, she had read a popular book entitled *Mother India,* which purported to be the truth about the great subcontinent. And was it? Bruce had never read the book, and he tried to convey the vastness of the place and the fact that he had seen only one small part of it. The papers had been full of India ever since its independence came about, full of the awful bloodletting between the Muslims and the Hindus, a recent history Bruce would just as well not discuss, knowing how causes and results were twisted and confused in the American media, and he was relieved when the talk turned to the astounding medical advances and discoveries that had come out of the war. They grasped at that, as if to squeeze some seeds of goodness out of the awful horror.

After dinner, he fell into conversation with Roberta. The two men had gone into Dr. Bacon's study to have their cigars and brandy, and Mrs. Bacon and Mrs. Steinmott were across the living room, immersed in their own conversation and recollections.

"You've had a real rotten deal, haven't you?" Roberta said softly. "I know we all have an agreement not to discuss

it, but I'm damned if I could leave here and not know how
hurt you are."

"A little hurt. I'll survive."

"Your dad talked to mine. I know the details in a rough
kind of way. According to the few knowledgeable people
I've spoken to, you've done nothing wrong."

"Ah, bless your heart, and the devil with all that. Now
tell me about you and the practice of medicine."

They talked for hours. It was close to midnight when the
Steinmotts rose to leave. Bruce had topped off the wine at
dinner with three brandies; and now he felt warm, tired, and
quite sleepy, and informed his folks that, if they didn't
mind, he'd stay overnight. It was a very strange feeling to be
in his bed in his old boyhood room. While the Bacons kept it
as a guest room, they had changed very little in the room,
and crawling under the sheets and the comforter, Bruce felt
a wonderful sense of security. As when a child, when the
sheets and comforter were neck high, he had felt beyond
danger. Now, he was suffused with a warm glow. He had
drunk just enough to mellow him and yet not enough to
trouble him, and for the first time in months, he fell asleep
almost instantly.

When he awakened in the morning, he was almost totally
disoriented. Where was he? In the instant of not yet being
fully awake, his life was like something he had dreamed.
Then he was awake, and reality returned.

He had breakfast with his father and mother, the kind of
breakfast he had eaten there long, long ago, bacon and eggs
and bran muffins and two kinds of jam and coffee. He shared
a taxi with his father, who went out of his way to drop him
off at Seventy-sixth Street and Lexington. When he opened
his door into his living room, he saw Molly curled up on his
couch and sleeping.

As he stood staring at her, she opened her eyes, blinked,
stretched, and then came to him and threw her arms around

him. He returned the embrace, holding her tightly to him. This time, *his* eyes were clouded with tears.

"I was calling you," she said. "I called until four o'clock in the morning, and then I knew that something awful had happened, and here I came, my darling, with what I could have of you, and your place and your books, and oh, Jesus, I was so scared, and I don't give a damn where you were, only that you're here and safe."

"I was with my mother and dad, and it got late and I decided to spend the night there. Why didn't you call me there?"

"Ah, darling, I cannot call there, don't you understand?"

"Have you eaten? Have you had breakfast—or dinner, for that matter?"

"No, and I guess I don't have a job either. I should have been there for breakfast at seven, and it's past eleven now, and I don't give a damn, with you alive and well. Anyway, I hate waiting tables. I'll get something selling stuff."

Bruce took her to a saloon on Third Avenue, where, confessing that she had not touched food since lunch the day before, she downed an enormous plate of hamburgers and fried potatoes. Finally, filled with food, relaxed, she smiled at him, touched his hand across the table, and said to him, "You ran, my dear one—ah, don't deny it. I understand it only too well. I think you want to love me, but I'm also frightening to you, and underneath, in your heart, you blame this whole rotten committee mess on me—"

"No!" he interrupted. "No! Absolutely not! You are wrong as hell."

"Then why did you run, dear Bruce? Don't lie to me. I know you better than you know me. You can go to bed with a woman who talks of herself as being built like a brick shithouse, but no way can you commit to her. My dear, sweet Bruce—now please, please believe me, and I am going to tell you that you can get up from this table and walk out of here and never see me again, and I will not be on your

conscience or ever trouble you again. I am free. But we have
nothing unless you are free."

"You could do that?"

"I damn well could."

"And the love you speak of?"

"I love you and I'll love you all my life. What the hell is
love? Handcuffs? Chains? If you had gone to bed with some
dame last night, I might think that your brains were in your
gonads, but I would not toss my love away."

"And you did think that last night?"

"No, you damned fool. If I had thought that, I would
have rested easy. I thought that you were hurt."

"Where now?" he asked as they left the restaurant.

"I'm tired. Let's go to your apartment. We neither of us
have a job."

But before they left for Washington a few weeks later,
something happened. Bruce got a telephone call from a Peter Johnson at the Temple Press, a small publishing house in
San Francisco. Johnson, a youngish easy-speaking person—
if one could decide such things from a voice—told Bruce
that a friend of his, Johnson's, had sent him a copy of the
manuscript. It was a copy, Bruce recalled, that had never
been returned, even though Bruce had written and telephoned for it.

"True," Johnson said, "my friend lifted the manuscript
and sent it to me. His company had already turned it down.
He had no right to do what he did, and I hope you will
forgive him. On the other hand, I think it's a fine and important piece of work and we want to publish it, and we don't
give two damns about Mr. Hoover and his night riders. We
can't do a big printing, but at least we will bring it into the
light of day. We expect to do a first edition of five thousand
copies, and we can only offer an advance of five thousand
dollars. But we will publish it, and do it honestly and decently."

Both the contract and the check arrived before the date

set for the trial, so there was something to celebrate on the train down to Washington. Bruce ordered a bottle of champagne, and he and Molly and Sylvia drank to destiny. "Howsoever," as Bruce put it, and Sylvia said, "Here we are on our way to trial in a Federal courthouse for no crime whatsoever, and toasting the First Amendment to the Constitution."

"I'll drink to that," Bruce said.

"Unless they find out what your Peter Johnson is up to and shoot him."

"Not likely."

"Now that we've voiced our trust in the First Amendment," Sylvia Kline said, "let's get back to reality, and the worst mistake we can make is to think that this trial is of no real importance. Until now, they've limited their attack to left-wingers, people who might or might not be communists, and of course, under the Smith Act, the twelve Party leaders. This time, they're reaching out. The only connection they can make for you is India, and that's a contrivance on their part. As far as your past in this country is concerned, it's snow white."

"And don't think that doesn't trouble me," Bruce said. "Not to realize the misery of those Depression years is nothing to be very proud of."

"We're not dealing with that," Sylvia said. "We're dealing with the misery of these years, so put away the guilt and listen to me."

If he could only shake loose from the absurdity of it, he could put his mind to work. Had decent people in Germany also taken shelter in the absurdity? When you took away all the catchwords that went with war and power—courage, glory, patriotism, motherland, honor, and all the rest—you were left with this strange animal called man scrabbling in the mud, driven by a lunatic lust to kill, lost to compassion, and motivated by lies that reached back in history like beads on a string.

"Bruce?"

"Should we order now?" he asked them. "I had the chicken last time," he reminded Molly. "Unlucky. I'll have the ham steak this time."

"Yes, order," Sylvia agreed, shaking her head. "You lack indignation, and I can't understand that."

But he hardly touched his food, and that said something to both women. Gently, Sylvia said to him, "I want you to know what I think will happen. My guess is that they will pick out two points. One, a government witness, recently in the Party, who will swear under oath that you are a communist. Now, they will not prosecute for perjury, because there's no way they could make it stick in a perjury trial, but they'll use it for the contempt. Secondly, they'll fix on your unwillingness to testify about Molly. Will you change your mind about that?"

"No."

"We've been through this half a dozen times. I don't think you're taking a sensible position. Neither does Molly."

"To put it mildly," Molly agreed.

"I mean," Sylvia explained, "that if I could tell the government attorney that you are willing to rectify the contempt by answering questions about Molly, he might just be willing to drop the charges. It's a fairly common practice."

"No. No way. And what about your government witness?"

"I would hope that if the testimony about Molly is cleared up, they might drop the other thing as well."

"Do you remember," he reminded Sylvia, "that you told me it was stacked? I've grown up, my dear. They don't give a damn whether or not I testify about Molly, and I'm not going to crawl on my belly to plead with swine. The breed isn't strange to me. I stood in a concentration camp and looked into open graves."

Molly shook her head, and Sylvia sighed and gave up on an old argument. Afterward, she said to Molly, "I don't know whether he's simple or wonderful, but if you find me another like him, I'll take a chance."

The jury had come in with a decision in the trial of the twelve leaders of the Communist Party, U.S.A. They were found guilty. Bruce and Molly read the headline story in the *Washington Post.*

"So it begins," Bruce said.

"Guilty of teaching the overthrow of the government by force and violence," Molly said. "Poor devils. They couldn't overthrow a proper doghouse."

"You know them—I mean personally?"

"I know them, but personally is a difficult question. They tend to hide behind the image. I've been around just long enough, Bruce, to know there are no heroes. We're all shabby, and when we get into a position of power, we're even shabbier. We have our saints, but they don't get into positions of power. That's the pity of saints, they're such a quiet lot."

That night, making love, she said to Bruce, "I never meant you in the shabby lot."

The first morning in the gloomy Federal courthouse, the three New Yorkers were bemused by the entrance of a former mayor of Boston, an old man in a wheelchair, who wept and promised to sin no more, after which the judge suspended his sentence. The judge, Harwood Wilson by name, had thin lips, a delicate nose, and two cold pale blue eyes behind his gold-rimmed glasses. He had a habit of pursing his lipless mouth and blinking rapidly. Molly whispered that she could never trust a man with two family names, and Bruce said that was because she was shanty Irish and lucky to have any name at all. Sylvia said that once the trial began, Molly would have to wait outside, to which Molly said, "But I can be helpful."

"When you're a witness," she said firmly. "Now get out of here and leave it to me. I'm going to start with a motion to vacate the indictment. It's hogwash anyway."

Molly left the court, and Bruce watched Sylvia in amazement, a most remarkable young woman. He was relaxed now; they had come together, he and Molly, and it would be all right. He had told her the night before, "You're the good thing that happened to me. Whatever my life is now, it's better than it could have been any other way." And now, watching Sylvia, he felt that she too was perhaps the best he might have done in the way of a lawyer, just a smart kid who would give it her best shot, and that was all right.

She moved for dismissal of the indictment. Judge Wilson agreed that he would hear argument. Albert Button, the Federal attorney, watched Sylvia with interest. He was a tall man in his fifties, with a heavy stomach, and perhaps conscious of a bad physical comparison to the young woman he opposed.

"There has been no contempt," Sylvia said, "and the House vote as well as the indictment are entirely without merit. My client was asked whether his friend, Molly Maguire, was a communist. He refused to reply to this question on grounds of honor, since it would put him in the role of an informer, giving evidence against a woman who was his dear friend. But Miss Maguire was at that time a writer on the staff of the *New York Daily Worker,* a professedly communist newspaper that employs only communists. This is public knowledge, and in her writing for this paper, Miss Maguire has identified herself as a communist at least thirty-three times. So there could have been no question on that subject, and her political identity was well known to the members of the House Committee on Un-American Activities. Therefore, it is evident that the question was purely a provocation, designed to entrap my client by playing upon his sense of right and wrong and simple human decency. I think it is to the credit of my client that this committee should seek to entrap him by concluding that he, as a fine person, might well be pressed into an act of contempt—or at least an act which would allow them to charge contempt—simply by honoring his beliefs."

The Federal attorney sat behind his table during this, smiling slightly and occasionally exchanging glances with his assistant. When Sylvia finished, he rose to speak.

"I find my opponent's argument very touching, but I must remind her that the question was asked not simply to identify Molly Maguire as a communist, but to open up a whole line of questioning concerning Bruce Bacon's relationship to a notorious communist. It was not his refusal to state her political preference that put him in contempt, but his summary decision to close off that line of questioning completely by announcing that he would answer no questions relating in any manner to Molly Maguire. A brief glance at the records of the hearing will confirm my argument. To dismiss this line of questioning as a provocation would undermine the total work of the committee. That, Your Honor, completes my argument."

He sat down. The judge sat motionless, staring into space. A black courtroom attendant poured him a glass of ice water, and the judge sipped at it, not as a person in thirst, but as if assuring himself that the water was water. He wrote a few words on the pad in front of him, and then he looked up, smiled, and said, "I have heard your arguments. The motion is denied. I suggest we go about selecting the jury."

They began the selection of the jury.

"Where are you employed?"

"The Treasury Department."

"Where are you employed?"

"General Accounting Office."

"Where are you employed?"

"The Justice Department."

"Where are you employed?"

"I work for Congressman Field Bixton."

"Where are you employed?"

"I am a housewife."

"Where is your husband employed?"

"He's a statistician at the State Department."

It went on and on. Sylvia asked whether she might approach the bench, and standing before the judge, she asked quietly for a change of venue.

"This is the wrong time to ask for it, Miss Kline."

"I have not tried a case in Washington before. The entire panel is government-employed."

"A jury will vote the evidence, Miss Kline."

"I still request a change of venue."

Patiently, the judge said, "You forget that I shall charge the jury. We are trying a misdemeanor here, not a capital crime. I resent your implication that your client cannot get a fair trial here in my court."

"With all due respect, Your Honor, a man accused of being a communist these days cannot look for a fair trial in any court in these United States. Do you think the jurors are exempt from fear?"

"Your client is not accused of being a communist. This is a contempt citation we are trying. Now, I will hear no more on this subject."

When the day was over, they had a jury. "I feel stupid," Sylvia said at dinner that evening. "I never should have taken your case. There are lawyers who could do it better, so much better."

"I doubt it," Bruce said. "Lewis Carroll put it neatly: first the verdict, then the trial. It doesn't make a damn bit of difference, Sylvia, whatever you do."

As a matter of fact, Bruce felt, she pleaded her case very eloquently in her opening statement. She began by explaining the purpose and history of congressional committees, the fact that they had been set up so that Congress, in framing legislation, might have the right to gather whatever facts were pertinent to this legislation. This gave Congress a right to inquiry that was backed by law to the extent of a misdemeanor—in that anyone who refused information could be charged with committing a misdemeanor.

"However," she told the jury, "not by the fullest strength of the imagination could Bruce Bacon's testimony about a woman who was his dear friend be considered pertinent to the drafting of legislation. In fact, the past few years have proven that the Un-American Committee has offered no new legislation and plans to offer none. I shall show that their purpose is persecution, not information or inquiry. They have taken a privilege of Congress and turned it into a police weapon with which to subvert the Constitution of the United States. My client has done no wrong. He is not and never has been a communist. He was chosen by the committee so that they might extend the boundaries of their terror."

Albert Button, the Federal attorney, was neither eloquent nor foolish. His opening statement was short and to the point. As Sylvia Kline had anticipated, he said that he would prove to the jury's satisfaction that Bruce Bacon was a communist and that his attitude before the House Committee constituted a gross act of contempt of Congress. His first witness was Gerald Crown, counsel for the Un-American Committee. Both he and Button had printed copies of Bruce's hearing, which had been entered as evidence.

Button said to Crown: "Is it correct that you asked the defendant, Bruce Bacon, whether Molly Maguire was a member of the Communist Party?"

"May I consult the record?" Crown asked.

"Please."

Sylvia rose to object. Evidently, Button had anticipated this, and he said, looking at the printed record of the hearing, "May I revise that question, sir? Will the stenographer strike my previous question?"

"Objection," Sylvia said. "There is a deliberate attempt at confusion here. Each of these men has the hearing record in hand."

The judge was looking at the record now.

"The question was asked of Mr. Bacon a bit later. I regret my error. The record is changed accordingly."

"I see no harm done, Miss Kline," the judge said. "The confusion has been rectified."

"Then," Button said to Crown, "consulting the record, I find that the question about communist membership was not the first question put to Mr. Bacon in that matter of Miss Maguire. What was the question before the communist question?"

Again, Sylvia rose to object. Button's clumsy formulation simply displayed the word *communist* again and again. It was a trigger word, requiring neither proof nor reflection.

"You don't have a valid objection, Miss Kline, but I do suggest that Mr. Crown consult the record. He may read from it."

Button smiled and agreed and turned to the jury, placing the hearing record in context with all the gentle forbearance he could muster. Crown read from the record:

"Crown: 'Molly Maguire. Do you know her?'

"Bacon: 'Yes, I do.'

"Crown: 'Do you know that she is an employee of the *Daily Worker*?'

"Crown: 'Mr. Bacon.'

"Bacon: 'Yes—I'm sorry. I was thinking.'

"Crown: 'Concerning one Molly Maguire. I asked you whether you know that she's an employee of the *Daily Worker*?'

"Bacon: 'You know that as well as I do, and your question is pointless. Now I have something to say to you. Since I am here as a witness before a congressional committee, I will answer any—'

"Nixon: 'Will you please answer the question!'

"Bacon: 'I will answer any question about myself. I will not answer any question about Molly Maguire. I have broken no law. Neither has she, and under the law and usage of this land, I am not required indeed to answer any of your questions. If I do, I degrade myself.'

"Crown: 'Is Molly Maguire a member of the Communist Party?'"

At that point, Button held up his hand. "That will be sufficient, Mr. Crown. According to the record, Mr. Bacon refused to answer any other question. Is that so?"

"Yes, sir."

Button turned to Sylvia. "Your witness."

Sylvia turned toward the jury, and Bruce could guess that, once again, since they had been chosen, Sylvia was trying to find an open face, a hint of compassion somewhere, even a shadow of anger; but the faces were lax and loose and meaningless. They were required to sit in a jury box; they were not required to listen or think, and they knew how they must vote. Nevertheless, she smiled at them. She was attractive when she smiled.

"Mr. Crown," she said, "I want you to continue to read from the record at the point where you left off."

Button was on his feet with an objection, holding that cross-examination could only be on what had been read.

"I think not," the judge said, a moment for benevolence. "You opened and introduced the whole record."

"Please, Mr. Crown," Sylvia said.

"I have watched," Crown read from the record, "and written about a world conflict to rid this earth of Adolf Hitler and Nazism. I find your tactics no different from his."

"Thank you, Mr. Crown," Sylvia said. "And now, just to clarify things, when Mr. Bacon made that statement, he was referring to the House Committee on Un-American Activities. Is that not so?"

"Yes."

"And to clarify it even further, he was referring to practices that opened the way for Hitler and the creation of Nazi Germany?"

"No. There is no comparison."

"But you just agreed to a comparison. That is all. Thank you."

Button was on his feet again. "Did you agree to a valid comparison, Mr. Crown?"

"No, I did not."

"Thank you," Button said, offering his own smile to the jury.

Lunchtime, Molly informed them that she had shared the witness room with a snake.

"Well, we're sharing the courtroom with some."

"Be specific," Sylvia said.

"His name is Lucas Gregory. He used to be the religion editor of the *Daily Worker.*"

"Come on. You're kidding. Religion editor on the *Daily Worker*?"

Molly leaned over, kissed Bruce on the cheek and sympathized that illusions die hard. "We don't teach atheism, and to tell you the truth, very few reds are atheists. It's just too damned hard, especially since so many of us come from Catholic and Jewish homes. One religion is substituted for another, and if you don't think that socialism and the brotherhood of man is religion, you're missing the point. On the *Worker,* the religion editor is supposed to analyze politically the various positions of the various religions, and that used to be the job of Mr. Gregory. About six months ago, when the going got rough ˙and the communist leaders were indicted, Brother Gregory got religion himself and became a witness for the Feds. Or maybe he was a plant from the very beginning. Who knows?"

Sylvia nodded. "He'll finger Bruce?"

"That's my guess. He'll finger him as a Party member."

"Isn't that perjury?" Bruce asked.

"It certainly is. But he's their witness and they decide what is and what isn't perjury."

"But it's Bruce's statement that he's not in the Party.

Can't they get Bruce for perjury?" Molly asked. "That's what scares the devil out of me. Perjury's five years."

"No way. Forget it, Molly. I explained the situation to Bruce. There's no way they can prove perjury, not even with a lousy D.C. jury. They'll use the tactic here as a tactic, that's all."

Which was exactly what they did, shortly and to the point. Button called Gregory, and then Button said, "Let it be noted that I am reading from the record, already entered as evidence, of the hearing of a subcommittee of the House Committee on Un-American Activities. Quote: 'Mr Crown: Now I will ask you: Are you now or have you ever been a member of the Communist Party of the United States?'

"Mr. Bacon's reply: 'Not ever and not now.'

"Mr. Crown: 'Very well. Have you ever been a member of a communist front organization?'

"Bacon: 'You'd have to be more specific.'

"In reply to Mr. Bacon's request, Mr. Crown, counsel for the committee, specified: 'You spoke to a group called the Broadway Forum, at the Murray Hill Hotel. The Broadway Forum is on the Attorney General's list of communist front organizations.'

"And in response to this, Mr. Bacon said: 'I don't belong to the Broadway Forum, if indeed it has a membership. I was invited to speak to a group of journalists, and I did.' "

At this point, Button returned to his table, dropped the record, and turned to Lucas Gregory and said, "You have heard the material read from the record of Mr. Bacon's examination by Mr. Crown, as counsel for the committee?"

"Yes, sir."

"I would like you to keep it in mind. Were you ever a member of the Communist Party, Mr. Gregory?"

Gregory was a stout, prim little man. No more than five feet, six inches in height, he had pink cheeks, pale eyes, and a bristle of sandy hair. He was in his mid-fifties, wore a pince-nez, and answered questions with a beseeching smile.

Afterward, Sylvia remarked that he made a convincing witness, to which Molly replied that he had certainly had sufficient practice.

Before answering, Gregory placed his pince-nez in his vest pocket—he wore a neat, vested worsted suit—and stretched the moment. No quick, top-of-the-head answers for him. "Yes," he said, "I was a member of the Communist Party for twelve years. Prior to that, I taught in the divinity school of which I was a graduate."

"And what led you into the Party, Mr. Gregory?"

"Misplaced idealism, sir. I saw it as a road toward true Christian socialism and the eventual brotherhood of man."

"And why did you leave the Party, Mr. Gregory?"

"Because I found that my expectations were cruel delusions. I found that this so-called Party of the Working Class was a tool of the Soviets—"

Sylvia objected. "My client is not on trial for being a communist, which he is not, and neither is the Communist Party on trial."

"Do you intend to connect this?" the judge asked Button.

"I do, Your Honor."

"Then I'll allow it and overrule your objection, Miss Kline."

"Nevertheless," Button said to Gregory, "you became the religion editor of the *Daily Worker.*"

"That is correct, sir."

"Now let me ask you this, as an expert in Communist Party tactics, is the Broadway Forum a communist front?"

"Absolutely. It was organized by the Party for a very specific purpose."

"And what is that purpose?"

"To introduce innocent people to aspects of the world as seen and interpreted by the Communist Party."

Again, Sylvia objected to a definition of the Party being imposed on the jury before any evidence had been presented, and again the judge overruled her objection.

"Would the Broadway Forum present a speaker who was not a communist?"

"Possibly—on some very few occasions. But for the most part, the speakers are card-carrying members of the Communist Party."

"I see. Now in your opinion, Mr. Gregory, is Mr. Bacon a card-carrying member of the Communist Party?"

Sylvia leaped up with her objection. "Your Honor, how can he offer an unsubstantiated opinion as evidence? I object most strongly!"

"He is an expert witness, an authority on the subject. He offers only an opinion. I am sure Mr. Button will elicit the reasons why Mr. Gregory holds this opinion."

"Yes." Button smiled. "And what is the basis, Mr. Gregory, of your opinion that Bruce Bacon is a card-carrying member of the Party?"

"Well, sir, like this: one, he spoke at the Forum. Two, he included no criticism of the Soviet Union in his remarks. Three, he spoke of connections with the Communist Party of India, which would have been unlikely if he were not a member of the American Party. Four, he spoke without notes—"

"What exactly do you mean by 'without notes'?" the Federal attorney asked.

"I mean, sir, he appeared thoroughly trained in his subject—which for the most part was an attack upon an ally of the United States, namely Great Britain."

"I see. Now does that sum up—is that the extent of your feeling that Mr. Bacon is a Communist?"

Bruce, sitting behind the defense table alongside Sylvia Kline, could not believe that what his eyes and ears perceived was actually happening. Never would he have believed that a process so crude, so lugubrious, so inept, could be taking place in the capital of his own country, the United States of America. Thinking of the trial before it took place, he had imagined some brilliant and intricate contrivance, done with wit and Machiavellian intrigue, a parade of glossy false witnesses who would weave a web of destruction about him. But instead, a stupid and unbelievable little plot was being spelled out to a bored, blank-faced jury who were obviously indifferent to the matter at hand. The Federal attorney's small invention would have stumbled badly if not for a friendly judge, and the placing on the witness stand of a man so witless and indifferently corrupt as Lucas Gregory was an act of desperation—where no desperation was required.

"There was a fifth reason," Gregory said, smiling, "but it appears to have slipped my mind."

"No matter, Mr. Gregory, your four good reasons are sufficient for our purpose." He turned to Sylvia with a slight bow. "Your turn, Miss Kline."

"Thank you," Sylvia said, not rising immediately but sitting and staring at Lucas Gregory as if he were something she could not comprehend. Then she sighed, shook her head sadly, and rose and walked slowly around the table. She stood staring at the table for a long moment, and then she picked up a clipping of newsprint and said to Gregory:

"This is a clipping from the *Daily Worker*, an issue in October of nineteen forty-five. I will enter it as evidence, and then I have certain questions pertaining to it." She handed the clipping to Judge Wilson, who read through it and then handed it to Button. The clipping was entered and stamped, and then Button asked permission to approach the bench. Both he and Sylvia then went to the bench, where Button entered strong objections to the reading of the clipping.

"I know how you feel, Mr. Button," the judge said, "but you called Mr. Gregory as an expert witness. This speaks to his work in the Party." He handed the clipping back to Sylvia, who then read it aloud to the jury:

"From the *New York Daily Worker*, October twenty-seventh, nineteen forty-five: 'I have spoken to pastors of four Christian faiths, and all of them agree that the incredible defeat and destruction of the Wermacht of Nazi Germany by the Red Army of the Soviet Union must be seen as an act of divine providence. If we are to say that God is in history and that God moves with history, then certainly the communist movement is an expression of the will of the Almighty. This is not my construction, but one that reflects the thinking of the four Christian ministers I interviewed. Of course, my thinking is Marxist in content, and I might put it differently.' This is something that you wrote at that time, Mr. Gregory, is it not?"

"I can hardly remember every piece I've written. But if you say it carries my byline, I wrote it."

"And the opinion it offers of the Communist Party is quite different from the opinion you expressed a few minutes ago under the questioning of Mr. Button, is that not so?"

"If you say so."

"I do say so," Sylvia said, turning to the jury. "And the opinion it offers on the Red Army and the Soviet Union is also quite different from what you expressed here in this courtroom. Is that not so?"

"My eyes were blinded to the full reality—as were the eyes of many, including the President—"

"A plain yes or no will do. The opinion was different. Is that not so?"

"Yes."

"Is it true, Mr. Gregory, that you became an agent for the FBI while you were still pretending to be a loyal Party member?"

"No. That's not true."

"Do you know when the Broadway Forum was organized, Mr. Gregory?"

"No, I don't."

"Then let me inform you that it was organized in March of nineteen forty-six. That was after you left the Communist Party, was it not?" And when there was no response from

Gregory, she snapped, "Answer my question, Mr. Gregory!"

"Yes, after I left the Communist Party."

Sylvia walked to her table, spreading the pile of notes and selecting a single sheet; and staring at it, without looking at Gregory, she said, "You are a professional witness, aren't you, Mr. Gregory?"

"I don't know what you mean by that."

"I mean that during the last two years, you have appeared as a witness eleven times—five times in contempt of Congress cases, four times in the trial of the Communist Party leaders and two other similar trials, and once in a perjury trial. Do you get paid for these appearances?"

"I get my expenses."

"And that's all?"

"Sometimes other payments."

Sylvia nodded. "You work hard at betrayal. Are you being paid in this case?"

Button rose to object to Sylvia's characterization of the witness. The judge upheld him. Sylvia rescinded the characterization, and asked Gregory whether he had ever attended a meeting of the Broadway Forum.

"No. I don't go to communist meetings. I have no interest in them."

"But you are an expert witness on their content. How can that be if you never attend any of them?"

"Because I know how the Party works."

"Without being there? That's remarkable. Did you know that Eugene O'Neill and Sinclair Lewis and Robert Frost all spoke at the Broadway Forum?"

"I didn't know that," Gregory replied, his confidence increasing. "I don't keep track of every speaker."

"And Father Le Grand, a Paulist priest? Are these people communists?"

"If they spoke at the Broadway Forum, they have a relationship to communism."

"And what exactly is a relationship? I am a little uneasy in the assumption, but it would appear that you are a human being, and since I am also a human being—"

Button rose to object.

"—we have a relationship, although I am not proud of it."

Button objected to Miss Kline's constant demeaning of the witness. The judge had not been listening intently, and he called both attorneys to the bench.

"She constantly insults the witness. The witness is an honorable man, a former minister of the Gospel."

"Enlighten me," the judge said.

"She calls him nonhuman."

"I simply said," Sylvia protested, "that he appeared to be a human being. That's hardly an insult."

"Let it pass," the judge said. He wanted to get the day over.

"The objection, Your Honor?" the stenographer asked.

"Overruled," the judge said. It made a better record if some of the government's objections were overruled.

"I asked you before and I ask you again, what precisely is this relationship you speak of."

"A connection with the Communist Party."

"You've heard Senator McCarthy characterize the Secretary of State as a communist. Does he have the same connection with the Communist Party?"

Button was on his feet, objecting.

"He introduced the Broadway Forum!" Sylvia protested. "Mr. Button opened the door."

"Senator McCarthy has no connection with the Broadway Forum," Button said.

"I suggest you save it for your closing remarks, Miss Kline," the judge said. "I'll allow the objection."

Sylvia turned to Gregory and said, "Do you have any proof of your assertion that Mr. Bacon is a member of the Communist Party?"

"My experience tells me that he is."

There was no rebuttal. The government finished its case, and left Bruce dumbfounded. "Is that it? Is that all?"

"Apparently," Sylvia said.

"And that's what they're putting out to convict me?"

"I'm afraid it's all they need."

At dinner that evening, Sylvia sat depressed and silent as Bruce reported to Molly on their day in court.

"What do you make of it?" Molly asked Sylvia.

"It's perfunctory," Sylvia replied. "It's a charade. The law says that there must be a trial, and so we are having a trial. The verdict is in, but we are having a trial. I'm not earning the five hundred dollars a day that I'm charging you, and when you come right down to it, you don't need a lawyer."

"Of course I need a lawyer."

"I'll ask for a dismissal tomorrow," Sylvia said. "They have no case and they've presented no case. In any court that dealt in proper law, the judge would throw out the case. Judge Harwood Wilson will not. What gets to me is not that they're playing dirty; I expected that; but their moves are so stupid and obvious that I anticipate each one. That's what gets to me."

Bruce couldn't make love that night. Rigid, he drew back from Molly's hands. Each rejection of her was, as Molly realized full well, a matter of blame that left him cold and filled with an anger he couldn't express. He would deny that he held her in any way responsible for the position he was in; he would deny that he had any fear of prison; but both denials were unreal, and underneath his claim to total objectivity was fear and blame, both very real—and both capable of immersing him in guilt; and it was not guilt alone but a terror that, unable to conceal the fact that he blamed her, he would lose her. It was the thought of losing her that put things in proper order. It was not Molly but Greenberg who had brought him to the Broadway Forum, and it was not

Molly but Legerman who had made the connection with the Bengali communists.

Unable to sleep, he lay in silence for more than an hour, and then softly and tentatively asked Molly whether she was asleep.

"No."

He rolled over to embrace her, and she welcomed him, wrapping her arms around him.

"I love you so much," he said. "There's no way I can tell you how much I love you."

"And you blame me."

"No, I don't blame you. Maybe sometimes for a little, and I know how crazy that is, and then I am terrified that I might drive you away."

"You'll never drive me away," Molly said.

"You know how much danger I've seen. I told you about the time I was trapped in a foxhole, interviewing a GI, and a counterattack rolled past us. I spent the whole night in that hole, and God Almighty, I was so scared, but not this way. I've never been frightened this way before. They take away my rights, my strength, my belief, my whole lifelong faith in this beloved country of mine. I know you grew up in poverty and bitterness, and I understand completely why you're a red, but I grew up with my belief in this country never tested, not even during the war. Oh, I know we produced bastards during the war, men like Patton, but they were part of the need to win; America, the golden God-anointed power that destroyed Hitler. And now, a few years later, I'm here in this lunatic courtroom, being tried in a scene out of Lewis Carroll. I don't know how to deal with it, Molly. Your Party leaders accepted it as the logic of their lives. I suppose for years you've all been preaching the corruption of our system, and now it confirms what you believe. But I can't stop believing the other way."

"Then believe your way, darling, and this is a filthy, momentary aberration. We'll live through it, believe me."

In the morning, at breakfast, Sylvia told them that the way the judge was pushing it along, they might very well wind up today. "I have only one real witness, Bruce, and that's Molly. What about our character witnesses?"

"I called Dad last night. He'll take a very early train and be here before the noon break. On the other hand, I called my one-time editor, and he said that the board felt it would be an improper position for the press to take—almost a matter of a conflict of interest. I spent four years in college to learn less than I've learned in a few days in the capital of my country."

"Don't sweat over it," Sylvia said. "We'll give it our best shot, which is just about all we can do."

But with Molly in the witness stand and Sylvia facing her, Bruce felt that he would have been better off if he had come down without a lawyer, dispensed with the jury, and told the judge to do whatever he had been instructed to do. Quickly, no fuss, no expense. Well, he had missed that, and here he was, clinging with a very thin thread to the efforts of two women.

Molly wore her sober gray flannel full skirt, a white cotton blouse, and her hair gathered in a bun at the back of her neck. Her lips were red, but modestly so against the milk-white of her skin. Usually, she wore no makeup, but in this case Sylvia persuaded her that one of the points held against communists was that the women tended to go without makeup. While Molly protested that this was apocryphal, she agreed to lip rouge. Noticing the way both men and women in the jury stared at her, Bruce wondered whether she might shorten the odds.

Sylvia began with name, origin, and religion. "Please tell us what is your religion?"

"I'm a Catholic," Molly said.

"And what church do you belong to?"

"Our family," Molly said, choosing the words carefully,

"are in the parish of Father John Boyle's Church of the Sacred Heart in South Boston."

"And do you attend that church?" Sylvia asked.

"When I'm in Boston."

"And what is your occupation, Miss Maguire?"

"I am a journalist," Molly replied, relieved that she had limited her evasions—not lies, she told herself—about matters of religion. Sylvia had talked her into that, but Molly did not believe for a moment that such religious definitions would mean a thing to the blank-faced jurors. "I work for the *New York Daily Worker*."

"And that is a communist paper, is it not?"

"It is."

"And you are a member of the Communist Party."

"Yes, I am."

"How long have you been a member of the Communist Party?"

"Twelve years or so."

"Do you know the defendant, Miss Maguire?"

"I know him very well."

"Would you point to him?"

She pointed, unable to repress a smile. Bruce grinned back. The torpor and depression of the previous day had gone.

"Let the record show that Miss Maguire pointed to the defendant, Bruce Bacon."

Molly began to giggle. Bruce stifled his laughter, and the judge chided Sylvia.

"What is your relationship to the defendant?"

"He is a dear friend."

"And how did you meet the defendant, Miss Maguire?"

"I met him the evening he spoke at the Broadway Forum."

"Was he at that time a communist?"

"No. Not only was he not a communist, but he had only the vaguest notion about what communism was."

"Did you ever try to convert him to your point of view?"

"No. For one thing, he is stubborn. For another, he was so immersed in his devotion to his native land that he refused even to begin any such discussion. Whereupon, we avoided it."

"Have you any opinion as to why your friend, Mr. Bacon, was called before the House Committee?"

"Yes, I have. I believe they are using their power to intimidate liberals who have no connection with the Communist Party—"

Button stopped her with his shouted objection: "The House Committee on Un-American Activities is not on trial here!"

Both attorneys went up to the bench. Bruce's father entered the courtroom, and Bruce motioned to him to sit beside him for a moment. "Dad, good to see you. You'll have to wait outside in the witness room until you're called."

"How's it going?"

Bruce shrugged. "We'll talk about it." He nodded to the attendant, who led his father to the witness room. Sylvia was saying to Molly, "Why do you suppose Bruce Bacon refused to answer any questions concerning you?"

"I think he loves me—I hope he does. He considers that to inform on me in any way would be dishonorable and leave him in a position where he could not live with himself. There is a long tradition, especially in Ireland, the country my parents came from, about informers being beneath contempt—"

Button objected, and the judge said with annoyance, "Why don't you leave the rhetoric to your lawyer's closing remarks, Miss Maguire?"

"I was trying to answer the question."

"The question itself is improper," Button held.

The answer was stricken from the record, and Sylvia asked Molly whether she had any scruples about answering questions about herself.

"None whatsoever."

"Then if the House Committee had subpoenaed you instead of Mr. Bacon, all their questions would have been answered."

Again Button objected. The judge motioned them to the bench, and Sylvia said hoarsely, "A man is on trial because he will not inform on a woman he loves. The House Committee's purpose is obtaining information. That is the purpose of every congressional committee. Your Honor, I am making the point that such information was readily available. Miss Maguire would and will testify and answer all questions."

"Your presumption. The House Committee is one thing, the evidence presented at this trial is something else. If the House Committee desires to hear from Miss Maguire, they have the right to subpoena her. You should know, Miss Kline, what the rules are in this court. You are permitted to practice law in the District of Columbia on the basis of knowing those rules. Now let's get on with it."

Sylvia Kline went on, trying to prove the innocence of Bruce where communism was concerned and the decency of Bruce where informing was concerned. But neither innocence nor decency was effective in that courtroom.

In his cross-examination, Button asked one question: "Do you and Mr. Bacon share the same apartment?"

"No, I live on Twenty-ninth Street. Mr. Bacon lives on Seventy-sixth Street."

"I have no other questions of this witness," Button said.

As far as Bruce and Molly could see, like running a race, it was clear the courtroom today and get them out of here and do it in all speed. Bruce's father took the stand as a character witness. Sylvia spent half an hour eliciting facts about Bruce's innocence and all-American Eagle Scout patriotism—to the point where it turned Bruce's stomach. He did not enjoy the picture his father painted; he saw that picture reproduced a thousand times, in the young West

Pointers he had met overseas, in the clean-cut CIA opera-
tives, in young men scurrying around Washington; yet his
father told only the truth without exaggeration, his son
Bruce Nathaniel as he had raised him and seen him.

"Did I do all right?" he asked Bruce afterward. Dr. Bacon seemed to his son to have lost weight, a man smaller,
thinner, pleading with the world to leave his son, who had
done no wrong, alone. What was happening could not be
happening, because in his world there was no place for it, no
reason for it, no comprehension of it. His friends at the
hospital club discussed Senator McCarthy and his two assistants, Cohn and Schine, as if they were creatures in another
world, with mockery and distaste and occasionally laughter,
but never as participants in their own lives. What had happened to his world? His wife blamed it on Molly Maguire,
but sitting next to her at dinner, he had to reject his wife's
assessment.

Molly was no longer the wary, defensive woman who had
come to dinner that night. She watched Bruce with a loving
eye that missed nothing, her manner gentle and caressing
without being obviously so. She was a strong woman, broad
hips, a wide pelvis. As a medical man, he noticed that. She
would bear children easily.

"We must not be too upset, any of us," Sylvia told them.
"If we lose here, we can appeal it, and even if we lose the
appeal, it's very rare that a contempt sentence is more than
a few months in prison, and even then it's usually suspended. There might be a fine of a few thousand dollars."

"We won't worry about the fine," Dr. Bacon said.

The next day, Sylvia made her closing statement. The first
part dealt with the traditional role of congressional committees, as instruments with which to gather information to be
used in framing legislation. "And that is entirely proper,"
she said. "Without the right to gather information, Congress
would be partially blinded, and it is fitting that no information should be denied to a congressional committee, even

this one. But this committee is not being used in the sense
that it was intended for. It has been turned into an instrument of terror. It has undermined the Bill of Rights, and in
its new guise, it has created a climate of fear that pervades
this nation. You may say, If one is honest and has nothing to
hide, why should he fear the Un-American Committee? All
he has to do is to tell the truth. But what purpose does the
truth serve when the government can procure a professional
witness like Lucas Gregory, who will swear to anything?
Here, during the past few days, you have seen an honorable
and gifted man put on trial for no crime, for no wrongdoing,
for no harm done to anyone, accused falsely and put in
jeopardy, his good name darkened, his place in society so
damaged that all his work and reputation as a brave and
generous war correspondent have been tarnished. For years,
risking life and limb beyond the call of duty, he brought into
millions of American homes the story of a great and terrible
war against tyranny and the same subjugation of the human
spirit that you have witnessed in this courtroom. I plead for
a verdict that will find him innocent of anything but human
decency and a proper love of his country."

On the other hand, Albert Button, Federal attorney, was
brief and to the point: "The act of being contemptacious
consists, among other things, of refusing to answer questions
put to one by a duly constituted congressional committee.
The record shows that Bruce Bacon has so refused. You
heard the record read and you heard the refusal stipulated.
The Congress of the United States found the defendant in
contempt, and this finding has been verified in this courtroom. I ask you to find the defendant guilty of contempt of
Congress."

Judge Wilson, in his charge to the jury, repeated the Federal attorney's explanation of the contempt of Congress process. Then he went on to say, "Many extraneous matters
have been brought into this trial, and without speaking to
their merit or lack of merit, I must tell you that none of

those extraneous matters are at issue. The only thing at issue is whether the defendant, Bruce Bacon, has engaged in contempt of Congress. You know precisely what such contempt consists of. You will now discuss the evidence presented and decide upon a verdict."

The jury filed into the jury room, the court was adjourned, and Bruce and Sylvia joined Molly and Dr. Bacon in the witness room. Dr. Bacon was wondering whether it made sense for him to remain in Washington. He had canceled all surgery for these two days, and he wondered whether the jury might be out for the rest of today into tomorrow.

"I think not," Sylvia said unhappily. "This is one of those handwriting-on-the-wall things. They'll take a vote and vote guilty, which they have most likely finished by now, and then they'll stretch it to a half hour to make it look otherwise than ridiculous."

"Oh, no," Dr. Bacon said. "I can't believe that. I listened to your closing remarks, and they were most eloquent. I don't see how anyone could be unaffected by them."

"But the jury didn't listen," Sylvia said bitterly. "They were thinking that in a few hours it would all be over and they could go home and shuck this commie case. The jury have their jobs and their families to think about, and they will not be drawn into ideology."

As she finished, an attendant came to usher them back into the courtroom. The jury were filing into the jury box and taking their seats. The foreman remained standing.

"Have you come to a verdict?" the judge asked the foreman.

"We have, Your Honor." The foreman handed a slip of paper to the attendant, who handed it to the judge. Judge Wilson read it and handed it back to the attendant. The attendant handed it to the foreman, and then the attendant said, "Everyone please rise."

The foreman said, "We find Bruce Bacon guilty of contempt of Congress."

It was exactly thirty-one minutes since the jury had left for the jury room.

Enter Here

Three weeks later, they returned to Washington for the sentencing. After a meandering homily, Judge Harwood Wilson sentenced Bruce to a year in Federal prison, minus a day, and set bail at five thousand dollars. Until now, he had been free on his own recognizance; now, found guilty and sentenced to prison, he was subject to a reasonably high bail —or perhaps unreasonably high, according to Sylvia. Molly's reaction was tears. Bit by bit, the action against Bruce was splintering her pretense at a tough, unbreakable will.

Sylvia fought to remain calm, to be a pillar of assurance and strength. More and more, Bruce was coming to appreciate this slender, gentle woman, self-effacing on the one hand, rocklike on the other. She offered both of them the hope of the appeal, and that hope lasted the three months that passed between her filing and the decision. In that time, the important factor in Bruce's life was the signing of a contract with the Temple Press in San Francisco for the publication of his book. With that, the years since the war would not have been wasted and meaningless. He had at least an anchor to the world he had returned to.

His folks gave a small party in very quiet celebration. They had become as involved with the book's publication as he, and they brought about a dozen old friends of Bruce and the family together.

Molly refused to come, and when Bruce pressed her, almost in desperation, she stubbornly refused to be persuaded.

"No," she said, "it's out of the question. I'll be damned if I'll be exhibited as a curiosity, the cheap Mick from Boston, with the wild red hair that probably came out of a bottle. Well, mine did not come out of a bottle! No," she went on, easing a bit, "that's not for me, Bruce. I'd only spoil it. You go and enjoy. The party's for you."

"That's crazy," he said. "What's come over you?"

More tears again. She lay in his arms, sobbing. "Oh, Jesus," she said, "I can't do it. I can't make a year without you. I can't. Bruce, my life's coming apart. It's coming apart at every seam."

"Suppose it were me instead of you—I mean you picked up and sent to prison, and I'm out here waiting."

"You're a man."

"I hope. But there's more strength in you than I ever dreamed of having, and I'm not going to jail. Sylvia says the sentence is as outrageous as the trial. She feels we can get a reversal in the Court of Appeals."

"Come on, darling, Sylvia's not that foolish. Not one of the convictions have been reversed in the Appellate, and we've drawn a judge named Prettyman, and according to Sylvia, he's death in these cases. My dear God, Bruce, I want you to hope, but it'll be worse if you hope too much and then all our hopes are shattered."

Molly did not go to the party, and Bruce's mother took heart. She felt that if only Molly could be taken out of the picture, everything would reverse itself and her son would not have to go to prison, and as unreal as such a conclusion might be, a part of her believed it. She was psychologically unable to accept the fact that there could be a lack of justice in her country. Such things happened elsewhere, not here; and she was most careful and gentle as she asked Bruce whether Molly was ill.

"She couldn't come," Bruce said shortly.

But Molly was right about the Appellate Court, and some

six weeks after the party that Molly had refused to attend, that court rendered its decision.

Sylvia Kline called Bruce and asked him to come down to her office, but instead of the formal cool handshake that usually went for greeting between them, she threw her arms around him, held on to him for a long moment, and then pulled away, embarrassed and full of apology. She bent her head, pulled a tissue from a box on her desk, wiped away her tears, and said, "Please sit down, Bruce. Forgive me. You don't know how hard I practice not being sentimental, but this—it's like everything I believe in washed out."

"They turned us down."

"Yes." She tried to keep back more tears. "Let me read you something. It's a few paragraphs from the majority decision. You have to understand what is happening.

" 'If Congress has power to inquire into communism and the Communist Party,' " Sylvia read, " 'then it must have the very same power and the very same and wholly legal right to identify the individuals who believe in communism and those who belong to the Party. The nature and scope of the program and activities depend in large measure upon the character and number of their adherents. Personnel is part of the subject. Moreover, the accuracy of the information obtained depends in large part upon the knowledge and the attitude of the witness, whether present before the committee or represented by the testimony of another. We note at this point that the arguments directed to the invalidity of this inquiry under the First Amendment would apply to an inquiry directed to another person as well as to one directed to the individual himself. The problem relates to the problem of inquiry into a matter which is not in violation of law.

" 'In our view, it would be sheer folly as a matter of governmental policy for an existing government to refrain from inquiry from potential threats to its existence or authority until danger was clear and present. And for the Judicial Branch of government to hold the Legislative Branch to be without power to make such an inquiry until the danger is clear and present would be absurd.' "

Then Sylvia added, "It's very scary."

"In other words," Bruce said, "you don't need a crime, you don't need a witness. You just put people in jail when you wish to put them in jail."

"That's about it."

"And now it's my turn. When?"

"There's still the Supreme Court. They have refused to hear any of the other cases, even when the First Amendment was invoked, and we're rather naked when it comes to constitutional argument. You invoked nothing. You simply told them to go to hell and be damned, which was very brave of you, but doesn't help us now. Also, it's very expensive."

"Do we have any chance?"

"Bruce, what can I tell you? There's always a chance of something, but nothing has changed. Truman is still President. McCarthy is still the honcho night rider, and people are more terrified than ever. It might give you a few more months on the outside, but I must be honest, and the way I see it at this point, nothing can alter the verdict. The bitter truth of it is that the Supreme Court cannot hear these cases. If they reverse on even one case, it would break the dam, and they haven't enough guts to do that."

"Then I might as well get on with it and do the time, and get it out of my life."

"I want you to think about it, at least overnight. Talk it over with Molly. I'll get us enough extra days to give you the time to wind up your affairs."

"And then?"

"We go down to Washington, and you surrender yourself formally . . ." She hesitated. "Well—that's it. You're in jail."

"Do I get the bail money back?" He was speaking slowly, carefully. "I know I get it back. But when?"

"After you surrender—a day or two. Don't worry about it, Bruce. I'll take care of it and deposit it wherever you say."

"I want you to give it to Molly. She's waiting tables again, and I know how she hates it. The five thousand dollars will take her through the year. Isn't there any way, Sylvia, you can help her find a decent job?"

"I wish I could. Bruce, you don't go from the *Daily Worker* into a decent job."

"And I want you to bill me today—for everything. I have enough money to take care of that."

"Don't worry about the bill. I'll get to it."

"When? When I'm in jail?"

"I'll get to it. There's no hurry. I'm not starving, and you can still sign a check in jail."

"And one more thing I'm going to ask of you: Can you get me eight days?"

"I think so."

Bruce looked at her, the small, regular features, the bright blue eyes, and dark brown hair. Birdlike, people might say, but when she spoke or smiled or wept, something happened that lit up her face and made it quite wonderful.

"I owe you so much," Bruce said to her. "I don't know how to repay you, and I certainly can't afford to pay you what should be paid for what you've done. More than a lawyer—you've been a fine, dear friend. God bless you."

"On the other hand," she said, in control now, "I've been with you and Molly all these long months. That's payment in kind."

Molly was in control of herself when they met for dinner that same evening. She worked breakfast and lunch, never the evening hours, which would have kept them apart too much. Through the meal, she talked little. She was turned inward. She listened as Bruce reported on his meeting with Sylvia. When he had finished, she was silent for a while. The dinner ended. The coffee came. It was a small, inexpensive

Italian restaurant, and the hour was late. Only one other table was occupied. Bruce ordered brandy, and when it came he poured his into his coffee. Molly looked at him inquiringly.

"I did it that way in North Africa. It's not great. I just wanted to remember the taste."

She did the same thing. "I'll remember too."

"You are a damn strange woman."

"I think you said that a couple of times. Maybe I'm not so strange. Maybe you're strange." She tasted the coffee and made a face. "That's what you want to remember?"

"More or less."

"However," Molly said, bringing it out of nowhere, "I don't give up. I don't give up and I don't accept anything the way it is. You're going to jail in a few days, and you're going to be there for a year, and the way the Feds make the rules, only your wife or father or mother or your lawyer can visit you, and I'm none of them, and if you want to walk out of here and not see me for twelve months, that's one thing; and that's all right, and I can take it and go on living, but not as your girl. On the other hand, if you love me, I want to marry you, now, before you go into the slammer."

"Molly—darling, we only have seven or eight days at the most."

"We can set the world on fire in a week. We can get our Wassermans in the morning, get married at City Hall, get the sleeper to Boston, and be married by a priest that day. The priest is for Mom. Otherwise, she'd die, and I can't take away from her the one sustaining thing she has. If you love me?"

"I love you. Let's hang on to that and tell me what I do about Dr. Bacon and his wife."

She was eager and alive now. "Don't bedevil them with it. Write to them after you're in jail. Tell them when you come out we'll have a great wonderful party, and I'll marry you again. I'll marry you as many times as you want, but one thing I will not do is weep in my pillow for twelve endless months."

"And what priest will marry us in Boston, with you a Catholic and me a Protestant?"

"That is no problem—absolutely no problem. Bernadette has a Jesuit, Paul O'Hara, who's madly in love with her and pleads with her to stop being a nun so he can stop being a Jesuit and marry her, and he'd marry a Hindu to a Muslim if Bernadette asked him to."

"What are you telling me? That these shenanigans go on in the Catholic Church, a priest marrying a nun?"

"Hold on, hold on, and keep it soft, because this is an Irish kind of thing and we're in an Italian restaurant and the Italians might take a dim view of our talk and toss us out on our respective ears. Who said a priest marries a nun? If she left her calling, she would not be a nun, and if he left his calling he would no longer be a priest. It happens, and sooner or later it will happen with Bernadette, but it has to wait because my poor mother would agonize too much. And furthermore, if we were not married in the church, I couldn't sleep with you without agonizing myself."

"But you've been sleeping with me for a couple of years. You are crazy—absolutely crazy."

"My love, we weren't married."

"God help me."

"Oh, He will, He will," Molly pleaded. "And now marry me—please."

"Sure," Bruce said. "No sweat. First thing tomorrow. And now let's pay the check and get out of here, and have one more night in bed without guilt."

"Ah, you're a wonderful, fine, Christian broth of a lad."

"Absolutely. And you're the strangest damn communist I ever heard of. I'm going to Boston tomorrow night to be married a second time to a Catholic lady by a priest who is in love with a nun, and I'm doing all this of my own free will a few days before I am going to be put away in the slammer for twelve long months. What did I miss? Yes, married to a card-carrying member of the Communist Party. God help me."

"All right," Molly said, "I'll explain once more, and listen carefully. First thing, we never mention your first marriage. Mom doesn't know about it, none of my family do. We don't lie, we just leave it off-stage, so to speak. About my first marriage, my husband was Jewish, and as I told you, the church doesn't recognize it. So in a Catholic sense, I never was married. This is not something I like. It belongs in the Middle Ages, but it is a fact, and the marriage was performed by a justice of the peace. Now there are different ways we can go. For one thing, the priest can simply witness an exchange of vows for the State of Massachusetts, but I don't think Paul will go that way. He might insist that no mass is offered or he might want it outside the rail, but I don't see any reason why. I think he'll make it very ordinary."

"And you're not worried about—"

Molly smiled. "What? Sin?"

"All right. You're a Catholic. Sin."

"Oh, Bruce—can't you understand? In my book, there's only one sin, to cause pain to another. I don't believe in any heaven or hell except what men make right here on earth, and now let's finish with this kind of talk and go home to bed."

The wedding in Boston was very simple, in the small chapel of a big church, with only Molly's mother and her two sisters and brother-in-law present, and Father O'Hara diplomatically avoiding questions and pitfalls. Bruce was amazed at how easily and undisturbedly the Maguires accepted the situation, as if life was a street where the turnings could not be anticipated and should not be cursed. On his part, Bruce alternated between moments of love and pleasure and moments of sheer panic. He had lived until now a life that was filled with futures; and now he had stepped into a world without any real or predictable future. He had been inaugurated into membership in the world of the poor and powerless, where a couple of stiff whiskies eased both pain and promise. He was very conscious of Molly watching him constantly, aware of every reaction on his part—so as to speak like a mental angel trying to anticipate and ease his hurt.

Father O'Hara, a lean, ascetic-looking man, shook Bruce's hand warmly and told him that he had been following the case. "A bitter, awful injustice," he said, and Bruce, on the other hand, replied that he hoped no harm would come to O'Hara.

"What harm?" O'Hara answered. "I'm revising some priorities, but doing no wrong. You married a fine, strong woman, and you're a proper man for her. Just let things work their way out."

One way with the bus was enough. They returned to Joe Carlino's house, where Mary had set out a huge repast, and Molly put her foot down and said, "The hell with saving. We'll take the sleeper back and have at least that much of a wedding night."

Molly stayed sober, with the instinct that someone had to stay sober and get Bruce onto the train when the time came, and Bruce and Father O'Hara got slowly and warmly drunk, opening their hearts to each other. Each lived with the guilts of an insane world and listened to mankind's pain. "Each of us are cursed with it," O'Hara said after an hour or so of talking and drinking. "You're a blood brother, Bacon, and you'd make a good priest and so would I if we could find us a church without sin. But as it is, we'll do the best we can and carry some poor, bleeding little church with us, which is a drunken, Irish way of blessing our uneasy burden. Perhaps the Irish drink because they have such a profound love for the music of words, and with liquor the words come easily. There's a profound truth in the fact that in the beginning was the Word, and the Word was with God and God was the Word, but I'm too besotted to see more than a tiny sparkle of light behind it. When you get out of jail, hale and healthy, God willing, we'll see something of each other."

There were some friends of Joe and Mary, and an old lady who had come over to America in the same steerage as Mrs. Maguire, and the four Carlino kids, and it all made for a packed room and a great deal of kissing and hugging and tears before Molly got a barely ambulatory Bruce into a cab and down to the station and into a bedroom on the New York sleeper.

"A sleeper," he said. "Oh, but you've gone stylish, Molly Maguire."

"I'm Molly Bacon now. Please to remember."

He was not the kind of drunk who loses the sense of things, and when Molly showed him a cash gift of five hundred dollars that her mother had given her, he shook his head unhappily and insisted that the money be returned. "How can you accept it? She's so poor."

"She's not poorer for this five hundred dollars. Oh, Jesus, my love, you don't understand things."

"I try."

"I know you try, I know that. Let's go to bed."

The last evening with his parents was more difficult. To be married and to keep it from them was, in the end, absolutely inconceivable; but before going to have dinner with them, the night before he left for Washington and prison, he went to his father's office in the Columbia Presbyterian Medical Center up on Washington Heights for a private talk. He felt it was best to be alone here, and Molly felt it best that she avoid the dinner as well. He argued against her decision, but she would not be moved.

"You simply don't understand them. They're the most decent, open-minded people you can imagine."

"I'm filled with guilts," Molly protested. "I can't be easy with them. They make me feel that I've robbed them."

"But that's your impression. You're making it out of the whole cloth and it has no validity."

"Oh, but it has."

"I want you to come."

Still she would not come, and he had to accept that. His father found it harder to accept. Bruce was waiting in his father's office in the hospital when Dr. Bacon walked in, still wearing his green gown. He took it off, trying hard to smile, telling Bruce that he had been three hours in the operating room, tossing the gown aside, and going to his desk for a cigar. "I'm getting too old for it," he told Bruce, "sixty-seven next spring, the legs go, the knees hurt—too old," trying to avoid a four-letter word called *jail,* trying to pretend that a year out of his son's life was not also a year out of his life. He lit the cigar, his hand shaking just a trifle but not so little that Bruce didn't notice it. "I should give up these damned things. That's what I tell my patients." In disgust, he threw the lit cigar into the ashtray on his desk. "How are you, kid?" he asked gently, blinking and trying to control tears. He used to call him kid before the war.

"I think I'm pretty good, Dad—all things considered."

"Yeah. Scared?"

"A little. What was it Tolstoy said—that a writer, above all else, should experience war and prison."

"That helps?" the doctor asked, smiling.

"A little."

The doctor took a bottle out of a drawer in his desk. "Golden Wedding, sweet as sugar. I never got a taste for Scotch." He poured two shot glasses, and passed one to his son. "Here's to you, Bruce Nathaniel!"

Sweet or not, the whiskey burned like fire. "Water?" his father asked.

"No—no, I'm all right. You know, Dad, if I could say I did something to earn this jail sentence, I mean if I were one of the communists they're putting away, I could say I'm giving a year of my life for my beliefs, for principles that are as important as freedom. What makes me empty is that I am not one of them. I am being sent away because somewhere along the line I was taught that you don't inform on others."

"That's a pretty big principle."

"Maybe, maybe. That's what Molly said. Tell me truthfully, Dad, what do you think of her?"

"I like her. You know that. She's a beautiful woman, decent, open. Hell, how much do any of us know about another?"

"You know we intended to get married?"

The doctor nodded, waiting.

"The point is that under Federal law, only lawyer, wife, and family get visitation rights. Facing that, Molly and I felt that we had to take some action. Well, we did. We got married."

Dr. Bacon waited, saying nothing, while Bruce spelled out the story, and then Bruce waited, sick over the mess that the whole business had become, wondering what his father would say, what he could say. What he finally said was "You should have trusted me, Bruce. You should have known me that well. But maybe no son can know his own father, any more than we can know our sons."

"If I don't think of you as my father," Bruce said, "but only as Dr. Bacon, I think I'm privileged to know you. You're a gentleman in this strange damned world where the word has lost all its meaning. That's why I came here and spelled it all out. I don't know whether we did the right or wrong thing. We're not thinking very straight. Molly has given many years of her life to a movement that lost its way somewhere along the line, and now its people are being hounded and persecuted and jailed as if they were the early Christian martyrs, and none of them quite understands how it came about. If anything, they are the most innocent and naïve people I ever met, and on the other hand, stubborn to death and ready to be jailed or die or anything else that's necessary to do what they think they must do to bring about the brotherhood of man. They've been isolated, beaten down, driven out of unions they organized, with the whole country turned against them, every newspaper in America calling them demons—and so help me God, Dad, the only thing I can compare them to is our Boy Scout troop when I was a kid, as crazy as that sounds. And as crazy as it sounds, the illusions are not so different, and this is what I've married, a wonderful, crazy woman who believes in Karl Marx and Jesus Christ and the church and the Communist Party and the working class and the brotherhood of man, and me, Bruce Bacon, whatever that is."

"Whatever it is," his father said, "it's a pretty good thing. Your mother and I haven't done too badly. I want you to bring her with you tonight."

"She doesn't want to come."

"Then see to it that she does, that she changes her mind. Come at seven-thirty, and by then I'll have had this out with Elizabeth, who is quite someone in her own right. We'll expect you."

It took a half hour of argument, but in the end she gave in. "It probably means my job," Molly told him. She was working the dinner hour in a small Italian restaurant on Fifty-second Street, and here it was already four o'clock and too late to find a replacement. "It's a hell of a thing to do."

"Molly, God damn it, I'm going to jail tomorrow."

"I would have seen you later, you know that. Don't make a Federal case out of this one, and for God's sake, let's not have a quarrel. I couldn't stand that." She called the restaurant, and Bruce could hear the explosion at the other end of the wire. "I'm fired," she said, putting down the telephone. "Oh, Jesus, I'm getting scared."

"Look, darling—please, dear good wife—" He put his arms around her. "Sylvia will pick up my bail money after we surrender. That's five thousand dollars, and I already told her that the money goes to you. That'll take care of everything, and I still have a few thousand in my bank account, and you have power of attorney over that, so you'll be all right and you'll have a break to try to get a decent job."

"Waiting tables is a decent job. Don't give me that kind of thing. Bruce, we're married ten minutes and we're tearing each other apart."

"No, we're not tearing each other apart. We're high-strung and we're frightened."

She clung to him. "All the things to do," she said. "I have to get rid of some of this junk. I'll keep the wing chair and the books, but the rest goes. I bought the wing chair second-hand, but I love it. But I have to find room for your stuff."

He led her to the bed. "Come on, baby. We'll lie here for a while and let the knots work themselves out—just lie here and be next to each other." They stretched out on her bed, clinging to each other, and then they dozed off. It was almost seven o'clock when they awakened, and Molly rushed to change into her gray skirt and white blouse.

"I should wash my hair, but there's no time," she said. "I'll tie it all in back and it won't look too awful. Should I wear makeup? I never know how people like your folks feel about makeup."

"You look beautiful."

She was subdued, like a very young girl, when they arrived at the Bacons' apartment, and then surprised and amazed when Elizabeth Bacon put her arms around her. At first Molly held back, but then she let go and accepted the small, thin body of the older woman against her own. Dr. Bacon made cocktails, and dinner revolved around a handsome rib roast. The conversation was as ordinary as they could make it. Dr. Bacon talked about the hospital and his work, and Mrs. Bacon finally intervened, explaining to Molly that it was one thing to have an internist bring home his work, and something quite different where a surgeon was concerned. Bruce turned the talk to the theater. He and

Molly had seen Arthur Miller's *Death of a Salesman* a few weeks earlier, and Bruce's mother complained that they rarely got to the theater anymore. "I miss it," she said. "I really do miss it." About Miller's play, Bruce and Molly had divergent opinions. Bruce liked it; Molly was untouched. Faulkner had received the Nobel Prize for Literature a few weeks before, and Dr. Bacon wondered whether Sigrid Undset had ever won the prize. No one could remember, but Molly, who had said little, told how she had discovered Sigrid Undset in high school and had fallen madly in love with *Kristin Lavransdatter.* Elizabeth Bacon was pleased. She and her husband were both great fans of the school of Scandinavian writers, and the talk turned to Hamsun and Bojer. Bruce, as always, observed Molly, amazed at how relaxed and easy she was. Elizabeth Bacon did not give in to any tears, an agreement reached with her husband, and when they finally got down to discussing the details of Bruce's incarceration and what their visiting privileges would be, it was done as a matter of course. Dr. Bacon already had spoken to Sylvia Kline, and now he assured Bruce that he would stay in touch with her and do whatever was necessary, and when the evening was over, they all embraced, and Elizabeth Bacon told Molly, "We won't have another wedding, but we will have a good party and celebration when Bruce comes home."

When they arrived at Molly's apartment, she had fallen into a dark, brooding spell, and when Bruce argued that his parents had taken her to their bosoms, Molly shook her head hopelessly. "They covered every normal feeling. How can I ever know what they think—how can I know what you think?"

"Only by what I say and do. We're different—but that doesn't change anything that we have in common, and I mean a long love and friendship. I think being married to a man on his way to jail spooks you."

"Maybe. God knows! Let's go to bed."

The alarm clock exploded their sleep at five-thirty in the morning, and an hour later they had met Sylvia at Pennsylvania Station and were on their way to Washington. They had breakfast in the dining car, where Sylvia spelled out the process. "We go first to Judge Wilson's courtroom, where I've arranged to make one more plea—this time to suspend your sentence. There have been a few halfhearted columns of criticism and distaste in the *Times,* the *Tribune,* and the *Washington Post,* very milky stuff. After what happened in Hollywood, they're beginning to worry about so many writers being sent to jail. It smacks too much of a full-fledged police state, and with the Hollywood Ten, you and a dozen others from here and there, Europe is beginning to realize that something most peculiar is happening here. Some say that Mr. Truman is planning something against Russia and this is all buildup, but God only knows; and if the administration feels it is moving too fast, they may just advise Wilson to suspend sentence. Anyway, it's worth a try."

"And if he says no?"

"Then it starts. We say goodby, and Molly kisses you, and I shed a few tears over being such a lousy lawyer—"

"And he kisses you, and we both tell you what a great lawyer you are," Molly interrupted. "I feel so helpless."

"And after everyone kisses everyone?"

"They take you downstairs to the holding cells, and there you're fingerprinted and photographed, and then, from what I could learn, they put you into one of those prison buses and shuttle you off to the District jail. But that's just a holding jail, although it's pretty big. Eventually, you'll be sent from there to one or another of the Federal prisons."

"Where? Which one?" Molly asked her.

"I don't know yet. But when they decide, they'll let me know. I've already written to James Bennett—he's the chief of the Bureau of Prisons—and asked that as a world-renowned writer and a person of flawless character, you be given some kind of special treatment."

Bruce stared at her over his plate of sausage and eggs. "You said all that about me?"

"I said it because I believe it. Anyway, Bennett has the reputation of being a thoroughly decent man, and if the letter does nothing else, it will open a dialogue with him—which I want. You know, a good part of this country may be brown-nosing McCarthy and his lunatics, but there are still good people around, and I want you to know that, Bruce."

Bruce tried to remember her words, standing with Sylvia in front of Judge Harwood Wilson, who stared blankly ahead of him as Sylvia pleaded, "My client is not a criminal, not a communist, only a writer and a gentleman, and as a gentleman he could not bear witness against a woman he loved."

"You've made quite a romance out of it, haven't you, Miss Kline?"

"I am not pleading for a criminal, Your Honor. He does not constitute a danger that must be removed from society."

"Neither does he have some destructive disease. Or does he, Miss Kline?"

"No, Your Honor."

"He appears to be in excellent health. Doesn't he, Miss Kline?"

"Yes, Your Honor."

"I don't think a year in prison will harm him. You will recall that he was offered an opportunity to purge himself of contempt by answering the questions he had originally refused to answer, and this opportunity to purge was rejected. He has only himself to blame."

"I referred to that, Your Honor."

"No, counselor. The law is specific. He has broken the law, and his sentence is what the law allows. Your motion is rejected, and the prisoner, Bruce Nathaniel Bacon, is remanded to the Federal marshal."

As the marshal led him away, Bruce looked back at the two women who had become so very much a part of his life,

one his lawyer and the other his wife, two women so unlike
any women he had known before the war as to suggest a
different species. They tried to compose their faces and pretend to no tears by not wiping away the tears that already
filled their eyes. The marshal swung him around to lead him
into the corridor. At this point, he was immensely relieved
that the waiting was over. That took a weight off his shoulders, and now he was genuinely interested in what lay
ahead, a new place to cover, to experience, and to write
about. If he were a fiction writer, he might have been able to
imagine and anticipate it; but he was not a fiction writer,
and all through his life he had discovered that what he
imagined and anticipated was never the real thing. To lie in
a wet shellhole, pleading for the rain to stop and for the
guns to stop, and pleading without any belief in the God he
was pleading with, was as far from any of his reading as
anything could be. So here was a reality, and he had twelve
months to study it.

Routine at first. The Federal marshal had snapped handcuffs onto his wrist, and in the elevator kept a firm grasp on
Bruce's arm. He was a big man, an inch more than Bruce's
six feet, and fifty pounds heavier, mostly in a large paunch
that pressed against his belt. He had no voice, opinion, or
pleasantry, and therefore became simply an ambulatory object who led Bruce out of the elevator and into an area
where there were other marshals, tables, desks, and a holding pen.

Here the handcuffs were removed, and Bruce was fingerprinted. Then he was given a cloth wet with cleaning fluid to
wipe the black ink from his fingers, and then he was put in
the holding tank, an iron cage about fifteen feet square. He
was still wearing his suit, sleeveless sweater instead of a vest,
tie and blue shirt, and topcoat. He had in his wallet fifty
dollars and a driving license and identification, namely, an
insurance card and his membership card in the Newspaper

Guild. Also, his father's professional card and Molly's picture.

There were three other men in the holding tank, one black, two white. The black man was heavy, fat, and middle-aged. He grinned and said, "Welcome to the Ritz, sonny."

The second man, dark, heavy mustache, sat on a stool, crouched over, staring at the floor. The third man, young, curly black hair, two or three days of blue beard on his cheeks, said, "That motherfucker don't talk."

"Who did you kill, sonny?" the black man asked.

"He's a banker, done in the investors, the assholes."

"You a banker, sonny?"

"I'm a writer," Bruce said.

"Assholes put money in banks. I break my ass to get it out, but put it there? No way."

"You never had enough money to put in a bank," the black man said.

"Yeah? Yeah? How the hell would you know, shithead?"

"Say that word!" the black man shouted. "Just say it!"

"Shut up, both of you!" a guard yelled.

A few minutes later, sandwiches were brought, two slices of rye bread with a slice of salami between, each sandwich wrapped in paper. The man on the stool didn't budge. The guard tossed him the sandwich and he let it fall to the ground in front of him. Bruce stared at the sandwich with distaste. He had no appetite, no desire for food, and the black man, who was devouring his own sandwich with large bites, said, "If you don't want it, sonny, give it to me." Bruce handed it to him. The young man with the curly hair said, "Share, you motherfucker, share." The black man grinned and pointed to the fourth sandwich, lying on the floor. The young man yelled after the guard, "Coffee—where's the coffee?" The man on the stool kicked away his sandwich, and the young man picked it up and ate it. A guard came by with tin cups and a pitcher of a dark fluid that was hot but tasted of nothing in particular.

A half hour later, the gate of the tank was opened and Bruce was told to step out. "Bacon, B. N., right?" the marshal said.

Bruce nodded.

"Come on. I'm taking you out of this nuthouse to jail. It'll be an improvement." And with that, he snapped the handcuffs on Bruce and led him through a passageway to where a panel truck with iron gates and two facing benches was waiting. There were six men in the truck, four black men sitting together on one bench, two white men on the bench facing them, all of them handcuffed. Bruce was told to sit next to the two white men. The gates were closed and locked, and the truck drove on out of the Federal building.

It was raining, a properly gloomy day for such a ride. No one in the bus spoke. Looking at his watch, Bruce saw that it was only three o'clock. Incredible that so much had happened in a day that was far from over! He closed his eyes. Was this real? Was anything real? The circumstances that had brought him here blurred over. Looking out of the gates at the rear of the truck, he realized that they had passed through a stone archway, where high wooden doors were closing behind them. Then the truck came to a stop, the gates were unlocked, and they were told by a guard to get out. Their handcuffs were removed.

What was strange and unusual—a little more than everything being strange and unusual—was the silence. No one spoke, no one complained, no one protested. He was perhaps a little better dressed than the other men in the bus with him, but otherwise they were perfectly normal-looking people. Nothing marked them as criminal.

The seven men were marched through the walled yard and into the prison. Gates opened and closed, electrically operated, and then he was in a hall with counters and cages on each side. He was told to empty his pockets; and his wallet, watch, keys, and small notebook were put into an envelope and marked. Then he moved on a few steps to another counter, and here he was told to strip down to the skin and fold his clothes and put them on the counter. In this hallway, the walls painted government green, the gloom hardly broken by the small bulbs in their ceiling sockets, he had a feeling of being in some surrealist hell, and this feeling was intensified as the other men stripped naked and took their places on the bench alongside him. The look of the place, the guards in uniform, the line of naked men huddled on the bench—all of it brought back the image and memory of the concentration camps in Germany, where the inmates were stripped naked before going to their death in the gas chambers. He couldn't escape his thoughts; he was a writer and he dealt in images and memories; and the comparison became even more poignant when, after their clothes were put in bags and marked, they were led into a long, tiled shower room where ceiling jets, controlled from beyond a glass panel by the guards, sprayed them with hot water. There was a basket of bars of brown soap, and a microphone voice told them to wash up and soap up and wash up again.

Then they went into another tiled room, where there was a wide metal bin filled with an antifungus solution. They walked through this and then they were given towels. Again, as Bruce dried himself, the silence penetrated and disturbed him. For the moment, his world of words had vanished.

Then, still naked, they went through a cursory medical examination by two physicians, and then they were marched into another room, where Bruce was given underwear, blue shirt, blue cotton trousers, socks, and shoes. He sat on a bench and dressed himself.

Then they were taken into the prison proper, where the cells rose in four horseshoe-shaped tiers. Bruce was separated from the others, and the black prisoners were separated from the white prisoners. He was taken to the second tier. The door of a cell opened by remote control. "There's home, Bacon," the guard said. Home was a cell that measured six feet by eight feet and contained two beds, one on top of the other, a toilet bowl with no toilet seat, and a sink —and another prisoner. He was a boy, no more than seventeen, blond, blue-eyed, slender, and with delicate features. He stood at the other end of the cell, eyeing Bruce with what appeared to be a mixture of fear and suspicion.

"My name's Frank Jenner," the boy said.

"Bruce Bacon."

"What are you in for?"

"Contempt of Congress," Bruce said, smiling for the first time since leaving the courtroom.

"What the hell is that?"

Bruce shook his head. "Hard to explain. Well—refusing to cooperate with a congressional committee, for whatever that's worth."

"You didn't kill anyone?"

"Oh, no. I'm not here for killing anyone. What makes you think I am?"

"I didn't think you are. I just asked."

"Why?"

"Because this here row of cells, twelve of them, they call it death row. They keep condemned men here until their appeals wash out, and then they send them off to Leavenworth."

"Who did you kill?" Bruce asked.

"I didn't kill nobody. It's the only empty cell they got, so they put me here after I was raped. You never been in the slammer before?"

"First time," wondering how the boy could put it like that, casually, as if it were an ordinary daily happening.

"What do you do?"

"I'm a writer."

A loud scream of bells filled the prison.

"We eat now," the boy said. "You can follow me if you want to. The doors will open in a minute."

With a great clanging, all the doors of all the cells opened simultaneously. It was a scene Bruce remembered from every Hollywood prison film, the tiers of cells, each tier horseshoe-shaped with a narrow outside passageway, one tier piled upon another, and in the well at the bottom, row after row of the long metal tables at which the convicts had their meals. Bruce, following the blond boy, went down a circular staircase and got into a cafeteria-style line. He picked up his aluminum tray, knife and fork and tin cup, and moved on to where the food was being served. His tray was divided into four sections. Behind the counter, convicts served the food.

"Potatoes?"

Bruce nodded. A large spoon of potatoes was slapped onto his tray.

"Turnips?" Another serving spoon full of turnips.

"Carrots?"

"Hash?"

"Bread?"

Two thick slices of bread were slapped onto his tray. Whatever had happened to justice in his country, nutrition was not one of the victims. He moved on, carrying the food-laden tray, sliding into the first bench that was not already filled. He sat there then, viewing his pile of food without pleasure, sick at the thought of consuming any food at all. Meanwhile, two large, hard-looking convicts on either side of him were noisily and enthusiastically putting away their food. The noise was gusto and chewing, since no talking was allowed at mealtime, but a whisper in his ear asked whether or not he intended to eat.

"I can't eat."

"You leave food on the tray, you do ten days in the hole."

Bruce knew about the hole. Everyone knew about the hole. All the literary and film and media images that were drummed into Americans for hours every day had come to life for Bruce. The hole was a cell without windows, without light, without a bed or a proper toilet. The hole was terror, isolation, and madness, but to be put into solitary confinement for leaving food on a tray—

"He's right," the convict on the other side whispered. "You want help?"

"Please."

With quick movement, the two convicts divided the food, half on each plate. Bruce breathed a sigh of relief while the two convicts shoveled his dinner into their mouths. They thanked him and he thanked them, all in whispers that left lips motionless. Bruce was relieved. He felt silly but relieved, and he was determined to limit his food in the future. The hole was not a pleasant thought. He was sufficiently aware of himself to know that he was an oddity, his tall, stalwart height, his horn-rimmed glasses, his slight stoop that came of years of crouching over a typewriter. His full mouth of teeth separated him from the run of the prisoners, their mouths full of gaping spaces. Already, he was beginning to characterize them. Here and there was hostility, anger fixed and unremitting, but most of them appeared to be neutral, wary, but neutral, poor people, gaps in their teeth, as if poverty could be measured in the mouth, young most of them, and white. The blacks were elsewhere.

Back in his cell, the electric gates slammed closed, the boy, Frank Jenner, told him that he was sleeping in the top bed but if Bruce wanted the top bed, he could have it. Bruce was just as satisfied with the bottom bed. The boy was trying to make a friend—or at least to neutralize an enemy. He was trapped in a system where everyone was his enemy. He was a sexual prize. "Just don't be afraid of me," Bruce said. "I'm straight. I won't touch you." He listened to himself speaking, amazed at what he was saying. Out of one world into another world, and nothing resembled what he had read or seen. He was promising a kid that he wouldn't rape him. It wasn't a question of homosexuality; it was a matter of

prison. It had happened once. Jenner told him how it had
happened, his eyes full of tears that he fought to keep back.
He wanted to be a tough guy, but he had no equipment for
it. He was born in Tulsa, Oklahoma, raped and brutalized
by his father as a child, a runaway at age twelve, two years
in a home for runaways in Denver, and then a runaway
from there, and finally in the District of Columbia, working
for an old black gardener and living in a corner of the old
man's shed. Among others, the gardener worked for Judge
Bradford Jones of the Appellate Court. Jones had a daughter who was fifteen and sexually adventurous enough to get
herself into a situation where Frank Jenner had fondled her.
He claimed it was a single time, a single embrace, but the
judge discovered them and had Frank arrested for carnal
knowledge. The boy had been here in this penitentiary for
seven months now, no hearing, no indictment, no bail.
"Who would go bail for me?" he said to Bruce. "I'll rot
here. I'll die here."

Sleep came hard and slowly that night. Bruce lay in bed, a
bed with no sheets, just a blanket and a pillow, and listened
to the moans beginning. The boy in the bed over his said,
"That's what makes me crazy, Mr. Bacon. It makes me
crazy to listen to them every night. They moan and they
whimper and they pray to God not to let them be executed,
and shit, I can understand, because who the fuck wants to
sit down in the electric chair, but they do it all night."

He slept and he awakened and the whimpering and pleading went on, and he slept again, bits and pieces of sleep. The
next morning, after a breakfast of oatmeal and coffee—
which Bruce devoured with sudden raging hunger—they
were led up to an exercise room on the roof, a closed room
with a ceiling of reinforced glass, so that while light entered,
there was no sight of sun or sky.

The convicts milled around pointlessly. Some walked,
others stood still. It was an aimless motion without function
or purpose beyond the fact that they were not in their cells.

Here and there was a little eddy. A large, heavily muscled man sat cross-legged, dealing cards to four others, a handsome man whose life force fairly vibrated. "A lifer," Jenner told Bruce. "He'll never get out. He's just here waiting for transfer. Everyone's waiting for transfer except me." Bruce tried to imagine that life force squeezed into a cell for an entire lifetime. The man was in his thirties—middle age, old age, the vibrant muscles withered, the hair turned white, and all of it in a cell. The thought chilled him; it cut deeper than the cries of the condemned that had awakened him during the night. His guide and informant, the blond boy who stayed close to him, pointed to another eddy. "The Purple Nose Gang," Jenner said, and then went on to explain that they were a gang of bank robbers who had blazed a trail across the country, their disguise and trademark a Halloween children's mask with a bulbous purple nose and a mustache. They were crouched in a circle over a piece of paper, on which one of them was laboriously making a diagram. "They're planning their next job," Jenner said. "They do it every time we're up here. They're crazy." But why not, Bruce wondered, in a world that was only less insane outside than it was in here.

He noticed that there were no blacks in evidence. The separation between the black prisoners and the white prisoners was complete, as if the state were willing to impose every indignity and punishment on the convicts except the peculiar pain of being in the same place as a black man.

In the tiny cell that he and Jenner occupied, there was a chair and a small table about twenty inches square. Bruce asked for writing paper, and it was given to him by the guard, long sheets of lined paper, and with it a sheet of instructions. "You do not write about the prison: you do not write about prisoners: you do not describe prison conditions. Any such reference will be removed from your letter."

He wrote to Molly, "My dear darling wife: I have been here only two days, yet it seems like eternity. I am con-

vinced that the first thing that happens when one sets foot in
a prison is a total rupture of one's time sense. A second
becomes a minute and a minute becomes an hour. So when I
say that I miss you and think of you constantly, it is because
in part of my mind, it is a long time since I held you in my
arms. I have learned that this place is mainly a holding
facility, and that with some exceptions, most of this population are held here no more than a few weeks. Then the men
are moved to one or another of the prisons in the Federal
system. Where I will be sent, I have no idea, but I'm sure
you or Sylvia will be notified.

"You will note that I am learning prison talk. The convicts are referred to as the *population*. The prison is called a
facility. The euphemisms are the *officers'* talk. The convicts
call them *screws* and a number of other things that would
simply be excised if I put them down. We in the population
build time. Thereby the main function of a man in prison,
building time, getting from one hour to the next. Some *fight
time,* and they go crazy. All this phony expertise comes
from the fact that we have been instructed to write nothing
about the prison or our conditions here, which does make
letter writing difficult. I don't think I violate the rule by
saying that a certain amount of reading matter is provided.
A library cart is pushed along the walkway and stopped in
front of each cell, and you have your choice of the books on
the cart. They are mostly fiction and a very odd choice indeed. One of the books, I noticed, was titled *The Great Escape*. It was so worn as to be falling to pieces, and no doubt
a bitter disappointment to its readers. I thumbed through it
and found it to be an Edwardian memoir of some kind, and
the escape was psychological rather than literal. I chose for
my selection *The Count of Monte Cristo,* not only a satisfy-
ingly fat volume, but something I had missed in my youth. I
knew enough of the plot, however, to realize it might be
comforting, since my fate was so much less severe than Ed-
mond Dantès's.

"As far as my own health is concerned, I'm in excellent shape, and facing the monster is a lot less awful than thinking about it. The few men I've spoken to snort down twelve months and say they can do that kind of time standing on one foot. But since most of them are repeaters and spend most of their lives in jail, I don't find their expertise very comforting. However, while not on one foot, I'll come through it all right, and learn something in the bargain. As I said earlier, excluding the afternoon they brought me here, I have spent only two days in prison and I think I've learned more about capital punishment and crime than I knew in all my years outside. Let me add one thing: I love you very much."

His letter to his mother and father was more flagrantly cheerful.

He spent eleven days in his cell, and then he was called out for transfer.

Mill Bog

The guard at the door of his cell block said, "You're moving on, Bacon. Anything personal in there?"

"Some notes."

"Give them to me. They'll be returned to you when your term is up. Anything else?"

"I'm halfway through my book." He was now reading *The Forsyte Saga* because it was long, the specific of first choice from the library cart. He had never read it before, and he was delighted with it and halfway through it. "Can I take it with me?" he asked the guard.

"No, leave the book. Take your toothbrush, toothpaste, and shaving stuff. That's government issue."

Jenner sat on his upper cot, knees drawn, head bent, his eyes full of tears that he was trying to hide. Bruce had left something with him. It had taken a few days for Bruce to draw him out, and then they talked for hours. Bruce talked about defending himself. You don't accept it, you don't accept anything from those sick bastards. You fight it—every inch of the way. Now Bruce, the first man in his life who wanted nothing from him, who could answer his questions, and who could make life something other than a meaningless nightmare, was going away. He'd never see Bruce again. He'd never have a friend or a defender again.

Bruce reached up to him. "So long, kid."

He wouldn't take Bruce's hand. He said, "Shit, get your ass out of here! I don't need you!"

"Pussy ass," the guard said.

Bruce said nothing. He followed the guard down the circular stairs to the room where he had surrendered his clothes, and there the same brown bag was handed back to him.

"Bacon, Bruce Nathaniel. Take these and get dressed. Throw your clothes into the basket. Your valuables will be turned over to the marshal and they'll go with you to your destination."

The eleven days in the cell with Jenner had constituted a valid separation from the world. His own clothes were strange to him, and he put them on in a sort of daze. Where was he going? At least he'd get out of this red brick medieval madhouse. After he had dressed himself, he was handcuffed and taken through the rooms he had traversed on his way in and through a pair of high iron doors into the courtyard. It was a cold, dismal day, the rain light but fine and cutting, about nine o'clock in the morning now. He and the guard waited under the projecting arch of the doorway, sheltered there from the rain. They waited in silence for about ten minutes before the car came. Bruce resisted an impulse to ask the guard where he would be going. He disliked asking questions of any of the guards, disliked speaking to them, although common sense told him that they were civil service people, doing what job they were fit for and, where he was concerned, doing nothing to provoke a personal vendetta. It didn't help. He hated them.

The car, a big, four-door Buick, was let into the yard through the high outer gates, and it pulled over to where Bruce and the guard waited under the arch of the doorway. The guard then gave the driver, a United States marshal, the bag containing Bruce's wallet, keys, and watch, and an envelope with his transfer orders. The guard opened the back door and motioned for Bruce to get in.

"Take off the handcuffs," Bruce said.

The marshal, a large, round-faced man, said, "They'll

come off when we get where we're going. Suppose you get in and relax."

Bruce bent, stepped into the car, and found the seat comfortable enough. The back section was separated from the front by a metal screen, and when the driver got in, the doors automatically locked. Bruce was still in the grip of the excitement of leaving the cell and the prison and tasting at least the partial freedom of sitting in a car and moving through the city. "Can you hear me?" he asked the marshal.

"I can hear you."

"Where are we going?"

"West Virginia, a facility called Mill Bog. Now listen, Bacon, we'll be spending the next few hours in this car, so just you sit back and relax and be a good guy, and we'll have a nice easy trip. I don't know how much time they slapped you with, but like I tell everyone who sits down in back of this car, the penalty for trying to escape is five years tacked on to the time you already got."

"I'm not going to try to escape, so why can't you take these damn handcuffs off?"

"I don't bend the rules, Bacon, so just sit back and enjoy the ride. If you have to piss or take a crap, tell me about it."

For the next half hour, the rain and mist obscured the view; then the sky lightened, the clouds began to break, and shafts of sunlight cut through. The window alongside Bruce was slightly open, and the sweet cold air was like a benediction. They were riding through farm country that soon began to give way to rolling, wooded hills.

"What's it like—this place we're going to?"

"Light security. That's as good as you can get in a Federal facility. It's a work prison, so you won't get bored, and it's in the middle of a Federal forest. A long way from anywhere. You could be going to worse places, believe me, and now shut up and let me drive."

About an hour later, they stopped at a gas station with a roadside coffee bar. The marshal stood at the toilet door while Bruce used the bathroom, and then he ushered Bruce back to the car and locked him in.

"Hungry?" he asked Bruce.

"Not so you could notice."

"How about a doughnut and a cup of coffee?"

He munched the doughnut and sipped the coffee with appreciation. Road signs told him that they were passing through Charlottesville. He saw people in the streets, men, women, children, stores, cars, policemen at traffic crossings —there was the whole world that he had once been a part of, free to come and go as he wished. Now he was in a cage, a trapped animal.

The farms became fewer, and the rolling forested hills turned into low mountains. The sky was blue, spotted here and there with cotton balls of cumulus clouds—a cold, clean fall day, the air clear and pine-scented. His depression disappeared. How could he be depressed in a land so wild and beautiful? He began to look forward to his destination. What was a light security prison? Well, whatever it might be, it could hardly be worse than the soul-shrinking place he had come from. Another hour passed, and now they were winding up into the flat-sided mountains of the Alleghenys. It was a totally wild, primeval, and beautiful place, the air full of pine scent, the leaf-stripped birches columns of white supporting a roof of old maple and oak.

The prison was like nothing he had expected, the entrance without gates or walls, only a sprawling building of wood and stone, painted government brown, situated on a slight rise; and beyond that a great sweep of green lawn, with World War Two–type barracks spotted here and there around it, all of it more like an army camp than a prison.

The marshal parked the Buick in front of a sign that said MILL BOG CORRECTIONAL FACILITY, opened the door for Bruce to step out, unlocked his handcuffs, and tossed them back into the car. Evidently here, at the end of anywhere or nowhere, handcuffs were a redundancy. He led Bruce into the building and into a room with a long bench, counter, and wooden lockers behind the counter. To the guard behind the counter, the marshal said crisply, "Here he is. Bacon, Bruce Nathaniel."

The marshal delivered the bag of Bruce's possessions, received a signed receipt, left Bruce and the building, and drove away. The guard, studying Bruce thoughtfully, asked, "You're not one of the Hollywood crowd?"

"New York," Bruce said.

"Right. The foreign correspondent. Very well, Bruce, come along and we'll get you some prison clothes."

He led Bruce into another room, where he told him to strip down to his skin—and pointed to the door to showers. As before, Bruce showered and walked in disinfectant, and then returned, towel wrapped around him, to be led into a supply room.

"Size forty-four?"

"That should do it," Bruce agreed. He was given jeans washed endless times, blue cotton shirt, undershirt and shorts, heavy socks and shoes, a heavy U.S. Army jacket, and a new set of toilet articles. His watch was returned to him. He was told that the money in his wallet would be considered a deposit, and that he could draw a dollar a week canteen money for cigarettes, shaving cream or soap, and candy. "Your clothes will be cleaned and returned to you when you're released, as will your other possessions."

Bruce dressed himself in the prison clothes and then was directed down a corridor to a room marked *Orientation.* There were about a dozen plain kitchen chairs in the room, but only two were occupied, both by men in convict clothes. In one, a slight man with pale blue eyes and light hair, in the other, a young man in his twenties. Bruce seated himself, and at first there was silence from all three of them. Then the older man—he looked forty but turned out to be twenty-nine—the one with the sandy hair, turned to Bruce and introduced himself. "Clem Alsta—what the hell, we're going to be here a while. Might as well know our names."

"Bruce Bacon."

"Harry O'Brien," the other man said. He grinned easily. Bruce was to learn that he was a bank robber who for years had done very well by walking into small suburban banks, presenting a brown paper bag, and asking the teller to fill it up. He never carried a weapon, and since he moved from state to state, he ended up in a Federal prison five years before. At this day of transfer to Mill Bog, he had two more years to serve. Alsta was another case of two more years to serve. In the merchant marine, in nineteen forty-three, he had killed another seaman in a bitter fight. He had been sentenced to fifteen years, and now, with his time off for good behavior, he had two more years to serve.

"A damned peculiar place," O'Brien said. "No bars on the windows, no locks on the doors. I could get up and walk out of here."

"To where?" Bruce wondered.

"It's minimum security," Alsta said. "You don : walk out, because if they bring you back, they don't bring you back here but Leavenworth, which I know about, and then you get five more years on your time. So you got to be a dumb son of a bitch to walk out of here."

Bruce looked around the room. It was clean, the walls painted pale green, on one wall a steelpoint engraving of Lincoln, on the other a portrait of Franklin Delano Roosevelt. There was a small table at one end of the room, an American flag, and a chair behind the table. The dozen kitchen chairs were placed in three rows of four. A sign on the wall read *No Smoking*.

Just being there, the three of them sitting alone in a room, became a sort of psychological medicine. No guard, no one to keep them from walking out if they wished, and when, after fifteen minutes or so, Bruce went to the door and peered out, the corridor was empty. It was a valid cause for reflection, Bruce decided: first, a committee of obsessed, half-demented congressmen, then a court where the scales of justice were fixed and soldered into place by a thin-lipped and apparently heartless judge, then a prison that was neither cruel nor kind, only as mindless as the hundreds of electric doors and gates that rolled back and forth constantly—and now? It is most interesting, he told himself, to be a citizen of a country so advanced, so civilized as to offer this strange prison, and so helpless before the onslaught of a few hundred primitive lunatics who could do as they pleased and say what they pleased and make a mockery out of all of it.

Then the door opened, and his off-the-cuff philosophy was laid aside.

The man who entered the room and walked up to the table, half seating himself on it, appeared to be about fifty years old and overweight without being obviously fat, a thoughtful face, and pale, intelligent eyes. He wore gold pince-nez, which he polished before he began to speak.

"You are here," he said to them, "in a minimum security facility of the Federal prison system. I am the warden of this institution, and my name is Craig Demming. I am also the final court of appeal. I am a good master or a harsh master. That is up to you. You have all three of you come from penitentiaries of one sort or another, so you are well aware of the difference between this prison and other prisons. Mill Bog comprises twenty-two acres of space. This area is surrounded by an invisible barrier, and this barrier is marked by small white signs that say *Stay Inside.* There is one of these signs every forty feet around the entire circumference of the twenty-two acres, and while you are part of this prison population, you are not permitted to step across that invisible line without specific permission to do so. In this institution, the only door that is locked is the door to the pantry. There are no guns anywhere on the prison grounds. If we should need an armed presence, we call in the state

police. By Federal law, you will be granted three days a
month for good behavior. Troublemakers lose their good-
time deductions. Let me also say this: in the twelve years
that this facility has been in existence, there have been only
eight escape attempts. They were all Kentucky men, moonshiners, who became homesick and walked out of here. They
were picked up by the police in their hometowns and returned here. Now let me tell you why no one to speak of
escapes from this prison without walls. No one in here has
more than two years to serve, and this is the best place in
the system to do time. However, if you do decide to escape
and you are returned, as you surely will be, you will be
penalized five years of your lives, and you will not do the
time here but in a maximum security penitentiary. So it's up
to you. This is a work facility, and tomorrow you'll be assigned to your jobs."

He finished as flatly as he had begun, turned, and left the
room. The three men sat in silence for a long moment, and
then O'Brien said, "I'll be damned."

"What do we do now?"

"Wait here, I suppose," Bruce said.

They only had to wait a few minutes, and then a guard
came into the room and told them to follow him. He led
them down a slight hill into the grounds of the prison
proper. Bruce noticed some houses on the hillside, away
from the prison grounds, and guessed correctly that those
were the homes of the warden and the guards. From the hill,
where the Administration Building of the prison stood, the
offices and admission section, Bruce saw the prison grounds
as an opening in the forest, twenty-two cleared acres surrounded by a wall of trees. At the far end of the opening,
there was a large frame building, the dining room and
kitchen. There were four one-story barracks, army style,
and two smaller buildings, one the library and meeting hall,
and the other a hospital. At the edge of the cleared land, a
big garage shed with trucks and tractors. All of this was

subsequent information; at the moment, the three men were led to the hospital building, which contained eight unused beds. There, the guard turned them over to a convict who held the job of hospital orderly. The guard disappeared, and the orderly regarded them without pleasure. "My name's Mac Olsen," he said. "I'm in charge of this place, and here's where you sleep tonight and make work for me." He pointed to a door. "That's the crapper. Use it if you need it. Dinner's in ten minutes, so pick a bed and stretch out if you want to."

"Which bed?"

"Any bed. I don't give a damn. You're here for one night." Olsen was a tall, skinny man with a twitch in one eye, bald, and in his middle years. He was depressed and unfriendly.

The dinner bell rang with a sound audible anywhere in the twenty-two acres. It was twilight as Olsen led the three men down to the mess hall. By now, Bruce had drawn out of Olsen the fact that Mill Bog, at capacity, housed one hundred and sixty men, roughly half of them black. The black men worked with the whites, but lived and ate separately. They had their own barracks, and the mess hall was divided. As one entered, it was whites to the left, blacks to the right.

The tables in the dining room were made of long ten-by-two-inch planks, as were the benches. Each of the three men was assigned to a separate table. Each table seated ten men, five on each side. The meal consisted of frankfurters, cabbage and potatoes, bread, thin coffee, and a small piece of cake for dessert. The meat was limited to two frankfurters per man, but there was ample cabbage and potatoes. Bruce, fiercely hungry after a long day with practically no food, ate everything in sight, and then walked out of the dining room and across to the hospital, where he sat on the steps and stared up at the starry sky. It was cold, the air clean and sweet. O'Brien and Alsta joined him and lit cigarettes. A loudspeaker, up at the Administration Building, came alive:

"Irene, good night . . . good night, Irene, good night, Irene,
I'll see you in my dreams."

"Not like Leavenworth," Alsta said.

O'Brien's cigarette glowed, but he said nothing. Bruce
had already observed how little men in prison talked. It was
an odd thought, but it occurred to him that if Molly were
here with him, it wouldn't be bad at all. Now the prison
camp was in darkness, the black walls of mountains all
around it and on the edge of the mountains to the west, a
faint and fading aura of blue-white light—a strange and very
beautiful world. The song on the speaker system finished
and faded. New York and Washington were without substance or meaning for the moment, and for the first time,
actually, since the contempt process had begun, his indignation faded.

The lights were coming on in the barracks; muted sounds
of speech; the tang of O'Brien's cigarette in the air; and from
the direction of the barracks where the black men were
quartered, ripples of laughter.

"I think I'll turn in," he said to the others. For better or
worse, they were his companions. All sorts of people would
be his companions. He'd survive that and likely profit from
it. He went inside, undressed, and crawled into bed. He was
asleep in a matter of minutes, emotionally and physically
exhausted.

He woke early in the morning, before sunrise. His watch
told him that it was five minutes before six o'clock. He
dressed, shaved, and then went out to sit on the steps and
watch the morning light glow behind the mountains. At
half-past six, the silence exploded in a crash of the bells, and
over the next half hour the convicts poured out of their
barracks toward the mess hall. Bruce and his two fellow
newcomers joined them. Bruce was ravenously hungry, as if
making up for all the days without appetite, and he did
away in short order with the bowl of oatmeal and the bread
and milk that came with it. Now, in daylight, he was able to

look at the prison population more or less objectively, young
men, most of them, no single type, no specific type. No one
addressed questions to him, no one asked him his name,
who he was, what he had done. Apparently, that would
come in its own good time.

Through with breakfast, he walked back to the hospital,
to find his bed stripped and new linen folded and waiting. So
with O'Brien and Alsta. They were told to make up the beds
and wait outside, and after some ten minutes, a guard came
over and told them to follow him. Alsta went to one of the
barracks, Bruce and O'Brien to the other. Each was directed
to an empty cot, the two cots ten beds apart, each with a
pillow and folded single sheet and two army blankets. The
barracks was empty, except for Bruce and O'Brien, and
when they had finished making up their beds, the guard told
Bruce to wait there while he went off with O'Brien.

Alone, Bruce wandered around the barracks, the long
rows of beds and the lavatory stretching through the back,
like the post of the letter T, a row of twenty pots without
wooden seats, reminding him for all the world of the hotels
in North Africa after the landing, where everything not
nailed down had been stolen, including the toilet seats. He
went back to his bed. A small wooden locker at the foot of
the bed proved to be empty when he opened the lid, but it
was an admission that people in prison might possess things.
Then he sat on his bed, mildly puzzled that he had been left
alone there, yet content to sit quietly and think about all the
many things that needed thinking about. In England and
France and India, he had seen prisons that might well be
models for a small corner of hell, and here was a prison
designed with common sense that did not squeeze its prisoners to death with either punishment or boredom, but put
them to work; and it was a prison designed by the same
society that lay silent and afraid under the threats and rav-
ings of a handful of semidemented men. Only here he was
an anomaly, a freak of sorts, a political prisoner, which was

something neither the prison system nor the country had ever thought through or even contemplated.

His musing was confirmed when the guard who had taken O'Brien away appeared and informed Bruce that the warden desired to see him. "Just go up to the offices," the guard said. "Main building." He pointed the way.

Left alone, Bruce walked up the slope to the building that had greeted him the night before. There were no walls. This was a strange prison, indeed; he could just go on walking.

He walked into the Administration Building, and the guard, sitting behind his desk at the door, asked him his name.

"Bruce Bacon."

"Yes, the warden's expecting you. Down the corridor at your right."

The door he opened was marked *Warden Demming,* and a middle-aged woman, sitting at a desk and typing busily, stopped to assess him. Evidently he was singular enough to define himself, and she simply pointed to a door that led to the inner office. The office was simple—government issue, a standing flag, a big portrait of Lincoln, another of Roosevelt, and a map of West Virginia. The warden, seated behind his desk, told Bruce to sit down and then surveyed him thoughtfully. After a moment or two of this silent study, he asked Bruce what he thought of prison.

"The District jail gave me the impression that nothing has changed very much in the past two thousand years, but this place—" He shook his head.

"Yes, this is an interesting place. About twelve years ago, Mr. Bennett, the head of the Federal Bureau of Prisons, sat down with a group of penologists to try to make something civilized out of the prison system. They came to some conclusions. If there are no locks or cells, a prisoner can't break out, and if there are no walls to go over, he can't escape, and if you give him work and treat him decently, he won't escape. It works. In twelve years, there have been only eight escapes, homesick mountain people mostly, and we just phone the local police, who pick them up. But we keep a pretty low profile. We don't want newspapers writing about us, and we don't want to be analyzed out of existence.

"Now let me tell you why I'm telling you all this. To begin, I read you every day in the *New York Tribune.* I had a subscription then to the *Washington Post,* the *New York Times,* and the *Tribune,* and I read every dispatch you wrote right through the war. I had a son in the service, a rifleman who was killed on the fourth day after the Normandy landings, and during that time, there were sixty Quakers in this jail, religious pacifists, and I had to make my peace with that. I think you helped me. What you wrote was different from what the others wrote. I don't know exactly how, but it was different.

"OK. Now you're here. I don't know what the hell is happening outside, and I don't know whether you're a communist or not, and I'm not going to ask you. You're here, and this is a work camp, and I got to find a job for you. About sixty percent of our population here works in the woods, logging. We work with the rangers who mark the trees they cut to thin the forest. Then we cut them, drag them to the mill, saw them, and ship them to Federal prisons. We have our own sawmill, but it's dirty, dangerous work, and I don't see you there. The rest of the population works in the kitchen, the garage, and on the grounds. You're not a mechanic, are you?"

"I'm afraid not," Bruce said.

"Well, I have another idea. Have you ever done any teaching?"

"No, again."

"You'll work it out. Half the men in your barracks are Kentucky moonshiners. Decent, deeply religious folk, but they make whiskey because if they don't, they starve. No other way for them to earn a living. Also, they're illiterate. A few of the younger ones can read and write a little, but for the most part they're illiterate. Most of them are repeaters. The local circuit judge knows their case, and he puts them in here for six months or a year. It would be a damn good thing if you could teach them to read. How about it?"

"I could try," Bruce answered slowly.

"It has to be an evening and weekend thing. They work in the woods during the day, and they're the best lumber people we have—"

"You know," Bruce said, "I've never done anything like this before. I never taught. I suppose I could give it a try, but I'm not sure I'd be any good at it."

"You can't make it worse."

"No, I suppose not."

"We still have the days. I'm trying to think of something that might be of some use to you. I think I'll put you in the motor pool, down at the garage. You'll learn what makes a car work. You won't go in as a mechanic but as an assistant. And by the way, evening work is optional. You can turn down the teaching if you want to."

Bruce thought about it for a while, and then he shrugged. "Sure. I'd like to try the teaching. The other thing—yeah, I'd like that. I sat in a cell in Washington for eleven days. That's unbearable."

"Good. We'll see how it goes. If you can't hack the teaching, let me know."

Five days later, Bruce wrote to Molly: "A very strange prison, my dear one. No walls, just small signs that say *Stay Inside.* According to the warden, it's worked out as a psychological prison camp. Give the men a full day of interesting—within bounds—work, tire them, treat them like human beings, and you'll have a calm, orderly prison. It works. It seems that every prisoner spends the first couple of nights lying awake and planning his escape. Once he has it worked out, he puts it on hold. Why risk it unless he has to, and many of the men here are living better and eating better than they did outside. I compare it with that medieval chamber of horrors that they first put me into, and I muse a good deal over the contrary and many faces of this country of ours.

"The food is not great, but there's enough, and we each get a glass of milk each day and oranges or apples, plus the regular food.

"We sleep in an army barracks type of building, cots set side by side. The cot on my left sleeps Lemuel Ward, a huge, tough gentleman from South Carolina, doing the last two years of ten years for manslaughter. He must weigh two hundred and fifty pounds, and none of it is fat. His background, what I know of it, is complex, interesting, but nothing you'd want to share with kids at night. He is both respected and feared. He has taken a great liking to me, thank heavens. He named me 'Professor,' and the name has stuck, and by now all the convicts call me that.

"The bed on my right provides an interesting counterpoint. It is occupied by a middle-aged man, name of Jackson Hill. He is a Kentucky mountain moonshiner. Half the men in the prison are moonshiners, Kentucky and West Virginia, and I'm told that if they didn't make whiskey, they'd starve, so it's a running battle between them and the revenue agents. They're very religious folk, and very often in the evening they'll do a little Bible reading—that is, one will read and the others will listen, since nine out of ten are illiterate, which I will tell you about later. But the other night, they were listening to some reading, all of them—that is, about seven or eight—gathered around Jackson Hill's bed. Lemuel Ward was listening respectfully. Ward doesn't say much, mostly just listens. He works in the woods all day with one of the lumber gangs, and after dinner, he sits crosslegged on his bed and makes ornaments out of the cellophane wrappings of cigarettes, a sort of prison art that I never saw anywhere else.

"Well, I'm lying there in bed, reading, and next to me the Bible-study group is in full swing with a sort of argument erupting. I must mention that the Kentucky men are treated very respectfully. They are dangerous fighters, and while it takes a good deal to rile them, once they're in a fight, they fight to kill. So while the Bible discussion made noise, everyone endured it. Finally, Jackson Hill turns to me and asks me do I know any Bible? So I'm in it, and the passage they're working over is that line where Jesus says, *Suffer little children, and forbid them not to come unto me.* Jackson Hill says to me, 'Now how about that, Professor? Here's a good man, Jesus Christ our Lord, telling little ones to suffer. Ain't there enough suffering when the poor kid grows up?'

"Now, Molly, I have to pause and mention that the warden asked whether I would undertake to teach these Kentucky men how to read and write. Like a damn fool, I agreed and I put up a notice on the bulletin board, but nobody showed up. Now come back to Jackson Hill's question; I explain to them that when the Bible was translated in the time of King James, three hundred years ago, *suffer* was used mostly to mean *accept* or *endure* or *tolerate.* So the line in the Bible, I explained, did not mean that Jesus wanted children to suffer, but that He wanted nothing to stand between Him and children. To us it appears simple and obvious, but it was a light breaking out to these mountain people; and not only did this little incident make me an authority on biblical puzzles, but that night a dozen of the Kentucky men turned up for the literacy class.

"Now bear with me. How do you teach illiterates? I don't know, I don't have the vaguest notion, and try as I might, I could not remember when I learned to read or how I learned to read. So I had to invent a system. The first time, I dealt only with the alphabet, the sound of the letters. We went over that for a whole evening, the sound of letters and the shape of letters. Then, last night, I started with a few simple three-letter words, like *cat, rat, dog, bed,* and *pop* and *mom.* Amazing how quickly the mountain people learn. I'm as excited over this as I was going out on my first newspaper assignment. It's like opening a box of something wonderful.

"So much for the volunteer work. My regular job at the motor pool is something else. The chief mechanic at the garage is a man named Dude Baxter. He's from New Orleans, where he was a driver for one of the local mobs. He was given eight years for being involved in the murder of a prostitute, and he is serving the last twelve months here at Mill Bog. Here's one for you on your women's rights crusade. He and his buddy, both drunk, beat this prostitute to death. A so-called honest woman would have put them both away for life if not the death penalty; but since it was a whore, they got off with short time. Baxter is a pig in human form, and I work not to annoy him, but I learn very little. I'm a sort of a gofer. Get me this. Lift this. Hold this. I think it's good for me. It turns my mind away from any sort of cockeyed pride I might be building out of this experience.

"And now, my dear Molly, a word about what this place looks like before I finish. It's called Mill Bog because there are cranberry bogs all through the mountains here. The mountains rise all around us, and the fact that we're in a Federal forest preserve gives the place a feeling of the forest primeval, since the trees are thinned and cultivated. There are times at dawn or early sunset when this place is beautiful beyond belief—an odd thing to say about a prison.

"So there it is, my love, until the next time I write, an attempt to give you at least a feeling of where I am."

He could have devoted a good deal more space to Dude Baxter, but that would have served only to worry Molly, and where she was concerned, he felt that her time was harder to build than his. That was the prison phrase, building time. That was the sane way to do it, to build time; those who went mad, as many of them did, those were people who fought time, who tried to conquer it, tough, mean people who could come to no terms with themselves. Baxter was that way, ugly and heavyset, tiny cold blue eyes that were full of hate. He watched Bruce, and Bruce felt his eyes. Bruce worked at the garage three weeks before things came to a head. Baxter's hatreds were institutional: he hated anyone who wore glasses, he hated anyone who read books or newspapers, he hated anyone who spoke intelligible English, he hated anyone who had any part of education. He said to Bruce that morning, "Bacon, I'm short a lug."

At best, his speech was none too clear. Bruce handed him a lug wrench, and he flung it at Bruce, missing his head by inches. "You motherfucken ignorant commie bastard! I asked you for a lug, not a lug wrench, you dumb shithead! Don't you know what a lug is?"

His voice bellowed out, and all the talk in the garage came to a stop. The other convicts working there stopped movement as well as conversation. They waited. Bruce remained where he was.

"Motherfucker, I asked for a lug!"

"I heard you."

"Get it!"

Bruce's thoughts had been elsewhere. He should have known that Baxter wanted a lug and not a wrench. If he had been paying any attention, he would have taken a step around the truck and seen that Baxter had a lug wrench in his hand, but he hadn't, and now he had precipitated the moment Baxter had looked for and waited for. What now? There were eight other men in the big repair shop, and tonight everyone in the camp would know what Baxter had called him and how he had responded.

"Not when you ask like that," Bruce said.

"How should I ask for it, asshole?" Baxter said softly.

"Politely," Bruce said. "Not like a damned barbarian."

Baxter grinned and said, "Take off your fucken glasses."

Bruce stood motionless, his heart hammering, asking himself, What do I do now? Then Baxter hit him in the stomach, and as Bruce doubled over, Baxter kneed him in the testicles, and Bruce crumpled to the ground, his whole nervous system exploding with pain. Baxter kicked him in the head, opening his forehead with the toe of his boot. The blood ran into his eyes, blinding him. He was unable to move, paralyzed with pain. As Baxter moved to kick him again, one of the Kentucky men who worked in the shop yelled, "God damn you, Baxter! That's enough. You'll kill him!"

Baxter slowly and deliberately passed the sole of his boot over Bruce's cheek, bearing down hard enough to rub off the skin. The mountain man pushed Baxter aside, and he and another convict helped Bruce to his feet and half carried him over to the hospital, where Mac Olsen helped lay him on one of the cots.

The two convicts who had helped him into the hospital had to go back to the garage. Olsen shook his head, filled a bowl with warm water, and washed the blood off Bruce's face. He had a cut lip, he was bleeding from the nose, and half of one cheek was without skin. His stomach hurt like hell, and as the pain of the blow to the testicles eased, the pain in his stomach increased.

"Can you talk?" Olsen asked. "What happened? He kicked you in the balls?"

"Yes," Bruce mumbled.

"Baxter?"

"Yes."

"You got some bad cuts around your face. I'm going to take the towel off and wash them out with peroxide. It's going to hurt like hell."

"So what? I hurt like hell now."

He bit on his lips as Olsen washed the cuts with peroxide. His nose had stopped bleeding. Olsen put a small piece of tape on his lower lip, closed his head wound with two Band-Aids, and taped a nonsticking, two-inch-square pad over his cheek.

"Do you think you could get up and walk?" Olsen asked him.

"I can try."

"How does your crotch feel?"

"Lousy."

"Let me have a look. Pull down your pants."

"Are you some kind of defrocked doctor, Olsen?"

"I'm as close to a doctor as you're going to get here, so you better damned well do what I say. I was a medic doing this under fire when you were writing your fancy stories, so just keep your mouth shut and do what I say. I want to see your balls."

He helped Bruce get his pants down, fingered his testicles gently as Bruce winced with pain. "Pull up your shirt," he said. The flesh below the breastbone was turning blue. He pressed. "How bad does that hurt?"

"Not too bad."

"I don't think there's anything broken inside. How old are you, Bacon?"

"I'll be thirty-five."

"OK. I think your cheek will heal nice and clean. Pull up your pants and take a few steps."

Rolling over, Bruce put his feet down and stood up, swaying a bit. He took a few uncertain steps.

"Good. Now lie down again. It's still almost two hours to lunch. Just lie here and rest. I'm going to give you a couple of Anacin, and that'll help keep down the pain."

"What do I tell the guards?" Bruce wondered.

"Nobody's going to ask you. The guards don't mess with this kind of thing, and by the time we eat, everyone in camp's going to know what happened."

As Olsen said, no one asked him what had happened. In the afternoon, he went back to the garage. It still hurt to walk, but he managed. Baxter avoided him, and nobody asked him to do anything. He hung around until the bells clanged, but none of the men working in the garage actually acknowledged his presence.

There was no class for the illiterates that night. His belly hurt, his testicles hurt, and his cheek burned like fire. He lay on his cot morosely, and finally Lemuel Ward, sitting cross-legged on his bed and working his cellophane craft, said to him, "You know, Professor, you got to take care of Baxter. You don't take care of that motherfucker, that motherfucker's going to push you into a hole in the ground. Or get the warden to take you out of that motherfucken garage."

"What do you mean, take care of him?"

"I mean break the motherfucker's back. Kill him. Beat him to an inch of his lousy motherfucken life."

Bruce smiled ruefully and winced with the pain. "Lem, I never had a fistfight in my life. I never hit anyone. I don't think I could."

"Hell, you were with the motherfucken army right through the war."

"I never carried a gun. I was a correspondent. I never fired a gun in my life."

Ward put aside his artwork, swung around to face Bruce, and dropped his voice. "Professor, you don't go up against a motherfucker like Baxter with your hands." Ward had one adjective, which doubled as a noun. "That's motherfucken bullshit. You take a heavy wrench and let the motherfucker have it when his back is turned. Just make goddamned sure that the motherfucker can't walk for the next six months."

Bruce shook his head hopelessly. The pain woke him several times, but he got through the night, and after breakfast he turned up for work at the garage. Baxter acknowledged him. "Take a broom and sweep this place. It stinks of dirt."

One of the men came over and held out Bruce's glasses. "I found them," he said. "They're not broken."

"Did I tell you to give them to him, you shithead?" Baxter reached out for the glasses, but Bruce got them first. There was a moment of tension, and Bruce waited for anything to happen. He tried to keep his hands from shaking as he put on the glasses. Baxter grinned. "Next time, motherfucker."

Bruce swept the big shed. It was agony, yet he got the job done. One of the men passed by and said softly, "Work easy, Bacon. Fuck that lunatic."

He piled into a can the oily waste and debris that he swept up. "Put it in the hole in back!" Baxter yelled at him.

There was a shallow hole behind the garage where waste and waste oil were thrown and where the men urinated, since there were no toilet facilities in the garage shed. Bruce picked up the can and carried it around the building to the back—aware that Baxter was following him, and as he was emptying it into the pit, Baxter kicked him from behind, propelling him forward into the filthy, oily pit. Bruce hardly felt the blow. He was conscious of only one thing, that he had to stay on his feet and keep his cut face out of the filthy, sticky mess in the pit. He dropped the can and somehow kept his balance, staggering knee deep, but not falling. He stood in the muck, swaying back and forth.

Grinning, Baxter said, "Pick up the can."

Bruce picked up the can. It was half full of muck. He climbed out of the pit, and now Baxter walked toward him and shouted, "Empty it, you dumb bastard!"

With a single motion, Bruce swung the big metal can around and flung its contents into Baxter's face. It was the last thing Baxter expected, and trying to dodge the sticky mess, he slipped into the pool of waste. Screaming curses at Bruce, trying to clear his sight, he scrambled out of the muck, but at this point everything rational had left Bruce. He was overcome by a kind of maniacal rage he had never experienced before, and as Baxter got out of the pit, Bruce slammed the metal can down on his head. Baxter fell, sprawling outside the garbage pit, and Bruce, reason gone and all control gone, began to beat him with the heavy metal can. Again and again, he brought the can down on Baxter's head, bending the can out of shape—and then the rage disappeared and it was over, and trembling, sobbing, he stared at the man lying in the oily mud, his head in a pool of blood.

He staggered into the garage, sobbing, trying to mouth the words that would say he had killed Baxter. Someone ran for Mac Olsen, and another ran to the back, lifted Baxter, still unconscious but not dead, and carried him into the garage, where there was a single old cot used as a bench. Covered with blood and filth, Baxter was a sorry sight. Bruce, crouched on a stool, his face in his hands, tried to summon his thoughts to explain what had brought him to this. His life was over. He had killed a man, and he would never leave prison or see Molly again. He would wear the black mark on his soul and conscience until the day of his death, the bar sinister of a life made worthless and useless. For the first time in his life, he had struck and slain another human being; and now, not only did every muscle ache with pain, but a worse pain was constricting his soul.

Meanwhile, Olsen had arrived with his black bag and two clean towels stuffed into his shirt. Any accident at the garage, as he well knew, called for clean towels. "I need hot water," he shouted. "One of you assholes run to the kitchen and get me a kettle of hot water. On the double." Meanwhile, he was wiping the blood and filth from Baxter's face. He wrapped a towel around Baxter's head to stop the scalp bleeding, and then he took a stethoscope out of his bag and listened to Baxter's heart. Then he snapped at Bruce, "Bacon, get your ass over here and stop feeling sorry for yourself!"

Bruce rose painfully and went to the cot where Baxter lay.

"What did you hit him with?" Olsen asked.

"An oil can. Is he dead? He's dead, isn't he?"

"He's not dead. You can't kill a bastard like Baxter. He has a bad concussion and maybe a fractured skull. There's a phone in the garage office. Dial three hundred—that's the main office—and tell them that we want an ambulance and a doctor. Meanwhile"—turning to one of the mechanics—

"get your ass up to the hospital and bring back the stretcher."

Bruce went to the garage office, still not out of his nightmare but not a murderer at this moment, and told the guard who answered the telephone that they wanted an ambulance and a doctor at the hospital. When he returned to Olsen, now the center of interest for every convict working in the area, the water from the kitchen had arrived, and Olsen was bandaging Baxter's head.

"He's alive?" Bruce asked.

"He's alive. Did he hit you again?"

"Kicked me."

"Where?"

"The hell with it," Bruce said.

"Get a hose and clean off your shoes and pants. Then come up to the hospital. I want to see where he kicked you."

The convicts parted their circle to let Bruce through to the water hose. No one spoke, but a few grinned and nodded. There were no guards near the garage, and Bruce would come to realize that this was the deliberate policy of the prison. All arguments and fights were handled by the prisoners. The guards not only did not interfere, they made themselves scarce—even though by now everyone on the prison grounds knew that Bacon had taken care of Baxter.

The stretcher arrived, and Baxter was placed on the stretcher and carried up the rise to the hospital. Bruce followed along. He wanted to help Olsen undress Baxter, but it hurt too much to bend over. Baxter was still unconscious.

"He could be like that for a day or two," Olsen explained. "He's had a bad concussion. I couldn't feel any fracture in the skull, but from the cuts it says he's been hit hard, and there are probably some hairline fractures. That won't kill him, and as long as he's not dead, it won't go on your record or take away any good boy time. Up at headquarters, they know the whole story about yesterday and it's valid self-defense. He'll lose good time, you won't. Now drop your pants and show me where he kicked you."

"It's becoming a habit," Bruce said.

"Red, turning blue and ugly as sin," Olsen told him. "That son of a bitch kicks like a mule. There's some skin off, but not like your cheek. I'll clean it off with peroxide and put a Band-Aid on it. I'll give you six aspirins, three and three. You're a big guy and you want three. It'll deal with the pain now, three of them, and then if you wake up with pain at night, take the other three. Go back to your barracks and go to bed."

He slept through lunch, woke up at dinnertime, went to the mess hall, where every convict who caught his eye gave him the sign of approval, thumb and forefinger in a loop, and then went to bed again. He refused to think about his attack on Baxter. It horrified him to discover what violence he was capable of. It made no difference that he was provoked; provocation was no excuse for his behavior. The thoughts were short-lived; he was asleep almost instantly.

The following day, he learned that Baxter had been taken to Alderson for x rays and after a few days would be shipped to the prison hospital at Lewisburg. He would not be returning to Mill Bog, a fate that no one in Mill Bog appeared to regret, nor was there any indication that he would not recover completely. The diagnosis, as Olsen was informed, spoke of severe concussion and two hairline skull fractures. No one spoke about the incident once a day or two had passed, and neither the warden nor any of the guards ever referred to it. However, Bruce learned about Baxter's vicious treatment of the black prisoners who worked at the auto pool, and one of them went out of his way to thank Bruce and shake his hand. Bruce's reputation went up several notches and the attendance at the evening literacy classes almost doubled.

All of which gave him no comfort, since the situation in his mind remained very clouded. He had tried to kill another human being, and only his inexperience in the business of killing had saved his as well as his victim's life. He left the incident out of his letters to Molly, and he kept postponing Molly's visit—at least until his face healed. A man who had learned the trade at Leavenworth, where he had served many years of time for the theft of over a hundred cars, was put in charge of the garage, and Bruce began an introduction into the mysteries of the internal combustion engine. He began to face the fact that he liked working on the big woods trucks and the tractors. It was the first time in his life that he devoted day after day to working with his hands, hard physical work, and he discovered that his body and his mental outlook were both changing.

Too tired to conduct his classes at night, he switched them to Sunday; and then, a month after he had come there, he was called up to Warden Demming's office, where the warden said to him, "Bacon, you and I both live in a world that confuses us, or am I mistaken?"

"I certainly share your confusion."

"I don't for a minute believe you're a communist, and I'm not going to ask you; but Washington has issued an order that no communists work in education. I think it's stupid and uncalled for, but there it is. I don't make the rules."

"You mean you want me to stop working with the Kentucky people?"

"That's what it is."

"It's a shame," Bruce said unhappily. "It's just the worst damn shame. They were beginning to read and write. I don't know how to tell them this—so help me, I don't."

"I'll come to your next class and take the heat off you."

There was some measure of relief in this, along with Bruce's disappointment. He had taken to the teaching, inventing his own methods, excited as a kid when they worked, playing with all sorts of theories on the subject of education; but on the other hand, he now had his Sundays back, to do as he wished with them. And his face was healed. It was time for Molly to visit.

He wrote to her, "We still have sixteen days before Christmas, and while you can't bring gifts, you yourself will be the most wonderful gift of all. Talk to my mother and father. I wrote to them asking them to come. They're not young, and I hesitate to ask them to drive down alone. On the other hand, from all I've been told, the train trip is miserable, and if you want my innermost feeling, it's that they shouldn't come. Not only is getting to this place an ordeal, but I am afraid of the effect on my mother, even though I have written to them in more glowing terms than this place deserves. Little things. I have lost weight—all to the good. I weighed one hundred and ninety when I came here. I'm twenty pounds lighter now, my nails are broken and beyond cleaning, and my hands are the hands of a mechanic—none of which bothers me, but Mother sees such things and she'll be worried sick. Also—let me be frank—for the few hours you'll be here, I want you to myself. I don't want to divide my love. I think of you constantly, trying to make an image of how you look, having internal conversations with you, having dreams about you.

"It's very cold here, and as I write, it's beginning to snow, just the first powdery sprinkling. At night, when the sky is clear, one is overwhelmed by the mantle of stars. We're almost three thousand feet high here, and the air is like wine. I am allowed two hours of visiting time per month, and while I've not yet done two months here, the warden will allow me four hours, since I don't want you coming again next month. The trip is just too hard. I must tell you that most of our time together will be in the visiting room, although perhaps we will be able to walk outside for a while. They do occasionally bend the rules here.

"So please write when you receive this, and tell me exactly when you plan to come. I'll count the hours."

She came alone, driving down in a rental car, putting the

chains on herself, a competent woman who would not be stopped by a snowstorm. She was no one to play games with, and she knew him too well not to see the scars on his face and demand an explanation. "I didn't want to write to you," he said. "Now that you're here, I can tell you." Her eyes filled with tears as he told her what had happened. "Don't tell me you're proud of me. I'm sick over the whole thing, and it's a damned undeserved dispensation that I didn't kill him."

"I'm proud of you," she said. "I love you. You're a strange, crazy man, but I knew that when I took up with you. If I could be with you here, I'd just as soon have it that way. The world's gone crazy outside. They're playing with their new atom bomb toys and stoking up for a war with Russia."

"I have a subscription to the *New York Times.* Some days I don't even open it, it's a world so vague and far away. I'm reading *War and Peace* again. I read it years ago, when I was seventeen. A book like that should be read twice, three times. God, if I could write such a book, I'd say that my life had some meaning."

"Your life has plenty of meaning, and speaking of books, I have the proofs of a book called *Invitation to the Theater,* by a writer named Bruce Nathaniel Bacon."

"You're kidding."

"Cross my heart."

"Where? Did you bring them?"

"They're locked in the trunk of my car. Shall I get them? I wasn't sure of the rules."

"I could have them. I'm sure I could work that through Demming, although the rule is that all printed material must come directly from the publisher. On the other hand, I don't know if I want to expose the stuff at this point."

"And you may not be wrong about that," Molly said. "Sylvia has some evidence that the vendetta against you is being sparked by that lovely British outfit called M-One and the Limeys are totally pissed off about accusations that they conspired in the killing of six million Indians in Bengal. We both think it's just as well that no one should see the proofs until the book is published."

"Why did you bring them then?"

"I can't do these things without consulting you. Sometimes I feel that they're weaving a damned web around us. I met a couple of Indians, embassy people and both of them Bengalis, and they said you're absolutely right about the famine and there's a pile of evidence put together at Calcutta University, and a squabble going on between the top brass there as to whether it should be released. The Indian government isn't looking for trouble with England, and they're trying to sit on the stuff. Anyway, your publisher feels the same way, and he doesn't want anyone to see the book until it's in print and until printed books go out for review. The way I hear it from friends out on the Coast, Peter Johnson is going all out on the book and with his own money. He's quite a character out there. But I have to have your agreement, and if you feel I can give you the proofs here and that no one else will see them—"

"No. Oh, no. You see, anything I have here in prison is subject to confiscation. It might be that technically they have no right to confiscate a set of printer's proofs, but you'd have to go to court to prove it."

"Johnson called to ask whether there are any copies floating around. I have four copies of the manuscript."

"That's it."

"If you want me to, I'll proofread it. I won't change a word."

"I'd like that. If you have the time?"

"Time? Darling Bruce, I'm in prison for a year. I got a damn good job at Fred's Steak House on Fifty-sixth Street, and I work the dinner hour only. The tips are good. I haven't gone under a hundred a week since I'm there."

The conversation was done in whispers, since the visiting

room was filled with people, men, women, children. Bruce knew that this happened every Sunday, but he had never been here before on Sunday. The mountain women came with their children, lots of children with cornsilk hair and wide, staring eyes, dressed very properly and neatly. Appalachia, Bruce knew, was the most poverty-stricken area of the nation, but the moonshiners were a little better off than the unemployed miners and the farmers who tried to scratch a living out of the rocky soil. They used shoes as a mark of distinction and they paid as much as forty dollars a pair. They were allowed to keep their Sunday shoes in prison, and they would put them on each Sunday, rubbing them to a high polish. They were uneasy with words, and for the most part they sat in silence with wife and child during the visiting hour. There was another room for black prisoners, separated by a thin partition from the white visiting room, and in contrast to the whispers in the white area, a great bubble of voice and laughter and weeping came out of the black section.

"We work together," Bruce explained to Molly, "but we don't eat together or live together—a beautiful expression of the looniness of society carried into its prisons."

But then, like the others, Bruce and Molly sat in silence. They had talked and talked, and then their talk ran out. Bruce had hoped that they might at least take a short walk outside, but an icy rain was falling and he never put the matter to a test. Four hours spent in a room with ten or eleven families began to choke them—and they sat in silence. But then the others departed, family by family, and the last hour of the visit was theirs alone. They were able to embrace, to hug each other, pressing their bodies together, to stand clutched in each other's arms, each filled with overwhelming anxiety for the other.

Then she left, and the visit was over and time began. Time, which had never occupied many minutes of his thoughts, began to preoccupy him. He searched the library for the few theoretical books on time. He listened to men who told him of their absolute suffering when it came to building time. For them, hours became days and days became weeks. He was taken back in his thoughts to the Boy Scout camp of his boyhood, summers that lasted forever, that were concocted out of the pure joy of childhood, a joy never really repeated in the adulthood of any person. The prison barber was an old black man, and sitting in his chair in a little shed off the mess hall, he asked the old gentleman what time was.

"Don't you know, sonny?"

"I'm afraid not."

"Time's like a loop, old cowboy lasso. Angel's got it, and you got all the sweet summer days when you was little, slow, slow. God's got it, time passes like it should. But ifen the devil get hold of it, he stop time. He stop it cold. That's what happens in the slammer. Time stops, and man we suffer like little Jesus till God frees us."

"And when is that?"

"Day you walk out of here, sonny—day you walk out of here."

Heavy snow began, and work in the woods came to a halt. Most of the men spent the day in the barracks, where some of them read books and some read magazines and some read comic books, and some just sat and watched the snow through the windows. It fell slowly, hour after hour, fat, lazy flakes turning over and over and over. The bunkhouses or barracks were warm enough, their steam-heated pipes fed from a central source by an endless supply of branch limbs from the cut trees. But tempers grew short in the close confinement, and every now and then there would be a burst of angry sound from an argument that rarely came to anything more than words. Nobody wanted ventilation because the area near the open window became icy cold; and as a result the barracks would fill with pipe and cigarette smoke and the smell of men's bodies. There was a strange prison game, aptly called Tactics, which was said to have come out of the wartime prison camps. It was played by four players, four chess sets, and four chessboards, the boards split and rearranged, and it went on for weeks. There was a game going in the barracks, and each day a crowd of men would gather around and watch it in silence. Bruce would join them every now and then, brooding over what a strange thing prison was. But whereas the heavy snow brought days of leisure to the woods gang, his own work at the auto shop went on. They dug through the snow to the garage, to fit the big army trucks with chains and to have everything ready for work in the snow. When the snow stopped, leaving the world a white and green pine wonderland, the trucks began to roll and the woods gangs went out again.

In the white world, they had a Christmas dinner with plum pudding—one half the mess hall white, one half black, and at least the voices mingling in the carols they sang.

It was a strange, strange world, this prison camp in the mountains of West Virginia. He lived in a community of convicts, but for the most part they were simple, easygoing men, himself the only middle-class person among them, poor people with commonplace Federal crimes, stolen autos across state borders, stolen checks from the mail, making moonshine and paying no revenue tax and selling it across the border in Ohio, fifty cents' worth of mash distilled into five dollars' worth of a hundred and eighty proof whiskey, doing a quick mugging or purse snatching in the District of Columbia, and himself there for contempt of Congress, the only one of his kind, in prison for a crime he could explain to no one. There was little violence in the prison. People worked hard all day, eight o'clock in the morning until five o'clock at night, and for the first few months, there wasn't a night when Bruce didn't go to bed with his muscles aching. But his muscles hardened and he reached a stage where he knew what a carburetor was and where spark plugs went and what they did and what was a cylinder and a piston, and he could even make a fair stab at a transmission. He could dismantle the treads of a Caterpillar tractor and he could fix and sharpen a chain saw.

All this knowledge and skill was as remarkable to him as achieving the power to transmute base metal into gold would have been to an ancient alchemist. One day, the warden called him up to the Administration Building and told him that James Bennett, the head of the Federal Bureau of Prisons, had sent out notices that all communist prisoners in Federal prisons should have the privilege of writing and the assurance that whatever they wrote could be taken out of the prison.

The John Bunyan syndrome, Bruce thought to himself, and then asked, "Why?"

"I suppose he finds what's going on out there not to his liking. He's an honest man. He also specified you. He wants you to be free to write; and if it's necessary to find you a typewriter, I guess we can dig one up."

"I can understand that. This prison is one damn remarkable place, and I wonder whether there's anything like it in the world. He wants it written about. I think that's a mistake. If I write about it, those morons in Washington will close you down. Anyway, I'm not a communist, and I don't want to write. I like what I'm doing."

"You do?" Demming asked him. "Is that the truth?"

"It's the truth. I like it."

And then Bruce found himself puzzled by what he had told Demming. Did he like it? Could he, he asked himself, spend the rest of his life as a garage mechanic? He admitted to himself that he couldn't, and he tried to fight through to an understanding of that. More and more, he was looking into himself, admitting to himself that he didn't have the vaguest notion of who he was or what he was or what his motivations were. Of course he could supply superficial answers to all of these questions; he was Bruce Nathaniel Bacon, he was six feet tall, had brown eyes and straight brown

hair, and weighed one hundred and seventy pounds or so.
He was a writer, a newspaperman, and a Christian; and that
last gave him pause. He had never thought of himself or
announced himself as a Christian before. Why now suddenly? Was it the John Bunyan thing that had called Christian into his thinking? He didn't know. The world was filled
with things he did not know, and a few months in prison
had put him through a process of unlearning. He wrote to
Molly: "I have the feeling that my head was like a squirrel
cage, endless movement, endless desperation, endless plans
to fight whatever brought me here. Now it's stopped. I look
at things, and I see everything in a new way. Not that I'm
any smarter, but I seem to see things for the first time. I'll
give you an example. I'm lucky to be in this prison. I listen
to prisoners who have been to various state prisons. They
agree that the most terrible are the Virginia state prisons,
only a few miles from here. There, they hang black prisoners
by their thumbs—yes, by their thumbs for a whole day.
They put prisoners into solitary in a hole five feet deep, four
feet high, and four feet wide. They beat men across the feet.
I sit sometimes in the evening with the cons with our pipes
—I learned to make and smoke a corncob pipe, the poor
man's comfort—and I listen to their stories. They appear to
have a desperate need to tell their stories, and they want me
to write about them; and I have come to believe that whatever men do as criminals, they are far less criminal than the
men who control our state prisons. In this year of nineteen
fifty, we have by and large, except here in Mill Bog, learned
nothing that makes the conduct of our prisons any better
than they were in ancient Babylon.

"I can give you another example. You know how we always talk outside about anti-Semitism and how we despise
it, and how so many of our friends are Jewish. Well, here in
Mill Bog there's a prisoner whose name is Cline. He's a
large, fat, whining petty thief, and no more Jewish than I
am. But somehow it's gotten around the prison that Cline is

a Jewish name and that Abe Cline is Jewish. Actually he comes out of a small fundamentalist total-immersion Baptist church in Macon, Georgia. He is intensely disliked, and whenever he tries to join any group, the men turn on him and say, 'Get the hell out of here, you lousy Jew bastard.' Most of the Kentucky men here have never seen a Jew, but they decided out of their distaste for Cline that he's Jewish, as have all the other men. Cline comes whining and pleading to me and begs me, 'Professor, I ain't Jewish. You can tell them I ain't no lousy Jew. You can make them believe that, can't you?'

"I don't have enough charity for that, and I shun Cline as much as the others do, but the experience has taught me more about anti-Semitism than anything I ever encountered. Again, it's looking at something for the first time."

Time passed, and it became January and then it became February, and then March with its wild winds and cumulus clouds flung across the blue sky, and the snow melting and the whole wilderness around them vibrating to the awakening of sleeping life. Most prisoners marked their days on the wall behind their beds, a practice Bruce followed, and one day he counted the marks and they added up to one hundred and fifty.

It was the day Molly came for the third time, and this time his father came with her. It was not a good visit for Bruce. He had adapted to Mill Bog, and when they came here to him they found a stranger. His lean figure made him look taller. He carried his body differently. His hands appeared to be larger, his fingernails broken, the grease dirt ingrained. He realized how bad it was for both of them, but there was nothing he could do about that. Loneliness had come to Molly like a straitjacket drawn ever tighter and tighter. She had moved away from the Communist Party, in part because she felt that any presence there might be harmful to Bruce, in part because she felt that their insistence on defending every move of the Soviet Union was a path of self-destruction. Her left-wing friends had dropped away, indifferent to Bruce's fate. She was convinced by now that Bruce's search for the truth about what had taken place in India was at the bottom of all that had happened to him. Seeing Bruce shattered all her inner strength, and it had something of the same effect on him; and as for his father, the man had suddenly become so old, so helpless, and inarticulate as well. Bruce's eyes filled with tears as he embraced them, each in turn.

"I think I'll wait a while before I come back. Do you understand that, my love?" Molly asked him.

He understood all too well.

He built time, and time passed. The snow melted and the forest returned to life and the trees put out their leaves as proof that winter was not death but only an interval before reawakening. The deer, hungry after the winter cover of snow, came nosing around the prison camp, intrigued by the smells of food and men and somehow knowing that this was a place without guns, and once a black bear came and ripped their garbage containers apart and would not depart until he had eaten his fill, for all the shouting and gesturing by the kitchen crew.

And in good time, it was July and summer and the men in the garage stripped to the waist as they worked in the heat, and Sunday was a time to stretch out on the grass in the shade and watch the clouds in the sky or to sit on the steps of one of the buildings and talk and smoke a corncob pipe. Sometimes, Bruce sat with the Kentucky men, listening to their endless discussions of the best method to build a still and the best proportions of grain and sugar to make whiskey and the best way to get it over the border into Ohio; other times, he would write to Molly or his folks or sit quietly somewhere and let the day be gentle; and once a month, he would be on garbage detail.

The garbage detail was rotated. There were men who hated it, because after gathering the garbage that had accumulated in the prison, the garbage truck would drive to the saw mill, a mile and a half from the prison, and pick up garbage at the mill. The smell of mill garbage was hideous beyond belief, and there were men who couldn't stand it. Bruce didn't mind the smell, and the excitement of getting out of the prison, first to the mill and then three miles more to the dump, more than made up for enduring the smell.

On this Sunday afternoon in July, Bruce was out during the afternoon with the garbage truck. When they came back to the prison, he was interrupted on his way to a shower by Mac Olsen, who said, "I got four more reds up in the hospital for quarantine. Drop by. Maybe you know someone."

"Not likely," Bruce said.

But after he had washed, curiosity took him to the hospital. The four newcomers were sitting on the steps outside, watching him as he approached, and then, suddenly, one of them leaped to his feet and cried out, "I'll be damned! Bruce Bacon!"

It was Hal Legerman, a little stouter, a little older, but very much the same man he had said goodby to in India five years ago.

Going Home

Bruce wrote to Molly: "Forgive me for letting last week go by without a letter to you. I have some explanations, but no excuses for causing you worry and anxiety, and I eased my conscience by deciding you would call my mother and ask whether she heard from me. I do hope you did so. You know, writing to my mother is a most painful task. I do love her and I know that she lives for me, and I have been away so much, my four years at college and after that the years of the war; and now here I am gone for another year. Well, I set out to write a long and proper letter, struggled with it for two evenings, and then felt so despairing at even the very thought of letter writing that I put you off to the next letter day.

"A lot has happened here since my last letter—or at least a lot for a place where one day is so much like another. I was out doing the garbage last week, which means taking my turn to pick up and deliver to the dump, and when I got back, four new political prisoners had arrived. Or reds; either way; but I feel the proper designation is political. You remember the story about Thoreau being put in the local jail because of his refusal to pay taxes to support the Mexican War, and Emerson came by and said, 'Henry, what are you doing in there?' to which Thoreau answered, 'Ralph, what are you doing out there?'

"Of course, that's an old saw and when I was in college, I sort of assumed that Thoreau was the first, last, and only

political prisoner in our history, which really says something about the teaching of history. It never occurred to me
that the thousands of strikers and protesters who had been
tossed into clink might also be regarded as such. I did get off
on this, but when I write to you I tend to become discursive,
perhaps because I have no one here to whom I can really
talk and who will know what I am talking about. Or has
that changed?

"Let me tell you about the four new arrivals who turned
up last week. Begin with Hal Legerman. You'll remember
my telling you about our meeting in India. He's become
quite a success as a producer on the Coast, and he's one of
the group that were subpoenaed by the House Un-American
Committee. He and his friends stood their ground on the
First Amendment—but why am I telling you all this? You
know their history better than I do. The second member of
that West Coast group is Oscar Hill, the writer, and that set
me back on my heels. He's written some of the best short
stories I have ever read, and I place him right up there with
John O'Hara as two of the best short fiction writers in this
country. That he should have been shackled and dragged off
to prison shames America. I can accept the fact that I put
my nose into that famine story, and that now the associated
characters in M1 and the CIA are slapping me down, but to
do this to Oscar Hill is an outrage. The third member of the
Hollywood contingent is Fritz Scharnoff, a successful director and not a nice man at all, indeed a consummate pain in
the ass.

"Let me define him a little more specifically. The day
after the four men arrived, while Demming was still trying
to decide where to assign them, they were put on lawn
mowers. We have some two dozen ancient hand mowers
that are constantly in and out of the shop for repairs, but
with the exorbitant labor pool that we have here at the
prison, it's easier to put twenty-four men on twenty-four
hand mowers for a few hours than to buy a big power

mower that would do the whole job. Our green, rolling lawns are the warden's pride and joy. A very hot summer day. I'm down in the garage, doing my stint, when Fritz Scharnoff comes storming down to see me. Four o'clock in the afternoon now. The lawns are mowed. Scharnoff says to me, 'How do you turn someone in?' I ask myself, Is the man crazy? I ask him what he means, and he tells me that while he was breaking his back in the hot sun with his lawn mower, two other convicts with mowers were sitting in the shade. I said to him, 'Mister, you're in jail. Those cons are earning twenty cents an hour. Sure they're goofing—why not? But if you turn them in, you'll be dead in the morning. Real dead. No heartbeat.' Do you know, the fool didn't believe me. He said he made the films where that kind of thing happened. I had to get Legerman to read him the rules, and it left me wondering what kind of organization your friends run with characters like Scharnoff in the membership.

"Anyway, we come to the fourth convict I met in the hospital. His name is Professor Lewis Duprey, and he is or was the head of the Department of Romance Languages at New York University. I don't know whether he's a communist or not, but he's here because he belonged to an organization that maintains a hospital in Toulouse, France, for the sick and wounded survivors of the Spanish Republican war against Franco. I imagine you know more about that outfit than I do, but he was on the board of directors when the House Un-American Committee subpoenaed their books and records and the list of their contributors. He voted not to give them the books or names, and here he is. He's an absolutely delightful man who takes his imprisonment with philosophical detachment and without resentment. Since he's middle-aged and somewhat overweight, Mr. Demming has created the job of librarian for him. We have a small library room with two tables and about eight or nine hundred books. Professor Duprey will not be paid the twenty

cents an hour that people like myself, who work in what are
called 'essential positions,' are rewarded with, but he accepts
that with equanimity. Oscar Hill was put in the hospital to
learn what he can from Mac Olsen, who's due for release
next month, and then Hill will be in charge. He's a sweet,
vulnerable, and talented man, and very excited about being
in charge of a prison hospital. I suppose all writers dream of
being something else—note the auto mechanic you're married to—and Hill has buried himself in the four medical
tomes the hospital contains. Right now, the hospital is
empty, so Oscar Hill has a breather in which to become a
doctor. Of course, there are some negatives in the picture.
You know that Dad gave me a subscription to the *New York
Times,* and every morning I pick up my newspaper at postal
and then stroll to the hospital—usually empty—where I use
the private toilet, a right earned by payment to Mac Olsen
of a pack of cigarettes once a week. The joy of a bowel
movement in private, accompanied by the *New York Times,*
cannot be overstated. Well, Oscar Hill has put an end to all
this by appealing to my conscience, my sense of sanitation,
my obligation to the sick—of whom there are none—and
prison rules. By offering to replace my weekly pack of
Camel cigarettes as a gift to Olsen, he swung Olsen to his
side.

"But I took my own small revenge as follows: Hill wanted
to know how one could get writing out of prison, and instead of telling him that the warden would facilitate it, I
suggested that he write on thin onionskin, which they have
in the Administration Building, shake the tobacco out of a
pack of cigarettes, roll up the onionskin, use it to replace the
tobacco, and then switch packs when his wife comes to visit.
He's very romantic, and believe it or not, he's doing exactly
what I suggest.

"So much for that. Legerman was assigned to the shop
crew at the garage, and since by now, with so many of the
original crew having been released, I am chief mechanic

once removed from the top—the top being a colored guy by the name of Sam Jones, who was trained by General Motors and who's brilliant—I made Legerman my assistant. Scharnoff created a problem. He is a total horse's ass; he earned some six hundred thousand dollars last year, and he goes around letting it drop. You can imagine how the cons react. Demming put him in the kitchen, but after two days, the chief cook booted him out, and finally he was put on brooms, sweeping the various buildings. He brought it on himself.

"Have I said anything about myself? Question: Can you count, dear lovely lady? I was sentenced, you will remember, to a year less a day—that is, three hundred and sixty-four days precisely. Now, Federal law gives me three days off each month for good behavior, and aside from my encounter with Baxter, which has been ignored by the administration, I am one of the best behaved cons in the institution. That adds up to thirty-six days, which means I will be released on October twelfth, two months and five days away. Suppose you tell me how that grabs you?"

A week later, a letter from Molly said: "It grabs me everywhere. The news of war breaking out in Korea filled me with horror, and all I could think about was the possibility that you would not be released at all, and certainly if this had spread into the third world war, my immediate fear, that might well have been the case. But it doesn't seem so, and all I can think of is that you'll soon be with me. I seem to repeat myself, with *all I can think of* over and over, but that's the way it is, and when I say all I can think of, I mean that nothing, absolutely nothing in the world is as important to me as putting my arms around you and getting on with the business of life and having kids and being together, and finding names for the kids and speculating on boy or girl and red hair or brown hair and blue eyes or brown eyes, and probably green. Which is all right too, because as you may have suspected, green is not an unimportant color to your

Molly Maguire Bacon. I have been reading up on old Nathaniel Bacon, and of course you know all that there is to know about him, but suppose he had not died so suddenly and the American Revolution had taken place a hundred years earlier, under his leadership, as it well might have. Oh, well, one can dream about such things. By the way, if the first one's a boy, shouldn't it be named Nathaniel? We'll discuss that. I've met Oscar Hill, a lovely and totally impractical man. I don't know your professor, but he sounds charming. How fortunate of your prison to have two professors, and as for the Hollywood director, I've heard about him. Oh, I've met good people and even saintly people in the movement, but with that, all too many Fritz Scharnoffs. But maybe I speak with some bitterness because I was formally chastised by the group at the paper for my petit bourgeois ambitions, and it's true. I have all the ambitions I listed above. I've had the class struggle, and I have paid my dues and so have you.

"Now for the good news. Any day now, if not already, you will be getting an advance copy of a book called *Invitation to the Theater* by Bruce Nathaniel Bacon. Please remember that I told you what a wonderful, extraordinary book it is, because I want credit where credit is due. Your publisher in San Francisco called twice, so we're old friends now; and I do like Mr. Johnson. The first time he called, it was to tell me that he had gone to press with a print order of five thousand books and already he had orders for seven thousand, so he was going to have another printing of ten thousand. The second time he called was to tell me that advance sales were over twenty thousand. He had bound five hundred copies and had sent them to newspapers and magazines and TV and radio stations all over the country. There are now thirty thousand copies in print, and Johnson assures me that he is moving very cautiously because he does not want to oversell the book. However, he feels that at this point it is selling itself, and he is still a month away from publication. I suggested that he put off the publication until you are out of prison, but he is becoming increasingly nervous and he wants the book to have the protection of the light of day. He feels that even the unproven implication that the British forces in India were responsible for six million deaths, a number that matches the slaughter of the Jews by Hitler, is earthshaking. He has put the MS into the hands of five Bengali residents here, two of them diplomats, and every one of them declares that you are absolutely right in the conclusions you draw; but to have them say that is one thing and to get them to make a public statement is another. The diplomats do not want a confrontation with the British at this point; they need British help too desperately, and the others are afraid that, as resident aliens, they will simply get tossed out of the country.

"Two other bits of information on this score. Both the FBI and the State Department have sent emissaries to the Temple Press. Oh, no, not for the world do they want to interfere with the publication of the Bacon book. We don't ban books in the United States. We are a free country, where freedom of the press is enshrined. But on the other hand, we are in the process of uniting and rebuilding a continent stricken by the war. Part of that is our ally, Great Britain. Wouldn't it be better to delay the publication of so inflammatory a manuscript? And of course the FBI man came with the usual half threat. The Director doesn't approve of the publication of the book. The Director feels that a patriotic American would not publish the book. Not real threats, only the feelings of that dreadful little man in Washington who speaks to God or perhaps feels that he is God. All of this over the phone from Johnson. He's scared, but firm as a rock. He wants to know whether we need money. He's prepared to advance you another five thousand dollars right now, bless his heart. Do you want it?

"So much for today. Send my blessing to Hal Legerman, the undaunted, and take care of Professor Duprey.

"I love you so much."

The morning after he read Molly's letter, Bruce was giving Legerman not Molly's blessing, but a mild reprimand and a lecture on pistons and cylinders. A truck engine hung from a chain hoist, and Bruce was explaining, "This, my friend, is an engine block. A cylinder block. The pistons move up and down in those holes, which we call cylinders, and that's what moves the truck. It doesn't matter how filthy and oily this shop is—the inside of those cylinders must be clean and pure. Absolutely and utterly clean and pure, virgin, not a speck of dust, but as smooth and unsullied as a baby's ass. There is an intercourse between piston and cylinder that must be honored and respected."

Legerman was nodding and grinning. "Sure. Absolutely. Do you talk to the others this way?"

Jones overheard. "He do. He sure do."

When they broke for lunch, Legerman said to Bruce, "I just don't believe it—Bruce Bacon running a repair shop."

"I don't run it. Sam Jones runs it. Keep that in mind, Hal."

"Got you."

"And damn it, I've driven cars since I was a kid, and I never knew what made the damn things run. I've had an eight-month course in auto mechanics, and I'm pretty good. That'll help if I can't make a living writing."

"I know. It's just a damned uncommon thing to see a jail turn a man into an auto mechanic instead of a seasoned crook."

"I suppose so. But there's no other jail like this in the country, maybe in the world, and I have the feeling that the warden doesn't love J. Edgar. Maybe this place is the way it is because it's so hard to get to."

"Maybe." The others were washing up. Bruce and Legerman were last on the line, just the two of them at the sink. "About Fritz Scharnoff," Legerman said.

"Tell me. You remember Groucho Marx's crack that he

wouldn't join an organization that would have him for a member?"

"It takes all kinds. This isn't India, where Majumdar lived on rice grains as payment. Scharnoff has taken in over six hundred grand a year. He's a rich and powerful man on the Coast. What brought him into the Party, I don't know. Maybe he had feeling about some things. But he's no way going to spend a year in this place, so don't trust him any farther than you can throw him. He's going to make a deal and sell us out—no question about it."

"That's a hell of a thing to say. How do you know?"

"Believe me."

"He can't sell me out. I never saw the man in my life. And God damn it, I am not a communist. I'm not putting you down, and I don't give a damn who is or who isn't. I'm just saying that I am not one."

"You don't need the truth to sell a man out," Legerman said calmly.

Two days later, Bruce's book arrived. As he unwrapped it in the barracks after dinner, a small crowd gathered around, the four newcomers, Lemuel Wood, Jackson Hill, Clem Alsta, Harry O'Brien, and a handful of others. When Bruce unwrapped it, a typographical dust jacket came into view, a pale lemon-yellow background and across it in large black letters: INVITATION TO THE THEATER. Someone said, "What is it—a movie book?" Others might have wondered. Bruce was quick to explain, "No, it's a book about World War Two. I use the word *theater* as in theater of operations, European theater, South Pacific theater."

That was understood. In one way or another, most of them had played some part in the war.

Underneath the title: *One of the most provocative and disturbing books of our time.*

His own name, BRUCE NATHANIEL BACON, was printed in large black letters across the bottom of the dust wrapper.

It was the most important event in the barracks since an

incident two years before, a time when one of the convicts got his hands on eight ounces of pure Acapulco gold. Everyone wanted to see and handle the Professor's book, and even Lemuel Wood put aside his craft work to demand a look at the "motherfucken" book.

Bruce reserved first rights. "Come on," he begged them. "Give me some privacy. Back off. None of us are going anywhere, and tomorrow you can handle it as much as you want. Meanwhile, give me a little privacy."

"You'd better make a lending list," Professor Duprey suggested.

"Give me a little time." He passed the book around so that everyone could have a close look at it, and then he pulled his legs up on his cot and opened the book lovingly. The jacket flap said: "Here is a book about World War Two that presents a face of war not seen before. It is a thoughtful, compassionate book that treats war and this war not simply as a struggle for freedom and a movement to wipe Nazism from the face of the earth, but as a human tragedy that has afflicted the entire human race and now threatens to destroy the human race. The story of the great Bengal famine of 1944 becomes a thematic component of Bacon's book, together with the Nazi murder of six million Jews and the genocide practiced against the European Gypsies. It is not an easy book to read, and parts of it are both horrifying and shocking, but it is a book that must be read."

The back flap of the dust jacket dealt with the current residence of the author—a Federal prison.

Bruce began to read it. He had to read it. Too much had happened since he wrote the book, and as he read it, he felt that an entirely different human being had written it. He had the very strange feeling that his purpose on earth was to witness the greatest tragedy in man's time on earth. He was no longer a witness. He worked with his hands eight hours a day in a garage, for which labor he was paid twenty cents an hour, and at the end of that long day, he had to fight to keep his eyes open to read a book, yet he had found a kind of peace. Perhaps if he had gone to a college other than Williams, say to Michigan or New York University, places where there were strong branches of the Young Communist League, his life might have taken a different direction; on the other hand, perhaps he had been more fortunate this way, in his position as an outsider, and perhaps that made his book something more than another account of war. Whatever his life had been, it brought him finally to Molly, and if it also brought him to Mill Bog, that only brought him closer to Molly. He thought a good deal these days about Ashoka Majumdar, and one day he asked Hal Legerman if he ever found out what Majumdar's fate had been.

It was a Sunday. Each Sunday morning, a Methodist parson drove up to the prison from Covington, Virginia, and conducted a sort of nonspecific Christian service—no preaching and many songs. It was well attended because it never lasted more than thirty minutes and the singing was good. Bruce went quite often, partly for the singing and in part for the walk in the woods that the minister conducted afterward, a forty-five-minute stroll through the adjacent forest. While the Federal forest was not virgin timber, it had been established more than a hundred years earlier, and it was a place of tall, splendid trees and somber semidarkness, with here and there a sun-splashed opening of cranberry bog. Bruce had talked Legerman into coming to services with him, and afterward he and Legerman and Professor Duprey trailed along after the minister on the woods walk. There it was that Bruce asked Legerman about Ashoka Majumdar. He explained to Duprey who Majumdar was and the circumstances of their meeting.

"He's dead," Legerman said.

"How did he die?"

"What's the difference? He's dead."

"I'd like to know," Bruce insisted.

"They beat him to death."

"Who?"

"The British."

"Then he never lived to see the independence?"

"No."

"How do you know they beat him to death?" Bruce asked.

"Oh, Jesus Christ—the last thing in the world I want to think about and be reminded of is Majumdar. Why the hell can't you leave it alone?"

"Because I want to know," Bruce said deliberately.

"OK. I know because they—they, his friends, brought his body to Chatterjee's house. Did you ever see the body of a man who was beaten to death?"

"Almost to death—yes."

"Then I've told you enough," Legerman said. "The difference between us, Bruce, is that your Christian leaders, as for example the good minister leading our pack, would say that you are blessed with innocence. I would say you are cursed with it. They would also say that Ashoka Majumdar is a fraud, an educated man and excellent writer taking his worldly pay in a grain of rice from each peasant who listened to him read. Majumdar was a Buddhist, and they don't have saints, only people, but some will say that his life was a pose and a fraud, because there must be an explanation. We live in a world where there must be an explanation for all happenings and there must be a pill for every ailment. Of course, when both fail, you can always kill people. That's the wonderful ultimate solution."

"Oh, come on," Professor Duprey interjected. "You're laying a heavy burden on Bruce. I'm not a Party member but I've been around the communist movement for enough years to be able to say that the wonderful communists I have known were blessed with innocence. The scoundrels, who are none too rare, are blessed or cursed with other qualities. This isn't India, Hal, and believe me, we are a society here in America today that could produce neither Saint John of the Cross nor Samuel Adams. Bruce left his book with me at the library, and I've read most of it, and he has a point of view that's new and clean and different—a sense of what murder is in its largest manifestation, which is war and genocide. You have no right to leap at him as you did."

"I didn't leap at him and I have the right. He is as fallible as any of us."

"I'm listening," Bruce said. "Please believe that I'm listening."

"Why do I have no right?" Legerman demanded of the professor.

"Why? Because you have locked up your brains. It's thirty-five years since Lenin laid out the blueprint for what is called the Communist Party. But then Lenin died and that wretched man Stalin stepped into his place. But since the Communist Party here in the States was organized some thirty years ago, nothing has changed. You made a set of rules and after that you stopped thinking, inquiring, adjusting, and as the years passed you worked the rules into a degree of lunacy. Can you look at the small thing, Bruce's wife being fired from the *Daily Worker* because she had referred to young Negroes as boys and girls, and not specify this as lunacy? And when Oscar Hill, as fine and sensitive a writer as you have in the Party, dared to criticize a book written by your cultural czar on the Coast, he was shredded to pieces by the brainless Party hacks. You learned nothing in all those years, and the only part of you that came to know and understand America were your singers and song writers, but when did a Communist Party leader ever listen to a writer of any kind? And instead of standing alone and proud, you wed yourselves to the Soviet Union, a society so different from ours that every lesson and conclusion you drew from it was absolutely wrong. You still defend that butcher Stalin, and you still try to convince the American people that no wrong was ever done to anyone in Russia. That didn't help Russia any more than it helped us, and when history called upon you to praise the Soviets for their courage and their destruction of the Wermacht and to criticize them as uninhibitedly for their destruction of democratic values like free speech and free movement and freedom from terror, you failed, you welshed, and instead you drove out of your movement every man or woman who dared to do what the Party should have done."

"Oh, no—no," Legerman protested. "That's too much, Professor. You're taking a bit from here and a bit from there, and lumping it all together. No, that indictment won't stand up."

Still, Bruce listened and said nothing. He was totally intrigued. Bit by bit, the maze of his existence was becoming understandable.

"Too much?" Duprey said. "I think not. Your whole leadership was arrested and put on trial in the Federal courthouse in New York City. They were as alone as they would have been on a lifeboat. Sure, your membership supported them—but who else?"

"All the media of this country damned us and the Soviet Union. You know that."

"Because your Party gave them all the openings. And from that, we suffered. Do you think they would have been able to throw a man like Bruce into jail if you hadn't given them all the openings? And now there's a sickly terror all over the land, and you gave them the weapon. Communism. Instead of giving the name the kind of nobility that Bruce writes about in India, you turned the very word into a criminal indictment. You allowed it to be used against anyone that mad dog, McCarthy, chose to slander."

"You can't blame us for that," Legerman protested. "You can't blame murder on the man who is murdered."

"Do you think Bruce would be here? Do you think I would be here if the Party had not become a symbol of guilt? You know how they defined it. A conspiracy to over-throw the government by force and violence. And the Party let them get away with that, because the Party was dying of its own condition."

"There were thirteen thousand Party members in the service," Legerman said.

"And where were they after the war? You started this discussion on the basis of innocence, and you did not like innocence."

"I still don't like it."

"But you see, both Bruce and I are innocents. That's why we are here. Bruce saw the evil in war—in all war, and believe me, that is a state of innocence. I saw the evil in the Spanish Civil War, and when the soldiers of the Republic, defeated, broken, came over the Pyrenees to Toulouse and desperately needed medicine and hospital care, I joined a group of people and we made a hospital and opened it to the Spaniards. That was our innocence. We see evil and we believe it can be overcome. We are foolish innocents, and by God, your Party should have protected us and fought for us."

"There was nothing left to fight with," Legerman admitted. "We tried to change things in ourselves. It was too late."

"Then what happens?"

"I don't know," Legerman admitted. "We failed. The kids will have to work it out, and maybe they'll do it right."

"If there are kids," Bruce said. "If the bombs don't fall first."

Bruce dropped behind, and Legerman and Duprey went on with their argument. Legerman had said something about guts, courage, and Duprey, his voice strangely shrill and very audible, said, "Guts, guts—you ennoble a man because he doesn't have the character to admit to himself that he is afraid—or too stupid to preserve his life—too stupid to preserve his life," coming back as an echo. Bruce shrugged, turned around, and headed back to the prison. He disliked arguments. He believed that few people were convinced by arguments. It took conditions of life to change a person's thinking. This he believed strongly. If Legerman had backed down, it was out of respect for Duprey; and Duprey, after long years of lecturing, lectured rather than argued. His was the voice of reason, backed by very careful and sensitive insights. Half through with Bruce's book, he had asked whether Bruce had dealt at all with religion.

"In my last chapter," Bruce had said.

"Are you religious, Bruce?"

"A religion that permits war or justifies it is no religion, and since all religions permit war and justify it, I have no religion."

"I'm a Quaker," Duprey said.

"Of course. I owe you an apology. But Richard Nixon sits on the Un-American Committee, and he's a Quaker."

"He is nothing," Duprey said slowly. "He lost himself somewhere, or perhaps he only lost his soul and forgot to return and look for it."

An odd character, Professor Duprey, Bruce thought as he saw Duprey and Legerman, still hotly engaged, disappear into the woods with the minister's group. Bruce enjoyed listening to them, but right now he wanted to be alone. Since the four men had joined him in prison, life had become more variegated, more interesting. Mostly, he would sit and listen, hardly ever projecting his own point of view. Scharnoff was downbeat all the way; in contrast, Oscar Hill was totally dedicated to the excitement of being in prison. He invested it with a fraternity of notable men and women, beginning with Socrates. Since he could not find the *Trial and Death of Socrates* in the prison library, he wrote to his wife to have whoever was keeping it in print send it to him. Like Bruce, he turned to *Pilgrim's Progress.*

Strange, interesting people, Bruce reflected as he made his way through the woods. They changed the quality of prison, but he was not sure that he welcomed this. He had spent most of his life with people who read books and newspapers and had ideas, even if the ideas were stale and often stupid. Here he had been discovering the curious pleasure of silence. When he worked, his speech was mostly limited to instruction; the speech of the men he worked with was limited to women and sports.

Silence was filled with other things, faint, distant sounds that entered his mind without disturbing it. This shadowed forest, with its mighty tree trunks, like columns in a cathedral, reaching up to a roof of leaves, was filled with awesome silence. Here and there, sunlight came through in narrow strokes, the golden shafts dancing with the tiny creatures of the forest air. It moved Bruce and in some small way exalted him, as if he had been let in on a great secret that few knew. It must have been almost like this when the first white men came to these ancient mountains.

He walked back to the prison alone. It was past midsummer, the dog days of August, the sun hot, the air still and heavy. He sat on the lawn, cross-legged under a tree. He must have dozed. He opened his eyes and saw Professor Duprey.

"Do you meditate?" Duprey asked him.

"You mean sitting cross-legged? No, I never learned. I'd like to."

"Mind if I join you?"

"Please."

"I can't sit cross-legged," Duprey said. "Too much good wine, too much good food, and now they put me in the library. I'm reading Proust. Never read him before, but if you tell anyone that, I shall deny it under oath. I am bored to tears. War is boring when no one is killing; prison is even more boring. That's the cruel punishment of being in prison, boredom, boredom, boredom. What was I doing, a Quaker in a war? I was with the Friends' Service, one of our ambulances. Boring, too. You know, the Buddhists have a myth about God, the spirit, the force, the mind of the universe, whatever. We'll call it God. God could do all things, make all things—space, the universe, the planets—create all that is or ever will be, and God was here forever because it was God who created time. But this great mind that created all that ever was faced a thing that He could not defeat."

"Boredom?" Bruce ventured.

"Ah, you know the story."

"No. But I'm in prison. Tell me how God dealt with boredom."

"Yes, that's the beautiful part of the story—a kind of special Buddhist beauty. Until now, God had created nothing that felt or saw or conjectured or reacted. Now, in the face of boredom, he shattered Himself into a billion, billion, billion fragments, and each fragment became a sentient creature, and in each sentient creature there was a tiny, infinitesimal part of the Godhead, and that tiny part carried only one instruction—to unite itself with all other sentient creatures so that one day God might be whole again."

"It's very pretty," Bruce agreed. "Did the Buddha Himself create the story?"

"Who knows who created it?"

"He might have done better to remain God and forget about the sentient beings."

"You're bitter?"

"No. Strange thing is, I'm not. But there are times when I'm filled with unbearable sorrow and not for myself. I envy Legerman. I have the feeling that he's unconquerable."

"He's a strong man. But he looks only in front. Your gift, Bruce, is that you can look in any direction you choose."

"If it's a gift. You see, Lewis, I learned that the most awful things can go on in the world, and there is not one damned thing you can do about it. I don't know enough about the Communist Party to measure your criticism, but I have a sense that you are right. My trouble is that I fell in love with a communist of great inner and outer beauty. I

said to myself, Trust this wonderful woman. I do trust her.
I'd trust her with my life. But I also said to myself, If she
belongs to that organization, then it's there. But she was
duped. When we needed it, it wasn't there."

"No one was there, Bruce."

Sunday became Monday, and a letter from Molly said
that she had put off her visit until mid-September. Her only
explanation was that she could not explain. Bruce was falling prey to a prison disease, psychological, that might have
been called "close to release." Apparently, it overtook every
convict Bruce spoke to, a terror that the convict would die
before the day of release, or be too sick to move, or he would
be told that he was denied his time off for good behavior—
or any one of a dozen other possible but highly unlikely
contingencies. It became more and more difficult to sleep,
even after a grueling day in the garage. His temper short-
ened, and he found himself snapping at the convicts who
worked in the shop with him. Legerman tried to help him.
"You're as healthy as a horse. You look younger and better
and certainly leaner than you did in India. You're not going
to die, and any day now, Molly will be here."

And Molly came, and the world brightened before it collapsed. She was waiting for him as he entered the visiting
room. It was midday on a cold, damp September Saturday.
Usually, visiting day was on Sunday or legal holidays. A
Saturday was permitted under certain conditions, and Molly
had sought this special permission with the excuse that her
boss would not give her Sunday—but, as she told Bruce,
with the hope that the visiting room would be entirely
theirs.

Saturday was also a workday, and the message came to
Bruce in the garage that he had a visitor in the Administration Building. He took the time to wash his hands as best he
could. His blue shirt was stained and dirty, but that was
from the nature of his work and he would not stop to
change it. Between now and his release, less than a month

away, there was no possibility of a visit from anyone but Molly, and he had written to her, half suggesting that she put the visit off, since the end of his term was in sight. She must have telephoned the warden for permission to come on Saturday.

She was sitting on one of the long benches in the visiting room, and she rose as he entered the room. Demming saw no purpose in taking a guard from his other duties and stationing him in the visiting room. If a prisoner wanted to escape, he would escape. There were no prison walls or locked doors here, so why give the prisoners a feeling that they must be watched? Thus, Molly was alone in the room, a tall stately woman in a long raincoat. She was hatless, her red hair coiled into a bun at the back of her neck, her smile full of sadness mixed with delight as he took her in his arms.

"You are beautiful," Bruce whispered. "Beautiful and wonderful. Each time I see you, I realize that I can't properly remember how wonderful you are."

"I like you too."

"Sit here."

They dropped onto the bench.

"I didn't mean I liked you," she said. "What sort of an awful word is *liked*? Only for teasing. Do you know how you look?"

"Filthy?"

"Lean and hard and brown. Is this room bugged?"

"No."

"How can you say that?" she whispered.

"I'm close to one of the guards and he talks to me. He told me that last month a couple of FBI men were down here, and they asked Demming how he felt about bugging the visiting room. He was incensed. He said that as long as he's the head of this institution, he will not have this room bugged."

"Thank God for that. I'm going to whisper, and don't interrupt me until I'm finished. A Russian, name of Josef

Dimitrov, defected to the British. Apparently, he's been a double agent for years, working with M-One. When it gets too hot for those creatures, they defect and become heroes in the West. Now, apparently, the creatures at M-One have gotten him to testify that you're a Soviet agent—"

"What!" He couldn't help the explosive response.

"Easy, darling. Yes, he will testify that you are a Soviet agent and that the Russians ordered you to take an assignment in India so that you could drive a wedge between Britain and America. The British are very uptight about this famine thing, and putting you down as a Soviet agent will undercut your book completely. The Labour government and the spy boys hate each other, and it appears that a British publisher wants desperately to publish your book. Johnson called me about it. He said the English publisher was offering an advance of twenty thousand dollars. I told him to take it."

"Yes. Of course. That's wonderful. That will really set us up. But the other stuff is sheer, unmitigated horseshit."

"I know that. And we don't need that money to set us up. The book is a national best seller, and there are already sixty thousand copies in print, and a paperback house is offering twenty-five thousand for the paperback rights, and Johnson has rejected their offer and intends to put it up for auction. I am told that's a new wrinkle in the book business. But the sheer, unmitigated horseshit can't be taken lightly. Sylvia has been notified that they will take you into custody here at this prison the day your sentence ends, and with the witness of this stinking Russian, they are going to indict you for espionage."

His heart sinking, an empty sickness inside him, Bruce whispered, "I don't believe that. It's too crazy. They don't make such things out of the whole cloth. It's movie stuff. It's not real."

"No, my darling, it's real. Do you imagine anyone could invent this kind of lunacy? I asked Sylvia whether they could convict with this kind of thing, and she said in a Washington court with a Washington jury, they could convict the Pope of bigamy—and a conviction with the charge of espionage, with this crazy war in Korea, could mean life imprisonment or even the death sentence."

Bruce shook his head hopelessly. "I can't face that." He was dying inside, slowly, agonizingly. He conquered an impulse to leap to his feet, scream, break his way out of there.

"On the other hand," Molly said deliberately, "you might very well face the charge and beat it. Sylvia thinks we could get a change of venue, and with that, away from Washington, with an honest judge, a jury might find you not guilty."

"And that's all we have to hope for, a jury that isn't terrified?"

"No. We have other things to hope for, and we are not going to wait for some rotten, cowardly jury to throw away your life. Now let me tell you what I worked out. Your release date is October twelfth, which is a legal holiday, which means it is a visiting day. October twelfth actually begins at one minute past midnight on the night of October eleventh; from that moment on you have served your scheduled legal time, and you are a free man with the right to walk out of here. No one can contest that. No one can charge you with attempting to escape. In the normal course of things, prisoners leave here some time between nine and twelve in the morning. I have made all my careful inquiries. Most prisoners are picked up by car. Others are driven to the bus station at Marlinton. Sylvia and I have been over this time and time again. On the eleventh of October, you will become increasingly nervous—only to be expected and of course people notice. You let it be known, subtly, that I will pick you up about noon the next day. By then, the warden will probably know that there is a hold on you, but he may not tell you until the morning of the twelfth. In any case, you are too nervous to sleep. I understand you get your city clothes on the eleventh, and it's reasonable that you put them on. Bedtime, you're too nervous to sleep. You follow me until now?"

"I think so."

"Do they have a bed check? I think you mentioned that they do sometimes?"

"Sometimes. It's uneven. Usually at ten o'clock. We rise early and we work hard. Most of us are asleep at ten."

"No dogs, are there?"

"No dogs."

"And what about a night watch?" Molly asked.

"I get your drift. Yes, two four-hour shifts. Ten-thirty to two-thirty. Two-thirty to six-thirty. But on cold nights, they hole up mostly. No one ever tries to escape. The last escape was four years ago. No one here serves more than two years, and the punishment for escape is five years."

"You won't be escaping," Molly said. "You're free. Listen, you don't sleep because you're too nervous to sleep. You sit on the steps in front of the barracks. You know the guards, and if one of them sees you sitting there, he'll understand, won't he?"

"I suppose so. But where does all this get us?"

"At midnight, you're free. You walk up to the Administration Building and around it. The moon will begin to rise toward one o'clock, so there's no need to hurry. If a guard sees you—"

"He won't."

"OK. Now the entrance to the driveway of the Administration Building is off Route Thirty-nine. Do you remember how that is?"

"Pretty well. I've seen it. I went out a couple of times to pick up supplies at Marlinton."

"Good," she said. "Very good there. You will turn left on Thirty-nine and walk down the road about half a mile. If a car approaches, you'll see the lights and you hide in the bushes or some such thing. I'll be in my car, parked, just off the road. I spotted the exact place. Now understand, my love, that even if this goes wrong, you've broken no law and you haven't attempted an escape. They can only bring you back."

"And you?"

"What have I done? You're a free man. You're my husband. You're leaving at an odd hour, so what?"

"And once we're in the car? What then?"

"The tickets will be bought for an early plane out of Charleston to Chicago, takeoff at eight A.M. Charleston is about a hundred and twenty-five miles from the prison, and between one o'clock and eight o'clock, seven hours—it's a lead pipe cinch. I'll bring you a long raincoat and a gray wig. You take off your glasses."

"Gray?"

"Not all gray. Streaked, you know. I'll wear a black wig. Just to delay the description. They may look for you in the morning, but they won't look too hard, will they?" Molly asked.

"Hard to say."

"You could trust—" She paused. "I don't know. Who could you trust?"

"Legerman?"

"Maybe. I think so. Maybe better to trust no one. Well, say they're ready to report you missing by nine?"

"I see what you mean. Why do we go to Chicago and what do we do when we get there?"

"My Aunt Constance—Mom's sister—lives in Chicago. I talked to her. She has a large old house. We go there and stay for a while. Joe and Mary will come out. They'll dye our hair, both of us. You grow a beard. We have plenty of money—Sylvia has power of attorney and will know where we are. If we stay a month, this will cool down and we'll go to Mexico. Mexico will not allow political refugees to be extradited. This has to change. This craziness can't go on forever, and we'll just wait it out. You can write and I'll have children—"

Bruce shook his head hopelessly.

"Bruce, what's the alternative?"

"Take our chances with the courts."

"We've taken our chances with the courts. What damned chance do we have? Twelve frightened people, all of them working for the government, all of them with their brains churned into mush, and all of them convinced that a communist is worse than the devil himself—"

"You mentioned a change of venue."

"Maybe, maybe—but, my darling, if they get you, it's over. They wouldn't grant bail. They want you out of their hair. That little bastard Hoover, well, no one dares face him or stand up to him or to McCarthy. You know that fat little guy—Parnell Thomas? The one on the committee? Well, the story goes that he began to prepare a file on J. Edgar, and believe me, there is plenty to prepare, and what did Hoover do but open his own file and indict the congressman. That's the way it is. Do you want to go into the courts?"

Bruce still shook his head. You didn't do things like that. It had not come to that. He stared at the woman sitting beside him—the cheeks more hollow, lines about her mouth, the dark mark of sleeplessness under her eyes.

"How much weight have you lost?" he demanded.

"Oh, the hell with my weight. We're talking about your life."

"What would you do if they convicted me?"

"I wouldn't have to kill myself. I'd be dead already. What the hell is wrong with you? Those damn bourgeois illusions of yours have you by the throat! You're still a goddamn Eagle Scout! Nothing changes with you! They could chop your hands off and you'd wave the bloody stumps and sing 'The Star-Spangled Banner'! God damn you! God damn you! I didn't need you. I was doing fine, just fine. I didn't have to give you my life, and now you have it—" She broke into tears, sobbing hysterically. He put his arms around her and held her tight.

"Please, baby, don't—no, no, please. I'll do it. We'll talk about it. We have to put it together more carefully."

She dabbed at her eyes. "I wore this damn eye makeup. I wanted to look beautiful for you, and now it's running and just look at me."

"I am. You're the best and most beautiful thing that ever came into my life."

She had the mirror out of her purse. "I look like a clown, an oversized redheaded clown."

"No. You look lovely." He whispered, "You look like all my best dreams."

Pulling away from him, she said softly, "I'm all right now. Let's go through it again."

"You'll be alone?"

"Just me."

"Can you do it? It seems so damn complicated."

"Oh, no—no, baby. It is not complicated. When I leave you here, I'll drive to Charleston and buy the airline tickets. Allegheny has two morning flights to Chicago, and I'm told they're rarely sold out. I'll buy two tickets on the morning flight."

"Suppose the airport is socked in? There's a lot of fog in these West Virginia mountains, especially in the morning. Suppose they stop all flights?"

"They'll stop incoming flights and put them into a holding pattern, but it's a very rare thing for an airport to stop the takeoffs. And if that happens, we drive. We'll drive straight on to Chicago."

"Wait a minute," Bruce said. "Why not drive? Why not drive the whole distance?"

"I thought of that. It's over five hundred miles, and it means going through the mountains, and the last thing in the world we want is to be picked up for speeding. Twelve to fourteen hours. We lose the whole time advantage. By flying, we'll be in Chicago by ten o'clock."

"Yes, that makes sense—" If any of it made sense. On the

other hand, the fact of life imprisonment was beginning to
sink in. Death he could grapple with and face; life imprisonment was another matter entirely. He called to mind a moment in the District prison during the days he had spent
there. How clearly he remembered the man sitting cross-
legged, dealing cards, his life force, his energy condemned to
rot in prison forever. They would not do it to him; he had
made that vow to himself. They would never do it to him,
because he would die first.

"Bruce?"

"We'll do it," he said. "If you're there, I'll be there."

"Trust me," she said. "I'll be there."

"The Night
That Covers Me"

Twenty-four hours after Molly had gone back to New York, Bruce was ready to dismiss the whole thing as romantic madness. To make his way out of the camp at midnight, to be picked up by Molly, to flee to Chicago and hide with her aunt; this was absurd—utterly and totally absurd. Such things were not done, and if they were done, they were not done by Bruce Nathaniel Bacon, and it was childish to imagine that they could get away with it, hide in Chicago, and someday make their way to Mexico. What would they do in Mexico? Bruce knew that people left their native land and lived their lives in other countries, but these were strange beings, unlike himself, and for him to leave the United States and live elsewhere was as unthinkable as death.

And death was unthinkable; otherwise, man would have gone mad in every generation. That was why he could face the thought of death, even romanticize it, because it was unreal; but the sense and quality of prison was very real indeed, not so much this strange prison camp in the West Virginia mountains as that cell in the District prison where he had spent those first days. That prison, with its electric gates, its club-carrying guards and tiny cells and holes where a prisoner suffered solitary confinement, its choking sense of hellishness, its foul smell of urine and excrement—that prison was very real indeed.

The first few nights after Molly's visit, he could not sleep at all. Each night was a blurred and endless dream, with every incident of past, present, and future crushed and scrambled, and question after question to be asked without answers. Like a person with a terminal disease, he longed for sleep and his mind refused the pleading. The world had crushed him too meanly, and he lived and suffered the desolate loneliness of all the men and women who had been imprisoned since man invented civilization and, concurrently, the jail. In prison, you were alive and dead at the same time. The luck that gave him the garage and heavy work from morning to night, to exhaust his body and numb his mind, would not be repeated. He would live his life in an iron cell. Like a pendulum, back and forth:

No, never. He would make the run with Molly.

No, that was insane. How could he drag Molly into this horror? He would trust the courts.

No, that was hopeless. He had trusted a court.

And how did he even know that there was a hold on him? How did Molly know? She said it came from Sylvia. How did Sylvia know?

He had to do it, if only because there was no way to get in touch with Molly. She would not return for another visit. Why hadn't he figured out some signal?

Then, one fine October evening, Warden Demming took him aside as he left the mess hall. "Bacon, let's walk a piece. I have some things to tell you."

Bruce nodded and joined the warden. They strolled slowly up the pathway that led to the Administration Building.

"Your release date is October twelfth. I'm sure you're well aware of that."

Bruce nodded.

"Your wife was here. Your attorney knew about it, so I imagine your wife told you."

"I'd like to hear it from you," Bruce said dully.

"Well, it's most peculiar. On the day of your release,

they're sending a Federal marshal down from Washington to take you to the grand jury sitting there—I mean in Washington. They'll hand you a subpoena, and then take you to Washington by car. Now I don't know why, except that it's one of those damned secret CIA affairs. I've watched you for a year now. I respect you and I like you—but God Almighty, Bacon, I am only the warden of a tiny prison. I don't know what goes on in the so-called higher levels of this nation, and so help me, I don't want to know."

"But if my sentence is up," Bruce said slowly, "then it's up. I've served my time. On October twelfth, I'm a free man."

"Yes . . ." uneasily.

"Suppose that on that day, I just walked out of here."

"I have an order to hold you."

"You mean you'll arrest me?"

"No, I have no right to arrest you."

"But if I walk out?"

"I would have to restrain you."

"How?"

"That's a damnfool question, Bacon. You know that. We have handcuffs here."

"Is it legal? Can you just cuff me and tie me up? Is that legal?"

Frustrated, angry at himself, at Bruce for putting him in this position, at a system that did things that made no sense whatsoever, Demming snapped, "How the hell do I know whether it's legal or not? I do what I have to do."

Bruce nodded and started to turn away. Demming grabbed his arm. "Bacon—for Christ's sake, Bacon, I don't like this damn thing. I wish to heaven there was something I could do."

"Yes. Thanks," Bruce said.

Demming held out his hand and Bruce took it. Then Demming stalked away toward the Administration Building, and Bruce walked back to the barracks.

Hal Legerman was waiting outside the barracks. "You've been in deep trouble for three or four days now."

"Just anxiety. I'm close to the end of the line."

"Bullshit, Bruce. What did the warden want?"

"Let it drop."

"Sit down here for a minute or two. It's a beautiful evening. We'll watch the sunset."

"I'm in no mood for sunsets."

"Do it for me. For an old friend." Bruce shrugged and sat down next to him. "I know you're out of here in another week, and then it may be five years more before we see each other again, because I'm going back to Los Angeles, and if you have any sense, you'll keep your beautiful Molly right beside you. Which deserves a brief homily."

"You're an odd character, Harold."

"You can say that again."

"Homily. Homily." Bruce grinned, the first time in days. "Where did you go to college?"

"You never asked me that before," Legerman said. "You know, you never asked me one damn thing about my past or who I was."

"In Calcutta, nobody has a past. The present is too absorbing."

"Homily. Do you need a college education for that? A dictionary will do as well. A homily is a moral discourse. Our friend Duprey casts a cool eye on my morality, but I always carry a piece of it around, mostly in my back pocket. I never went to college. My father wasted his life over a machine in a sweatshop, and my mother died of hunger, misery, and tuberculosis. There's all the background anyone needs. Now let me get to the homily—"

"If you must," Bruce said.

"I must. Now here it is. I met an Indian diplomat in L.A., and we got to talking about this famine that brought us together and which has given you so much grief. Oh, he agreed with all our conclusions, and in fact he assured me that there was ample evidence of the conspiracy. That being the case, I asked him why the government of India, newly liberated from the shackles of colonialism, did not broadcast to the world that a crime of unbelievable dimensions and horror had taken place. Can you guess what he said?"

Bruce shook his head. "No, I can't. We've talked about this before. I don't mean to put you down, Hal. I like you and respect you, but right now my brains are addled and I'm a pale, neurotic imitation of the man you met when you came to this place."

"We all are, Bruce. With this stupid Korean War going on, we all feel that we'll never be released. But let's talk about India for a few minutes. That's my homily. You wouldn't want me to waste it?"

"Heaven forbid. It's getting dark already. The summer dies so quickly."

"I asked you what you might guess that this diplomat said."

"You tell me."

"He gave me four reasons for their silence. First reason: they're still dependent on England for a good many things. They don't want to upset that apple cart. Second reason: their problems as a new government. Third reason: they don't want to feed a piece of fuel that big to the Communist Party. Fourth reason: people die in India, people die in Bengal. There are floods and famines, and in the case of this particular famine—who died? A part of the dead, a large part, were Untouchables, and their lives are not very much worth bothering about, and another part of the dead were Muslims, and since the Muslim rice dealers were involved, let them worry about their dead, and the rest of the dead were very poor peasants, of which there are all too many in India, and nobody, India or elsewhere, makes much fuss when the very poor die. So there is my homily, and the reason I'm boring the shit out of you with this is because at this moment you have a very poor picture of yourself."

"If that's your moral discourse, I can live without it."

"I suppose so. I can understand that. But the point I'm making is about you and your future. I may argue with Duprey, but he and Oscar Hill and you and myself—we're caught in the same noose. We feel the agony of poor people who die. We don't laugh about it or brush it off. Maybe there were ten thousand correspondents working that war for a buck and a big reputation, maybe only a few hundred, I never looked at any statistics, but you're different."

"Yeah, that's why I'm here," Bruce agreed sourly.

"I'm trying to reach you with something, and maybe I'm not putting it right. Do you know what Jesus said to the Jews?"

Bruce turned and looked at Legerman for a long moment. "You really beat the hell out of me," Bruce said.

"I try. Now I'll tell you what Jesus said to the Jews. Quote: Ye be the salt of the earth: but if the salt have lost his savor, wherewith shall it be salted?"

"He said that?"

"Your religion. Did you ever read the New Testament?"

Bruce smiled. "No, they never sent me to Sunday school."

"Enough of goddamn unappreciated homilies," Legerman said. "I'm going to bed and read. I'm reading John O'Hara's *Appointment in Samarra*. I found it in the library. The man writes like an angel."

"Thanks," Bruce said.

"Work easy," Legerman said.

Bruce sat on the steps of the bunkhouse while darkness filled the bowl where the prison camp lay. Ink poured into a vast receptacle, ink rising to the tops of the mountains that surrounded the place, a black cup with a rim of white light. Too much beauty is painful and fills one with nameless longing; it always speaks of things beyond our reach, and it shrinks the flimsy substance of the ego. The moral discourse on the part of Legerman had left him cold. Decency and compassion are better dealt with by someone not consigned to hell. There were men in prison who took it in their stride. They built time without giving it much of a second thought, and some of them were far more content in prison than they would have been outside. No one went hungry in prison—not in an American prison. They had clean clothes, decent food, and they lived in the company of their peers.

Of course, Leavenworth and Lewisburg were not Mill Bog, but they were what the convicts called good prisons. The point was to commit a Federal crime, and so keep oneself out of state prisons.

Bruce was coming to the conclusion that he would kill himself before he accepted a life sentence, and this, romantic and improbable, nevertheless brought him a sense of peace. It also decided him. He told himself that he would do as Molly desired, meet her on the road and make the break for Chicago. He would do anything for her, go anywhere for her, live anywhere, so long as they could be together.

It was a decision he had to come to, and once he had made the decision, he slept better. He was no longer confused from hour to hour, torn and anguished, and those feelings were replaced by excitement and anticipation. He had done something of the sort once before, when Legerman hustled him out of Calcutta before the British could catch up with him, and that had been successful, and there was no reason why this should not be equally successful. And with this came the expectation of seeing Molly without a time limit, without the misery of saying goodby a few hours after greeting her. It spelled freedom, and regardless of the danger that came with it, the taste of freedom was sweet and delicious.

The few days passed, and it was suddenly the eleventh of October. Professor Duprey shook his hand and said, "I shall miss you, Bruce. You are like a rock, and in prison one needs that." He didn't say he would see Bruce in New York. Word gets around in a prison; even a blurred sense of something impending gets around. Legerman said, "That pig, Scharnoff, had a meeting with an FBI man up in the Administration Building yesterday. Be careful what you say to him." Suddenly, he threw his arms around Bruce and crushed him in a bearlike grip. Bruce's eyes were wet as Legerman let go of him.

"All right," Legerman mumbled. "Second meeting. We have a few more to go."

Oscar Hill was more restrained. He still felt guilt for denying Bruce the privacy of the hospital toilet, the more so since no one had been injured sufficiently since he took over to warrant a bed in the hospital. He thanked Bruce for giving him the cigarette idea, and informed him that he had already smuggled eighteen pages out of the prison. Bruce felt miserable about that, but without the courage to tell Hill that it was a vengeful invention.

Scharnoff sought him out, slapped him on the back, and said, "Lucky bastard, you and that redheaded beauty of yours." The director, short and heavily muscled, grasped Bruce's hand, and in what is at times a gesture of hostility, attempted to crush it in his. Bruce crushed back, and Scharnoff winced in pain. Months in the machine shop had done things for Bruce's grip.

Lemuel Ward gave him a wallet done in his cellophane craft work, and Jackson gave him the name of a hamlet in Kentucky where there'd always be a glass of corn whiskey, one hundred and eighty proof, waiting for him. The convicts who worked with him at the motor pool had come to like him more than a little. Clem Alsta and Harry O'Brien turned his leaving into anger. He was leaving them. They reacted as if it were a blow struck against them. Sam Jones, the boss convict at the garage, held his hand for a long moment, and then shook his head, his eyes full of pain. "You made me a damned good mechanic," Bruce said. "I'm going to leave my book with you. I hope you find time to read it."

Tears in his eyes, Jones said, "You dumb white son of a bitch, I can't read."

For more than ten months, Bruce had spent every day except Sunday in the big garage and the sheds that adjoined it. He had forged parts in their big furnace. He had taken apart tractors and ten-ton half-tracks, and he had put them together again. He had worked on lawn mowers, bread-mixing machines, logging windlasses, commercial cars, pleasure cars, and trucks. Every problem he met had been solved by the intercession of Sam Jones, who had never learned to read.

Back at his barracks, he saw Demming, who was waiting to say goodby. Dressed in gray flannels, shirt and tie, and tweed herringbone jacket, Bruce presented a different figure of a man from what Demming had seen before.

"I hate to lose you," Demming said. "You and Jones run the best work force down in the garage that we have ever had."

"I'm not being released," Bruce said bitterly.

"You're being released," Demming countered. "You're being released from here. We'll have a check for you in the morning. Twenty cents an hour isn't much, but over a year it mounts up. I try to run a decent place here, Bacon. It's a prison, but it's probably the most intelligent prison in America. Mr. Bennett would be pleased if you were to write about it."

"How? With joy at being imprisoned decently without committing a crime? Do I praise the prison and at the same time damn the lunatics in our Congress who have put that filthy committee together? I've been what you call a good prisoner. I have not complained and I've worked hard. That pays whatever debt I have to the clowns who put me here."

"Come on, Bacon," Demming said impatiently. "Neither I nor the Federal commissioner put you in prison."

"That's true and I'm sorry for blowing my stack. On the other hand, you hold me here tomorrow until the next set of lunatics pick me up. You know, I don't think it's legal. I don't think you have any right to hold me tomorrow."

"It's legal. I got the subpoena today." He reached inside his jacket and handed Bruce a subpoena. "A Federal marshal will be here tomorrow to drive you to Washington. A letter has already gone out to your wife, informing her of the fact." He paused, staring at Bruce. "It stinks!" he exclaimed harshly. "It stinks to hell!" He put out his hand and Bruce took it.

He had given his extra tobacco to Lemuel Ward, cot to his left. His small store of four Milky Way candy bars went to the Kentucky moonshiner, cot to his right. The moonshiners, all of them heavy drinkers who dried out during their jail term, had a sort of frenzied desire for sweets. The gift was appreciated. Now, as daylight faded, Bruce sat on the wooden steps in front of the barracks, smoking the last of his last pack of Granger Rough Cut in a corncob pipe that he had made, and contemplating the sunset, his past, and his future. His year had not been entirely wasted. He had learned enough to get a job anywhere as an automobile mechanic. He could make a corncob pipe, and he could forge and hammer a piece of iron into something it was not originally intended to be. He could fix things, not all things, but a good many things. He had lost twenty pounds; he was in good health; and he had acquired a taste for tobacco, and now he was facing the rest of his life in another Federal prison.

If Mexico was to be their final destination, then how does one make a life there? He had never been to Mexico. He had studied German and French in college and reinforced them during his war years, but he knew not a word of Spanish. His vision of Mexico was confused and uncertain, pieced together out of bad films and books not much better than the films. Perhaps they could lose themselves in Canada? Perhaps the Canadian government would refuse to extradite them? His thoughts were becoming childish, and he shook his head to clear them away.

Darkness came, with the faint promise of a moon that would be over the horizon in another hour, and while they gave little light, the stars made a wonderful appearance, a host of dancing players indifferent to their earthly audience. A guard came by for his nightly check.

"Can't sleep, Bacon?"

"Later, perhaps. I want to get used to civilian clothes before I take them off." For Bruce the guards were nameless and faceless. Demming had once reminded him, "We need prisons, and as long as we have them, we need prison guards." Bruce had complained to Demming that the guards were brutal toward the black prisoners and almost fawning toward the whites. When Demming was away in Washington, they'd drive into the garage, begging favors—a new screen in the transmission, plugs, a carburetor, shocks. Demming answered Bruce's complaint, asking, "Did you ever know a kid wanted to grow up and be a prison guard?"

This guard on this night wanted to be friendly. In his eyes, a man like Bruce represented power denied to him, and that could or might be useful someday. How was not important; Bruce was not an ordinary prisoner. "You can't imagine how many of them do it. They get their clothes the day before release, and they got to put them on immediately."

Bruce nodded.

"Good to get out."

"You're right," Bruce said.

The guard went inside, did his check, and came out again. "Going to sit here all night?"

"For a while," Bruce said.

"You're lucky we got a touch of Indian summer. It'll be cold as a witch's tit a week from now."

"I imagine so," Bruce agreed.

The guard went on. The ripple of sound coming out of the

barracks behind him muted. The day began early in the prison. It was lights out at nine o'clock. At ten, the prisoners were mostly asleep. Bruce tapped out his pipe and put it in his jacket pocket. Molly didn't smoke, but she rather liked the scent of his tobacco. Now, as the prison slept, time stood still. It was eleven o'clock, and then, in what felt like an hour, it was eleven-fifteen. Bruce's heart was beating faster as he rose and slowly walked up the rise of land toward the Administration Building. The half moon had appeared, and it cast its cold silvery light over the prison. If he feared the possibility of being observed, he was also grateful that he would not be stumbling around in the dark.

The silence was thick, heavy, not the opposite of sound but a part of sound. He had once heard the expression "to listen to silence," and now, for the first time, he understood it. He could hear the silence.

He walked slowly, without haste. He made a circle through the grassy lawn around the Administration Building, and that way he reached the access road at the beginning of the driveway. He began to walk down the access road toward Route 39, and then, suddenly, it was there, Route 39. As he turned left on 39, he offered a pleading prayer, to what god or gods might be, that no car would come along. He told himself that if he were to see the glow of approaching headlights, he'd fling himself in the brush or the ditch or whatever was alongside him, since a man on the road at this hour of the night could only be a convict.

The half mile after he had turned left would stay with him. For one thing, he had no way to measure distance. He remembered that a mile was 1760 yards, but for the life of him couldn't seem to work out the distance of his stride. He reasoned that there had to be two feet between the toe of one foot and the heel of the other, and then it became fuzzy. Finally, he accepted it as a stride a yard. Over eight hundred steps at least.

He conjured up possibilities. Suppose she was not there—

what then? Was he to stand there and wait until dawn? Or
go back to the prison? Had he remembered everything correctly? Did she say to turn left? Could he be sure of that?
Suppose something had happened on the long drive down
here? And where would she be parked? Where he walked
now, the forest was so close to the road that a car could not
park without blocking the road. But hadn't she said that she
had already selected the parking place? She must have.
She'd driven up and down the road sufficient times to pick a
spot, but when she said half a mile, had she measured the
distance, or was she guessing at the distance? And now he
had lost count of his steps. How many—four hundred, or
was he already in the five hundreds? Shouldn't he be seeing
Molly's car now? Moment by moment, he expected a car
from the prison to come tearing down the road, or a police
car, lights flashing.

But the road remained dark. He tried to read the face of
his watch. She had said one o'clock, but that had not been
meant as a specific point in time. It was not "I'll be there at
one A.M. on the nose." He had taken care not to leave the
prison ground before two or three minutes after twelve, and
now it was only twelve thirty-five. Perhaps he was not to
expect her until one, in which case he would have to hide
somewhere by the road. Had he read his watch right? Did
he dare strike a match, the better to read his watch?

And then he saw the car, parked in a small enclave, just
enough space to hold a single car; and then before he could
test the reality or inquire, she was out of the car and had
flung her arms around him and was kissing him and sobbing
and trying to speak at the same time. "Oh, my darling, my
dear, wonderful darling, and you're so wise and wonderful,
and I was dying a thousand deaths waiting here and thinking of every horrible possibility, but you came because I
knew you would come and I prayed to the Blessed Virgin
and swore I'd light a hundred candles even if I don't believe
in anything except Bruce Nathaniel—"

"And cops and stuff. Come, Molly, let's go."

"Just tell me that you love me—just once."

"I love you and you make miracles, and I can't believe any of this, and please, let's get the hell out of here."

"Yes, yes. There's a little lever under the seat, and move it back if you need more room, and you drive because I can't even think straight."

Bruce, his heart still hammering, his hands shaking, managed to ask "Which way?"

"Straight on, and then we hit Two nineteen, and then we go south to White Sulphur Springs, west on Sixty, and we're home free. And we're going to make it."

His hand was shaking, and his glasses had clouded. He took them off to wipe them.

"Let's go," Molly said.

"Honey, you drive. I don't know what's wrong with me, but you drive, please."

"All right. Sure. I can imagine what you've been through these past few days, with your imagination, seeing yourself in prison—but you're not going to prison, not ever again. Slide over. I'll walk around."

"I love you. Thanks, baby. Later, we can switch. Are you tired?"

"I'm just fine," Molly said, skipping around the car and climbing into the driver's seat. "I stayed the night at Charlottesville, so utterly exhausted that I slept till noon. And I want you to understand that this is a class Buick we got here, first rate and three quarters full of gas. We won't break down."

She pulled the car out onto the road, switched on the lights, and rolled along at forty-five miles an hour. "Just nice and easy," she said. "We are not going to speed, and we are not going to stop or be picked up."

Bruce suddenly burst out laughing. He couldn't stop. "Yes," he admitted to Molly, "I'm sort of hysterical. You know, we have this little country place on Indian Lake, and when I was a kid, Mother said something about wishing she had black-eyed Susans on our place, and there was a field next door owned by a kind of unpleasant character, and I took a shovel and basket, and very early one morning I dug up a clump and replanted it on our place. I was so filled with guilt. I was properly trained, Molly, and I had never stolen anything in my life until that black-eyed Susan caper came along. Would you believe, I went to this character and offered to pay him? And now we've pulled off a prison break just as smooth as silk, and we're going to outrun the cops and be in Chicago before they know what we're doing, wearing some silly disguise—when do we try that?" He was laughing through everything he said, unable to stop chuckling. "It's crazy. It's absolutely crazy. I'm a respectable news writer."

"Your book," Molly said, "is running away with itself. Top of the *Times* nonfiction best-seller list. Scribner did a whole window display, and Westbrook Pegler denounced the store and denounced you and thought it would be a good idea to throw a brick through both of you. He called you 'another commie rat,' and Sylvia says we can sue him, but if we're going to be in Mexico, I don't really see how that's going to work."

"How do we get to Mexico?"

"All in good time. There are any number of ways, but I guess the easy way is to take a streetcar across the border at El Paso. There are at least a hundred people down there who've taken refuge, most of them in Cuernavaca, and I know some of them, so there'll be people we can talk to until you learn some Spanish."

He was still chuckling. "Just as crazy," he decided. "But it's all sort of demented, isn't it?"

"I have a thousand dollars in cash in my purse, and there's more where that came from. We're not exactly rich, but we've got some resources. Sylvia has power of attorney, so we can get money when we need it. It's in my name, so they can't tie it up."

She was high as a kite. He reached out to touch her, running a hand along her thigh. He was so tired, and all this was so much like a dream. The scent of her perfume; the sound of her voice; he had dozed and he awoke with a start.

"Where are we?"

"We just passed Lewisburg. We're on U.S. Sixty, headed for Charleston."

"I was dreaming. We'll be early when we get to Charleston."

"About five in the morning, I would think. I turn in the car at the airport. We'll have some breakfast—and then off to Chicago."

"I feel rested. Do you want me to drive?" he asked.

"Oh, no, baby. You've been through enough these past few days. Just lean back and rest and sleep if you want to."

He fell into a doze again, thinking how wonderful it was to be loved and cared for by this bold, confident woman, so resourceful and so ready to meet any situation life might present. He had given a year of his life to defend her honor and indeed his own as well, and that made him proud, and in that fuzzy land between sleep and wakefulness, he lived over his meeting with her, their dates and trials and small triumphs—

"Bruce!"

Her cry awakened him, blinking and then instantly awake as he saw in the distance the flashing lights of police cars. Molly increased her speed.

"Molly, slow down!" he cried. "We'll bluff it out—we'll talk!"

The car was hurtling toward the police cars, seventy and seventy-five and eighty miles an hour. It was happening too fast. Everything was too fast, and the memory of it was a jumble of his cries and Molly's desperation, and then they shot through the opening between two police cars, and then

Molly swerved to avoid a third police car, angled into the road and invisible until they were upon it. The car skidded wildly, spun around, and then slammed into a tree.

He regained consciousness in a hospital room in Charleston. He had suffered a bad concussion. When he was able to speak, he asked about Molly, and he was told that she was dead. She had died instantly of a broken neck when the car hit the tree.

The following day, Sylvia Kline and Bruce's father, Dr. Bacon, arrived at the hospital in Charleston. They found Bruce in his room, seated in a chair and staring morosely at the floor. Death and grief are difficult walls to break through. Bruce recognized them with a nod but no words. His head was bandaged. He had been cut around his scalp and had lost blood, but there was no fracture and he was free to leave the hospital.

Bruce rose and Dr. Bacon embraced him. The doctor had seen enough grief and death to know that words were not much use on such occasions. Sylvia's eyes were full of tears. She had to speak to him, but her voice broke when she tried. She walked to the window and wept, her back to Bruce and his father. Finally, Bruce said, "It's as all right as it will ever be, Sylvia, so don't cry anymore. I had it out with myself, and I can live with it." He fought back his own tears. "I can live with it."

"I saw the x rays," Dr. Bacon said. "Molly died instantly. There was no pain."

"Where is she?"

"Here at the hospital. In the morgue."

"They won't do an autopsy?"

"No reason to. And certainly not without your permission."

"I want to see her."

"Are you sure?" the doctor asked worriedly.

"Yes, I'm sure."

"We've made arrangements for the body to be taken t
Boston. I've spoken to her family," Dr. Bacon said.

Sylvia turned to them, trying desperately to control he
tears. "I must tell you," she said. "I'm your lawyer.
pleaded with her not to do this. I begged her. I want you t
believe that, Bruce. I should have stopped her. I should hav
stopped her."

"I should have stopped her," Bruce said. He put his arm
around Sylvia, holding her thin body to him. "It's over. It'
done."

He dropped back into his chair. He was very tired and hi
head hurt. "What do we do now?" he asked.

"If you can think of such a thing as good news today . .
what I mean is that I spoke to the Federal prosecutor i
Washington this morning, and they're dropping that insan
business with the Soviet defector. They have no case an
they know it won't wash, and if only I could have told tha
to Molly—" She broke down completely now, crouched in
chair, sobbing.

"If you want to see Molly?" Dr. Bacon asked.

"Yes."

"Do you want to come, Sylvia?"

She shook her head.

They went down to the pathology room. Molly's body
was in a cold locker, covered by a white sheet. Bruce folde
the sheet back. Strangely, there were no cuts on her face
just a single bruise, and her head rested on a cushion of th
red hair. Her eyes had been closed. For a long moment
Bruce stared at her, and then he bent over and kissed he
brow. It was cold as ice. He walked over to one of the lal
stools, sat down, and began to cry. From the time he was ten
or eleven years old, his father had never seen him cry. Now
he stood and watched his son weep. The pathologist and his
two assistants pretended not to notice.

"I'm all right," Bruce said after a moment or two. "I can

...old it back if I have to. I'll have the rest of my life to deal with it."

"No," his father said. "Time takes care of it. Time takes care of everything, believe me."

"You talk to the loved ones," Bruce said bitterly. "That's what a surgeon does. He talks to the loved ones. Oh, Jesus, why am I taking it out on you?"

"Because I'm here."

They went into the hospital cafeteria, where his father ordered coffee that Bruce couldn't drink. He thought, I am closed, closed all over. He tried to drink the coffee, and he couldn't. "Do you know, Dad," he said to his father, talking like a small boy explaining and begging to be forgiven for what he had done, "they weren't after us at all. The police cars. They had set up the road block because there had been a robbery and a shooting here in Charleston. At the prison, they never knew I was gone until the call from the hospital here."

"Molly couldn't know that."

"Why did I agree?"

"I think because you loved her."

"God help me." He pushed the coffee away. "Let's go back to the room. I have to talk to Sylvia. What do I do about Molly?" He couldn't say "her body."

"I took care of that."

"Yes—you said you did."

Back in the hospital room, Sylvia had composed herself, and she said to Bruce, speaking very precisely, "There are no charges against you, Bruce. I telephoned Mr. Demming, and he said that your departure from the prison, while unusual, was in no way illegal." She spoke very formally, fighting for self-control. "I also took care of the car. It was totaled. I informed the Hertz people of that fact. We have reservations for the five o'clock flight to New York out of Kanawha Airport. That's only two miles from here, so there's no great hurry."

"There was a United States marshal supposed to pick m
up at the prison?"

"He never came. They called that off."

"So it was all for nothing."

Sylvia shook her head dumbly.

"All for nothing, all pointless."

Two days later, Molly was buried in St. Augustine Ceme
tery in South Boston. Father Paul O'Hara took care o
things, and afterward everyone gathered in the Carlin
home, where Bruce found himself loved and embraced b
Molly's sisters and her mother, and no words of blame wer
spoken. Bruce got himself a little drunk and wept his ow
tears. He was still weak and uneasy on his feet, and he wa
grateful when Father O'Hara drew him into a corner an
instructed him to sit for a while and rest.

"You've been through a hell of a lot," O'Hara said. "Lif
and death and the loss of a beautiful woman who would se
any man's heart on fire. All the saints abandoned you, an
God was out to lunch."

"Yes," Bruce answered after a moment, "you could say
that, although it's a bit curious, coming from a priest. I wis
to hell you could comfort me or that anyone could, but tha
doesn't seem to be your line of work."

"No, I'm not much good in that line, and in a few week
I'll stop being a priest and marry Bernadette, who's almos
as beautiful as her sister Molly."

"So you've decided."

"I've decided."

"I hope you're happy. Where do you stand with God?"

"I read your book," O'Hara said. "That, and the Holo
caust and the war and your own experience—ah, God has
some explaining to do. But that isn't what I mean and feel.
I'm a Catholic priest, and that's hard to shake. You, being a
Protestant, would not understand that."

"No. And I've reached the point where I don't very much
give a damn about anything."

"That's a mistake."

"Oh?"

"A deep, serious mistake—because, you see, you are shedding your tears over a woman who gave a damn, who cared, whose heart was as big as the whole world. I know the whole story, and you belittle her, telling yourself that she was some wild and impractical left-winger with a crazy Irish soul and her feet firmly planted in midair. But that would sell her so short, so terribly short. You can argue her belief and say what you will about it—so long as you remember that whatever you say, it's part of the dream."

"And what dream would that be?" Bruce asked sourly. "Is it your dream of a heaven that doesn't exist, of a God that nitpicks this crawling lot of humanity to see who is Catholic and who deserves an eternity of boredom in that heaven that doesn't exist?"

"You're a bitter man."

"No," Bruce said, "not really bitter. Deprived."

"And you think you will never love again?"

"Something of the sort."

"Then I can give you one small comfort. You will love again."

"How do you know?"

"Because, in the simplest terms, you're a loving man. Ah, try to see it another way, Bruce. You come to our wake, and there you find a coarse lot, drinking whiskey and stuffing their faces, but think of it as an old, old rite out of a time when there was so much hunger that food was the blessing and the face of God and the definition of life as well, and what do we do at a wake but celebrate life? And it's life that connects us. We all die, but we all live because we are connected. And when you discover that connection, even for a moment, you touch God and you know what God is, and that's what Molly gave you."

Bruce stared at him without speaking.

"Do you understand me? Do you know what I'm trying to say?"

"I'm not sure."

"Give it time. Life is a wonderful thing, as lousy and painful as it is, still a wonderful, beautiful thing, and you have a whole life in front of you. What a fine gift that is!" He took Bruce's arm. "And now let's have some whiskey and food, and we'll talk about Molly and remember her."

America's Bestselling Author
HOWARD FAST

___THE PLEDGE 20470-4 $5.95

___TIME AND THE RIDDLE 20517-4 $4.95

The Lavette Family Saga

___#1 THE IMMIGRANTS 14175-3 $4.50

___#2 SECOND GENERATION 17915-7 $4.50

___#3 THE ESTABLISHMENT 12393-3 $4.95

___#4 THE LEGACY 14720-4 $4.50

___#5 THE IMMIGRANT'S
        DAUGHTER 13988-0 $4.50

At your local bookstore or use this handy page for ordering:

DELL READERS SERVICE, DEPT. DHF
P.O. Box 5057, Des Plaines, IL. 60017-5057

Please send me the above title(s). I am enclosing $_____.
(Please add $2.00 per order to cover shipping and handling.) Send
check or money order—no cash or C.O.D.s please.

Ms./Mrs./Mr._____

Address _____

City/State _____ Zip_____

DHF—12/89

Prices and availability subject to change without notice. Please allow four to six
weeks for delivery.

In 1355, Margaret of Ashbury did the most shocking thing a woman could do. She wrote a book.

A VISION of LIGHT

Judith Merkle Riley

Mid-wife, inventor, faith healer and mother, Margaret of Ashbury is an extraordinary woman with an astonishing tale to tell. But the year is 1355, and only a renegade friar with a mysterious past is willing to help her chronicle her incredible story.

The result is a mesmerizing tapestry of a time, a place and its people—and a portrait of a woman who will long be remembered as a heroine for all time.

A VISION OF LIGHT
Coming soon in paperback

Dell

For SPELLBINDING storytelling,
read the extraordinary
Asian Saga by

James Clavell

___	**KING RAT**	14546-5	$4.95
___	**NOBLE HOUSE**	16484-2	$5.95
___	**SHŌGUN**	17800-2	$5.95
___	**TAI-PAN**	18462-2	$4.95

At your local bookstore or use this handy page for ordering:

DELL READERS SERVICE, DEPT. DJC
P.O. Box 5057, Des Plaines, IL. 60017-5057

Please send me the above title(s). I am enclosing $_____.
(Please add $2.00 per order to cover shipping and handling.) Send
check or money order—no cash or C.O.D.s please.

Ms./Mrs./Mr. _____

Address _____

City/State _____ Zip _____

DJC-12/89

Prices and availability subject to change without notice. Please allow four to six
weeks for delivery.

For riveting,
realistic,
"what if"
disaster
novels that will
make you think
twice, nobody
writes them
better than this bestselling author.

___ **AIRPORT**
10066-6 .... $4.50

___ **THE FINAL DIAGNOSIS**
12508-1 .... $4.50

___ **HOTEL**
13763-2 .... $4.95

___ **IN HIGH PLACES**
14000-5 .... $4.95

___ **THE MONEYCHANGERS**
15802-8 .... $4.95

___ **OVERLOAD**
16754-X $4.95

___ **STRONG MEDICINE**
18366-9 .... $4.95

___ **WHEELS**
19414-8 .... $4.50

At your local bookstore or use this handy page for ordering:

DELL READERS SERVICE, DEPT. DAH
P.O. Box 5057, Des Plaines, IL. 60017-5057

Please send me the above title(s). I am enclosing $_____.
(Please add $2.00 per order to cover shipping and handling.) Send
check or money order—no cash or C.O.D.s please.

Ms./Mrs./Mr._____

Address _____

City/State _____ Zip_____

DAH–12/89

Prices and availability subject to change without notice. Please allow four to six
weeks for delivery.

Special Offer
Buy a Dell Book
For only 50¢.

Now you can have Dell's Home
Library Catalog filled with hundreds of titles, including many
books for teens like you. Plus,
take advantage of our unique and
exciting bonus book offer which
gives you the opportunity to
purchase a Dell book for only
50¢. Here's how!

Just order any five books from
the catalog at the regular price.
Then choose any other single
book listed (up to a $5.95 value)
for just 50¢. Write to us at the address below and we will send you
the Dell Home Library Catalog.

DELL HOME LIBRARY CATALOG
P.O. Box 1045, South Holland, IL. 60473

Ms./Mrs./Mr. _____

Address _____

City/State_____ Zip _____